SECRETS
OF THE WORLDS

Vol. 6 of the
Three Worlds Saga

Carol A. Strickland

Other books by Carol A. Strickland

Touch of Danger – vol. 1 of the Three Worlds Saga

Lost in the Stars – vol. 2 of the Three Worlds Saga

Stalemate – vol. 3 of the Three Worlds Saga

Worlds Apart – vol. 4 of the Three Worlds Saga

Mind Shift – vol. 5 of the Three Worlds Saga

Secrets of the Worlds – vol. 6 of the Three Worlds Saga

Applesauce and Moonbeams – wacky soft sci fi

Nothing Personal – ditto but wackier

Burgundy and Lies – sweet historical romance

Star-Spangled Panties – the full nonfiction dish on Wonder Woman!

Carol A. Strickland, publisher
www.CarolAStrickland.com

Publisher's Note: This is a work of fiction. Names, characters, places, and incidents are a product of the author's imagination. Locales and public names are sometimes used for atmospheric purposes. Any resemblance to actual people, living or dead, or to businesses, companies, events, institutions, or locales is completely coincidental.

Book Layout © 2017 BookDesignTemplates.com

Secrets of the Worlds/ Carol A. Strickland. -- 1st ed.
ISBN 978-1-941318-62-1 ebook
ISBN 978-1-941318-63-8 paperback
Some publishers require other ISBNs and you'll find them on those sites.

With thanks to Diana Francis, who gave me an extraordinary edit.
Also to beta readers Jaime Lee Moyer, Will Nuessle, and Lora Lindberg.

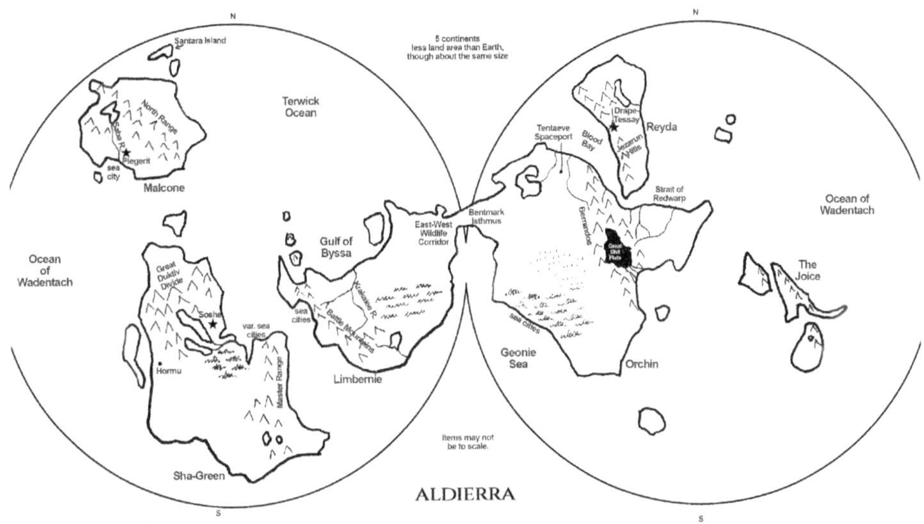

The Aldierran Ultimatum

I am Aldierra. I am your mother, your nurturer, the source of your life. I have loved you for eons but you have tried to destroy me. No more! I will not take this abuse any longer!

I am an advanced being and I need to evolve. I can do this with you or without you. Make your choice. Stand by me; support me and love me, and I will continue to support you, too. You will receive my bounty in abundance. And in turn you will evolve, become more loving toward each other. Happiness will come within your grasp.

But continue to forsake me, to destroy me and the life that lives upon me without remorse, and I shall have to destroy you. Lovingly so, for you are my children. But I say I will not take this abuse any longer!

DECIDE! You have three seasons to make your choice and act. Your deadline is the equinox.

Please, my children, do not forsake me. I have enjoyed your presence until these last few centuries. I wished to be your home as you matured. But sometimes you have to cull the herd, thin the seedlings so that others may survive. I will do this if you force me to.

DECIDE. By the equinox after next!

Inform my Chosen and I will know.

CHAPTER

1

Field Marshal Bracken's first humble request to the Affiliated Systems had been for food for his people. His world of Aldierra had failed at its invasion attempt of the AffSys capital, Sarastor. Now they were left begging. Since then the Starharts: Londo, Lina and Jae, had plowed through reports of Aldierran famines, food shortages… and food destruction caused by the hundreds of wars across the planet.

Aldierra was, to put it mildly, a horrific mess. Everything that could go wrong via human action on a world had done so there.

The three had been named the Chosen of the Three Worlds: Aldierra, Sarastor and Earth. It had been those sentient planets that had designated them such. Thrown into their new duties and a marriage that had come as a happy surprise to themselves as well as the few witnesses to it, the Starharts had managed mere days to prep and coordinate. Many of those had been filled with emergencies on other worlds. Now they were here. The first AffSys food shipments were about to arrive.

Londo Starhart prepared himself for a quiet but busy schedule. He made sure Jae and Lina were utilizing personal air filters so they wouldn't have to deal with the atmospheric conditions Jae had reported from his first mission to the planet. The three of them would be supervising, but would help Bracken's Majority Army as needed.

"What the orb?" Jae exclaimed as the three Starharts ported in mid-air over the Tentaeve spaceport.

The environment they found themselves in was bad enough. The atmosphere reeked of chemicals, burning, and general foulness. The low sky might as well have held clouds of mud. The city and its spaceport stretched grayly below them before fading quickly into the smog, away from the extensive field outlined with massive hangars designed to load and unload sizeable spacecraft.

Instead of landing space, it was filled with men.

Yes, sizeable platoons of soldiers waited for the shipments as ordered. But the vast majority of humanity on the field were uninvited civilians, as well as more than a few who wore uniforms of non-Majority Army military. Groups stood beside vehicles of every size, from land and air cruisers to primitive wagons. All wore masks to filter their planet's polluted air.

Londo handed Lina off to Jae to hold aloft via his Legion Array as they hovered over the venue. He let off a string of obscenities and then rubbed his mouth. His nose. He turned to his spouses. "I'll get them out of here," Lon promised.

"Not in time," Jae told him. "I'll set up… something."

"I'll contact the army for backup," Lina said and added before Londo could comment, "I'll get my guards first."

Lon nodded as his untrained bride ported away. He and Jae had made sure she realized the importance of her guards. She was still a neo, but seemed to learn fast. She knew what they all had planned here.

As a Legionnaire, Jae was an expert at leading during times of crisis. He began circling the area, scouting possibilities from above. Lon could see him settle sound protection around his ears, then give a chin-nod his way. Lon took a central position over the port. Some of the men below – and they *were* all men, no women in sight – began to look up and point.

Londo adjusted his translator. "We gave you instructions to stay away!" Lon could shout like no one else. His mammoth translated voice echoed off the tall buildings that ringed the area. Their windows rattled. "We have important work to do here. You are interfering!"

A part of him wondered at the translator. Maybe it was the volume it was having to handle, but it seemed off somehow. Still, people understood it, even if they did nothing about it. He'd look at the system… later.

"Food will be transported in an orderly manner. Anyone interfering with our system will be dealt with!"

That didn't seem to impress anyone. Instead fights broke out. People battled to be near probable landing spots for the hyperspace vehicles, sensing lapses in security when they'd be loaded. Someone started screaming in a keening, insane way that was taken up by several others in the horde.

Jae had a mic of his own, though it had to mechanically add volume to match Londo's. "This means YOU!" He pointed at several battles below. "We see you. You were told to keep this area clear. We made no announcements that we'd be handing out food here."

Shouts answered him.

"But we will." He spared Londo a pointed glance to quiet him as cheers broke out below. "Form a line if you can. Stand down! It will take us time to get this organized. Precious time; you are holding us up. It will take even more time to see everyone serviced. Hm.

"Let's say this: if you're here, your House will not receive food allotments from the transports. You will be responsible for carrying all your House's food home. If you haven't the capability to carry that right here, right now – we're giving out four weeks' supply – *go home*. Now. Get your food there instead. We mean it."

The crowd had stilled for the announcements. Then it started shuffling about to make room for people turning around with their vehicles. The majority were remaining. Scuffles ensued, but now a few on the ground were trying to stop them.

Londo held out an expectant, crooked arm as he felt a telepathic touch, and Lina ported into its support, her normally pale cheeks flushed. Somehow they were going to have to get her a version of the Legion Array that allowed for flight at the least. Her new levitation power wasn't that reliable yet. Cheerily his so-shapely lady waved her padd at him so he could see the program, and he nodded agreement.

A giant image of her appeared over the crowd. "I am Lina Starhart," she announced, her speech instantly translated. "You know me. I am Speaker for Aldierra. She spoke to each and every one of you through me just a couple weeks ago. You will listen to me."

All movement, all conversation, in the plaza stopped.

Lon couldn't help but admire his bride. He had no doubt that many men in the crowd did so as well.

"You will let the troops here transfer the cargo that needs to go into the transports. That's our first priority. That food will travel far and wide to provide for this territory's people who need it most.

"But there are many of you here. You heard what Jae – Neutrino – told you. We will give you rations–" the crowd broke into cheers – "but you have to be able to carry them all. You will need to queue up for them. Your House names will be struck from the lists we're using to distribute supplies. We'll operate clockwise." On some level Lon was as surprised as Lina that there was an Aldier-ran term for that. "Beginning…"

Lon felt her mentally link with Jae for information as to where he planned to operate from. She double-checked with Londo as well. Jae had chosen a spot farthest from where the first ramps had been set for the transport ships.

Lina pointed. "There. One. At. A. Time. No fighting or you'll go to the back of the line. If you're lined up here and you don't get your food today, well, there won't be any food here tomorrow for anyone in your House. We have a tight schedule. If you think you're not going to make it, *go home now.*"

Ah. Good girl. Now the crowd moved with purpose. And murmured. And shouted. And shoved.

"Calm the hell down!" Lon growled at the crowd as Lina gave him some serious side eye.

*******Like that's helping things,* **** she told him telepathically.

*******I have more experience at this than you, Lie. You're doing fine, but let me do this part.***

She shrugged acceptance and pointed to target a platoon of personal guards on the outskirts so he could see she was taking her own security measures. Then she ported to them.

Jae zipped down from another direction to land amid the nearest ranks of troops. "Let's get a squad to start making room for supplies over there."

Lon listened as his new husband continued laying out his strategy. That would do. He looked up to see the first of the approaching cargo superships emerging from hyperspace at the edge of Aldierra's atmosphere. Lon signaled it to take a holding position just above the port. The crowd wasn't clearing much. There was no room for it to land.

So he called Field Marshal Bracken, his best army liaison at this point, and Bracken assured him that mid-air transfers for the incoming cargo were not possible. "We don't have many large, empty aerial transports, Valiant," he said. "What we have we can have here by tomorrow, but not today. We have the required number of ground transports already lined up for this, but they will need room to load and exit."

"Start positioning the aerials in Sha-Green for tonight's shipments, then. We'll work as originally planned here. Good enough," Lon said, though he hated the thought of Bracken thinking he was praising him.

This being a spaceport, there was no dearth of odd equipment. Lon chose from bulldozers three times the size of those of Earth and lifted one into the air. As he descended with it in his hands, he yelled, "Clear the way!" at the crowd below.

They tripped over each other and screamed in their scramble. He paused just over their heads, the sheer bulk of the equipment terrorizing them to speed. Finally there was just room enough to set down the thing.

He took a moment to stand in front of its looming blade and pointed into the crowd. "I'm going thataway! Fair warning!" **Lina, get me troops to hold this line, please.** He took his time moving to the back of the bulldozer and lifting that end just enough so he could push it across the pavement. By then a few dozen soldiers had arrived. They gave quick salutes he returned, and assumed positions near the edge of the dozer's blade.

That blade struck sparks as it inched forward. The crowd screamed at its approach. Men climbed other men, clambering to get out of the way. Lon wasn't going to tell them that he wouldn't hurt them. Let them move.

"Anyone with a weapon will be arrested!" he reminded the mob as flashes appeared within it. "Their House members will be moved out of line and refused service. Get rid of your weapons!"

Lina—

Medics on their way, she replied telepathically.

She was excellent at this. His Lina jumped into situations and bulled her way through. She'd spent much of yesterday establishing connections with Aldierra's military supplies and support networks.

Her uniformed troops had managed to funnel a lane of foot traffic out one long boulevard, against the push of the crowd. As Lon's bulldozer crept closer, every civilian in front of it decided to turn the street into a full-width exit. Men carrying stashes of weaponry were part of the surge away from the plaza, moving quicker than most.

Londo chuckled to himself. Healthy fear, managed responsibly, could accomplish miracles.

He cleared a wide path to that road, then came around again, discouraging the men who'd tried to fill in what he'd just emptied. A triple-thick line of soldiers with force field shields were making it difficult for them. Good.

When he got a moment he checked his vest pockets, then swooped over to Lina and handed her a palm-sized disc. "It's set to detect their weapons," he said. "You don't go anywhere without checking first." Lina nodded as he showed her how to operate it.

Londo saw that Jae was finalizing his supply lines, poised to operate as efficiently as they could. Excellent. That was why Jae was a Legion Alpha Team Leader, the same as himself. He heard communications relay that Lina was ordering portable toilets for the crowd, to be delivered to Jae's contingent first, and clean drinking water, ditto. **Have them service the men holding these lines as well,** he told her.

Jae signaled a warning at both of them and Lon waited expectantly. A column of magenta light shot upward next to Jae. His image appeared over the crowd. In his left hand he held the jeweled Staff the Worlds had given him. Firmly he struck it upon the ground.

Every person in the area swiveled to look up at his image.

Lon heard sharp intakes of breath from across the tarmac. Jae's youthfully rounded face was arresting. Noble. People always took a few moments to recover from the awe he inspired. Jae was Feithi through and through, the product of a legendary race, now extinct… except for him.

If the sun had been out his golden hair would have blazed in contrast with his deep almond skin. As it was, his startlingly blue eyes seemed to meet those of the men below.

"I am the Minister for the Three Worlds, for Aldierra," he declared. The tattoo that showed he was one of the Chosen glittered gold above what Londo had learned was his Third Eye region.

Lon gave the back of his right hand a glance. It held a matching gold tattoo. Lina had one of her own, just above her heart.

"The line forms here. First come, first served. You heard the conditions for how you will be expected to behave. Line up quickly. Line up peacefully. There will be water available for you as you wait. There will be toilet facilities available…" Jae went on in that manner for a few minutes more, and then his image disappeared.

That staff was such a good trick, Lon mused. No one could touch it but the three of them, unless Jae aimed it in a targeted manner. It made everyone pay attention to Jae for a few moments.

Jae had his Staff. Londo, his amazing new Shield. Lina had her Flute. Marvelous gifts.

It was time to get back to work. Lon hovered over the crowd as the first ship lowered, then held a position just above the cleared section. He secured angled transport ramps to it. A nearby land truck eased closer to link in, mindful of the crowd.

Damn. Non-weaponry fights were breaking out. He needed to be here, to get this operation into motion or they'd never complete the day's activities. Jae? No, though he hated to add more to her duties…

Lina. He told her how to order her personal and borrowed troops to police the brawls. **Be assertive. Don't be polite.**

I'll do my best High Commander Valiant impression. Hup hup!

He smiled at that. **Give a yell if you run into trouble. Make sure at least five of those guards stay close.**

He kept track of her through the next hour or so as her group stopped dozens of fights. She seemed to calm things down well, but noticed that some fighters disappeared from in front of her. Ported. Likely to the back of the line, he thought. They should go home.

He wrestled with the connections between a second interstellar transport and yet another truck when he heard Lina having problems.

Hate to bother you.

Give me a sec. He rushed the job, but not so much that the machinery couldn't work through it, then flew to her aid. This fight involved more than two Houses. Orange-skinned men in different colored House garb snarled at each other as runnels of blood soaked their clothing. Two of Lina's guards had guns pointed at the participants when they should be guarding Lina. He didn't see any obvious weaponry on the fighters, but then he hadn't yet had a chance to fully investigate Aldierran tech.

"Stand back!" Londo ordered the crowd as he swooped in. While some drew back, others surged forward to take advantage of the confusion to place a final fist in another's face. Lon dug into one vest pocket and flicked two black rectangles their way, then another toward another man. Within instants the rectangles inflated into large pillows that were unaffected by air friction. With Valiant's mighty flick behind them, they slammed into the men, knocking them to the ground without hurting them badly.

Lon waved his hand to signal the pillows' electronics to deflate and return to him. He had time to tuck them into his pockets as the men hauled themselves back to their feet. "Who started the fight?"

"They did!" "They did!" "No, they did!"

They screamed at each other. One was almost incoherent in his fury.

"SHUT UP!" Lina yelled from where she stood between the factions. Her translator also had excellent volume capabilities.

Londo glanced around, taking the measure of these bastard clowns. "Any witnesses?" he asked the crowd. **We'll have a quick trial here,** he explained to his wife.

It took several moments for one to say, "I saw it from the beginning, Valiant. Er, Protector."

These days he did have several titles. Lon gave a nod that the man should proceed. He told his story, bowing every third word to Lina and occasionally to

Lon. The big bruiser in orange and red had been heckling one of the others because the lowliness of their House meant that Mr. Orange and Red should go first.

"Is this correct?" Lina asked Mr. O&R. Of course he didn't agree. He told how the others had tried to break line, pushing him back.

Lon might be a new telepath, but he could easily sense the story being concocted for the first time. It needed a better plot.

The other two main fighters also accused O&R of instigating the fight. Four more crowd witnesses confirmed.

The remaining fighters were merely defending themselves. For the most part.

There's something else involved, but it's vague, Lina told Londo. **Essentially this is the true story.**

Lon nodded once to her as he turned to Mr. O&G. "Fighting in line," he declared. "Holding up our processes. Delaying others receiving help. I believe we've already stated what would happen if that occurred. Speaker?" He nodded at his wife.

"B-but–"

Lina straightened her shoulders. "Punishment is given as promised. We will take note of your House. Hope it was worth it. Have a nice trip."

Mr. O&R vanished, followed by the rest of the group with him. Their fancy transport required Londo to dump it a few miles away.

He returned and looked around to see how everyone else had reacted. He matched looks with the head of Lina's guards, who gave him a crisp chin-nod. "Everyone good here now?" He grinned at Lina. "You've got to teach me that teleportation trick. It's so handy."

She was adorable when she smiled at him. Tall for a Terran woman; just the right height for him. Pale skin, dark hair that showed red highlights in even this wan mid-morning light. A figure he would always crave. Bright green eyes that were sparkling now because she adored him with a feeling that was ever so mutual. His head waggled with pride.

"It is indeed," she told him. "Thanks, hon. This just started to get too big for me. I think I can handle things from here, though."

"Speak up if you need help."

Over the next hour of emptying out the first transports, Lon looked up to see his wife's image hovering over the mob. She informed it of more fights and the punishment it engendered. "Hope they brought good walking shoes," she razzed the perps. "Hope their food supplies at home hold out until the next shipment. Their House is now on our shit list."

Ground transport after transport left the arena. Things finally seemed to be settling into an efficient process on Londo's end. But Jae's lines took much longer. Often Jae had to explain holdups in that they were consulting computer records to confirm how many people each supplicant House needed to feed. Many did not take that well. Everyone was getting precisely the same amount of food for each person in their household. Some found this unfair.

Still, he was managing. Jae not only looked like the ultimate elfin Prince Charming from out of a fairy tale – well, a fairy tale that had lived in Lon's fervid imagination for years and not one for children – but he was also one helluva Team Leader.

Lon snorted when small buildings popped up around Jae's station. A peek inside from his position revealed that they were portalets. He looked around to see men shuffling forward – some quickly – toward the facilities. Otherwise these men would just face a vehicle or crouch down on the pavement and do what needed to be done.

Ah, Lina's face appeared again above the crowd, informing the civilians in rough terms that they would indeed leave the toilets clean when they exited. Anyone not using the toilets but doing their thing elsewhere was responsible for cleaning up after themselves, punishment provided if they did not.

Lina would know to have portalet replacements lined up. Right? How would the portalets be cleaned out? Would these people merely dump the waste into the nearest river, or onto a street? The three of them would be cleaning up this world. Might as well begin at–

It's handled, Lina assured him.

Lon's pleased surprise in that simple statement delighted her. **I do have a few organizational skills,** she told him with a silent laugh.

They had so much to learn about each other. This marriage was going to be fun. **So I see. I'll observe and take notes.**

After another hour they broke for lunch and some burrito-type wraps. Jae grimaced over his.

"I asked people in line to recommend local street food," Lina told him. "This was what I could find that passed the food poisoning tests." She gestured at her earrings, which contained such sensing tech. "The vendors don't seem to be regulated for safety."

"Or taste," Jae muttered. "Maybe it's just a cultural thing we'll have to get used to."

Ah, so it wasn't just Londo's taste buds being picky. That made him feel better. He'd just chowed down on the food because he was hungry. He could eat solid acids and not be harmed, but usually acids didn't taste that great either. They weren't as bad as rust, though.

The two men shared sips from a variety of beers Lina brought. "They all seem safe," she told them, though only one had both good flavor and aroma. Lina made a note about them. Lon made a mental note that she'd ported in a bottled water from Earth for herself. It took only a few minutes for her to safely port over two hundred parsecs between worlds.

"Another thing," Lina told them. "There are a lot of injured people here. Not from fights. From disabilities and illnesses. Yet they're here to help their Houses get the supplies; they're that desperate."

"I'd noticed the ambulances," Lon said.

"Yeah, we got help through to the worst of the bunch, and I made notes to have medics visit the Houses involved. If sick people are coming here to work, there must be sicker ones at home. Why aren't their Houses caring for them?"

After the break Londo busied himself with hooking up the next transport to receiving equipment. Four flying vehicles shrieked into the plaza. It was obvious these didn't come from the army the Starharts were working with, and sure enough Bracken immediately reported, "Those aren't ours," into Lon's com system.

They targeted the massive hovering warship and flew in tight, menacing loops around it and the wide conveyor belt that extended to the ground. Robotic shippers herded the cargo down. Lasers flashed from the flitters, and the bots tumbled off. One of the flitters landed on top of the ramp, while the others held defensive positions above it. They fired at several army squads, easily discernable because of their uniforms.

But Londo swooped to rescue the robots before they could smash against the ground. He set them and their loads on the pavement and then leaped back into the sky. Lasers flashed at him, but he held out his right arm to will his Shield to appear. It caught the charges to absorb them without any kind of backlash. He could have commanded it to reflect, but who knew where those reflections would go?

He enlarged the Shield to catch a few poorly-aimed blasts before dismissing it to wherever it went when he didn't need it. Grabbing one rogue vehicle by a corner, his fingers sank through the metal. With a swift movement he tossed it high to the west, then seized the next one and did the same. Then the next. The one on the ramp got the same treatment, though he made sure no food had been stashed within. There it went, up into the sky, uncontrolled!

He pointed silent direction to army troops who rushed in to tackle those pirates who were still standing on the ramp. They sprinted crazily, trying to find an escape route. Then he flew off to follow where he'd thrown the aircraft.

One man jumped from the ramp, but telepathic rapport told him that Jae had been watching and took off to catch him in mid-air before Lina could port him.

Within five minutes Lon was back in supervisory mode, and a new video of him dumping the vehicles at an army prison played above the crowd.

Already air ambulances had arrived to see to the injured. Lina directed the crowd to let the aid through.

Jae had to deal with one House who'd felt they could take advantage of the interruption to grab extra rations. Lon was happy to see Jae's squad unload that House's vehicle and send them away, foodless. Now it was Jae's head that appeared above the crowd explaining the crime and punishment.

Jae kept his line in order. He requisitioned volunteers to help, one from each House in line to rejoin their Houses later. That seemed to reduce the number of skirmishes in his line.

Even with the spectacular warnings and the proof that Houses indeed were getting their supplies, the afternoon's heat ignited tempers. Army troops spotted more trouble in multiple spots before Lina could personally attend to them all.

The troops packed their prey into black bus-sized floating transports. Whether they took anyone to the end of the line, to jail, or dumped them in the middle of nowhere, Londo couldn't tell and at this point, didn't much care. He had twenty billion other people to worry about.

Gentle flute music filled the area. "Greensleeves." Lon's breathing eased. He realized that he'd been holding a lot of tension in his shoulders and back. A few breaths released that, and he sighed in relief.

Under the calming spell of Lina's Flute, the fights slowed and then stopped. There were a few shouting matches, but no fisticuffs, no weaponry. The threat of violence and frustration, of House honor and need, hung in the air only to dissipate. One after another the emptied warpships took off to higher climes to return home. They were replaced by the next in line to be unloaded.

A local film crew that had arrived around lunchtime came by to interview Londo as he waited for a new ship. He reminded their audience of the schedule and their rules. He mentioned the punishments that had been meted out today.

"In the coming months we'll be helping you all with food production," Lon told them. "Instead of having to import food from the AffSys, we'll see that Aldierra has enough food to feed its own population – and the distribution channels to accomplish it."

With the signaled approach of one of the afternoon's warpships, Londo concluded the impromptu press conference and stretched.

All right, he decided in those spare moments. This Aldierra business might require a little more work than they'd expected. They'd deal with it. Then he turned his attention to the final cruisers.

CHAPTER

2

The three of them… no, the *ten* of them: Lina, Lon, Jae, plus seven cats in hard plastic carriers appeared in the lobby of The Landmark Fifty, the hotel Jae had reserved for them. Both Londo and Jae blinked hard in the sudden light before looking about at their new location, but Lina was momentarily discombobulated as she finished her interstellar port.

They'd completed distribution at the Aldierran spaceport, then ported to Legion HQ on Sarastor to collect some items. From there they went to Starhaven, their home-in-progress on Earth, and then back to Aldierra. At top speed the trip would have taken a hyperspace vehicle more than a week, but Lina accomplished each leg in two minutes. She was responsible not only for the instantaneous transportation, but for the more time-consuming biofiltering and electrical balancing that interstellar ports required, performed just outside of normal space.

It had been a long day. She was pooped but glad she could complete this final, so important port.

The cat carriers sat at their feet in varying stacks, along with fifteen suitcases, one enormous crate of security equipment and assorted weaponry, two cat trees, one crate of kitty litter, one of human food, one of cat food, a smaller one containing cat toys, a tower of litterboxes of different design… and a pile of boxes that Jae or Lon or both of them for all she knew, had packed in addition to it all.

They planned to stay a while.

— — —

Lina had never been to this world just to gawp. Today in the mob she'd been focused on particulars, not the big, cultural picture. Now she took the time to drink in some atmosphere.

The hotel sparkled with cleanliness, though it smelled musty. The dark-floored lobby was wide, encompassing several deserted sitting areas and what might be a bar, but with a low ceiling that cast a pall of claustrophobia throughout. Lina didn't think that the windows lining the area were anything but video screens giving a window-like illusion, like Legion HQ on Sarastor used for security reasons.

As Lina took her time looking around, her husbands greeted two Aldierrans who stepped forward to greet them. "Greetings, honored ones," the darker man's words came through the translator. "Here I am manager. Honor is ours. Hotel is ours. Conditions are ready." He bowed deeply.

But the words he actually said were audible over those the translators offered.

And they were quite different.

Both Londo and Jae did double-takes at the marble-sized translators that floated next to them.

"Could you say that again?" Jae asked as he reached to enclose his with his hand.

"Very honored to have you with us," the manager repeated. "Ours is not the largest hotel in Plegerit, but we believe it is the best. Everything is ready for you." He paused as he watched their reaction, then continued lamely, "I am the manager."

Londo and Jae looked at each other, then glanced back at Lina.

She shut her open mouth. "I heard it as well," she said. "All day long I've been thinking there was something wrong with the translators."

The manager took in the sight of her and dropped to his knees. "Speaker," he breathed. He riveted his gaze to the floor.

"Oh jeez. Please don't do that."

Lina stared at her translator marble. Had she really not noticed that they could understand Aldierran? Had any of them not? Had this ability snuck up on them gradually throughout the day? Aldierran now was a smoothly delivered language from her ears to her mind. Before it had come in hesitant spurts and odd word choices through the translators.

Londo stepped forward, his translator turned off. Lon was a prince of a man, Hercules in the flesh, though he was crazy more powerful than the mythic hero.

"Let's try this again. Sir." Lon spoke Aldierran. Or rather, Lina now knew, Farrani, the Aldierran language. The manager looked up at him. "I am Valiant, and this is Neutrino, and you seem to remember the Speaker here. Er, you may rise."

"The Speaker," the manager said in awe. Behind and beside him, a small squadron of assistants had assumed similar positions, gazing at Lina in wonder.

They were distinctly carroty orange in skin tone, though two were much darker than the others. Orange was the reigning Aldierran skin color, like peachy browns were back on Earth.

These were all brunettes, and it struck Lina that she'd never seen an Aldierran with a beard. Was that to adhere to fashion, or did beards not grow on Aldierran men? Were the face masks most men wore not amenable to beards? Was being a brunette part of the uniform? Field Marshal Bracken and most of his subordinates had had olive hair – but maybe that was part of *their* uniform. On Sarastor, Lina had seen people who'd changed the color of their eyes to match a particular day's fashion.

When standing, all these men seemed to lack Londo's height, which was 6'4". Jae stood four or five inches taller than him – difficult to tell for sure because Jae had such a mass of thick, blond hair that fell to his shoulders – and Lina was four-ish inches shorter than Lon, which was about the same height as these guys. She'd like to say she was getting used to being the shortest person in the room, but the opposite had always been true before. She was a stranger to all these Out There peculiarities.

Oh, how things had changed since she'd met Lon!

Jae had chosen the target of her port to be the lobby of this hotel located in Plegerit, which was a secondary or perhaps tertiary capital on Aldierra. Both Lon and Jae had been adamant about them not staying in the world's capital, Drape-Tessay. "We need to de-centralize ourselves as targets," they'd explained to her. "But we still need to be close to the action."

Plus Plegerit was right on top of where they'd determined their primary work would begin.

The hotel had been secured and cleared of customers. There remained this group of employees, plus two more across the room who stared at them from behind a half-wall. All were men. There were more men elsewhere in the hotel carrying on normal hotel duties, but any who weren't on staff were members of the Majority Army who'd already claimed rooms and offices to help coordinate this project with the larger military units around the world.

"Yes. The thing is, we brought translators." Londo held his translator marble between thumb and forefinger. "We've been having difficulties learning Aldier-ran… uh, Ferrani, what with just running into your people what, less than a month ago? From out of nowhere, it seemed to us. The translators were just beginning to truly learn your language."

"You may all rise," Jae told the remaining kneelers magnanimously, who also got to their feet.

As they stood, the manager seemed as if he didn't know what to talk about first. "Your speech is clear to me," he decided upon. "You sound like native speakers. Your system must be very good."

"That's the thing," Londo began.

"We aren't using it," Jae finished for him. "Suddenly we understand you. Perfectly, I believe." He glanced to Lina, who was crouching next to one of the cat boxes.

"Same here," she said. The wails of her cats had caught her attention. The three Starharts had covered the cat carriers' gates with towels to darken them so they wouldn't be frightened by the absolute blackness of the interstellar port, but still the cats screeched in dismay. Even a tiny sound came out of Katie's outstretched mouth. She was usually silent.

"You're fine now, baby," she assured the cat inside. "All that dark is gone now. See?" She leaned over another box. "See, Moosie? All better. It's reality again. At least now we know what that final bit with the Sentinels was. Lon, this probably has something to do with your accent."

The answer had come to Jae and Londo as well at almost the same moment. Two days ago they'd been summoned by the Galactic Sentinels, the race who ran the Ruby Brigade that patrolled much of the galaxy. The Sentinels lived at the center of the Milky Way. The Starharts had taken the rogue Ruby Guard Paul Granger to Aum to face trial. Once he was imprisoned, those almost immortal beings had done something to them had caused a mighty sting on the right sides of the back of their necks, even Londo's invulnerable one.

In the time since Londo's (studied) French accent had been absent. They'd commented on it. Been mystified. What had the Sentinels done?

"I wonder if it's only for Farrani," Jae mused.

Lina peeked into the final carrier. "Fafhrd's asleep. Nothing fazes her."

"Are you sure she's just asleep?" Jae asked from a crouch behind her. "She looks–"

"Not dead." Lina reached a finger between the bars of the gate to stroke the ancient black cat.

Jae nodded and stood back up.

"We'll need to help program the translators," Londo said before returning to the subject at hand. "Small, private hotel is what we were aiming for. Is our security in place?"

"Yes sir, they arrived yesterday. They've been–" A pained look came over the hotelier's face, his mouth scrunching ever so slightly– "making adjustments to our own system."

"Good. Good. We'll clean up when we leave."

"We are known for our security!" the manager insisted.

Lon granted him an understanding smile. "We require a little bit more than even Aldierra's best. You understand. We're here to help save your world."

Lina gave the staff a watery smile as she stood. She hadn't known what to wear. Where were the women on this world? Jae said he'd seen a few when he'd done his first-contact mission. She'd spoken to three women Lon and Jae had saved from a flood the other day, and she'd also seen a couple in the secret video Jae had shot on that mission. They'd been wrapped in long robes. Was that normal garb? Outdoor winter apparel? She'd have to learn quickly, along with everything else about this world.

"Are we really going to die?" the lighter fellow of the crowd blurted. His companion elbowed him. "Well, you want to know as well," he huffed.

Londo whispered the exact translation to his translator.

Jae stepped forward. "No one has to die if everyone works together. Aldierra is angry because her humans have mistreated her and each other for so long, and so badly. We're here to help. We're going to do everything we can to change the world for the better."

That brought a deep bow from both gentlemen. Then they turned to Lina as if expecting her to make some kind of Planetary Announcement.

"We're so pleased to meet you," she said instead. "What Neutrino said is true. Thank you for your warm welcome. This is the entire Starhart family. Our cats are in these boxes. They are pets, not food. We look forward to staying in this lovely place."

"We appreciate your effort," Lon said.

"Yes, Valiant. Of course! Anything you need, you have but to ask."

"Can you show us our rooms, please?" Lina asked. "I'd really like to let the cats out of their carriers. They don't like them." Molly was gnawing at the metal bars on her door. Moosie was beginning to howl again. "It usually means they're going to the vet, you know? Cats don't like change, and this is a pretty big one."

"They are Starharts now," Londo said.

"Starharts do what Starharts need to do," Jae said. "We survive."

— — —

Lina hoped that was true. In the past weeks invulnerable Londo had died for a few minutes, and she'd come a hair from dying herself. And being lobotomized. And being tortured and raped. Jae was the healthiest of the bunch. She held back an ironic chuckle and asked the universe to continue to keep them all alive and as healthy as possible.

Here they were in this Aldierran hotel. Along with a sour chemical or musty smell, it reeked of exotic luxury, with its shiny stone floors and expensive-looking draperies and fringe. Golden accents glistened on each surface. Of course the ceilings were quite low. Both Lon and Jae had remarked on the lack of good Aldierran headspace even in the ceremonial areas they'd previously visited. Lon had just a touch of claustrophobia, and was looking forward to instituting a change in this world's architectural styles.

This group of Aldierran men wore spotless purple uniforms draped with gold braid and what looked like military medals on their chests. It was rather startling to see their skin such natural shades of orange, brighter than Terran skin, because with just a tweak or two Aldierran skin could have set itself in the Terran range.

Lina sighed. It could happen the other way as well, that Terrans could tweak to look more like Aldierrans. She should get over her prejudices. Skin was technicolor Out Here.

Shock at the lack of female presences set in with a vengeance now that things had slowed down. The three women Lina had met said women were kept locked away in dark places that assured they'd not try to escape. Aldierran women were slaves, though they weren't called that. They were just "women."

Girl children were not wanted, so many were killed at birth. Yet the men of the planet were desperate for more women. Did they not see the correlation?

Well. The three Starharts were here to begin the mission to change Aldierra in every way they could.

But could they do enough in nine months?

— — —

They walked instead of porting to their floor. Both Jae and Lon had insisted on the entire hotel being given over to their use, including that of their new security personnel. They hadn't specified just how long this would last because they had no idea.

The Aldierran Patriarch had given them carte blanche for the duration, and announced it planet-wide. Thus the hotel manager couldn't refuse. They'd assured him they would pay for their stay, which mollified him.

Ca-ching, Lina mused, but Jae whispered to her, "Don't worry. Even though we still don't have a final number from the Tour, we know we have more than enough to finance the Aldierran part of Three Worlds through Deadline. Besides, I gave Stoan a memo to make sure you were getting paid for all the Legion porting you're doing. That alone should pay for this place." He gave a little snort.

The preliminary estimate of how much she'd been paid for last week's Mind Control Tour was enough to fizzle every circuit in Lina's mind. She dealt with that by ignoring it. Besides, both Jae and Lon were hugely rich, due to them being famous megaparaheroes and all. Jae was becoming interested in money and financial systems, so they'd thankfully given him that part of their project to oversee.

On the way Jae discussed with the manager what security measures were being instituted, and Londo used his paravision to double-check through the walls and wiring. One of the crates they towed had material that was supposed to add to such things.

Lina attended to her frantic cats as carts rolled the baggage down the halls. For years they had lived with her in North Carolina in her small house out in the boonies. Then the cats had spent the last two weeks at Starhaven, the estate Londo was building in the Rockies. Most of the time since all this chaos had begun, they'd had only stranger cat sitters and not their mama or new daddies to comfort them. Now they were on Aldierra, where even the filtered hotel air smelled pretty awful. There'd be no familiar smells for them.

The cats' vets had given her mild tranquilizers to soften the transition for them. She couldn't ask the Legion doctors for a recommendation as the AffSys didn't contain cats, at least not as pets. Lina didn't know if they had any pets at all in their culture.

Their new quarters on the top floor opened to a very large room as low-ceilinged as the lobby had been, but not lower, thank goodness. In fact, the manager – the not-trying-to-seem-nervous Mr. Primmi – had remarked at the high ceilings, intended for only the most elite of guests. The walls were a stark but glossy light gray except for a smallish photo of Patriarch Lupoff, the head of the Great Council of Military Governors and as far as they could tell, supreme dictator. Lina thought removing that would come near the top of her immediate to-do list. She didn't want that arrogant old man staring at her.

There were some settees scattered about, all of them black and none of them looking like something you'd want to curl up on with a good book. Well, it was good enough for an entry room, she supposed. People wouldn't overstay their welcome.

A couple of dreary area rugs with gold edges sat in front of the settees on the shiny dark floor. Lina tried to scuff her foot on the expanse without anyone noticing. It seemed like it could be really slippery. Bad for cats. Bad around a bathroom, too. Did it continue throughout the suite? Maybe they could get some more rugs with a little color to them. Then again, they wouldn't be here long, would they? No need paying for furnishings for a place they'd move out of in a week or so to permanent quarters.

As soon as everyone hotel-related cleared out, Lina and Jae set about freeing the cats from their carriers. Londo placed two litterboxes around the large chamber and filled them.

"Not in the entry, please," Lina told him. "How many rooms do we have? Does this place have a swimming pool? I brought my suit."

Londo looked around with a disapproving expression. "Somebody tell me they can see some color in here somewhere."

"It stinks." Jae spread his arms to command the devas of the place to clear the air. He changed things: matter and chemical reactions and such. Dealing with devas of nature was his primary mode of work.

Lina took a testing breath and smiled in relief. "Thank you, Jae. Oh, it's better already. We need to get something to do this so we don't keep working you."

"I'll get a system," Jae replied as one of the cats ran to him.

— — —

Londo counted cats as they emerged, starting with the short-haired gray tabby who was sweet on Jae. "That's Ember." Then there was the chubby tri-colored cat Lina described as "calico," shyly peeking out to take in the new conditions. Lina had said it was rare for a calico to be male. "And Obi. A sensible name I can remember. Fat Cat is Obiwan. I think we have five main bedrooms, plus something they called 'women's quarters.'"

Before they'd said their vows at their first wedding, Lina had made sure Lon knew that her feline herd was a part of the contract. He'd countered for a promise of two kids, minimum, at some point. Deal. When Jae signed on for the second wedding, Jae had agreed to the terms as long as one of those kids would be fathered by him. Deal.

Big black cat with big ugly nose bolted out of his box and came to a skidding stop fifteen feet away from Londo to survey the room. "You're Moose. Well-named. And uh… Oat… no, Bran. Bran, that's your name." That was the smallest one, a regular short-haired brown tabby. Bran-Bran; the name was doubled for some reason, even though it had been shortened already from something Lon couldn't recall. Bran bounced around, then attached himself to Lina's ankle, where he'd been for the past two days since they'd returned from the Tour. A mama's boy. "He and Obi are best buddies. Do I get extra points for knowing that?"

Lina grumbled at the concept of "women's quarters."

"You know you won't be staying in women's quarters."

"But it will be interesting to see what those consist of," Jae said, the gray cat purring in his arms. "Go on, Lon."

"Um. Ember. I've said that already, right?" Here was the other black cat, this one sleek like an Egyptian leopard, but– "Old… old… Fafhrd, that's the one. Where do you get these names, Lie?"

"She was my first cat, and she wasn't a *gray* mouser," she told him as if that explained everything. "I was reading a lot of Leiber at the time."

"Who else? Oh, Molly."

The chubby, unpleasant ginger cat hissed at him for daring to use her name. Okay, he'd call her Fat Cat 2. She shed a significant proportion of her mass of medium-length hair with every movement as she checked out her new kingdom.

"Is that everyone? Wait, here's Katie." Fat Cat #3. Well, maybe that lush fur of hers made her look chubbier than normal. She was a beautiful, fuzzy tortoise-shell with a dark coat underneath her patterning; friendly but aloof, whatever that meant, according to the notes Lina had left for pet sitters. The important thing was that she didn't like to sit on laps. And apparently she didn't think too much of Molly. Or was that Moose? The lack of lap sitting suited Londo just fine.

"Check," Jae confirmed. "Very good."

Londo made a face at him. "I've been studying."

"And you just passed the exam," Lina said. "Jae passed his yesterday."

Jae made a superior face at Londo.

A soft buzzer sounded and Lon saw Lina flinch, probably because she'd been witness to too many security breaches these past weeks. This sounded like one of those, and this suite wasn't surrounded by Legionnaire guards.

A man's voice came over the sound system: "Field Marshal Bracken to see the Starharts," it said.

"One of our security force," Jae explained to Lina.

"I met my personal squad this morning," Lina said. "Well, a few of them."

"We have plenty just for this building," Jae told her before he glanced Lon's way.

"Bracken," Londo said, and he couldn't withhold a growl. He met Jae's look. Of anyone, Jae knew he would never forgive the field marshal for having indirectly caused the death of Aiko, his former love. It had been a part of Aldierra's failed invasion of Sarastor, a case of an impersonal war, but still…

"He's the best person we can deal with," Jae reminded Lon, who grimaced.

"I know. That doesn't mean I have to like it."

They all turned to the front door as Jae gestured acceptance to the room's computer system. An outside guard opened the door ahead of Bracken, and then stepped back, securing it from outside.

Bracken nodded to them all, adding a subservient bow to Lina. His uniform was only a third covered with medals. He stood at average Terran male height, and had a slight middle-age paunch. Londo understood that such wasn't common on food-starved Aldierra; a bit of fat was a sign of status.

Bracken was head of the Majority Army, the Greens.

"Welcome to Aldierra," he said as he looked at them before checking out the entryway. "We are at your service, whatever you need. My people and I have taken a suite of rooms on the third floor. We were working from there this morning, making sure monitoring and communications were online. I hope this accommodation is acceptable to you."

Jae stepped forward to greet him, as Jae had known him the longest. Jae had been on the first-contact mission to Aldierra as well as teaming with Lina and Wiley to stop the invasion that tricked Bracken and his fleet. "We appreciate the recommendation," he said. "And the guards. They seem to have been efficient at securing the place."

"Yes, thank you," Lina said. She offered a few more bits of polite small talk. Londo took the moment to try to adjust his thinking, and Bracken unwittingly aided him by drawing it out.

"The Minister," here Bracken again nodded to Jae, the appointed Minister of the Three Worlds, "indicated during his time with us that the way we live is quite different from what you are used to. I was thinking I might explain the facilities, perhaps give some suggestions. And as long as I'm here, where I believe I am unable to be overheard by my own forces, perhaps it is a good time to help make plans for what you will be doing on my world. We shall often have to operate around the military, rather than alongside it."

Surprising. Ever so slightly Londo cocked his head at Bracken. "Very good," he said.

Bracken gave him a small bow. "Protector." Then Bracken regarded the pile of luggage curiously. He spotted the various cats, whom he'd met at their wedding.

"Not for eating, Field Marshal," Lina reminded him.

Nod. "Speaker. I will inform others of this. Aldierra has many types of rodents about this size or smaller – a few larger – and those are definitely hunted, though many are difficult to catch. For the most part, they don't taste particularly good." He gave a pause. "Your Farrani is very complete. I don't see a translator."

"Long story," she told him. "Gist is: we don't need them anymore."

Lon said, "We'll be updating the translators that everyone on our side of the language has. It might take a week or so before the system can flesh out the vocabulary. If you link your linguistic systems to ours at that point, we can update yours as well, so people can stop talking in such a stilted way."

A genuine smile came to Bracken's face. "That would be a relief, Protector. Thank you."

Lina picked up three empty litterboxes and began walking across the room. Lon grabbed the litter crate to follow, and Jae with Bracken walked beside them, taking in the new quarters and using Jae's Legion sensors to map out security features. The survey would copy to Londo's systems as well.

"The Sha-Green shipments came through with no problems," Bracken reported. "Only nine or so Houses showed up, and were escorted away."

"Were there any injured or sick people among them?" Lina asked.

"I will inquire, Speaker. We will investigate and offer aid."

Just after the entry came a room the size of a smaller hotel ballroom, plus six offices off to the side.

"This suite is extremely prestigious," Bracken said. "This would be used to host formal gatherings among the military or perhaps including civilian officials."

"Likely we'll use it for that as well," Lon said.

A kitchen sat between two good-sized, informal rooms. Bracken pointed out how the smaller rooms could be closed off from the larger so modest-sized committees could use them. He gestured at an electronic wall box. "Privacy modes," he explained. "For exchanging secrets. Often such modes will include the ability for certain armies to listen in."

"Not here," Jae said as he double-checked. "We gave our guards instructions that this suite would maintain absolute privacy. They've done a good job, but we'll be adding more to what they did."

"I haven't gone through everything yet," Lon said. "I'll make sure it's all secured within two hours."

But Lina had stopped at the kitchen. She set two water bowls on the counter and, after experimenting, turned on a faucet. Water a weak shade of yellow came out.

"You must be kidding me," she said.

"What's wrong?" Bracken asked.

"Just look at it." Lina pointed, but Bracken shook his head in incomprehension.

Lina opened a crate and rummaged through it as Jae came closer to see the evidence.

"We'll get a purifier for this as well," Jae said.

"A purifier for the entire hotel would be best," Londo said. He'd anticipated a number of small tasks needed before they could settle in for the night. He reached into one of his vest's many pockets for his padd and began to motion at it. "There. Ordered. I'll install it in a while, Lina, if you bring it here."

"Will do."

"It'll take some finagling to match the systems…" Lon mused. He motioned for his Array to coordinate with other systems to figure it out for him before he glanced at Bracken. "You may be used to dirty water, but we aren't. Cleaning your world's water is one of our priorities."

"Both natural water and municipal systems," Jae said. "We need to learn how you treat your wastes as well."

Bracken nodded. "I'm sure you'll find those deficient." He sighed. "I'd never thought of it that much before I met you, but we do seem to have our problems in so many areas."

"Let's begin with getting you some clean air and water," Jae told him. "And distributing food to those who are starving."

"Handouts." Bracken seemed to whisper the word to himself. "We are to be… pitied. Reviled."

"No," Londo said, "the food is a temporary measure until everyone can figure how to get your people to raise their own food efficiently, as well as distribute it in a fair manner. Purify and supply their own water. Maintain clean air. Eventually we'll turn off the weather control as well."

"Weather control?" Bracken's shock showed clearly.

"Aldierra hates weather control," Lina told him. "It seems all worlds do. Earth doesn't have it but Sarastor does. We'll be getting rid of it there as well."

"Later," Londo said.

"Yes, after we get Aldierra through the Deadline."

"Though it might help if we did it before then," Jae offered, and both Lon and Lina gave him considering gazes. Jae kept his own list of personal priorities and schedules in his head. Lon knew he himself occasionally lied even when it wasn't necessary, but Jae sometimes kept things too close to his vest. Jae had a tendency to do things that kept him apart from others.

In Lon's opinion, that's why Jae talked so much. He would go silent then seem as if he'd realized he'd done so. That spurred non-stop random chatter to cover it up. Lon theorized that Jae didn't want others to begin guessing what his Feithi opinions were.

Well, the three of them were married now, and were all telepaths who shared minds on occasion. They would adjust accordingly. Londo would persuade Jae to let them know what he had in mind. Literally. They could accomplish more if they worked together.

Lina found two bottles of water and poured them into the bowls. Then she set them on the floor. Oat… Bran-Bran was the first to sample, followed by three more of his siblings. Apparently porting was thirsty work for cats. Lina refilled the bowls.

"I guess the hotel caters as needed?" Lina surmised from the small size of the kitchen. "Didn't we learn about the dangers of catering during the Tour? Do they do room service? Can we buy from random restaurants so we're safe? I'm not keen on poison in the food."

It did seem to Lon that everyone had tried to poison her and her staff during the previous week's Mind Control Tour. Both husbands had worked hard to keep more than a few attempts hidden from her so she didn't have to shoulder that worry as she worked. They hastily reassured her that such would not happen again. Bracken said that he could personally assign a trusted cook and staff to work for them.

"That would be acceptable," Londo said. What kind of food did they serve on this world? He hoped they could find out soon. His stomach was thinking about signaling for dinner.

Lina nodded. "Thank you. But Field Marshal, I also need to know where I can get food to feed the soldiers who will be working with us in the field. Water for them. Toilets. Shelter. Clean-up. Transportation in and out of all that, plus for the volunteers." She heaved a heartfelt sigh. "Before we're through there might be thousands upon thousands."

"Maybe millions," Jae put in helpfully.

"Right. It's not going to be as colorful as what Jae and Lon do, but–"

She didn't finish as they came to…

"Women's quarters," Bracken announced. He began to walk past but stopped when they didn't proceed with him.

It was just one circular interior room, smaller than the informal rooms. This held a dozen cots plus pit-like toilets that were to the side but still in the open. In front of these were what might be primitive clotheslines that could provide some privacy in use. Two large pots sat nearby with sturdy handles.

"For clothes washing?" Lina theorized. A trough-like sink on the opposite side held storage beneath that revealed a few wide but shallow buckets.

"For bathing," Lina decided. She pulled one out to demonstrate. "A standing bathtub. You step in and then bend down to get your water for washing and rinsing. Spring and them were used to this kind of thing. You bathe when you are called by a man for sexual service."

Londo pointed at the wall, the inside of which only he could see. "No hot water available. They'd be cold baths, cold laundry."

"Women don't feel the cold like we do," Bracken stated.

Jae stood by the one door to the windowless room and held up an electronic box. "A lock," he said. "It completes the prison."

Londo cursed quietly. How many women were on this world? Were they all in this situation? Were some in worse ones?

"I don't see eating facilities here," he said as he looked around the room. "No clean water available. No food storage cabinets or food service items. Are the women just starved, then, unless they're called forth to service the men?"

Lina's glare at Bracken should have paralyzed him. "We don't treat our *animals* this badly."

"But. But." Bracken looked around the room as if seeing it in a new light. "They are... *women*."

"Field Marshal," Lina said icily, "women are human too. Just as one hundred percent fully human as men are. Perhaps in this instance, a little *more* human." She looked down at the floor. "Yes, Aldierra, this is a priority for us. I'm sorry we didn't make that clear to you before."

"Definitely a top priority," Londo said and hoped the planet heard him as well.

"But..." With visible effort Bracken shut his mouth.

Jae gave Lina a chin nod to the outer hallway.

The brighter note in Lina's voice seemed forced to Londo. "Let's set up a litterbox or two here. This is now the official cat shit room. No cat trees in here, please. We'll find a window with a nice view and set those up there. Now where's a real bedroom?"

CHAPTER

3

From within the wings, Lina Starhart watched her husband address the hotel's theater crowded with reporters, sociologists and documentarians.

"The primary rule here is: Wear. Your. Vest." Londo targeted the audience with his worlds-famous Valiant Warning Scowl. "Poke your nose one millimeter into public space, and you'd better be wearing it. It's for your own protection. Aldierra is a violent planet. It holds twenty billion people, and all of them are either terrified or angry. Or both. Violence is brewing if not boiling under the surface. *Don't* be the one who winds up a target."

If the failed invasion hadn't shown that, then yesterday's fiasco certainly had. Lina was still reeling from the impact of her new job. She needed to adjust her mindset; change gears. A week ago she'd been teaching psychic techniques to eager students. Now she was running an out-of-control rodeo that stretched over an entire world.

Thank goodness they'd had last night to reassure each other. And do other things.

Lon looked so hot when he orated. Dark hair that he insisted on keeping combed into military order when it looked so sexy when mussed. His honey brown skin was electrifying to touch, especially since both of them had been denied that sense for so long. Of course in public he dressed in tight black pants and boots, that black hunter's vest over it… His nose might be a bit larger than average, a bit like Julius Caesar, but he wore it so well.

Woof.

"Violent," Lon repeated for the *n*th time, snapping her admiring attention back to the occasion. He was speaking in Farrani. Offworlders all had translators relaying the message.

She glanced at Jae to see how he was taking the speech. His focus was fully on Londo, as it should be, especially since he was repeating Lon's words in Pan-lingua for the translators' program.

Would she ever get over the rush of Jae's stupefying looks? That was shallow of her, right? He was layers of intriguing personality, skill and intellect as well; shame on her. But he stood a few inches taller than Lon, his skin warm almond, a shade darker than Londo, with mysterious blue eyes. The tips of his pointed ears barely peeked out of a generous mass of shoulder-length blond hair. When he smiled…

It wouldn't be wise of her to reach out in hopes of Jae offering his hand to clasp. His role as the third in their marriage was secret except to a handful of people like Bracken. There would be no smiles, no touching, no intimate laughs when they were in public.

But now he looked at her from the corner of his eyes, and the left side of his mouth quirked. His eyebrows raised and lowered a fraction of an inch. With a grace that almost masked his move, he sidled over and they stood together, only the air around their bodies palpably meshing.

Lina took a long breath to savor his calming presence. This would have to be enough. They had work to do.

This project was starting from scratch, and it was a rush job. Deadline was a mere almost-nine months away, and it involved the entire world of Aldierra.

Darn those Three Worlds anyway. They'd known for a long time that this was coming. The Worlds had thrown the three of them together; they'd fallen completely for each other… and now they had no time to deal with the personal side of things because Aldierra thought everything had to be hurry, hurry, hurry.

When at the very least were they going to get a honeymoon?

Since her own Speaker for the Three Worlds costume was only days old and hardly famous – yet – Lina wore one of the orange-trimmed vests over it. On front and back it held the circular symbol for them, the Starharts, since it was recognizable from a distance, unlike the more detailed logo for the actual Three

Worlds. That had a horizontal format and was only used as a stripe reaching across the left front shoulder, like a name tag might.

Oh – Lina made a note on her padd. She needed to requisition name tags for everyone, with built-in locators. Just in case. Aldierra was a violent yadda yadda.

This morning the Starharts had included a warning in a global telecast that anyone wearing this vest with its symbol was never to be harmed. Punishment for disobeying would be brutal.

Right now they didn't know what, but Londo had made it sound very bad indeed. "We'll handle it if it comes up," he assured the two of them in private.

Lon was so regal there in the spotlight. How had he ever chosen her? How had Jae?

She'd heard the speech as he'd rehearsed. She glanced at her padd, where she'd stored so many, many notes from their Aldierra discussions.

You need assistants, her spirit guides whispered inaudibly.

I know. It's in here. She bobbed the padd up and down as if the guides wouldn't know what she meant. **Give us a chance to begin like we'd planned. We need to set foundations, hire a staff, but we also need to get these people off and running. Just because Aldierra's antsy doesn't mean you have to be too.**

Something angelic patted her reassuringly on the shoulder, and Jae turned to her as if he could sense something as well. She nodded to him. He tilted his chin as his eyes moved, as if searching for that spiritual vibe. Then he gave a one-shouldered shrug and surveyed the crowd, still murmuring into the translator.

The big question came from the crowd to Londo: "When exactly is this Deadline?"

"The Ultimatum was given on Aldierra's solstice. Currently it's summer in the northern hemisphere; winter in the southern. We have three seasons to turn this world around and save every citizen of it. Deadline is two equinoxes away. That will be the first day of spring in the northern hemisphere and first day of fall in the southern. The date is Carvun first, and if the planet is exact, and we may expect this to be so, 1523 hours in the prime time zone."

"I'm still not sure how this Ultimatum was sent, Valiant…"

Lon gave a little smile at that and motioned to Lina, who stuck her head far enough out from the wings so people could see her. "My wife," Londo explained.

"She's a telepath, a psychic. Now an interstellar transporter as well. Then-Admiral and now Field Marshal Bracken of Aldierra owned a large crystal globe that was unknowingly linked to the sentient being who is the very world of Aldierra. Lina came near it, and suddenly she was telepathically broadcasting the Ultimatum to every living Aldierran human."

"It wasn't my decision," Lina called so people could hear her. "Aldierra just borrowed me. I was along for the ride."

Lon nodded. "We've discussed this. Neutrino [Jae lifted his left arm to wave identification to the audience] has theorized that Lina was utilized to step down Aldierra's frequency to one that could more easily communicate with humans. It helps that Lina has been talking with worlds and spirits all her life."

By now Lina was used to lots of people in college class-sized amphitheaters looking up to her. This time were gathered documentarians and sociologists of just about every color and variation to be found in the galactic sector containing the Affiliated Systems. The capital planet of the AffSys, Sarastor, was one of the newly announced Three Worlds. Many other people in the crowd with skin tones on the bright side of orange were natives here on Aldierra. All those were men.

Some attendees were from Earth, the last of the designated Worlds, whose sector neighbored the AffSys as well but from another direction. They looked more than a little mystified at all the advanced tech they had been given: cameras and lights and sound equipment, all contained in baseball-sized floating globes. They wore computers less than pocket-sized that were worked via hand gestures or even glances. The Terrans had been given interfaces so they wouldn't have to learn all this Out There tech overnight, but it would still be a rough learning curve, the same one Lina was going through.

Ugh, tech learning curves. The worst.

Londo had taken a Valiant stance, legs wide and fists on his hips, his scowl in full play. Marbles floated above the various groups, translating as needed. "Violent. Things will probably get worse before they get better. It's also grossly polluted. Wear your breathing masks. Goggles likely wouldn't hurt. When in doubt, either don't touch something or wear gloves."

Londo let his gaze sweep the audience. "Never drink the water. *Never.* Scan any drink you might be offered to make sure it's safe. Hell, scan the food as well.

If you think you need it, and I'm especially talking to the women here, call in for more guards. They are being paid well to protect you all, so put them to work."

Her beloved Jae looked as determined as Londo. Here on Aldierra, not a member of the AffSys or even its sector, the "Last Feithi" had only been a rumor until their brief broadcasts had begun the other day. Like his people, Jae could control the very nature of matter. He could change subatomic structure, reformatting it into new elements. He could heat things up by ordering atoms to vibrate faster. He could alter blood chemicals to either save or stop someone in their tracks.

Even in galactic boondocks like Aldierra, Feith had been an almost mythical world of a peaceful and advanced people. Now only Jae remained. He was resolute that Aldierra would not wind up destroyed like Feith. It had not been the planet Feith that had destroyed every bit of life on that world, but rather evil and jealous individuals from the AffSys. If the Aldierrans didn't shape up, the end result would be the same for them.

Lina stepped front stage to help with the video show as Dr. Wilder Mem-Bazer watched the session, his image on a nearby monitor. She didn't have to look at her friend to know how pleased he was to witness this potentially monumental change to galactic history. He radiated intellectual excitement that one didn't have to be a telepath to pick up.

The middle-aged Wiley had a warm teal complexion. His short violet hair was sedate and styled, but soon Lina knew it would stand higgledy-piggledy as he ran his hand through it with all his ponderings.

With his brilliant scientific five minds Wiley investigated all things he could think of. He could think of a lot. He'd insisted on making thorough records of this experiment, and had congratulated them for considering that already. However, Jae had put his Legionnaire friend and mentor in charge of coordinating the people in the room and others like them who would be arriving soon. That would be one less thing off their shoulders.

Wiley thought he could fit these objectives around his Mega-Legion duties, for he served there at the same high levels as Jae and Lon, if in a slightly different capacity. "If worse comes to worst, I shall incubate another mind," he'd declared.

Jae had given him a doubtful look, but shrugged. "Whatever it takes."

It helped that Wiley had paid the interstellar transportation and supplies for the civilians here. Jae and Londo both brought home Legion wages whose amounts made Lina dizzy, and last week she herself had earned... well, she wasn't quite sure how big the figure was, but it was *big*. Big, big, BIG. Large enough to awe both Lon and Jae, though the final figures hadn't come in yet.

She had come up with a way for the sector to defend itself against the Yanist-Glory Empire, which was located in yet another neighboring galactic sector. Now that the threat of Mind Control was neutralized, the Empire could no longer encroach on the AffSys' sector... until they devised a new way to conquer planets.

The worlds in the AffSys sector had considered that important enough that they'd paid Lina and her support staff an enormous amount of money. Wiley had explained that it was actually cheaper for them to do so than to maintain their defense budgets at the levels Mind Control required.

At this stage there was no way to tell exactly how far the money would stretch, but everyone assured her that they were good for a long while. Still, savings when they could get them were much appreciated. Plus by flying this crowd in on his dime, Wiley had relieved her of the effort of having to port them here using her new interstellar transporting power.

It didn't look like it from the outside, but porting bunches of people or large objects could get tiring quickly.

Lina gestured to guide the puters through the AV display. "What we want from y'all," she told the group as she folded Farrani into the Southern-style pronoun, "is documentation of the situation here on Aldierra. We need records of how the world is now, how it changes, and how it stands once we hit Deadline."

The audience murmured their worry at the mention of the Aldierran Deadline. Lina said, "No one who is non-Aldierran will be harmed by a bad outcome of the Deadline. If there is one. Which is what we're here to prevent. What they like to call 'the Doom' or 'Doomsday' – *please* don't encourage those terms – is for Aldierrans only, one hundred percent."

She nodded as they took that in. The Aldierrans in the bunch didn't seem relieved.

"While we're looking for the overall picture, or distinct studies on different aspects, we also want stories we can run on popular news programs. Short, upbeat bits. Closeups on the average Aldierran, how they're coping or what they're doing to help out. Cute kids. Try to emphasize hope for a bright future. If you can't find that, well…"

"Show what you find," Jae told them. "We need a true historical record as well as, well, propaganda. Let's hope future historians can tell the difference."

Deadline Doom was nine months away. Aldierra would exterminate every human of her world unless they showed her they would honestly and actively change their ways.

The three Starharts were starting from scratch. The Great Council of Military Governors, with the Patriarch sitting at their head, had assured them that waiting a week or two before the Starharts came to Aldierra would give the Council time to come up with all kinds of strategies and campaigns to get the job done.

They hadn't done squat.

Lon told the crowd that there were video examples in the people's kits, and that they should keep in touch with Wiley's special office. At the first sign of trouble, they should yell for help. Jae added that the new planetary teleportation system they'd just installed, which was mechanical and not of Lina's doing, was available on a limited basis. Then Jae glanced at Londo expectantly.

Londo gave the crowd a commanding chin-up sign of dismissal. "I'd like the non-Aldierrans to remain," he told all. "We need to make sure everyone is immunized and has their cultural cues, so no one accidentally causes an incident."

The Aldierrans obediently filed out. When the doors closed behind them, Lon took his Regal Stance, nearly an At Rest posture. He didn't scowl. He allowed no emotion to show on his face. It might as well have been one of Jae's cataloged expressions that he used to keep his tangled emotions private.

It had been a huge concession for Lon to agree to revealing this much of their secret. Lina could feel him clench in anticipation.

"Aldierran culture includes polygamous marriage," Londo told the assembly. "The low ratio of females to males happens because of violence and neglect inflicted on women. Marriages usually contain multiple men with one wife. We are presenting ourselves as a marriage unit to the Aldierrans. All three of us are now 'The Starharts.' You will not question that. You will not ask Aldierrans if they believe it. You will treat it as fact. We Starharts need to be people the Aldierrans can identify with."

A lie. Londo did have a habit of lying. Their only huge argument so far had been about his lies. He'd promised to tone them down... for her. Now he was lying to how many people?

Polygamy did show up in the AffSys, but there it was a shocking slavery or impersonal sex-for-hire arrangement. Earth? When it was done it was for the misogynistic purposes of the patriarchy. In the few cases that were the exceptions, Earth had no support system for such, no way that the participants could function to best effect.

Feith had treated both the dual-Triune and the full Triune with dignity and honor. These were meant to reinforce emotional attachment and increase spiritual growth.

But Feith was dead.

Non-Aldierrans thought the marriage contained only Londo and Lina. It had been two-ish weeks now since the final, secret Triune wedding.

"And do check with our medics on the way out to see that you're up on your shots."

With this story Londo encased her and Jae in his lie. Lina didn't like it, not one bit. She'd said so, but Jae had remained quiet.

Anything for Londo.

How did Londo condone his lie? Something larger than their commitment to uphold Feithi tradition kept him from revealing the truth. Maybe kept him from revealing his own truths to himself.

She'd asked Jae about it and he'd told her not to nag Lon. "Do you not think that Lon will eventually come out?" he'd asked.

Lon was too tied to virtue and honor and all that – truly using it as a basis for his life – not to come around. The only question was: how could she and Jae make sure it was sooner than later? Already the situation strained at her. She could feel Jae's anxiety at it as well, but he kept his darned "masks" on, hiding his emotions from public view.

Anything for Londo. They both agreed on this.

For now.

Absolutely, one day Londo would relent to let the full truth out. One by one in his life, Lon had lost too many people he loved. His bio father. His bio mother. The friends who had also been experimented upon for years by the aliens who had kidnapped him when he was a toddler in order to turn him into another Maximus. He'd watched in succession as their bodies had been taken away. Even his dear Aiko's death was barely a month past, though she'd been a mega-powerful Legionnaire.

Prejudice and misunderstandings ran deep. An announcement like this would turn some of the special people in his life against him. He didn't think he could handle that well, not with the stress of this Deadline upon them.

Still. Jae had lost everyone, all at once, when his planet had been destroyed. He was the only survivor, the Last Feithi. But he'd been a boy and was quickly offered help afterward. He'd had acres of psychotherapy through the years. Lina heaved a sigh. Likely that's where all his masks came from. He needed to hide within himself from the misery the universe had presented him with.

Londo's therapy hadn't arrived for years, after he'd rescued himself and been found and then adopted by Maximus. Now there was this marriage. Not even Maximus – no, she should remember to call him "Hal" – the most famous para-hero in the galaxy, knew their secret.

Yet.

Lina vowed to keep her eyes open so she could be ready to cushion any blow that unveiled the secret too soon for Londo to handle.

Unless of course she couldn't stand it anymore and did it herself.

– – –

Londo received Hal's call almost immediately after the event.

"Of course I heard this," the sectors-famous hero declared hotly. "I have Wiley funneling me feed he thinks I should know about your project. What the hell is all this?"

"All this?" Lon replied innocently. *And so it begins*, he told himself.

"That you're making people think you three are married!"

"Oh that. It's the Aldierran way. They'd just assume it. This way they can identify with us. We're one of them."

"But– A threeway!"

"It. Is. Normal here."

Hal let out an audible growl as his usually calm features contracted into anger on the screen. His deep brown face became even more dark. "We do not do scandal."

"No scandal," Lon repeated. "That's why we're doing this. Otherwise it would be a scandal."

"Rands do not have scandals!"

"I'm a Starhart now."

"I don't care. Rand, Starhart. No scandals!"

"But on Aldierra–"

"I'm talking the rest of the galactic sector, AffSys and beyond. What will people think? You know some will believe this."

"How about Feith? Jae told me that they had polygamy there."

"Feith? You mean the dual-Triunes? Not the same thing."

Dual-Triunes were one step below the Triune, a more open kind of marriage the majority of that world's population had had. "In general."

"Not the same. There it was honorable. They had a way of arranging things; I don't know. But at any rate, Feith is dead. You can't bring that up as an excuse."

"But–"

"But nothing. Get your PR people on this, especially before the news leaks on Earth. Drive home that this is a ruse you're playing."

"But–"

"Nip it in the bud. I'll talk to Stoan, see what–"

"Do not talk with Stoan!" Lon interjected. "I am the Legionnaire. I will talk with my commander when and if I deem it necessary." He took a breath. "I'll let my assistant handle this, as needed."

"Your assistant is new."

"But comes highly recommended. I'm on informal leave from the Legion, so his job load is light. I'll set him on this. We'll get it straightened out."

"Well…" Hal's features relaxed. "I suppose…"

"Everything will be fine," Lon reassured his father. His heart clutched, hoping Hal would believe him. He must. He couldn't lose Hal's support.

"See that it is."

CHAPTER

4

Londo's task list for the day was lengthy. He pondered as he hovered over the air vehicle lanes in the dark and gritty clouds above Drape-Tessay, the primary capital of Aldierra. It was set on the smallest continent, Reyda, located in the northeastern quadrant.

Day One had not gone as planned. The food distribution snafu had almost been disastrous. Despite Hal's protestations about the Triune, though, this semi-reveal might work. It was a lie to some, not a lie to others. A good compromise, and it would hurt neither Lina nor Jae. They'd get over their upset.

Not only would this have the Aldierrans working smoothly with them, but it would also get non-Aldierrans used to the idea of the Triune, whether they thought they were in one or not.

The three of them would escort the Aldierrans through this Doomsday Deadline alive and well. Lon had no doubts. Every Aldierran must surely be committed to doing all they could to help their world. With all three Starharts helping, how could they lose?

Lon pictured the celebrations at Deadline, after however Aldierra the world signaled that they had all passed their test. He hoped it would be as obvious as the Ultimatum had been. The people would be over-the-top relieved. So happy. They'd cheer Londo and his spouses as the unrivaled heroes of the moment.

He could see the parades with him, Jae and Lina in the front. Tickertape raining down, or whatever this world did. People standing along the street as they rode by, cheering.

The other worlds would be celebrating along with them. They'd be rewriting their history books. Londo's face would come next to "legendary" in the dictionary. Or at least next to Hal's. Playfully he planned the right portrait shot for the entry.

At that moment – that very moment when the tickertape was falling everywhere – he'd tell everyone the truth about the Triune.

And they would still love him.

– – –

He'd have to make sure their Aldierra plans went smoothly if he wanted that tickertape parade. A schedule everyone abided by was the only way they were going to get through this. Thankfully today's food distribution points were reporting all-clears, with Bracken's people overseeing aerial transfers.

This operation needed better outreach than just Bracken. Those bastards on the Council had disregarded every suggestion the three of them had given.

Communications were needed. Lon had to know the truth of what was happening throughout Aldierra. Quickest way to do that was to utilize the Majority Army. The Majority Army was overseen by Bracken, who was overseen by the Council. The telecasts the three of them had been making had been funneled through systems administered by the Council.

To quote just about every character in his beloved *Star Wars*, Lon had a bad feeling about this. Someone else's finger was on the button, not Lon's.

According to Bracken, there were at least fifteen major wars currently across the planet. But Jae was right: they had to take things step by step, not get distracted by… people getting killed.

Innocent people getting killed. Maimed. Terrorized. The children…

Londo fisted his hands and clenched his eyes shut. He'd been fighting such all his life. This time he couldn't rush to help. To protect.

He was Protector of Aldierra now.

A triaged organization came first. Then he could protect better, with Jae backing him up. And Lina.

Ah, first thing: Lina must be protected with more than just a squad of five men. She had zero defensive training.

He took his padd from a vest pocket and set that as top priority on his task list.

He added an item about Jae's protection as well. Jae had a tendency to get injured on the job, even though Jae was one of the most dangerous people Londo knew. Superb in offense and even defense, but not invulnerable.

Now. Other things. Organization. Take those problems with food distribution, for example. Many things had been revealed with that, and he'd spoken to a number of military types already about what they'd encountered.

Lon screwed his mouth in concentration. This Doomsday threat wasn't helping at all. It had ramped up terror more than he could imagine. "You couldn't have given us more time and less panic?" he asked the air and hoped that Aldierra heard.

He checked. Yes, here was a report relative to stress levels. Suicides. Good god. Look at the curve. It had exploded as soon as Lina channeled Aldierra's Ultimatum of Doomsday.

He searched wider. Riots. Bad before; cataclysmic now. Murder: ditto. Assault, thievery: ditto, ditto.

He was now acquainted – Lon balked at the idea of saying "friendly" – with the man who was ultimately responsible for Aiko's death. Bracken would be the topmost in rank in the military, next to the Patriarch and perhaps the Great Council.

Patriarch Lupoff seemed ineffective in anything but playing politics and war. Politics and power struggles roadblocked getting positive things done. Political aspirations too often initiated negative actions.

Bracken would have to be their liaison to the Council. Sure, Lupoff had given the Starharts free rein during the emergency, but Lon wondered how good Lupoff's memory would be about that as the project continued.

Londo made notes.

The armies of Aldierra were vast and many. As far as Jae could figure out, armies had been set in typical "us vs them" tribalized conflicts to keep the people from going about their normal lives. Propaganda held the population in constant fear. These were the strategies that kept the armies in power and awash with money, things that ensured that the Council remained the Council.

Aldierra was at war with itself.

The Council was the biggest power problem on the planet. Jae bet that they were controlling all the armies and not just the Majority one. He could be right.

Lon wondered: Time to make a covert move to ensure the other priorities went more smoothly? Time to gather allies, in spite of themselves?

— — —

"Field Marshal," Londo said as he advanced toward the uniformed Aldierran. Bracken wasn't wearing the full display of medals across his chest today, only six, since he was in the everyday comfort of his new private office. The dark walls were broken up with maps and military symbols and a stern portrait of the paunchy Patriarch. "I would like to talk with you, if you have time. Or even if you don't."

Lon nodded at the three men who waited on Bracken, padds paused expectantly in their hands, even one with papers.

"Of course, Protector." Without turning, Bracken instructed the aides, "Give us privacy," and they left quickly.

Lon checked his own padd. "Privacy" was a relative thing, it seemed. There were listening and viewing devices hidden in a handful of spots here. He wondered if Bracken knew? He dug in a pocket and released a tiny electronic globe into the air. It created a zone of absolute security around him and Bracken, delineated by a dark perimeter.

"This will take a while." Lon gestured to the field marshal's desk and chair there. He pulled up his own to the side and laid out several padds, instructing them to project multiple screens.

The picture that came up most sharply to him was the one in his mind: Aiko. The legendary heroine had been impaled like a golden butterfly by the fragments of a bomb. She'd managed to tell him that she'd always love him before... Before...

It was because of Bracken's war.

It took every bit of Londo's strength to pull himself past the empty black hole left in his soul and back to the present. "I have some ideas. Field Marshal, how would you feel about repurposing some of your armies? At least for the duration, but possibly beyond?"

Bracken took his seat. "I was expecting this. Our Majority Army would be the easiest and best place to start. And if we are truly private, which I believe we are," he glanced at the dark bubble they were in, "call me 'Bracken.'"

"Is that a surname? A first name?"

"It's the entire name. Once a man reaches a certain level of… distinction, he is allowed to pare his name down. My family calls me 'Bracken.'"

"Very well. I am 'Londo.' 'Valiant' will do if you want to say it under more official circumstances."

"Or 'Protector?'"

Lon gave a Gallic shrug. "That's a title I'm still getting used to. Let's keep it for formal Aldierran business."

"Very good."

"Now about the armies. Instead of offensive actions, I'd like to use as much of them as possible for building a new world. This will require much demolition of what is holding this world back, and construction of new structures, new wild-life territories."

"Wildlife?" Bracken sat back in his chair.

"Animals don't have enough room or resources to thrive," Londo explained. "Some of our preliminary actions have been to retrieve the studies various Aldierrans have made through the years that show where the primary migration routes originally were, where the huge forests were that, among other things, replenished oxygen and supported the type of life that inhabited them."

Bracken rubbed his beardless chin. "That sounds like…"

"Cities will have to get smaller. Entire cities will have to be moved, and ones we're keeping will have to be remodeled to house the relocated people and their workplaces."

"Entire… cities?"

Londo nodded, gauging his reaction. This couldn't be a time when he could offer compromises to make people feel better about him and his own actions. Time to set some boundaries, some lines that couldn't be crossed.

"We have a Deadline," Lon reminded the field marshal.

Bracken looked ill. "So we do. It… I'm not sure…"

"I have some preliminary notes." Lon gestured at screens, which Bracken in turn peered at.

A broad cityscape bloomed perpendicular to the wide desk. The view looked down from the sky.

"This is Plegerit. With the Saba River," Londo said before triggering an overlay with lines and arrows, as well as small boxes with animal names in them.

"These are the original migratory routes. You can see how Plegerit built right over them as well as the river. We will remove all artificial structures from this area."

"But this is… an established city. Government and army facilities. People's Houses. Businesses. Agricultural complexes."

"I will relocate them. A balance has to be made of people's needs to those of the flora and fauna of the world. Aldierrans need to learn to share."

Lon could see Bracken's eyes tracing various routes.

"They'll also need to learn to care for and maintain it. This will provide more employment than you currently have. Several of our information sources think this. We hope it will make up for the jobs that will be lost during this larger transition."

"Larger?" Bracken looked sharply at Londo.

Lon added more layers to the view, these increasing the greenery of the landscape below via time lapse. Trees and meadows, brush and clear streams spread across the map, beginning at river's edge. The edge of Plegerit retreated from all of it.

"That's what we're here for," Lon said. "We're going to change the face of your world even as we start changing your people's attitude toward it… and each other. I don't know what they'll think of being relocated – I'm sure it will be rough in the beginning – but the geoengineering is a subject not open to debate. It *must* happen."

"It's a beautiful vista," Bracken said slowly. "But…"

"It's very possible to achieve," Londo assured him. "We'll need additional input. Lots of input on every matter you can think of about every phase of this, and more. It needs to be thorough but fast."

Lon waved at his screens and just the level with the map of Plegerit and the boundaries of the first phase remained. "This sector should be evacuated within eight days. We have to move on this. Big world. Short deadline."

"Eight days?" Bracken's voice held a momentary squeak.

Lon frowned. "We three have talked about this. Tell the people if they balk that they have two weeks maximum," he said. "One week if at all possible. If everyone works together, they can help others move one week, then the first ones can come back and help the remainder, and so on."

Lon triggered a world-wide map with pinned focuses. "Plegerit won't be the only high-population area affected. The people in these spots also need to be getting ready. We hope within six weeks we'll be working throughout."

Bracken blinked rapidly at the view. He licked his lips. "Yes. Six weeks. Fast indeed."

"I'm finalizing some house plans with Aldierran experts, plus some business templates that people will be able to customize. It will make the process speedier, but we hope it will also give the occupants a feeling that they're helping to design all this. Because they will be." Londo rubbed his nose. "The first versions may be a little rough. We'll improve over time as long as we get good input."

Bracken triggered two screens that replaced his desk top. "I have been thinking about our situation. Here is my own list, and not that of the official Majority Army, or one from the Council. And here…" Even more screens, set at reading angles. "…Are some resources I've contacted already. Or to tell a larger truth, many of these are resources I've been meaning to contact."

"Excellent!" Londo transferred the data to his padd. "We'll be studying all of this." He paused to give the field marshal a level look. "With your help, that is. We will be relying on you. On what you can suggest, as well as, well, your political and military clout. Am I too frank?"

"No. No, not at all. It's good not to have someone dancing around a problem instead of dealing with it directly."

He seemed like he was thinking deeply. That he was about to say something, but stopped.

The field marshal stood up and paced around the back of his desk, then began to circle to the front of it. He stopped. He frowned and Londo could practically see dark clouds gathering around him. Then in a blink, they disappeared.

Bracken's right hand formed a fist. He brought it down hard on his desk, through the insubstantial screens. "I am yours, Protector of Aldierra, in this Deadline problem. In helping our world for once, instead of reaching out to draw others into its misery. I. Am. Yours." Then he glanced side to side. "This is truly private?"

"As private as private can be." This had obviously been a major issue for Bracken. As field marshal he'd devoted his career, his life to the military and its aims. Bracken surprised him. Humbly Londo bowed his head. "I and we are honored, Bracken. We will all try not to disappoint you or your efforts."

Then Lon flashed him a grin. "With you, we can likely get twice as much done. Now, let's look at item number four on my list…"

— — —

They'd removed sofas in the smaller rooms and replaced them with office desks and chairs. There was also a central conference room to use now, right next to the kitchen.

Wiley contacted them from Sarastor to explain that Stoan Kinrol, the commander of the Legion, had okayed him altering their sensor earrings to handle wider communications than before. They'd be able to use them to communicate with whatever staffs they hired, as well as various normal communications media, plus the Legion could patch through in case of emergency.

"Tell him… thanks?" Lina murmured. Stoan was an awful, accusing person who delighted in arresting her. Perhaps he'd seen the light? Jae and Lon both thought highly of him.

Their earrings were always recording, per Wiley's programming. They stopped when they encountered a sexual situation the three might find themselves in, but otherwise every moment was memorialized somewhere. Lina felt very sorry for whoever would be slogging through the records sometime in the future.

Well, these would come in handy. Lina and her husbands replaced the studs on their earrings after Lina had ported them in. Wiley gave a finger twitch on his screen and everyone's padds loaded instructions.

More technology to learn. Oh joy. Didn't Lina have enough to do already?

— — —

Among Bracken's recommended personnel was a personal assistant for Lina, a man named Lt. Twofence. She housed him in one of the smaller rooms on the floor below and asked him to hire more to take different shifts. At some point she should go downstairs and meet them all.

Lon had rough-installed water and air cleaners in the building, but needed some more thingies to perfect the system. Jae had put together such gigantic supply lists that when Lina was given the signal to port from Sarastor, the equipment and tech doodads for both had to be aimed to land outside on the street because they wouldn't fit inside the hotel. Jae had been digging through that all morning.

He'd done so humming and singing nonsense songs, Lina noted. Lon whispered to her mind to explain that Jae had always been a tech geek. Once he'd come to the Legion as a young teen, he'd taken up with Wiley and ensconced himself in his labs, hoping to avoid undue curiosity from others in the Legion community. Over the years he'd been a valued assistant (and sometimes guinea pig) for Wiley's experiments.

Lon chuckled and admitted that he'd been a guinea pig as well. He'd joined the Legion as a teen less than a year after Jae did, though he was a little older than Jae. He relished hanging around Jae, and if Jae were in Wiley's lab…

Wiley was now also a close friend. Wiley had been intent on learning just how Lon had been experimented upon by aliens when he was a kid to turn him into another Maximus, but he backed off doing his own experiments once he realized how much psychological damage that process had caused Londo.

Whew, those had been big ports. Still, Lina was rather proud because more and more she was able to port larger things. She wondered what her limit was, but decided she didn't need to kill herself to find out.

The three Starharts had planned on taking different shifts so they could best cover the entire world as needed, but this introductory phase would concentrate on daytime outdoor work in the Plegerit area. Lina's workday would be different from her husbands' as she was coordinating materials, information, and people around the world.

They' aimed to have at least a couple of meals together each day so they could talk.

"About non-business as well as business," Jae had insisted. Talking was also only one possibility of what they could do together if their schedules meshed.

This second day's schedule had begun much earlier for Lina than it had for Lon or Jae.

"Your turn." She greeted Londo as he entered the room they'd designated her office, which they'd lined with computer links and screens. They managed some very satisfactory kisses above a thorough hug, but didn't go farther than that.

"I'm beat," she said. Lying on the desktop next to her, Obi must have agreed, for he was fast asleep.

"There are at least fifteen ships of various medical people arriving today starting in about an hour. It should be on your padd if I did things right. Medics, doctors, researchers, sociologists. I've got them quartered here in Plegerit, plus Drape-Tessay and Soshe. Wiley's already given them translators and vests, and they're bringing their own supplies, both food and medical. He would like you to give them that 'Welcome to violent Aldierra' pep talk you made yesterday. You might want to tape that so you don't have to repeat yourself in the future."

Lon glanced at the wall clock designating this time zone. "Looks like you've been up for nineteen hours. I don't want you exhausted by all this. Have you eaten lately?"

She checked beside her acti-board, where an empty cup sat along with a saucer with crumbs. "I think so. Unless Moosie ate that. And no, no caffeine today. I'm following doctor's orders. I just wanted to get a head-start on my new schedule."

After she'd kinda overdosed on stims during the Mind Control Tour last week (in order to save the galactic sector, she reminded herself), Legion Medical had sworn her off any stimulants for three months.

"Good. I want you healthy."

"Wiley also played a game with me," Lina told him. He raised his eyebrows at that. "He talked to me in several languages."

Lon waited for her to get to the point before he made a guess. "You understood them."

"All of 'em. Apparently – assuming this works on you and Jae as well – we are now omni-lingual, thanks to the Sentinels."

He reared back in amazement and blinked a few times. "I am going to try this out. It sounds fun."

"It is."

"And also uber-useful. We should send the Sentinels a very generous gift for their kindness. But first:" He leaned forward to give her a no-nonsense glare, although the silly angle of his mouth counteracted the effect. "You. Healthy. And rested. Hit the sack. I'll have breakfast waiting for you when you wake up."

Lon was at mid-afternoon in his shift. Jae was at a similar point. He'd done his doodad unpacking and then taken off to recruit likely civilian volunteers, about a third of a world away. He'd used the mechanical transporters they'd set up last week so she didn't have to be distracted from her own work.

"In a minute," Lina told Lon. "Here's what I've found so far from the major eco-groups that aren't areas we're already targeting." She gestured to turn the screen in the air so Londo could see it:

"Nuclear waste in oceans and at poles especially

"Red tides, caustic jelly along shorelines and in rivers

"Chemical spills along waterways of all kinds

"Wacko ocean currents

"Solid pollution at all oceanic levels

"Fish kills: why? How to treat?

"Giant refuse fires, like tire fires – no way to extinguish

"Forest and grassland fires

"Almost no rainforests

"Epidemics"

That one had a sub-note:

"Mutated and/or old diseases once thought eradicated"

The list went on, with "Nessie/Godzilla" listed at the very bottom.

Londo pointed. "What's this?"

"Lake and sea monsters," Lina said as she rubbed her eyes. "Most seem the shy sort, but one or two of them attack people."

"I don't blame them." Lon stood there surveying it all. "You want me to prioritize for us?"

"With a list this long we need to give the more minor stuff to our army of infinite volunteers." Lina flexed her back. "I'm still trying to find people to organize that, to free up Jae. Can you ask Bracken how we can best split this between military and civilians? We should divide it, first into land and sea matters, and then subsets of that, don't you think? Each group can have their own specialty. But that may reduce communications. I want them talking with each other, sharing ideas."

"We have to start somewhere." Londo pulled Lina to him and kissed her again. She smiled sleepily. He then shoved her toward the bedroom.

"I'll play with the cats a while and work on this before I head out again," he promised.

"Don't *you* forget to eat."

He mumbled something in her general direction and sat down to make some calls.

— — —

But it couldn't be bedtime yet, no matter how loudly her mattress called to her. There was so much to do. Lina stood alone in one of the extra bedrooms.

She didn't move as she tried to rouse herself a little more, just for a few minutes. Then she crooked the first two fingers on her right hand and tapped her upper left chest, as if there were a *Star Trek* Starfleet badge there.

"Captain's log," she said as she clenched her eyes closed. Surely this was too silly. But it was the only way she'd remember to do this, and it had to be done. "Uh, puter, insert date and time here. I'm not sure what it is, Aldierra-wise. What is it?"

The suite's puter's voice told her as her earring recording system took it all in. "How many days until Deadline?" Again, the puter reported. "I hope that registered on this," Lina told her earring. "Anyway, captain's log. Earring. Puter. Earring-puter, whatever, this is going to be how I signal I'm doing it. Make a note of my hand action and salutation. Always add the date and time and how long it is until Deadline and note it out loud so I can hear it."

Wiley had firmly requested they do this journalling. She recalled the day's events and narrated them into digest form. Occasionally she had to tap her right earring to bring up the audiovisual it was always recording where she had book-marked something in her day that needed noting. The new earrings let her do that, which was a lifesaver. Everything was working fine, except…

"Puter, can you set up a filing system? I need to know who I've met. Oh, starting from when I first landed in Legion HQ, if you can. Request permission from Wiley to get info from when I was in his lab, okay?

"Their faces, their names and any titles they have. What we talked about. Can you summarize it? Just a paragraph or two for each. I'll try to add what I think was important. If I meet them again I want to be able to bring up that information for reference, but I don't want to have to go through pages and pages of mate-rial." She gave that a thought. "Unless I specify you to do that for someone."

Puter assured her that it could do such a thing.

"Good. Well, I suppose that's it for today, official-wise." Lina sighed. "But on a personal note, it sure is odd to hear Lon talk without that accent of his. It was so sexy. It was also just a tad not natural. I think Lon used it to set himself apart from Maximus, you know? But he just doesn't seem Londo without it.

"Now, Jae's accent – that was Lon having a joke. Jae wanted to learn English, so Lon gave him a language tape with a really thick Irish accent because Jae has pointed ears like a leprechaun. That's an Earth being from the Timeless Realms. Har-har, funny once or twice, but I couldn't understand him half the time. I'd just smile and nod, like I was agreeing with him, and then try to switch things back to Lingua. It's a relief not to hear it. Jae's English is now Standard Ameri-can English, which suits me just fine."

She pressed her lips together for a moment. "I think I still have my American accent. Southern, that is. White Central fairly urban North Carolinian, if we want to be more specific. The difference is that that's my native accent. Neither Lon nor Jae grew up speaking English. I assume whenever they speak their native language that they use the accent they had as kids.

"But it sure would be nice if Lon got his accent back when he speaks a language other than French. Now he can't even fake it. I'm not sure if he can fake other accents. One of his joys is to do impressions of people. He's really good. Have you heard his Maximus impression? It's amazing.

"I wonder if it would be awful if we sent a message to the Galactic Sentinels asking to restore Lon's accent. It's such a piddly thing, and they have such important work to do. It was incredibly nice and handy of them to give us the translation thingie that they did. Like a million, billion thank-you points to them, right? No, just forget I mentioned it." Again she heaved a heart-felt sigh.

"Captain out."

CHAPTER

5

Thanks to advance work, the Starharts had many groups outside of the military government gathering information for them. By now Lina had thoroughly researched more mundane subjects than had her husbands: where to find portable toilets for upcoming worksites; who provided catering or military ready-to-eat meals in the area? What were the main transportation routes available to the places they were planning to work in? Where were earth-moving equipment and operators, and who needed to be contacted to make use of them?

Jae and Lon would be doing the shiny stuff. For the most part she'd remain behind the scenes as supply and transportation.

She put out a planet-wide plea that groups who were already working on their world's and society's problems, should get in touch with Three Worlds with ideas about what kind of help they needed. After all, three people were not going to solve everything alone. She set up two suites on the army levels of the hotel to house the preliminary contact teams. It would do for a start.

A glance at her watch confirmed that her husbands' meeting with architects would be winding up soon. She checked with Legion HQ's medical section parsecs away on Sarastor. The people she'd requested were ready to port in.

Two minutes later, three Aldierran women appeared in front of Lina. "Here you are," Lina told them cheerily as they clutched each other. "Welcome home."

Although her porting was instantaneous, Lina held her interstellar portees outside normal space for about two minutes in order to equalize electric potential and filter out contagions. Those two minutes of interstellar blankness could be terrifying for first-timers. These ladies had only travelled to Sarastor via hyperdrive ship, which took days.

She motioned them to seats. Beside each sat a refreshing drink that Lina had tasted to see if it lived up to the description. Not anything she'd call "delicious," but it would do.

During the Mind Control Tour Jae and Londo had quick-scouted part of Aldierra. They'd saved the three women from drowning after a dam break, and the women had been taken all the way to Sarastor not only for medical attention but also gentle debriefing as to the state of women on their world.

They'd lost their families and homes in the flood. Dawn was a young woman in her twenties. Her mother had cut off her nose when she'd been a little girl. It was to discourage men from coming near her.

In returning from Legion Med she now wore an artificial nose that didn't look very real, but was in the right general shape of what should be on her face. She'd refused cosmetic surgery to get a more realistic one. Well, that was her decision, and Lina admitted to herself that she could now look at Dawn and not get completely weirded out.

Hope was much older than Dawn, though Lina's notes from Sarastor said she was only in her early fifties. She didn't look it; life had been hard for her. She'd lost daughters and a granddaughter who was about to give birth to the flood. How young did women here begin to have children?

Spring was from a different House, and the closest people she'd lost had been her sisters. She was in her late twenties and had borne daughters who had been killed after birth as a matter of family tradition.

"You've thought about this," Lina confirmed with the women as they awaited the meeting they'd been asked to attend. They nodded. "Good. Now, the next room will hold all men. Well, I'll be there. But you will too. You represent the women of the world. We understand that different Aldierran cultures may have different ideas about these designs, but we'll deal with that later. This is just to flesh out our rough ideas. Basic templates."

"Are you sure it should be us?" Spring asked in a quavering voice.

"I'll be there," Lina repeated firmly. "You've already met Londo and Jae. You know they want to help. They're on your side."

The women looked at each other uncertainly.

"Take a deep breath," Lina instructed. "Breathe in your own strength. Breathe in the strength of your sisters, your daughters, your mothers. All the women throughout this world who have come before you. You will do fine. Wonderfully. You'll be helping this and so many generations to come."

"Will there *be* another generation, Speaker?" Dawn asked.

Lina gave her a conspiratorial grin. "If we have anything to say about it, there will. We may have to cheat a little to get it done." She stamped her heel on the floor and looked down. "You didn't hear that, Aldierra."

The world's gentle laugh echoed in her mind. Underneath her absolute frustration with her humans, Aldierra was a nice world. Then again, all the planets Lina had ever spoken with were nice. "But this is mainly the job of you and all your people, women and men alike. Stand tall and let them know your power."

Take your own advice, Lina, she ordered herself. She straightened as she led the group into the meeting room. It was a comfortable size for the ten Aldierran men there, plus Londo and Jae. The four women did not crowd it.

Wiley stood next to a 3-D screen hovering above the floor. He too was a startlingly realistic hologram as he was actually back in Legion HQ. His uniform was his lab coat over a baggy yellow jumpsuit, though Lina had seen a more streamlined version of it he hauled out for important occasions. Today it was something in between.

He would have looked quite scientific if it weren't for the myriad of rings on each finger. They were computer and sensory controls. Wiley not only had five minds, but the last time Lina had inquired, he was up to seven visual-type sensory inputs he could choose from. This began to explain why his eyes had a tendency to operate independently. If he were using more than one mind to concentrate on something, they would move in unison. Lina had also pointed out that the "wild eyes" manner scared people. It seemed to her that he'd toned it down since.

As Lina's group entered, Wiley's screen widened to show Andri Nemlor, subcommander of the AffSys Mega-Legion, by his side. She was tall, slender, and had medium beige skin. She was one or two years older than Londo. Though her hair was short it wasn't to the stubble stage so many Legionnaires who hadn't gone entirely bald preferred. But it was bright pink and matched her uniform.

She glanced at Londo and Jae, nodded, spotted Lina and gave another nod, and then turned to study her own screen.

Five women now; good.

"We have preliminary plans for women's shelters," Jae said as the screen changed its view.

Two of the Aldierran men muttered darkly to themselves. Lina made out "Don't see why…" before another one nudged the first in his ribs to shut him up.

Lina saw that the design had changed a bit from what Londo had proposed. "Small rooms," she observed.

One of the men bowed to her. "To allow more to live in the unit," he said respectfully.

"Could we get a picture of a woman in there?" Lina asked, and Londo waggled his fingers at the screen.

It was all the silhouetted woman could do to make her way around the bed in the mockup. She bumped into the walls several times.

"Gentlemen," Jae asked the group, "would you like to live in such quarters?"

"But these are for women," the previous man declared. "You can pack them maybe five at a time in a room this large. For example, the bed doesn't have to be that big. And beds can be stacked."

The other men murmured assent.

"Where will these 'shelters' be placed?" another asked. "Not too far from their Houses. The Houses should be able to keep track of their own women."

"Yes, too far gives other Houses proximity. They could steal the women for themselves."

The men began to speak loudly over each other. Lina saw Dawn take a breath.

"Excuse me," she said, and Lina was proud that her voice hadn't been a whisper. "Excuse me."

No one could hear her over the cacophony.

The women began backing away from the screen and into a corner of the room until they were huddled against the walls. Lina strode to the screen, the focus of the gathering, and put her fists on her hips.

"Enough!" she announced. "This meeting is over."

"But–"

"Apparently the Aldierran men in this room are unable to listen to women or take them seriously." She turned to Londo and Jae. "We need all-female focus groups. After that… Well, we'll see."

— – —

Within two hours thirty women stood in the main conference room of the suite. There were no men in sight. Andri's screen still showed her, but from a corner of the room, watching.

The women's dress showed striking variation in color, pattern, and wear, but always displayed a bulky cover-up fashion, even for half their faces. The three Lina had ported in from Sarastor were the exception, as they wore the tunics and leggings they'd been able to choose on that world. Their face veils had been relegated to neck scarves now that they were in the presence of only women.

Food and drink were located on a table against the side of the room. Some of the women shot straight to it upon arrival, shoving extra food into the folds of their mantles even as they filled their mouths. Lina tapped her earring and requested more food for the room.

Four AffSys women, all sociological architects, moved through the crowd. They set up duplicate screens and showed the women how to play with the views and run simulations on them.

Lina had to take five minutes to sit with one of the Aldierrans. She radiated pain. She had a raspy breath. Lina took her to a corner and talked to her quietly as she gently positioned her hands over the woman's upper left chest. "This is energy healing," she explained. "Your lungs are very irritated from all the pollution. Before you return home, I'll make sure our medics work on you in–" Lina chuckled – "a little more scientific a way than what I'm doing here. I've seen them clearing out people's lungs already. It's a bit startling of a treatment, but they sedate you so you're groggy. Takes about an hour, and when you sit up again you'll find you can breathe so much better. I'm just giving them a head start here."

"It doesn't hurt now," the woman said in awe.

"I'm glad."

The woman looked at the hands on her chest and then to Lina's face. "Can I learn this? There are many at home who have the same problem."

Lina poked out her lower lip as she considered. "That's a very good idea. I can port in energy healers from Earth, get them teaching on the air. Women do have access to TV? Usually these healers charge a lot of money for their classes, but I'll pay them well." She shrugged. "Maybe they'll do this for free, or for reduced wages. It's a very good cause."

"We can really learn?"

"You're alive; you can learn. And I know other things, other people, who could be teaching as well. Meditation. Lord knows this world needs to learn that. I need to do it more. General psychic abilities. Lots of interesting things." She wriggled in delight as she realized. "We'll have a full planet of psychics by the time we're done, maybe. Thank you for such a great idea. We'll put you first on the list to learn."

The woman just gaped at her as Lina scribbled a note and her name on her padd.

"You'll see." Lina smiled at her and then stood up. "I think you're done for now. It should improve even without the medics, but they'll give you a much more thorough session." Lina touched her earring and gave Lt. Twofence on the other end instructions to send female AffSys medics to attend to the crowd after their session was over.

He sounded doubtful. About attending to women's needs, or about female medics?

The women took another fifteen minutes to finish playing with their new computers. Lina stepped forward to the main screen.

Immediately one of the women piped up, "Will we be punished when we return, Speaker?"

Lina shook her head. "There is nothing to be punished for. We will make that very clear to your Houses. You can tell them whatever you want for what we're going to be doing. Tell them that you're helping to save your world and its people. That will be true enough.

"We've tried to get a cross-section of your population." Lina gave a wry smile. "There are approximately five billion women on this world, and here are a whole thirty-three of you." She shrugged. "Well, it's a start. We'll be refining this as we go along. But right now you represent all the continents, plus some sea cities, and we've tried to get a spread of economic conditions among you as well. Some of you are poor. Some are rich. Some have powerful husbands. Some have Houses with no power at all. All the opinions and suggestions given here will be considered on an equal basis."

Dawn, Spring and Hope were positioned near Lina. "These women have been aware of this project the longest. They've been able to think about it, and they've had a wee bit more access to Sarastoran technology than you all. They will assist.

"What we're going to build is women's shelters. Places to remove women from unsafe conditions and let them get on their feet. Recover."

As a group, the women gasped. "Shelters!" "Safe!"

"These *shelters* will be for women only?" a woman asked.

"Women and children," Lina replied. She asked the group, "Would men be welcome at such shelters?"

"No!" they replied as one.

"There are men who are also persecuted," Lina said.

"Then let them have their own shelters!" Two women cried the same thing at once.

From her earrings, Lina heard Lon and Jae's comments about that. Wiley drily added his own opinion.

"So be it." She made a note on her padd about boys and if/when they needed to be moved out of the shelters, to ask later.

"I'll remind you if you need it. Should be an interesting cultural note," Wiley's voice whispered in her ear.

Hope played with one end of the building on the main screen. "Look at the bathrooms!" she exclaimed. "Why are there doors?"

"For privacy," Lina said. "And over here are areas for changing babies. See the storage next to it? Diapers and wipes and creams and such."

"There are systems to clean the diapers," one of the Sarastoran architects pointed out. "Unless Aldierra doesn't want to use AffSys tech. Our toddlers and babies wear underpants that clean themselves. They need to be recycled once a day."

"Really?" Lina asked, but the women in the room had begun to spin the main view, stopping for a few seconds here and there just to spin it to another angle. They watched a moment as it stopped and then jabbered among themselves excitedly as they spun it again.

"We want your opinions," Lina instructed.

"Imagine if this building could be your dream home," another architect said.

"As a starting point," Lina corrected. They couldn't go so far as to put in swimming pools or places where men could be boiled in oil while the women watched. All that would likely be too expensive.

The view settled down. Dawn clasped her hands together and faced Lina. "How is sound in this? There should be quiet places for relaxation and… getting away from all the squabbling."

"It would be nice to have quiet places just to have quiet places," another woman added, nodding.

"Gardens."

"Multiple kitchens, too. How many people will live here? Not everyone wants to eat the same thing."

"We thought communal dining would be most efficient," one of the Sarastorans said.

A woman spoke up. "Have you ever tried to get a child to eat what everyone else is eating? If you feed the same thing to all, then you will wind up with starving children who would rather do that than eat even… *karkies*."

Hope added, "Babies and toddlers do not eat the same things as the older children. And some have… What did that doctor call them? *Allergies*." She used the Sarastoran word before attempting a translation to her own language.

Other women nodded at her wisdom. Lina tapped her fingers against her mouth as she thought.

"We should have thought of that, as in 'duh on us.' Duh! Well. We'll have different menus for the same meals," she decided. "The kitchen will be extended to provide prep and storage room for the extra food. The dining hall can remain the same size. Maybe we should have a smaller one to handle the kids who are particularly noisy at mealtimes? And likely there will be different schedules for meals, so not everyone eats at the same time anyway. What do y'all think? There will be at least one doctor or nurse in each center who can discover allergies, so that will help. Before long, we hope they will cure them."

The main screen split into smaller ones showing alternate versions as the various sub-groups came up with them. Finger wiggles and instructions to the computer stretched the plans and then replaced some walls. More finger wiggles from others placed silhouettes of women as well as children of different ages inside the diorama.

Ramps were added on almost everyone's screens. There were so many disabled, not only among the women but the children as well.

"Doctors," Lina muttered to herself and the people listening in. "Lots and lots of doctors. They'll need clinics. All-women as well as for men. Video medicine, of course, to handle most of it. Is anyone working on general triage of the population so we can attack this efficiently? Wiley, how's the outreach to AffSys medical students coming? How good is AffSys medical AI?"

An hour and a half later, the multiple screens had been narrowed down to just one. The women studied it before they nodded approval.

In her ear, Londo also muttered wonder at the amenities his own general residence plans had omitted or gotten wrong. "I'll fix them," he promised.

Lina nodded, though no one else in this room could hear his comment. "I suppose we'll offer final adjustments for each location before we build. Customize these a bit. But this will be the generic base."

Dawn pointed at the entryways. "What are these?"

"Quarters for the guards. We made them separate from the women's quarters."

"Men? I thought these shelters were supposed to be safe?"

Lina put in quickly, "You don't want men living with you at all, not even nearby, right?"

"Men guards – pfah!" Hope actually spat and Lina tried not to flinch. "We've seen the women at your Mega-Legion. Women can be strong. Women can shoot guns. Kill any man who tries to get in!"

That caused excited conversation. The AffSys assistants looked anxiously to Lina.

When it died down, Lina said slowly, "If we had women being guards we'd have to get them training. Weapons. Non-lethal ones. Psychological help so they don't just start shooting at any man who passes by. Or any woman whom they dislike."

The discussions wore on. When they finally came to a conclusion, Dawn leaned toward Lina and said, "Now about how you dress, Speaker…"

– – –

There was just. So. Much. Data to go through.

Londo tried to absorb it all as he sat at his new office desk. They'd had people gathering info for three weeks, if you started from Jae's First Contact mission. Things had snowballed from there, the pool of who they queried had vastly expanded, and what had accumulated was of mammoth proportions. Londo set his computer to organizing things as much as possible, but what could he use for parameters?

This was for an entire world. A world that had been going downhill for what seemed like a millennium. When had it suddenly become worse? When did it hit that point where the planet itself decided it had had enough? What was the absolute minimum they could accomplish in these nine months – only eight-plus months now – to make Aldierra change her mind?

At this point, an absolute minimum seemed to be a thousand times more than what they could accomplish.

Lon sweated through it as new info kept scrolling down and down his screens.

After a while he consulted the notes he'd taken with his spouses, as well as suggestions others had made. Bracken's armies had shitloads of suggestions. Those were surely the high notes. Londo adjusted his search and category instructions.

Once they'd settled on how they'd approach Aldierra's rampant ecological disasters – air and water first – he'd instruct the system to look for cultural emergencies. Maybe those would show some shared cause that they could tackle.

The list scrolled on.

Mon dieu, where did they begin?

Jae came into his office from his own office, where he had begun taping daily meditations people could stream once they began to broadcast. He was recommending twice a day. So far they had a library of six.

"Meditation will ease the worst of all this negative energy," he explained to Londo.

"Since when do you talk like Lina? Negative energy?"

"Since when do you speak with an accent again?"

"I do?" Lon clasped a hand to his chest. "I do? Zhe rain in Spain stays mainly…"

His accent was back! Yes, it wasn't truly natural any more but by now it had become a habit to stress it when he spoke. It differentiated him from Hal. And besides, he did have a slight problem with his "th's."

His shoulders relaxed. He breathed easier. He was himself again.

"Thank you, Sentinels," he murmured.

"Yes, thanks," Jae echoed. He drew a chair close to Londo and sat so he could put an arm around his shoulders, a hand on his arm. "I'd mentioned it in a report the other day, but didn't frame it as a request. They must have overheard. That was quite nice of them, wasn't it?" He squeezed Lon's shoulder. "And I bet Lina also said something. She once told me your accent was sexy.

"Lon, I've talked about negative energies before, I think a number of times, though it's never been the subject of a conversation. Weren't you paying attention?"

Well, maybe Jae had said such things now and then in the years Lon had known him. Maybe at those times Lon hadn't been kicked in the face by circumstance and dying for a few minutes and sentient planets and ridding the sector of Mind Control to notice.

"I've taken you for granted too often, Jae. I'm sorry." Londo kissed Jae gently and then surrounded him with a hug. "I really do pay extra attention to you but you know me: sometimes I get tunnel vision." Another kiss. Another, plus some squeezes.

Jae gave Lon a knowing smile between kisses. "You have to barrel through life. It's who you are. I wouldn't change that. Now and then we need a Valiant with tunnel vision."

There had been so many years when they couldn't touch each other, not like this. The fear of accidental injury had been too great. Lon relaxed fully into the warmth of their hug. "I'll keep an eye on this. You remind me when needed, *d'accord?* Now, besides lessening the negative energy around here, what do you make of this?" Reluctantly he broke the embrace to show his padd with the list.

Jae's eyes widened in consternation. He gripped Lon's hand as he checked the accompanying screen with its list of wars and riots, murders and suicides. Hissing softly, he let out a slow stream of air across his teeth.

"Where do we–?" Lon began but Jae gestured.

"You begin with the major polluters, as well as clearing and building. I begin by cleaning waterways and oceans. We have to lay the foundations. Alongside that we hit some major social problems, to balance things. The most occurrences first. That way we'll be helping the most people. We'll work our way–"

Lon checked the screen again. Now the list was numbered, largest number of incidents to smallest. It wasn't the best categorization, Lon could see, but it–

"Here," Jae said, pointing at the #3 spot.

"You're… kidding."

"No. I told you I'd heard about this. Murder is involved, which lifts it to number-one position. It's real." Jae gripped the edge of Lon's desk. "We'll need to make an official proclamation. An edict. Now. Then we can hand it off to others for enforcement while we attend to water and migratory routes."

"This is going to upset the armies."

"It's going to upset everyone. Prepare for feedback."

Lon gestured to bring up five more screens, some of them for communications. "I'll talk to Bracken first, see who he sends me to."

"Bracken will back us?" Jae said before biting his lip and then nodding to himself. "Bracken will back us."

"*Dieu merci.* We're going to need his authority to ram this through into people's heads."

But people were going to hate him for this.

— — —

The studio was next to the lifts on the second level of the hotel. Just a day ago it had been a plush if smaller suite of its own. Now it was filled with electronics arranged in rainbow displays, with ultra sound control throughout. Light and holograph systems were stacked up on shelves as well as liberally placed within the largest room. There was also a stage of sorts, and a variety of chairs to choose from, plus two tables. A lectern. A pitcher, glasses and plates were stored to the side. Lon's paravision picked out the directed microphones embedded in the ceiling.

Six civilian men worked in the suite. Three of them ambled around, checking readiness, one still working on cobbling some connections, while two sat in an adjoining room fiddling with electronics. One deferentially called Londo over to have him approve the link with the communications satellites Lon had hand-placed into orbit.

These satellites would not be subject to censorship from any source except the Starharts.

Forty-five minutes later they officially launched the planetary broadcasting studio, joined by the field marshal himself.

"This is an order for immediate release." Facing the camera with the no-nonsense expression that had guided an interstellar invasion fleet, Bracken stood at attention. Rows of medals glittered on his chest. "All citizens, military and civilians alike, are to obey." He nodded to let Londo come forward.

"From this moment forward," Londo ordered through the cameras, "homosexuality is not a crime. On any level. From now on, legal sex requires consenting adult partners of sound mind, period. We'll leave it to your legislators to figure out how sex between minors measures up legally, either heterosexually or homosexually, but even there mutual consent is required.

"Kids are going to experiment, but bullying can happen easily at those ages. Mistakes can be made on people too young to realize it in advance. Take that into consideration.

"No adult will be imprisoned, no adult will be punished, and certainly no adult will be killed because they have participated in a consenting homosexual act with another consenting adult. An adult in full possession of their faculties. That means no drugs as well as intellectual disability."

Jae joined Londo on stage. "Non-consenting sex will be prosecuted as rape," he added. "This includes non-consenting women. Females of any age. Males of any age. Non-consent equals rape. Rape equals a felony."

Londo held up a hand. "The Speaker would like a word," he told his audience, and Lina popped in.

She looked around to see what was what, nodded at Bracken, and said, "As long as we have everyone's attention, I'd like to add a request. I hate to make it an order but I will if needed.

"Y'all out there know that Aldierra has a big population problem. When the Ultimatum was given, the population was twenty billion and some. Now though it's been just weeks, it's significantly grown. Your world cannot sustain this. We are going to ask everyone to stop having babies for three years." She held up three fingers. "Three years."

Lon wondered how the hell they were going to enforce that. It made sense; it would have to become more than a suggestion soon. He'd have to research studies on China's attempt at population control, to find out if anything had worked there that the population had approved of.

This population wouldn't approve of this.

Lina continued, "If you're already pregnant and want the baby, no problem. Go ahead and have it, and good health to everyone involved. I hope your medicine in this area is up to snuff. We'll work at that.

"If you're pregnant and don't want the baby, arrange for an abortion. How easy are they to get here? Well, if you can't get one, contact us – put up our contact info, will you?" Lina asked a hidden engineer. "Good. We'll try to get a simpler contact system within the next couple days so everyone can remember it."

Lon saw Jae checking his padd. Abortion doctors. A call had already been sent out for volunteers to come to Aldierra.

"Um. Fetuses in later stages of development. Y'all know that the soul doesn't enter the womb until the fourth month earliest, right? Sometimes it doesn't come in until months after birth. That's according to hypnotic age regression studies on Earth. Has anyone here made a study? If so, we want to hear about it. If your healthy fetus is four months or older but it's not wanted, we need to talk about abortion alternatives unless there are health problems. We'll see what the AffSys has available.

"In the weeks to come we'll also be passing out birth control to both men and women of childbearing age. Oh – I've already run into people who don't know what that is. We'll be doing all kinds of informational programs about birth control and I suppose basic sex education. Whether you get pregnant or not can be controlled. Pregnancies can also be monitored to make sure everyone involved is healthy.

"If we don't get to you soon, just… control yourselves, okay? I'll be researching what y'all already do in the birth control area here. Use it. Just remember: no new babies for three years, please. At that point we'll all pause and check what a new plan of going forward will be."

She smiled apologetically at the camera and said, "Thank you."

CHAPTER

6

The surveys weren't finished yet, but Lon had studied plans for this migratory route on the continent of Malcone enough that he could start to rough things in. Buildings would have to come down, but so far he'd seen too many that weren't ready.

Lina, get some people to go through these buildings to make sure they're empty, he called. **A couple of companies, army companies. No, a battalion or regiment. We need this done quickly. Bring a good-sized group of guards too. People aren't happy about having to evacuate their homes and businesses.**

Got it, she replied. **Give me two hours to organize and get them there. I'm already working with a base nearby. Send a map of where you're working and we'll tick off places as we go through.**

Efficiency, thy name was Lina Starhart, Londo thought with a smile. He knew he could count on Jae to get things done, but now he knew his bride could as well.

They hadn't gotten married in order to form a business partnership like the Worlds. They'd married because they loved each other and wanted to be together. Plus have sex. And family. Mutual support. And sex.

Sure, they could have had sex without marriage, but… This included a complete intimacy and trust that came with pledging oneself to another for eternity. It added a depth to the situation that he hadn't anticipated.

A legal marriage cemented them into a social network, a safety net of sorts.

Oui. Marriage was a good thing.

He had friends who'd told him that marriage could get real tough now and then. Half of marriages didn't survive. He intended his to be one of those that did, and for that they just might need a safety net.

Lon sucked in a breath. Sometimes he could get a little rough in dealing with people. He might lie a bit. Might state things in a way that upset others.

Silently he reiterated his intention to be the best husband that Jae and Lina could have chosen. When the time came, he'd be the best father. And grandfather.

He hoped their current work wouldn't interfere with any of that. There'd been zero time for a honeymoon either. Couldn't avoid that. They'd have one that was twice or three times as long as a normal honeymoon once they were through the Deadline.

The world around him faded as he imagined that honeymoon with two of the sexist humans ever. Yeah. The things they'd do…

Sailboat and sunset had to be set aside, though. Smog, filth, and ugly buildings took their place in the here-and-now. He could begin with this commercial air transport hub. His paravision showed all buildings empty of workers, with blank interior spaces where electronics and office materials had been.

Ten minutes later Londo was covered with dirt. Dust was settling around him as the last walls of an outer complex dropped. Satisfying. A baby step, but every step–

He heard the sound of laser fire nearby. Guns made a unique, high-frequency squeal when they loosed focused light, a squeal his parahearing picked up.

With a leap, he hovered over a distant section of the hub's field to reconnoiter. Twenty-plus men were shooting at each other, ducking in and out of cover afforded by sheds and abandoned vehicles. They wore orange and blue uniforms, so they weren't members of the Majority Army. Three young boys were dressed in partial uniform. Rips and discolorations marred their facemasks, as if they were used issue, improperly maintained.

Their lasers kicked up dust clouds around them, fizzling edges of metal containers. Setting more fragile ones on fire.

"Stop!" Lon bellowed, and though some of the men clapped hands over their ears, most kept firing at their opponents, even while breaking into a run from him. One man dropped to the ground, hit on the back. Too late.

Some tried doors, only to find them locked. Others found an SUV-sized tank and jumped in. One man crouched on its floor, searching for a way to get it to start.

A hand through the tank's engine made sure it wouldn't. Lon used his para-breath to weld the doors shut. The men pounded on the walls.

For the rest, Lon squeezed their weapons to pulp in his hands. Then he scooped up the men in piles, to deposit them in a corral he set up with dumpster walls in the middle of the complex's field.

It didn't take long for a Majority Army flitter to land at Londo's summons. As the men were loaded into it, one of the Majority officers explained that this was the dregs of the hundreds of small wars going on around the planet. These battles cropped up here and there every day. Sometimes the soldiers only hurt themselves and their opponents, but other times any number of civilian bystanders were injured or killed by their activities.

Lon ripped the doors off the tank. The men inside sullenly filed out. "Not on my watch," he declared to them. "You people are getting in my way, and we've only started."

— — —

"Ready to go, Valiant," the control room called. "Coming up on the top of the hour."

Lon nodded and took a stance on the stage. He checked for the red light to come on as well as the director to give him a go-ahead finger signal. Red lights were more exact to his way of thinking than the fluctuating rainbow system the Aldierrans normally used.

"Good morning, good afternoon, good evening… Wherever you are. We'll try to organize these things so there aren't so many of them.

"As Protector for Aldierra I'll be coordinating with the armies of the world. All of them. From this moment, war is outlawed. Any and all hostilities will cease. I don't care what your reasoning for your war is. We'll be working with all parties to solve any problems in a peaceful manner that I hope you'll be able to live with. Who knows; you may even prosper.

"I've never seen so many soldiers." He shook his head. "They make up the majority of your population. *Eh bien,* without wars they are out of a job. Thank you for your service. We will put these rag-tag armies to work building and re-pairing your world. They're already organized to a point. Many of them have been trained in useful work that has little to do with killing. We'll train more in that fashion."

He shifted and looked away for a moment, his mouth moving left to right. "We are moving ahead on our plans around the world immediately. If the previous announcement didn't affect you, this one will: I'm sorry and I sympathize, but many of you will have to be displaced," he informed the viewers. "Check our maps and schedule."

From the chatter in the control room he knew contact information was now displaying. "This won't be pleasant, but we'll have an entire program about it soon to explain the why of it all. Please help each other as this is happening. It won't be painless. But those areas we've specified Will. Be. Cleared."

He dropped his scowl and tried to look pleasant, remembering that he had a tendency to scare people. "That's all for now. It's going to be difficult but I swear to you it will pay off.

"Try not to panic. Picture a better world and work toward that. Lina keeps telling Jae and me that if everyone put in five minutes a day to do something good for the planet or for others, our jobs would be lightened enormously. There are twenty billion of you.

"Remember: no more war. I will stop any warring I see, but I'd rather use my time to repair your world. Starhart out."

— — —

Lina drowsily came half-awake. No alarm. That was good. Odd, but good. Smiling to herself, she snuggled against the broad, warm back of Londo, and in his sleep he muttered some unintelligible something. He had such a deep, rich voice that could vibrate along every bone in her body, sending her into shivers of delight. Londo.

Behind her the bed shifted as Jae burrowed deeper into her hair, his breath tickling the back of her ears. How were both he and Lon here? Lina woke another few levels. When had their schedules coincided like this? Someone must have coordinated. *Thank you, someone!*

Here in bed at this moment no emergencies existed. Lina had some ideas about how to exploit that fact.

"Good morning, angel wife," Jae whispered as his arms slid around her silk-covered body. It seemed he had ideas as well. He had such expressive hands, his touch igniting potent sparks that raced to certain very sensitive places.

"Mm. Good morning, tom cat husband." She was about to turn over to face him when he said, "Ow."

"Ow, ow, ow. Ow!" He batted at something.

Now it was Lina's turn. "Ow!" From long habit she covered her eyes with a hand to protect them as Fafhrd lazily strolled over her head and face. "Faaaf! Get down!"

The sleek black cat regarded her. Lina reached to move her to a safer place. Where? Everything within reaching distance was filled with husbands.

"A little room, please, Jae." With difficulty Lina turned onto her back and set Fafhrd on her stomach.

Jae scrunched over, watching the Terran animal. "Does she do this every—" he began, but let out an "Uff!" as chubby Molly landed squat on his chest, her claws extended. "Hey! Get off! Get off!"

The cat eyed him skeptically, as if the only human who was supposed to be in this bed was Mama.

"It's okay, Molly," Lina told the cat. "He's family now. You remember Jae."

"Hi, Molly," Jae said, and rubbed her head. Molly squinted at him and then stretched out her neck, butting at his hand. Her claws retracted.

"Scratch along her jawline," Lina whispered to him, and he did so. Molly's eyes closed and she held up first one side, then the other for special attention.

"What's going on?" Londo asked. He rolled over suddenly and Molly's tail bristled, doubling in size. She hissed at him, claws digging into Jae's chest as she stood her ground.

"Gri-GACH!" Jae shouted.

"Molly! Get down! Molly!"

The orange cat spat and hissed again at Londo before she ran down the full length of Jae, claws extended all the way. "Molly!" he yelled. He grabbed the sheet against his neck and sat up.

Lina was struggling with Fafhrd, trying to get the tired cat off her. "Oh dear."

Molly's flight left hisses hanging in the room as she ran past other cats. From atop the headboard behind Jae, Ember growled deep and low.

"I thought we closed the door," Londo said, watching the ruckus. Two of the cats were having a fight. "Hey!" he told them. "Which– Who– Obi! *Euh*, Bran! Stop that!"

"They're not fighting, they're playing," Lina told him.

"How can you tell the difference?" The two males lay on the floor in 69 position, kicking each other in the face as they tried to bite each other's stomach. "Are you sure?"

"Sure. They love each other. They're best friends." Now Lina joined her husbands in sitting up, setting Fafhrd down on the lower part of the giant bed between her legs. She reached to take Lon's hand. "Believe me, when there's a fight around here, you'll know it."

Lon nodded. "Maybe I need to adjust the sensor on the doors today so it stays closed. But no cats on the bed."

"Aww…"

"Absolutely not." Lon's face took on a commanding stare, and then regret washed across it. His mouth formed a determined line. "Ask Jae. A few years ago I broke his arm. I was just rolling over in bed. Imagine me and… that one." He tilted his chin toward Fafhrd. Ancient, fragile Fafhrd.

Oh. If Lon's body wasn't attuned to who he was with, he was still Valiant the All-Powerful. He couldn't control it.

Ember clambered down to Jae's shoulder. Lina said, "You've learned a few things since then. We'll try some training sessions, see if we can do a loop between you and the cats."

"With cats? How are they…" His mouth remained open, though his eyes didn't meet hers.

Lina followed where he was looking. Katie was standing in the doorway, a garishly striped rodent larger than a mouse and smaller than a New York rat hanging from her mouth. She regarded them expectantly.

"I think it's alive," Jae said slowly, and Lon nodded affirmation.

"It won't be for long," Lina told him. "My cats are all good mousers, and Katie's the champion of the bunch. Why does this fancy hotel have rats? Good Katie. Yes, Katie-Darling, you're such a good huntress! Aren't you a good kitty-widdy! Yeees you aw, sweedie Katie-Pie! I hope it's safe for her."

Katie acknowledged the compliments with grace and took her prize into the bathroom to be dispatched.

"She'll be quick. She just wanted to show off."

Lina's husbands were silent as they regarded the empty door to the bathroom.

"You'll get used to them," she said, hoping it wasn't a lie. She rubbed a knee on either side of her to let the wish sink in.

Jae made a face. "Please tell me she's not going to eat it," he said.

"Um..."

"Oh sunfire. Can't we set it free?"

Lina shrugged. "They die from the infected bite eventually. This way's a lot quicker. Or I can get a shovel and club it to death; that's even quicker." She wrinkled her nose. "I hate doing that. Hate it."

Jae ran his hand down his face, glancing first at the bathroom door and then at Lina.

Her tiny smile was apologetic. He put his hand on hers. Lina leaned to him and explained, "I have barbarian carnivorous cats." Both men had agreed before they married that the cats were part of the deal.

Lon grunted. "But you say they're good mousers?"

"And ratters; also squirrelers and birders, unfortunately."

"I thought you fed them."

"Domesticated cats kill for sport. Katie and Moose are the only ones who actually eat–"

"Please," Jae said quickly. "I haven't had breakfast yet. No more talk about... eating..." He swallowed sourly. Ember was now stretching on the mattress next to him and he petted her. "You wouldn't do that, would you?" he asked the gray tabby. She rubbed up against his hand adoringly. He shook his finger at her. "I don't want you to do that!"

She rolled onto her back and wriggled in ecstasy to be in Jae's presence.

"She doesn't understand a word, does she?"

"She's a cat, Jae-bae. Even if she understands, she's signed an oath from the great Cat God to ignore you."

Jae frowned at Lina and then glanced at Londo, who was watching Ember disapprovingly. "No cats on the bed," Lon ordered. "Here's something she understands." He snapped his fingers and the sound ricocheted like a bullet. Lina jumped. Jae had tensed in preparation; he must have seen such before. But Ember jumped, too, staring at Londo.

"Ember," Londo said, "get down. You understand that phrase. Get down, Ember! You too, Fafhrd!" The ancient cat he picked up like eggshells, placing her on the floor next to the bed.

"But Londo," Lina began.

Lon gave her an even look. "No cats on the bed," he said again. "We have to show them who's boss. We start this marriage off on the right foot. We have enough bodies in this bed already."

Lina knew that if she said anything it would be the wrong thing. Ember and Jae looked at each other and Jae scooped Ember into his arms protectively.

He doesn't understand cats, Lina told Jae silently. **He'll learn.**

"I heard that," Londo muttered. "No undermining Team Leader. No mutinies on my watch." But he gave Lina's crestfallen face a smile. "That doesn't mean that we can't give the mangy things some breakfast," he told her. "I'm not a heartless–"

Bran jumped up on the bed, running lightly across Londo and leaping first to Lina and then to Jae before he jumped off. Ember hissed at him as he passed so close. Obi was right on Bran's heels, chasing him and garnering another jealous hiss from Ember.

"I know some cats who are going to be keelhauled!" Londo bellowed. "Out! Get out!" In a flash he threw off the sheets and chased the cats, flying through the air like a whirling arrow. He reached down to pick up a cat in each hand and lightly tossed them out of the bedroom. He didn't have to track Moose. The large black cat fled in terror from the flying parahuman. Fafhrd strolled out of the room with a cloak of dignity, ignoring Londo and pretending it was her own idea.

Lon stuck his palm in the way of a cat who had tried to come back through the doorway. "No cheating!" he yelled. "Go away! Go get some mice!" and the herd retreated in a scampering of cat feet. He turned back to his spouses, brushing off his hands triumphantly.

Jae looked at Ember, still in his arms. "But he's usually quite good with people," he assured her.

— — —

The scheduled rains had moved out of the area a while ago, and Londo arrived to check progress that had been done before it hit.

"*Câlice*," came out as a hiss, then, "Where the hell are the surveyors?!" he thundered, and the far-off buildings beyond the urban terrain he had cleared vibrated with his voice. "All surveyors, report in, in person! Now!"

The city of Tenita, adjacent to Plegerit, was fast becoming a ghost town at least in its center, where foothills paralleled the Saba River. Ending abruptly at the town's new edges, different levels of muddy bare ground lay around him, accounting for where scores of sub-basements had once been, where pipes and utilities had run, where underground transportation had been laid, and that transport hub had been. Here and there a tiny patch of green still survived. Londo had carefully avoided it as he had levelled the area's structures yesterday.

A fine mist of dust still hung in the air. Flexible orange fencing followed the contours of the land, preventing erosion. Programmed spool machinery had erected that as soon as Lon blasted through.

Clean-up vehicles the size of department stores squatted here and there, gathering up the detritus before scuttling off to waiting transport. They noisily replaced each other as they filled. Londo had made sure they skirted that green. People were marking those, and a few trucks carried landscaping equipment with which small squads could carefully dig it up, to move it to a more protected spot later.

Already Londo had had to stop some squads, since too many of them had lumbered in and dug willy-nilly, "preserving" what was now rapidly dying vegetation. They hadn't bothered to dig up root systems or to pack the plants with any kind of care. Now no squad could operate without a licensed landscaper in tow.

Lon had checked the licensing requirements as well and adjusted them. Aldierra was loosey-goosey about what it allowed its people to get away with. Loosey-goosey or willy-nilly; this world couldn't bear amateurs who had no idea what they were doing, but who blundered ahead because it gave them a wage and prestige to appear to be doing something constructive.

No wonder their invasion of Sarastor had failed.

Flitters gathered from points along the barrens to target him. Six of them. They settled to the ground, one barely missing a patch of green.

Lon's scowl deepened.

It took the surveyors forever to gather in a group on the ground.

"Sir?" one dared to ask.

Without saying a word, Londo fired up large screens so all could see. The surveyors took it all in.

He would be calm. He could accomplish more if he weren't angry. But he had so little patience for idiots, especially when a world and its people were at stake!

"I double-checked your marks before I started work today," he told them. The screens showed the patterns of the survey, laid out against the topological map of the area. Across the barrens, floating lights of various colors marked the pertinent points.

Lon told them, "*Here* is what they are supposed to be."

The surveyors all perused the screens and nodded.

"Eh-yuuh," the first surveyor said slowly as he traced the pattern with his eyes. "Yes, that's what we did."

Then Lon triggered a different color of patterns to overlay the map. A pattern quite different from the first.

"Do you see the difference?" Londo asked, holding himself steady.

"Oh, there," another man said. "And over there and there, I suppose. Did you want it closer?"

Lon tapped against the immaterial screen. "And here. You're more than a hundred feet off."

"Good enough," someone said.

"*Not* good enough!" Lon roared.

The men cowered and held their ears against the assault.

"What do you mean, 'good enough'? These are plans for infrastructure that has to last a thousand years! They've been checked and triple-checked, both by humans and computers. They've been worked out to the millimeter. So many projects depend on you hitting your marks exactly!

"Your work looks like it was done by drunks."

The first man opened his mouth and then closed it. "Uh. We'll do it again?"

Londo closed his eyes, gritting his teeth against what he wanted to say. He took two deep breaths and then opened his eyes again. "*Can* you do it right?" he asked the first man. "Does anyone here actually know what he's doing?"

He allowed his glare to travel over the cowering group. "If you can't, I need to find people who can. Maybe you could find supervisors who could teach you as we go and check your work. No one I know on other worlds who calls themself a surveyor would perform work like this.

"Aldierra cannot afford for her people to do sloppy work."

"We can—"

"*Are* you drunk? *Are* you on drugs?" Londo peered at them, then dragged a sensor from his vest.

He aimed it, waving it slowly at the group and checked the readouts. "Drugs. Alcohol. Other intoxicants."

"We'll do it again," another man declared.

Sourly Londo replaced the sensor. "That's what I'm afraid of. You'll show up for work, inebriated and inept. Well, my fine sirs, not on my watch. Not so long as I'm Protector of your world. I'll have sober people working on all Three Worlds projects, people who have been trained properly and who take pride in their work. People who realize that their literal future is riding on this."

"But Protector—"

"As of this moment, you are all fired. Go discuss this with whoever hired you in the first place. I want to have some words with them myself. If you want to get sober, if you want to show that you can do the job correctly, then they can hire you again – as long as they also hire someone to double-check your work and state of sobriety."

How he wanted to punch them! How dare they interfere with all the work he had to do!

He felt like throwing a full-out tantrum to rid himself of his anger. The last time he'd done so… Well, a few asteroids were now meteoroids. He'd been a young teen. That was when Hal had decided he needed better psychiatric treatment and reluctantly sent him to Sarastor. Mad Valiant was a danger to himself and others.

"Go!" Londo shouted. Then before he could meet with the contracting supervisors, he flew up, up, out of the planet's atmosphere.

A pocket in his vest thrummed, and he triggered a combination phone and Legion Array. A half-helmet rose up from the neck of his shirt, holding a bubble of air.

"*Allo*, Hal," he said. Hal was back on Earth.

"Just wondering how you were doing. You're starting to bear down today, right?"

Lon targeted a small asteroid and zoomed to it. "Yesterday we really got serious across a number of areas."

With one solid sock from his mighty right hand, the asteroid disintegrated into dust. It spewed in all directions, but mostly away from Londo.

"Uff."

"Everything going well?"

"No." Another asteroid, this one larger and not too far away. "People are arriving impaired to do their jobs. They're screwing up their duties, throwing us off schedule. Way. Off. Unh. Schedule. Unh."

Now satisfying dust and streamers of rocketing dribble. Ahh.

"Are you hitting things again?"

"I am not having a tantrum," Londo insisted as he neared an even larger asteroid. "I am letting off steam in a controlled and focused manner. So I don't kill anyone."

"Well. Good. If it comes down to it, see that you don't kill too many."

"I'll do my best."

SMAAASH!

Ah, oui. That was more like it.

Three more asteroids were reduced to space dust.

"Sooo… Got a plan of action yet? Beyond not killing your workers?"

"Barely. We made some official proclamations."

"Which were?"

"We outlawed war. Guess I'll gather the big weaponry and dispose of it as I come to it. Lina told them no babies for the next three years. We'll see how they obey that. We said rape was wrong and would be considered a major crime. Then we announced that homosexuality isn't illegal. They kill gays here."

Hal waited a long beat to react. "Tell me again how many women they have?"

"Not enough even to pretend that the entire population of men hasn't had regular sex with their own gender.

"I chickened out. I got Bracken to stand with us because I don't know how much publicly recognized clout I have here yet. Don't know what punishment will be for any of this, or how we'll be able to keep track of who's been arrested for gay activities, or who's been raping whom." Lon drew in a breath and let it out slowly. "But we will. Somehow."

"I know you will."

"God, people are going to hate me. For upsetting the norms. For offering false hope because you know we're going to miss some. A lot. But mostly, because we're trying to save their world, and to do that we've got to eliminate a lot of what they're used to."

"Son, you're the best Team Leader around. Give yourself a break."

They cleared their minds by discussing two cases Hal was concentrating on at the moment, as well as the latest acquisition to his model train collection. "I'm going to wire the lights in the display room to coincide with actual outdoor conditions. Or should I do it the opposite way, for contrast?"

It was a serious question for Hal, Londo knew, and they both gave it its due. Lon relaxed. Somewhere in this galaxy there was time for innocent fun and fantasy. Soon enough they returned to the problems of Aldierra. Londo made notes of experts Hal recommended and what he'd discovered on his own galactic travels.

"Thanks, Hal. We're going to need everyone here pitching in. Jae is rousing them as much as he can. He's got them doing meditation. I practically collided with some Earth dude in full bearded guru gear before I left the hotel today, heading for the broadcast studio. Lina ported him in because he specializes in teaching meditation. For all I know, she's got the Dalai Lama signed up to come here as well. She knows a lot of woo-woo people. Or maybe she knows people who know people, and they're all woo-woo."

Hal laughed.

"She's talking with as many Aldierran women as she can, but she doesn't want to leave out approaching men as well. She doesn't want to be seen as women-only. Jae and I don't want to be seen as men-only. Plus a good part of the male population here is just as abused as the women."

#Don't mess with your earring!#

"What was– That didn't quite sound like Jae."

Lon lowered his fingers from his left ear. "That was AI Jae. My new earring is programmed to remind me not to play with it."

Again Hal laughed but then he returned to the subject at hand.

"You need… I don't know what you need."

"I'm still unsure about how much I can trust the Majority Army. It's tightly organized and noted for discipline. But it has mixed priorities. I don't want the upper echelons telling the lower ones different things than what we're saying. They're after maintaining the status quo, if not increasing their own power base."

"You should organize your own army. A civilian one. Maybe divert some military units to your own personal use."

"*Ouais.* Jae's concentrating on the civilian side while I take the military. We'll see what we can do about that. Anyway, Lina's got a friend on Earth who's been working with the gay community for years. I don't know how well-known he is, but he's gotten a lot done, communications-wise. I think she's going to talk with him about coming here to see what he can suggest.

"Lina's going to be doing most of the hiring now, and the people she hires will be hiring others. We're trying to figure a way to make sure the hires are, well…"

"Worthy. Trustable. Any help from the Sarastor side?"

"Sarastor doesn't want to kill gays, but the people there don't want to acknowledge them to any extent either. They're not the accepted majority, so they don't count. As much. We'll get to that when we're done here." Londo groaned. "They're going to hate me too."

"Not everyone, son," Hal soothed. "Not everyone."

CHAPTER

7

They had a rough plan of action, including steps building up to large projects that Lina could arrange if she could navigate Aldierra's military system. Who and what was available for non-showy Three Worlds needs?

The people who worked with them had to be provided food, water, shelter, medical attention, transportation, and portalets. Lina soon knew all there was to know about portalets. She even had conferences with Terran and AffSys portalet people, enough so that she set up a manufacturing plant on Sarastor that would produce a pared-down, easy-to-clean and -manufacture design that relied on minimal tech. They joined an army of portable urinals. She kept acres of the things stashed in various spots around the planet, ready to be dispersed as needed.

She didn't neglect the civilian side of the population; civilians kept civilization running. Jae helped her discover scads of organizations that had been working on its various problems for ages. They needed to be organized to build off each other's efforts. Universities provided centuries-spanning ecological and social studies that had largely been ignored by government.

Now she knew how to contact groups of women, which entailed contacting Houses that were allied to each other. After that she had to go to other Houses and their allies who were at odds with the first Houses, then Houses that didn't have any particular alliances with others, Houses that were blackballed for some reason, and so on. Plus the Houseless.

She kept thousands of contacts on her lists, coordinated by the computer system Wiley and his assistants had designed for her. It helped that her padd was AI and could come up with solutions on the fly to problems as they came up.

Odd then that the way she dressed would pose such a dilemma.

Aldierra had different cultures. The ones she'd encountered so far wanted women dressed from the tops of their heads to their toes. It seemed a worldwide "given" that women only uncovered their right eyes, in order to, well, move about safely instead of having to feel their way through the world. That they had been granted an eye seemed a boon blessed upon them by the males of the world.

Lina tried walking through their suite with her left eye covered. She almost stepped on three cats, and tripped into the corner of a coffee table.

The first focus group she'd gathered on the subject had looked at other worlds' costuming and particularly liked some Indian kurtas and kurtis: loose trousers, long tunic, short sleeves, and various modest necklines – worn with a shawl, of course, to cover the face. Lina suspected the groups also liked the beautiful patterns and light fabrics that were so different to their regular wear. They left with files showing them possibilities for themselves.

The meeting wasn't helped in that her earring kept buzzing in her ear, asking her to repeat what the women had said for the translator to learn from. Women used a different range of words than their menfolk. Their social worlds were not the same.

As soon as she could she met with two more groups to get a wider sample. Her AI made suggestions and between it, the groups, and Lina's stubbornness (darn it, she had already spent enough time coming up with her Starfleet co-splay/costume a few months ago), came up with acceptable variations. Her tunic was now unbelted, its split skirt converted to side slits but still wide and flowy with a handkerchief hem. The square neckline only showed a centimeter of cleavage. She hated to get rid of her tights because they came with the built-in comfy shoes AffSys people favored. Instead she programmed regular shoes in the same general make and made sure the pants weren't so loose that she might trip over them. They were fairly short anyway, but not quite capris.

Boots, her guides told her, and she obediently added those to the shopping program. No telling where she'd be operating. With another thought she added a parka, jacket, and raincoat to the ensemble.

A couple variants that uncovered more skin were for soggy or hot conditions. Darned if she was going to overdress for a monsoon during a heatwave. All versions left her with her face fully exposed. Too bad; so sad.

The wardrobe would be made in the ombre green and dappled leaf pattern of her Starfleet costume. Her AI informed her that this was her "theme aesthetic."

In her mind Lina blew a juicy raspberry at society dictates even as clairvoyance confirmed that her new clothes were appearing or printing out or however it was accomplished, in Lon's apartment back on Sarastor. Her existing Starfleet duds could be used anywhere off Aldierra.

(Lina added a sleeveless variant of that for wearing on Earth, where she didn't have to kowtow to anyone.)

"Most of you have two eyes," she'd explained to the groups. "You should be able to use them. And protect them too."

So while she was in deep design mode, she had the AI take existing men's pollution face masks and make versions that were either pared down to essentials in a sleek way, or the same with a few frills thrown in. Some of the focus group had liked colorful ribbons braided through them. All the models would protect two female eyes as well as nose and mouth from atmospheric pollutants.

None of them resembled Darth Vader – unlike some of the men's styles she'd seen.

Lina set her chief military aide, Capt. Valehold, to arranging mass manufacture for immediate distribution. The Majority Army already had plants churning out military-issue masks, so this shouldn't be too difficult. She asked him to arrange a PR campaign telling Houses that face masks increased the distinction of a House's womenfolk.

Valehold didn't understand.

Lina didn't particularly care. Could she please get some *real* work done now? They had a planet to save.

She found working with the military aides she knew difficult. They were all men and trained to think that cultural norms were sacrosanct. And of course that women weren't entirely *human*.

None of her aides knew quite what to make of Lina. She was the holy Speaker for Aldierra, all hail. She was a mega-para. She was married to the uber-heroes Valiant and Neutrino.

But she was a (pardon the expression) *woman*.

The confused ways they looked at her drove Lina crazy. Still she worked with them as well as she could and continually explained the odd concept of women being humans as much as men were.

She began to understand why Lon sometimes banged his head against walls. Maybe she could tie a protective pad onto her head and do it too.

Lina's personal assistant, Lt. Twofence, was incensed at her choice of clothing. He fumed, his eyes practically rolling backward in fury, and told her it was completely improper. She must talk to his wife if she wanted a reading of what a true Aldierran woman felt about it all.

Twofence was her assistant. She needed to keep him happy to get good work, so she agreed.

The wife, Shurrone, was a cowering thing, stuck in a tiny compartment within their small military housing unit in the city. There she had two other husbands, none of whom she had chosen. Recently she'd had to give up her son to the husbands, since he was too old to stay with her in her woman's quarters. She was pregnant and sure this child would be a girl who would not live long.

"It is the Right of Daughter Refusal," Shurrone confided to Lina. "It only takes one husband, or even a grandfather, to refuse a daughter. This way it does not impinge on the honor of the House. They have the first month in which to decide to drown her or not." She leaned forward and whispered, "I've heard that in some places they just leave the baby out in the open, or dump her in a gutter. At least drowning is quick. Merciful."

Shurrone couldn't read. She didn't know numbers to any extent. She didn't know what birth control was. She wasn't sure how conception happened or how her own system handled it. She didn't know why or how she had periods, only that if they stopped she was likely pregnant.

"If I carry a girl and they find out, I go to a place where they get rid of it. Once I took some pills. It was messy and I hurt for weeks after."

"Was this your choice?"

Women didn't have choices. Women did as men commanded. Shurrone was satisfied that her female babies had been aborted. Better than carrying a daughter to term and then gazing upon her face, only to have one of the husbands kill her.

When they returned to the hotel Lt. Twofence looked angry when Lina told him she would not be covering her face.

"I thank your very wise and lovely Shurrone for her teaching and advice," Lina told him, "but I have chosen a different way to dress. I will represent myself as an individual deserving to look out on the world with my own two eyes."

"The Speaker can do whatever she wishes." He bowed.

– – –

A final focus group that afternoon had confirmed the costume. One variant, though, had to be re-hemmed and reinforced so that a woman who wore that style could harvest seahemp without injury. After all, Lina would be influencing style.

Now, *that* was a frightening thought! Still, fashion had to change here. Women had to be free to be able to *move* when needed. Lina could live with influencing that.

"This isn't cultural appropriation, is it? I've never quite understood that, when it's done with respect," she told Jae as she modelled the seahemp version. The groups had told her that women attended to seahemp only when men outside their Houses were not present. They were then protected by a guard of male members of their Houses.

Lina signaled some screens to show him the range of styles she'd settled on.

"Approved by an entire world?"

"Gathering seahemp and other ocean food sources seems to be a fairly widespread occupation for women in the warmer coastal regions," Lina replied. "If they can get away with wearing this, well, I don't want to sweat to death if it's hot. Maybe this will encourage others to dress for the weather, and for their men to approve of it."

Jae walked around her, tilting his head this way and that to take it in. "I've seen Terran clothing. This is modest compared to some things. Then again, maybe all the pictures Lon's been showing me through the years have been por-nographic."

"That's very likely."

"You do know that 'clothing optional' was a common choice on Feith," he added as he sat and put his feet up on the coffee table. He took a sip of the cocktail room service had provided. "My family usually wore more than the general population averaged. Of course we worked in forests and on rocky terrain. It was a rough environment. City dwellers didn't have to worry about everyday injuries. But I doubt–"

Lina's earring buzzed.

"Emergency port needed," came the call from Sarastor's Legion HQ.

"Sure thing," Lina responded and ported. These calls were getting frequent.

When she appeared in the Legion's Monitor Room, located on a security level Lina could not otherwise be allowed onto, the Officer of the Day who stood at a large control board let out an audible gasp.

"What are you wearing?!" It was Brügz, a former Commander and current temporary leader of Jae's Alpha Team.

A group of four Legionnaires skidded into the screen-lined, dark room, and their first impressions of Lina were not good ones. Their mouths hung open. One of them muttered a rude comment.

Damned Legion dress codes! The Mega-Legion did not like skin of any gender showing below the neck or above the wrist. Her mind searched through Londo's apartment downstairs. There was that slinky wine-colored robe. She wrapped it around herself.

"Sorry," she said. "Aldierran clothing. Acceptable Aldierran clothing. I've had it cleared through them."

"Not acceptable here." Brügz leveled an index finger at her. "I'll let it go once. This port is important."

"Yessir. I'll keep… something nearby I can change into," Lina promised. "For next time." Unless she forgot.

– – –

Jae had begun this project using military troops because that was easiest and quickest. Some of these men were from the Majority Army, but Jae had insisted that some come from the Red Army, and a few from the Blues, Violets and Oranges. They had different official names, but those were the ones they commonly used.

He'd train these and then they could train the civilians who were being recruited.

Jae made sure their work clothes were of no particular color. This way the "us vs them" social polarization problems would be minimized. They would learn to work together, eat and sleep together, strategize together, to see each other as fellow humans.

They were kitted out in durable dirt brown, moss green, and sand beige coveralls, with bits of a pastel bluish-violet that Lina had called "orchid," to represent the color that the atmosphere of this world should be.

Instead that atmosphere was layer after layer of murky gray and brown.

As was this river they stood by, gray and unhealthy green with yellowy vomit brown liberally mixed in. The men's facemasks ensured that not only did they not breathe in the rotten air of the world, but that they didn't swallow river muck.

Only the orchid trims differentiated the troops from the filth they were immersed in. Their clothing was warm and fairly watertight, but after many hours everyone would be cold, wet and mucky in general.

They should begin higher up on the slopes of the North Range, toward the source of the streams and creeks that formed the source of the Saba river. Instead Jae began here. He thought that change could be more easily seen in this larger environment, plus the terrain was easier. The men would be encouraged if they could see their progress.

The river was still narrow here and not too deep. Humankind had been dumping its refuse in it for centuries. Jae was surprised to see the occasional flit of a fish or some other water creature amid the debris.

A minor road wound its way nearby, and Lina had found a route to bring in equipment: excavators and loaders, with a line of trucks waiting to haul things away. There were trained people to utilize that equipment, but most of this would require manual labor.

Twenty billion people, Jae mused. Almost three hundred here today. He'd explained that they'd be clearing larger debris from the waterway. He'd placed the medical tent and notified Lina where food tents should go. A line of portalets had appeared just after he'd arrived, and he'd sent some men to position those in likely places. Camp tonight would be a short way down the river, and men were spared to set up those tents before returning.

Ah, screens began to pop up among the groups along the banks. They would show what lay beneath the water so the men could make plans of what should come out first, and how many it would take to handle it.

"Use your ropes!" Jae called to more than one team. "Keep eyes on each other!"

There would surely be injuries along the way but by the orb, he was going to do what he could to make sure they were minor.

Jae lent his back and Legion Array to the effort as one group heaved what looked like a turbine out of the muck. It must have weighed over a ton, but their enhanced ropes held and his gravity-defying Array let him pull much more than he could without it.

"Someone get in there and see if you can save any fish caught in it," Jae called.

A loader trundled over to take the wrack away to a truck, allowing the group to catch their breath. Jae nodded at them. "Great work. Now, stay hydrated. Take a break every hour, or after each big job like this."

As Jae moved down the line he found all the workers doing fairly well. There were more than a few stupid decisions that Jae noticed, and he put on his best teacher mode to show them the better approach. The stupid decisions continued, though at a slower pace.

"Slower" seemed to describe the mental state of too many workers. Were they mentally challenged? Jae brought up scans of the area and zeroed in on the eyes of the men.

Dilated pupils. Almost everyone had them, and the blood vessels in the whites of their eyes had also expanded to give them a reddened look. Jae groaned to himself, then sent a message to Lina to have her deliver a squad of Sarastoran medics here this evening.

He got a response from Londo, warning of workers who reported in intoxicated. *A little too late, Lon,* but something to keep in mind for Jae's other duties.

Drugs and dangerous work didn't mix. He scribbled notes to the others that it was popping up here, and then the signal for lunch sounded. The men pulled themselves out and away from the river with relief.

Jae had to instruct more than a few to wash up before eating. The concept seemed new to them.

But after lunch things changed. "Green Army, ho!" came a soft call from his right.

Jae didn't think he was supposed to have heard it. Had the men discovered their fellow armies in the group during their meal? Had they redistributed themselves?

"Blues, ho!" came a response. "Dirty greens!"

With that, two squads fell upon each other in deadly hand-to-hand combat. More men ran from their duties to join in.

"Stop!" Jae used the amplifier from his ring to make his voice echo in the river valley. "Stop now!"

But they paid him no mind. He pointed at the other groups, the ones who had not joined in, and nodded that they should begin their afternoon work. Then he leaped into the air above the fight.

He held out his arms to gather energy. He could sense the metabolisms of the fighting men, how excited was the living matter that formed them and ran through their energy pathways. He could feel the electrons raised to higher energetic levels. The bodies supported it in a manner that went far back into evolution: fight or flight. These men were trained to fight.

But Jae spoke to those pathways and the energy within them. He spoke to the bodies. *Calm down. Ease up. Easy, easy. Power down, down, down.*

One by one and then two by two, the fighting men reared back from each other. Their knees buckled. They had not strength enough to raise their hands or even bare their teeth. They collapsed upon the ground, sometimes in piles.

"Uh," was all they could say in their daze.

Jae called a pause to the squads along the river and projected screens above it so everyone could see his announcement. "There is no Green Army, no blue, no orange, no rainbow-colored. Not here. We all work for Aldierra. We are the Aldierran army. Instead of destroying, we build. We heal the world. We help each other as well as ourselves. We are no color…" he looked around at every-one "…except that of dirt. Instead of being the Dirt Army, I think we should call ourselves the Aldierra Army. Or even better, the Aldierra Corps." He raised his fist. "Aldierra Corps!"

Slowly the call was taken up here and there along the river. "Aldierra Corps! Aldierra Corps!" Until everyone who could lift a hand shouted, "Aldierra Corps!"

As for the fighters, once they'd recovered Jae had them separated and divided one by one into random groups, brown and dirt uniforms all.

CHAPTER

8

Londo stretched the sleep out of his shoulders and back as he shuffled to the kitchen. He scratched his head as he tapped the coffee maker's buttons. As had become usual in the past few days, there were separate piles on the counter of a number of breakfast selections encased in stasi-keepers, which would keep them fresh and at serving temperature.

Many had stickie notes from Jae describing what they were. These were dishes made by the hotel's service staff. Others held notes from Lina. Hers were from street vendors she'd encountered through her wanderings around the world.

He chose one from each spouse and took the cases to the breakfast table, along with his coffee cup.

Ah, home. A place he could relax. He hadn't been able to relax in weeks. Too bad Jae and Lina weren't around to relax with.

They needed more time together. "Two or three years to get this started," he continued his continuing argument, likely unheard, with the world around him. That was a lie. They should have begun this with at least three or five years before such a deadline.

But three years ago… Jae had been a little frightening back then. He'd had a tendency to appear fine, then erupt in rage at unexpected things.

Lina said that before she'd met Lon she'd been hiding deep within herself. She hadn't been able to touch others, she'd set herself so far apart from the rest of the fearful world.

And Londo… Well, he might have dealt with people a little more brusquely than he should have back then. He might have scared… or disappointed those around him.

But each of them had come so far. One of the last things Aiko had told him was that his bearing had improved a lot.

Dear Aiko.

He heard a sound rather than feeling anything, and looked down to see one of Lina's cats – Bran-Bran – climbing his robe. "Hello," he told it.

How did you talk to a cat? This couldn't be something the creature was allowed to do. "Get down," he ordered blandly. The cat ignored him.

Londo arrived at the table, set down his bundle and then the cup, and matched gazes with the cat. "Down," he repeated.

Instead Bran hopped onto the table. He sniffed the keepers as if they let odor escape, which they didn't.

"Has anyone fed you today?" Londo rubbed his nose. Surely Lina had set some kind of program to make sure–

#Londo, please feed the cats,# the voice of the local home computer told him.

He glanced at the clock. It was top of the hour, so the computer must have been set for this. Yes, it seemed a good time for cat breakfast, if they were to keep to any kind of schedule.

He asked the computer where the cat food was, how much to administer, and then emptied the cans onto many paper plates as he'd seen Lina do. Along the way the entire herd collected around his feet, meowing as if they hadn't been fed in days. Bran jumped down from the table to join his siblings. And yes, Fafhrd also came instead of sleeping through.

"Does Fafhrd need a pi–"

#Don't forget Fafhrd's pill,# the voice ordered. *#Give Lina a call if you can't administer it.#*

"Hum." Londo squatted to set out the plates, and the cats held back mere nano-moments before diving into their food. Some literally. They smacked their kitty lips as they ate. A couple made *ar, ar, ar* noises as it went down.

Fafhrd finished a very small portion and then looked at him expectantly. A cat that wanted a pill? Lon looked around for the prescription bottle and the pill gun that had to be used.

Then he remembered, and took the carton of unsweetened lactose-free milk from the fridge. Hm. He fished around cabinets until he found a small bowl and poured some in. How much? Maybe that much.

He put the bowl on the floor only to have every cat dive for it. He snatched it up, looked around, and settled for the counter next to the sink.

This was for Fafhrd, not the rest. He knew that much. The cats yowled at him except for Molly, who included a hiss in her proclamation about possession of the milk.

How to handle Fafhrd? Like a baby. She was a thousand years old. She was super-fragile.

Lon found a towel to wrap around his hands and then picked up the eldest cat as carefully as he could. Slowly he brought her up to the counter and deposited her on its surface.

Fafhrd drank about half the milk before she sat back on her haunches and began to bathe herself.

"Too much, eh?" Lon asked her but she ignored him. No, she glanced at him for one moment before returning to her task.

Lina, Fafhrd pill time, he called. He knew his limits.

He set down the dish of milk for the rest of the cats to fight over, and then washed his hands and took a seat for his breakfast. Though he didn't need the heat, he heated his coffee again. It was what was done, what was expected. He drank hot coffee as Hal had taught him. Just like norms.

After a while Lina popped in and gave Fafhrd her pill. It was as Lon had concluded: too complicated for a mega-strength being to perform. Lina had to grasp the cat firmly around the jaw and then stick the pill gun into her mouth, pill sticking out its end, then depress the plunger handle to release the pill down the cat's throat.

If Lon had tried that, most assuredly he'd have accidentally ripped the cat's head off.

"I'm never going to be able to do that," he told Lina as she massaged the cat's throat to make sure the pill went down Fafhrd's gullet.

"I know. Just give me a call and I'll do it. Thank you for feeding them." She squirted an inch of the smelly contents of a tube onto her index finger and then reached again into Fafhrd's mouth to scrape the gel onto the roof of her mouth. Fafhrd worked the stuff hard with her tongue, tilting her head this way and that.

"Milk?"

"Poured too much. Faf let me know, so now I know too."

She turned to give him one of her glorious Lina smiles. "You learn everything so fast." Then she heaved a sigh. "I wish I were like you that way. Learning curves. Blech."

He held out an arm and she came to sit on his lap for a few precious moments. He could actually feel her through their telepathic double-loop. The ability to touch was a miracle. "You amaze me how fast you've caught on to things."

Fafhrd jumped off the countertop to the floor. Londo tensed. "Should she do that? Should I have let her down?"

"Faf knows her limitations," Lina said. "If the day comes when she can't get down, she'll tell us in some way. She's very smart."

Lon nodded. "She's a Starhart."

They cuddled for the few moments Lina had free. As she told him what she was doing on the other side of the world, Lon took a long sip and settled back to taste the way the day was going so far, his arm around her waist. Rating: excellent.

His phone rang a tune: the fanfare from the earliest of the Maximus movies. Hal had called him first today instead of the other way around. He must have seen Lon's schedule. Lon made it available to his father. They worked together on many things, and they often conferred. Plus they liked to chat.

Lon smiled all during the conversation. Lina only joined in when Hal directed a comment to her. That was kind, her letting him talk with Hal. It was small talk anyway, Hal curious about some of the work being done today. Soon they signed off.

"I can't get over how close you and Hal are," Lina said. "That's so nice. You have such a bond."

"He's the greatest father I could have asked for," Lon replied. "Every day I remind myself of how lucky I was that he found me. That he had it in his heart to take me in and adopt me. If it wasn't for him…"

"But…" She must have heard that there was something in the way he said it…

"Every now and then… Every now and then I wish I had known my bio father. All my memories of him – such as they are – are of him and Maman fighting. Of him leaving us and Maman crying."

Lina pressed her lips together and then said, "But he had a nice laugh?"

Lon let out the slightest of chuckles. "That's something to remember, isn't it? A great legacy." Still, he could recall the love his maman had for him. Where was Maman? Her loss was a great hole in his heart.

"We'll find them eventually. After all this blows over."

"*Mouais.* Yeah." Londo took another sip.

— — —

Fifteen hours later Lina settled into her office chair as the 3-D picture came up on screen. This brand-new day was going to be one when she would be longing for a stim before it was done. Or just a chai latte. Ooh, she knew a place that made them just a bitty bit richer than others did. Hot liquid candy with a jolt, mmm.

But she was banned from caffeine for what, another two months, plus a bit. So she'd kinda overdosed on stims and trauma during the Mind Control Tour. She was better now. She'd be needing those stims.

Time to stop pouting and start work for the day. She should be working on organizing all this mess they were floundering around in. The guys were both relying on the Aldierran military's procedures to create a preliminary framework for what they were doing.

But the Three Worlds weren't the Aldierran armies. Three Worlds needed a Three Worlds way of doing things. She made sure to slot in ninety minutes to the schedule to confer with her old UNC business professor, who'd recommended a colleague from Northwestern, who'd recommended a colleague from Wharton. Dr. Hedgepeth had been informed of the general info Lina needed, and would pass that along so everyone would come prepared.

That meant today's schedule was full-up, so her big organizing task would have to be moved to tomorrow, which was good because then she'd know better about what the hell she was doing. Her first chore for today didn't have anything to do with organization, but it was needed to begin a change in planetary attitudes.

Lina didn't like confrontation. Someone had once told her – maybe it had been a few more times than that – that she was passive-aggressive. Perhaps she was, if she had to face down a jerk. But sometimes that jerk was too obtuse to see the "aggressive" part of that phrase and just viewed her as passive.

It was time to react in a more active manner like Lon when the occasion demanded. *Hup-hup! Punch!* But in a polite way. Not quite Bitch Lina mode. Somewhere around Jae mode, that time he'd yelled at her. He'd been precise and deadly with his words.

Oh, they'd been so confused then. She hadn't known what was going on, and Jae… Well, Jae had viewed the situation much as this one was: that an entire world was in imminent danger. Her actions had threatened to block his path in saving it.

They'd apologized profusely to each other afterward.

All her life she'd been willing to stay in the background, hidden.

Why? Because if she hadn't, her father would have punished her more than he did.

But what had that cost her? When she'd gotten a job she hadn't progressed far, though she pretty much ran her department and others unofficially from the sidelines. She'd developed invisible networks that helped her company prosper.

Since she'd gotten powers – since before she'd been named Speaker for the Worlds – she'd had to extend herself, first to save her own life and then to save Londo's. Then to save Sarastor from invasion, Olympia from a mad Ruby Guard, and a galactic sector from Mind Control.

Now she was in charge of saving the lives of twenty billion people. If she didn't step up to the plate, who would? Oh, Lon and Jae would, but twenty billion were too much even for them. She could lighten the load.

She had refused Lon and Jae's help with making this call. It was time to pull on her Big Speaker Panties (properly vetted by focus groups) and step into her own responsibilities. She had to learn to assert herself with a little oomph.

She could do this.

Her screen displayed the upper torso of a civilian man with slightly graying green hair, looking every bit as if he sat in the room with her. A whiff of something rather unpleasantly sour came with him, though he was dressed as spiffily as she'd seen any male Aldierran civilian. His suit was styled with jewelry that looked like colorful medals across his chest.

She hoped her smile didn't display as bared teeth. "Mr. Froregreen," she began.

"First Lieutenant Froregreen," he corrected her.

"Ah. My records don't note that you are still in the army."

"Well. I'm not. But I was." Maybe that explained the jewelry?

"All right. *First Lieutenant* Froregreen, first of all I should mention that people are filming me all the time, and we have some documentarians in my office right now. I hope that's all right with you."

Two of them had their cameras floating on either side of her screen, though the actual people were controlling them from the far corner of her office. She'd told them who'd she be talking with, and they jumped at the chance to be here. After all, this would be publicized.

"All right," 1stLt. Froregreen said slowly. "May I ask the purpose of your call? I am honored, of course, to be contacted by the Speaker to our world. Do you need money?"

That triggered another smile, this one more genuine. "Oh right, you're one of the richest men on the planet. Ordinarily I'd ask you about your life story. It must be fascinating. But I called you to talk to you about your factory– Well, all of them, now that I see the records. You have quite a network, don't you? Many different products, but all seem to have one unifying feature, besides you as owner. Anyway, your factories, plural, were cited over ten years ago for polluting well over Aldierra's lenient standards. Like by ten times."

For a moment he froze. Then his expression looked like he was tweaking it, commanding it not to frown. His featured morphed into a more unperturbed expression millimeter by obvious millimeter. "Speaker, that was well in the past."

"And now your levels throughout are at about fifty times the limit, according to last year's measurements. This is on average. Some factories are worse."

"Ah…"

"The courts told you to shape up or shut down."

"We have been on appeal."

"Yes, I've seen the reports of your court cases. They must have cost you a lot of time and money. At least if the system works the same as it does on the planet I come from."

"That's the way it works here as well."

Was his intonation becoming the one directed to a child? Was he talking down to her, as if she couldn't understand the issue?

"First Lieutenant," she said evenly but with determination, "you have lost your final appeal. In so many ways. We have decided. As of now, your factories are closed. All of them."

"What? Speaker, you can't–"

"I can and I am. To use a Terran metaphor, you are a very big fish in this world's pond. But for the nonce, we Starharts are bigger fish. With bigger teeth. As of this very moment, I inform you that your factories are closed. Permanently. Tell your employees. Tell your suppliers and your customers. Shut them down. We give you two days to allow for safe shut-down for all your properties. Two days for your employees to remove their lunches, their family photos, their memorabilia, personal files, and boots from their workspaces. I don't want a wisp of any kind of material, radiant, gaseous, liquid, or solid, coming from your factories."

"You can't–"

"Even as we speak," Lina signaled her contacts waiting throughout the world, "there are officials approaching your locations to make sure this goes smoothly. If any systems need time to shut down safely, tell them and let them oversee the process. I'll send experts if needed. I remind you: two days max."

"But–"

"And the record of this call will go public in order to show other big fish in Aldierra's pond of what has been done to you, so that they can mend their ways before the same happens to them. An example had to be set. Congratulations; it's you.

"Your employees will continue to be paid from your company profits until they find other work, not to exceed one and one-half years. They must actively look for jobs unless they are physically or mentally unable to do so, or endure a personal emergency of some sort. Retirement funds will remain available for them. Your executives' wages will be decreased by 85% for this same time period.

"I will recommend to the courts that they check up on your case, and if they find you need to be fined but that much of your company profits have been used up providing for your employees, perhaps the courts could take remaining fines out of your personal fortune."

Froregreen raised up in his chair, gripping its arms. His mouth snarled in sheer fury. His eyes were slits of hatred. "*Kopa!*" he snarled. "You *topi!* You'll never get away with this!"

The reporters in the room let out horrified gasps at his language.

"Oh, I'll have to translate that for our system. It's telling me it has no definition for it. Thankfully, I know it." Lina made a show of writing a note.

"I'll put a tickler in our calendar to make sure we check back at some point in the future, and remind the courts if it comes to it, that to deprive you of every cent you possess due to your crimes upon the ecosystem and populace of the planet would be cruel. They should leave you with," she shrugged, "something.

"Goodbye, *Mister* Froregreen."

— — —

Londo sat up in bed like a spring had sprung. Two cats fell off him and scrambled for safety on the other side of the room. Next to him, Jae rubbed his face as he woke up.

"My condo!" Lon exclaimed. He gave Jae a disbelieving expression. "I forgot to check on my condo! How could I forget?"

"Awf nmumbo," Jae replied, but rubbed his husband's shoulders. Then he patted them. "Don't worry."

Lon raked his fingers through his hair. "But I promised. I'm already… I think I missed the deadline I promised! After the attacks in Montreal I said I'd have everything fixed in… was it a month or six weeks? What day is it on Earth? I can't think!"

He grabbed his phone on the nightstand and called across star systems. "Kurt?" he asked the phone. On the other end was Kurt Campbell, his best-friend-who-wasn't-a-lover, and who also oversaw Lon's construction needs on Earth. "Yes, it's me. How are repairs to my condo coming? The building?" At the reply he groaned. And then cursed heartily in various languages.

"Things got away from me. You would not believe how busy we've been since the attack. *Mon dieu*, so many things have happened since. I forgot. What can we do? Can you hire more people? I'll pay as much overtime as we need, as long as everything stays safe. I promised everyone they could return to their homes soon. Uh huh. *Ah oui*, the streets were damaged as well. *Chrisse.* I'll be there…"

"He'll be there in nine hours," Jae spoke to the phone. "He needs to get some sleep first. He's been going full-steam."

Londo made a face at Jae for that, but gave in. "*Oui*, that was Jae. My nanny. Yeah. Yeah, we'll talk." He closed the conversation and sat there, staring at the phone. "Can I get this fixed?" His groan was low and drawn out.

"You will not worry about it right now," Jae assured him. He signaled for the next day's schedule to pop up. "You will get some sleep. You're beat. Lina will port you there in the morning. I'll get up now and start to cover some of your duties for today."

"But can I finish the job today? I mean, enough for Kurt's people to finish by the end of the week? He said that by some miracle I still had six days left. He might have bargained for more time already; I'm not sure. His crews haven't been able to attend to some of the basic structure. I said I'd do that part. It needs to pass inspection, too. That'll take time. If I concentrate on the exterior–" He slammed his fist into his other hand. "I don't have the same kind of equipment there as what I've been using here."

"You'll do what you can. I'm sure your neighbors will understand, especially if… if you throw money at whatever money buys in this kind of situation."

"Storage of their possessions. I'm already paying. I'll just pay for a little longer. And bonuses to thank them for their patience."

Jae sighed. "Money solves everything on Earth, doesn't it?"

Lon looked at him sorrowfully. "In too many situations, yes. It also causes almost every problem as well." He searched Jae's face. "How are you doing, *chéri?* With the secret and all. I haven't kept up with you on that either."

Jae kissed him. "I'm doing fine. Now go to sleep. Rest up. When you return from Montreal I want to see you exhausted because you've put everything you could into your work. You won't have to feel guilty about anything."

Uncertainly Londo lay back down. Jae smiled at him and spoke to his cells and the stress chemicals there. Slowly Lon's eyes closed. Jae sat there for several minutes before he released his hold on Londo. His husband slept naturally.

Then Jae carefully rolled out of bed. He'd have a long day ahead.

— — —

Lina was eating breakfast as Jae came in at the end of that day. She picked at it as he settled in. Then they had time for hugs, kisses, squeezes, loving small talk, and kitty pats.

"I saw that Foregeen, Froregreen thing," Jae told her. "Good work. Put some *skurny* fear into the folks around here who need it."

"Thanks." Lina returned to her gruel. "I ported Lon to Earth before I went to bed yesterday. Think I'll have him pick up something for us to eat on the way back, if he still has any functioning brain cells left. Is it my uncouth provinciality, or is the food here not that great?" she asked. "Have you found anything good out there?"

"We eat the military rations you arrange," Jae replied. He checked the counter for the dinner stasi-keeps that had been set out for his return, and sniffed at the latest offering. "It's calories."

"It's military issue, ugh. We need more than calories. Can you ask some of your people? What restaurants and such do they like in their areas? If I'm porting wherever, I can check them for us, get some take-out. Maybe find some caterers for your army corps."

"Will do. And my corps won't be all-army for long."

Jae sat down with his wife and picked up a fork. He turned it over. It was speckled with… something.

"Who's cleaning our kitchen?"

"Lon's soldiers." She looked up from her gruel with a disapproving expression, her mouth off-center as she frowned. "They don't do a good job, do they? And I want to know if they're treating the cats right. I'm getting… vibes."

"I'll install hidden cameras before I hit the sack. Think we still have some leftovers around here. Wish we could get some kol-vanaschen."

That AffSys house cleaning technology was forbidden outside the limits of that galactic sector. Weapons were fine; spaceships were perfectly okay. But cleaning service?

"Stupid Prime Directive stuff," Lina mumbled to herself. Advanced tech wasn't allowed for less advanced cultures… unless it was. There didn't seem to be any logic to it. The AffSys must view house cleaning as a dangerous, dangerous activity.

"I'll look into it. Again," Jae assured her. "Aldierra isn't that far behind the AffSys."

"Thanks, honey." She got up to empty the last part of her meal into the trash. "I don't like my assistant," she said. "Am I being mean? Picky? He gives me the creeps. His backups aren't much better. They not only have an Aldierran mindset, but an Aldierran soldier one as well." She wrinkled her nose.

"Have they done anything to you?"

"No. It's just… vibes. And the way they look at me." She brightened up. "I do like my guards, at least the ones I've had a chance to talk with. They're dedicated and in my humble opinion, really good at their job. I trust them." She rinsed out her bowl. "How's your staff? Your personal assistant?"

"Mine is…" Jae shrugged. "All right, I suppose. I haven't dealt with him that much yet on things that he actually has to think about. Do you think Bracken would have any ideas?"

"Bracken would prefer we only have military types in the upper positions. Would you like my assistant? He's fairly efficient when he approves of what he's doing."

Jae considered. "Let me check him out. I'll get Lon's input when he comes home."

"If he's conscious."

Jae felt for Londo's vibes, so far away on Earth. His husband was a combination of frantic, focused work and weariness. "Maybe I'll let him get some sleep before I do that."

— — —

It would have been nice if Lina could have visited Earth while Londo was there, but she had been too darned busy to come. And he'd been too busy that they might have taken a few minutes for lunch or just five minutes together.

Jae hadn't yet fallen asleep as he and Lina had both taken Londo's call from Earth, but he was on his way to bed. "It's done," Lon had announced. They could feel his utter exhaustion. There were tremors in his voice. "Inspectors come through first thing tomorrow, back again for the interior work the day after that, and everyone should be moving back within the next few days after that."

After a while Lina had been able to port Lon back to Aldierra and his bed. He'd literally fallen into it on top of the covers, next to Jae.

A day later Lina sat in the Catshit Room, empty except for the litter boxes and this one raggedy office chair, a yard sale find from a couple years ago. Five dollars but fairly comfortable and it rolled well. Lon made extremely rude comments every time he saw it, so she tried to keep it out of his line of sight. It would be wasteful to throw it away if it could still be used.

Dinner tonight had seen them all together. Well, it had been lunch for her. But it was so nice to be with her husbands and not have some emergency at hand. Lon congratulated her on the Froregreen thing as well.

Jae had pulled off a very long shift to return to his normal schedule. Though she was barred from stims, Jae wasn't. Londo had managed to do everything he'd had on his list to accomplish. The two of them had taken to bed after dinner without any newlywed exercise.

They all would have to do something about that situation. It was getting to be a problem.

But she was still flying high from the praise, just halfway through her day. Even a call from the Legion for her to perform an emergency port for them (she checked how she was dressed first) didn't knock down her energy. Best put that to use since they had so many more basic things to accomplish before they could really get things started around here.

Water, air, migration routes: check. Being attended to. War: check-ish. So far nothing had come up, which meant it hadn't necessarily been eliminated. Women and disenfranchised: still a long, long way to go in that department.

According to Jae's accountants, they had plenty of money. She wished her brain would stay awake long enough for her to understand what they told her about it in their meetings, but one financial term in, two amounts mentioned and discussed, and her brain turned off. Jae had laughed loudly once he'd noticed.

It was enough money that their finance people through the Legion refused to handle even a fraction of it. Jae was looking for a firm that could husband – now, *there* was a term – their funds to stretch them out. He was fascinated by money as a concept, and having so much of it was a fresh adventure.

Though her new earnings still hadn't sunk in on a personal level, Lina knew that with extremely judicious planning and scads of unpaid volunteers, they might just be able to get this Aldierra mission off the ground and into the air, maybe even for as long as it wanted to fly.

Hopefully the accountants would warn Lina and the others if funds were getting low. Heaven knew what they'd be able to do about it.

She stared at the curved white Shit Room wall around her, using it as a blank background for her plans. Everyone was going to have their duties in this, but Lon and Jae were paraheroes on a galactic sector level; they had to leave time for that. That left her, and she knew that one person would not be able to accomplish these goals, not by a long shot. An infinity shot.

What they needed to do was to get lots of hands involved. Professional ones in the important positions, not volunteers. The more the better. A thousand people could accomplish a thousand times more than she herself could.

She paused as the back of her brain sent some figures up to her. Eight billion people on Earth, twenty billion on Aldierra, three billion natives on Sarastor. Thirty-one billion. How much could thirty-one billion people accomplish? If everyone just put in a few minutes a week, how much was that?

It was time to officially organize this Three Worlds deal. Thirty-one billion people needed a structure that wouldn't collapse on them and wouldn't impede them either. A free-floating organization, there for direction, communication, and help, not for power. And on a more practical level, a structure that the three of them could afford and keep up, year after year, for as long as the worlds needed it.

So she sat, petted Fafhrd who came in to snooze against her shoulder, and thought. Her amazing uber-futuristic techno-wizard padd sat next to her on a small table. Plastic, brown, Dime n' Dollah Store. The table, that was. Cracked leg, but she'd glued it back to health. The padd held notes from every time they'd discussed what they'd be doing as well as those university experts yesterday, plus some Sarastoran ones she'd consulted last week. And Wiley's suggestions, of course.

Lina checked the padd for Terran time zones. The area she knew well was into nighttime mode, past closing for most places. But she had visited San Francisco. Surely a city that big would have an all-night paint or arts and crafts store. It was possibly still light there.

— — —

The paint store clerk looked up as the tee-shirted woman stood patiently next to his counter. "Excuse me," she said, holding up a can of white paint. "How fast does this dry? And is it really opaque? I mean, I know paints like to say they're opaque when they aren't."

They talked for a while and he showed her some faster-drying brands. She got a fill-up paint roller with several replacement heads and a whole rainbow of spray paint. She told him she was working on a mural, and asked where the nearest newspaper was. They did still have newspapers in San Francisco, right?

— — —

Lina shut her eyes as she spritzed the first big blob of red paint in the middle of the wall. Aldierra, the hot spot. A third of the way around the room from it she spritzed green for Earth, and then another third further on, gold: Sarastor.

Lon and Jae had installed all kinds of doohickeys in this hotel suite that would need to be torn out when they left. In comparison, having to get someone to repaint a wall shouldn't be that big a deal.

So she paced up and down the wall, spritzing little blips and blops here and there, then stepping back to see how it looked. She kept referring to their notes. Once she took out the roller and filled it up, covering some color-coded patches with white. If the paint dried on the roller, she had replacement heads so she didn't bother to wash it, only covered it with plastic wrap.

She spritzed again and nodded in satisfaction at her work while the puter played a classics rock playlist from Earth. As her day wore on she dared to sip from a 20-ounce bottle of Coke, fully caffeinated, fully sugared, to keep herself alert. They might have ordered her off caffeine, but this was an emergency. She wouldn't drink it all. Brownie points for that.

She tore off a twenty-five-foot length from the heavy roll of leftover newspaper newsprint. (Price: free.) Shakily she used that new backup power of hers to levitate to the ceiling and taped it in place six feet out from the wall using a roll of masking tape she kept on her arm like a bracelet. A ribbon of newsprint soon dangled all the way across the room from the ceiling. She floated in lurches down to the floor. She needed to practice levitation, but as it was she was getting by with it. Not a priority.

Using cardboard to write against, she made occasional notations on the paper. Back and forth along the fluttering newsprint, she walked and kept glancing from the abstract painting on the wall to her notes.

Spritz. Splat. She lined up things across from each other. No, that wouldn't work at all. She erased the wall using the white roller, then ripped part of the paper, replacing it with a new panel, copying a few things from the old piece. Now she ran tape from the wall to the paper, using it like string, spritzing to give the tape a color code.

She sat back and looked at the result a long time before she put up a second tier of newsprint, painting and writing on it in the same way, running the tape from it to the first paper and from that to the wall.

No, no, no! She shredded half of the second tier, then replaced and separated it so it didn't run the entire length of the wall, but rather had two shorter lengths. She shooed off the cats who'd come to play with the dangling pieces of tape. Two of them came in to investigate the bank of litterboxes.

There. She regarded it for some time as she checked against her padd. She walked her way through the chart. How exactly would this be accomplished? She got out new colors and assigned them meanings, spritzing out color samples on the side wall and penning in the legend next to each.

Go from here to here to here. Okay, how about this? Here to here to... where? She frowned at the paper banners as if they'd betrayed her. There. Was it all epicycles? Was it too much running around? Could this organization be done in a simpler, more direct way?

Flatten the hierarchy. Barney Fife's TV voice rattled her brain: "Nip it! Nip it!" What if something happened to one of them? The organization had to continue efficiently. And she didn't want to become a Manager. People changed when they became Managers. Make everyone a mini-manager; that way there didn't have to be Major Managers. Employees had to know the jobs of the people who were next to them in the organization. Also one level above and one below. Cross-training would be a must.

She tried to remember re-engineering theory, why it hadn't worked at her old job at Midnight Delivery. How would she have redesigned that place if she could have begun from scratch? If you considered every citizen of the Three Worlds as customers... But Three Worlds was a service organization; it didn't deliver product. Well, sometimes it would. Hm. Hm.

She remembered her friendships with the people at the Durham Red Cross, how Aisha there had taken her around a few times because she'd been bored and had explained the organization and exactly how it was totally screwed up to her way of thinking.

Lina recalled her county's housing council; she had worked as a volunteer assistant for its manager. They'd had such lofty plans, and she'd organized squadrons of well-meaning volunteers to help the professionals carry them out. They could swing hammers but not much else. Her manager had traveled to larger organizations in other states and come back with tales of what they were doing differently to get better results, though her county didn't have access to those kinds of funding. How would she have done it if she and her pocketbook were in charge?

She sang along with the sound system as she tore down, painted over, and retaped.

After a long while, even the singing couldn't keep her awake. She hoped this wouldn't anger the Worlds, that she would use her Flute for her personal needs, but this related to the Worlds' business.

She let the Flute fade into existence in her hands and then played a spritely jig on it. Not too loudly; her husbands were asleep, as were most of the cats. But the cats roused themselves and those who weren't in the room already scampered in. Though Lina couldn't dance, she tried a little boogie herself as she played, tilting her body back and forth to get circulation going. Oops– her lively dance really was the same movements as that kid on the Christmas *Peanuts* special. Londo had once asked her if that had been the only dance instruction she'd ever had.

Well, she might be uncoordinated dance-wise, but now she was awake again.

CHAPTER

9

Lina? Didn't you ever come to bed?**

***Go back to sleep, Jae. Sorry for waking you.**

It's dawn. I'm awake for the day.

You are? I lost track of the time.

You aren't on stims, are you?

Just the Flute and a little caffeine. I've only drunk half the bottle. Where's Lon?

You know how he is once he's asleep. He's out. You come to bed.

I need to finish up here while I'm hot. There's fruit in the fridge so you won't starve.

What in the orb are you doing?

Jae wandered into the room, wearing a robe and rubbing his longish hair into a mess. He stood blinking at the banners: crazily-painted squiggles and lines and circles all over the walls, paper similarly marked hanging across the room, eight flanks of it, with colored tape connecting points in a web. There was clear plastic covering the floor, slippery to walk on and wet with dollops of spilled paint. Ribbons of painted paper lay in low piles all over.

"You've returned to your artistic roots," Jae surmised. "This is modern-era abstract Terran art."

"Be quiet," Lina snapped, spritzing a violet crescent. "Give me about twenty minutes here."

It was more like forty, but Jae honored her artistic trance. He saw the legend on the wall, saw the three large circles around the room, and tried to puzzle it out for himself. At one point were two grouped symbols in light blue with strings connected to the big purple rectangle on the first hanging of paper. One was a non-convex polygon, making a kind of star, he supposed, and then some kind of bilateral figure, a curve with a long end to it that connected down the middle to its mirror image. In his woozy haze he hazarded a guess: labia. Star-labia.

Oh. He bet that that was the Terran symbol for heart. Did Terran human hearts look like that? Starhart. That was them there. He dried the paint on the floor as well as Moosie's feet and sat down on it to watch his wife as she paced, looking distantly at her work, critically. Measuringly. She had a great butt.

"Okay," she finally said and he snapped out of his daydream. "You're a citizen of the Three Worlds. Pick one."

"Aldierra," he said quickly.

"You've got a problem that you think the Three Worlds should handle. Pick a problem."

Jae frowned. He'd had some distressing discussions at camp yesterday. "I'm gay, and I've been caught three times. I'm scheduled to be executed in two weeks and the authorities aren't paying any attention to our decree."

"In that case they've probably got you in a cell with no communications," Lina said. "You die. Sorry."

"So I'm the lover of the gay guy who's going to be killed any time now, I don't know when because no one's telling me anything."

"Ah." Lina went to the far wall and tapped on the big red circle. "You're on Aldierra with a sociological and legal problem. You can operate on theory and go the sociological route, to our call center [she tapped her finger on the first line of paper, which only had the one block that Jae knew was the central call center because that's what purple was labelled on the wall], who connects you to ambassadors and scientists who will endeavor to talk or write a paper to convince the Aldierran public that your friend is a human being who does not deserve punishment for what he is.

"But along the way, they'll say what you need is immediate help, and they contact the call center, who transfers your call to the legal branch, which is where you should have called first anyway if you had any shred of common sense in you at all."

"Sorry," Jae said.

"That's all right, the people at the Call Center would have put you in the right direction when you called. Anyway, here at the legal center – and we have three of them, one for each planet – we have experts who know all about Aldierra's legal system. They get in contact with a branch of the research department who keeps a list of contacts that we need for any situation–"

"Any?"

"So it'll take some time to compile. Any situation, as I was saying, and they find someone who gives them the particulars on the case. The lawyers now know that they have two weeks to get your friend out of this jam, and they sic their legal lobbyist over here at Soshe – that's the capital where they do all the paperwork and legal stuff, right? – on the officials needed while they also pursue legal channels to bail out your friend, to get the charges dropped.

"With a safety margin that they determine, if the lawyers still haven't made any headway at, say they've decided on two days until d-day, they contact the call center–" she pointed at the purple block "–and they contact us directly. We take your friend out manually, any way possible, and the lobbyists–" she pointed at the sociology block "and the lawyers" at the judiciary block "cover our asses. If needed, we get the poor man off Aldierra until things cool down. In the meantime, you've been contacted at every important juncture and told how things are going. Maybe with that information you've managed to find your own way to help your friend. Hopefully you'll report back if you have; we need to know what works."

Jae considered as he petted Ember, his ever-present feline companion. Moose didn't object to being rubbed with his other hand. "But all my research has landed the cold eye of the authorities on me now, and they've dragged me off, incommunicado."

"Ah, our lawyers are aware that that could happen, and they're smart enough to know that if they haven't been able to get you to answer their calls for two days in a row that you're the one in trouble now. So they go to Soshe, who go to their contacts, and they find out where you are."

"And none of this came about because the line to Three Worlds Communications was tapped." Ember climbed off him to explore the litter boxes.

"Absolutely. This communication system must be untapped, unprejudiced, absolutely secure. People have got to know that they won't get into trouble for using it. And they have to be able to get the results they need. Everyone at the Call Center will have to be trained on how to redirect a call to get it where it needs to go."

Jae lay back on the floor looking at it all, his arms behind his head. "And everyone needs to be encouraged in incentive so that they can signal somebody that no one else might think of, in order to help. If they don't know the answer, they should ask someone."

"One huge team, divided into sub-teams that work together," Lina said.

"How many team members?"

Lina sat down on the floor next to Jae. "As near as I can figure, about thirty-one billion."

Jae smiled at that. "Payroll is going to be a problem."

"So we only pay the core people. This is a volunteer organization, maybe fifty percent of it. Sixty. Seventy. Maybe more. I'm thinking barter here, Jae."

"Barter?"

"Get a break on your taxes if you give two hours a month to the Three Worlds. Go to other participants and they give you a discount on something if you give them a discount too. But you've got to have your membership card, up to date and validated, to get in on it."

"And who keeps track of all this?"

Lina sighed. "I'm hoping individuals will. I've seen bartering organizations; they have everything on computers. Everything's broken down into units or monetary values. But not crypto currency. I don't trust crypto."

"Cryptocurrency is the way everyone works. I don't know about Earth, though. Okay. Widespread barter. Throughout three worlds." Jae wiped his face with a hand and then looked sharply at his wife.

She said, "I know some small-scale barter places with just a few thousand people on board. We can check them out."

He gave her a small, ironic smile. "Check your history, too. Five hundred, maybe longer years ago, Feith abandoned currency in order to develop a plane-tary barter system. That would involve about a billion people, maybe more. I don't know what the figures were back then. But somewhere in the history files, there are extensive records of doing this."

"Oh good. I'll try to track down some Sarastoran economics grad students who actually like to deal with figures and economic theory. They can research the files and give us the *Readers Digest* condensed version."

"You seem to have been hit with a spark of genius tonight, wife," Jae said, holding her close. "This looks good to me. Basically, it's all here; it should work."

"We can fine-tune as we go," Lina said, and he nodded.

"I'm slotting in once-a-week meetings to make sure everything's running smoothly." Jae noted it on a screen that popped up from his Legion Array ring. "Tuesdays good for you?"

Where is everyone? Lon's thoughts were sleepy.

"We're here," Jae said to the air.

Port me. Please.

Lon appeared standing up in the middle of it all, the paper hanging from the ceiling, the tape running in a cat's cradle everywhere, paint spattered and respattered all over the plasticked floor and white walls.

"What the *tabarnak* have you done with my house?!"

"Our house," Jae corrected. "Lina, how about if we run that tape from over here – that's publicity, right? – to over there?"

"Why would you want to do that?"

"We've got censorship on all three worlds at varying levels."

"Hm. If we take it directly over there, we could lose a level."

"Yeah. Do it."

Lina got up to restring and recode a new line of tape.

"It's going to take three coats at least to clean this up," Lon complained. He bent down to look at the legend and turned to compare it to the rest of the room. "Haven't you ever heard of paper, Lina?"

"That's it, hanging right there."

"I mean..."

"So I knew this was going to be a three-dimensional affair. I'm a visual creative."

"Well, I've had some ideas after we had our last meeting on this," Londo said. "I–"

Lina pointed at one section of the charts. "There. Did I miss some of your notes?"

Jae pointed to a couple other areas. "My latest ideas are here as well, Lon."

"Isn't that why we have combined business files?" Lina asked huffily. "I'm not going to do all this myself. I'm not going to leave you out. Make sure you record your ideas and notes. If you don't like the way I'm organizing the files, tell me a better way to do it."

"Here, Londo," Jae patted the floor next to himself. "Pick a world, one of the three."

"Earth," Lon said after he'd obeyed and sat.

"Okay, you've got a problem and haven't been able to get the local authorities to handle it. It's a Three Worlds problem, maybe. What is it?"

"I'm hungry."

"Okay, a hunger problem," Jae said, squinting at the paper, the connections.

"No, I'm really hungry," Lon said irritably. "Who wants to go out for breakfast?"

They went through the channels with Londo, describing someone who was starving on Earth. He scratched his head, looking at the display as he comprehended it. "You came up with all this in one night?" he asked Lina.

"This is all what we've been discussing," she replied. "I've been making notes. You've been adding to them, as has Jae, and I think I put everything into this. Plus I've been talking with Legion Communications, to see how they do it now and how they did it a century ago, so we can ease into this, technology-wise. I've brought in organizational experts. It's all been percolating in the back of my brain. I think it'll work. Probably not quite in this form, but it's going to be close. We'll make changes as needed."

Londo frowned at it all. Then he got up and began walking around. He pointed out some spots and aimed problems at them. "What if…" He picked up some tape and ran it to the next line of paper. "And then…" More tape. He ripped off some paper from the roll and hung it where he wanted it.

"Better," Jae said, and Lina agreed.

But now Jae was the one who began to rearrange. Before long, everyone was walking around, taping and tearing and spritzing, and getting paint all over their clothing. Lon spritzed directly at Lina.

"Why haven't you gone to bed yet?" And he spritzed her again, just to hear her shriek. Then they both laughed.

After a while they made what Jae announced would be final adjustments. The room was chaos. Tape hung everywhere, but the important parts were connected firmly to where they wanted it to go. A ball of discarded colored tape sat next to a sleeping cat. She in turn was partially covered with used but unwanted paper diagrams.

Jae set his fists on his hips as he surveyed the room. "I don't see any way to simplify it further until we get it up and running to see where the glitches are. It's pretty simple as it is."

Lon pocketed his padd, which he'd been using for organizational research. "It's a lot of people..."

"A lot of people putting in a small amount of time," Lina reminded them. "We have small cores of permanent staff and lots of volunteers. That can become one of the Three Worlds' goals: to get people to volunteer a few minutes each week to help out. A half-hour here, a half-hour there – it'll add up. And the more people do it, the more publicity we give it, the more people will want to help."

"Volunteer work is not the most reliable." Londo made a face. "But *oui*, we'll have to rely on it."

"She's thinking interplanetary and planetary bartering for the volunteers," Jae explained.

Lon sat on the rickety chair. "Barter," he sighed.

"Barter."

"Okay, it could work but this is still going to take one hell of a lot of money." He watched Fat Cat use a litter box.

"That's where the complete line of Valiant and Neutrino underwear and souvenir mugs–"

"And tee shirts," Jae added.

"That too," Lina nodded, "comes in."

Lon closed his eyes and shook his head at them. "We'll have to get the Worlds declared a charity."

"Aren't they?" Jae wanted to know.

"I suppose. We need to talk with my lawyer on Earth. Remind me to call him. In the meantime, where do we start?"

Lina pointed at the big purple rectangle. "Communications."

"I doubt if Legion Informational Systems will even consider taking this on temporarily," Jae said slowly.

"They won't even laugh at us," Lon agreed. "They'll just lodge a formal complaint, have us kicked out for even mentioning something like this."

"We won't use them," Lina insisted. "We start on Aldierra, with Aldierran communications."

"Problem," Jae announced. "Women on Aldierra. Gays on Aldierra. They won't want to talk to straight male operators, I bet. At least, a sizeable proportion of them won't. And we have House rivalries to worry about."

"Our pool of educated and skilled Aldierran women to work the phones might be small," Lina decided.

"So no Communications hub on Aldierra?" Jae asked the two of them.

"I don't think so. It'll take too much time to train folks. How about Sarastor?"

"*Non*," Londo blurted.

"Absolutely not," Jae said.

Their reasoning had something to do with AI and lack of focus among too many Sarastorans. Whatever it was, Lina would find out soon enough when they got to working on that world.

"So that leaves Earth," Lina determined.

Jae nodded. "Sounds like it. What's our other priority here?"

Lon wrinkled his nose as he thought. "What we're going to come up against, if they're as paranoid as you say they are, Jae, is privacy. Fear that what they say will be used against them."

"Agreed. Communications must be secure."

"We can do that. What's all this tape?" Lon pointed. "Is there one communications center or three?"

"First center is on Earth. It's also our largest, since that's where central HQ will be."

"Then come the outlying centers on Sarastor and Aldierra."

They argued some more and discussed, then agreed that some of the funkier potential problems were too distant to worry about now. Aldierra would be their concern until Deadline was passed.

"Many of these things will change as we figure all this out," Lina said. "We'll have to restructure from time to time. Maybe we'll discover that all this can be solved through, I don't know, just two levels. At which time we can throw everything else out. We can't afford to get stuck in Business as Usual just because it's convenient to us. I figure on weekly tune-ups for a month, then twice-monthly, until we can ease it down to yearly in a few years. Of course, we'll have to run fire drills all the time."

Londo rubbed his eyes. It was still a little too early for this. "Fire drill?"

"That's what we called them at Midnight Delivery. Pretending that something horrible had happened and then–"

Jae drummed his fingers on the floor, and the plastic drop cloth gave a rattling sound to it. "You're talking basic Legion exercises. Drills. Not just for fires."

"Just to see if everything's being handled efficiently. Time it as to how fast we can collar these things. Ask the operators and contacts involved if they see better ways to do it."

Londo sprawled on the floor, groaning. "It all sounds like work to me. Remember when we thought this would be a breeze?" Then he held up his padd, which he'd been checking for a minute or two. "What's all this?"

Lina peered at it, and Londo helpfully made it into a large, mid-air screen.

It was her personal notes about the two of them. What foods they had liked, how long they took to get ready for the day, where they stored which clothing, names of their Legion staff. Favorite colors. Clothing sizes. Funny things they'd said. Items they'd said they liked.

"Oh that. Doesn't everyone do that when they get married? We're in a rush here, so I needed to get an organized handle on it all."

"But I don't like *kennel* soup."

"That's not what you said the other day."

"I was being polite to our host." He deleted the item. "*Yark.*"

"Look at this." Jae let Londo see another portion of Lina's files.

Lon let out a soft whistle. "*Chrisse.* Slap a security filter on this, Lie."

"Uh. How do I do that?"

Jae kept scrolling. "Commissioners. Heads of state. Legionnaires. What they've told you. Families?"

"I need to keep them straight, as well as be able to bring things up with them. Starting off with, 'Did Billy like his new braces?' kind of eases in the conversation, you know?"

"I suppose."

"You guys need to add to this. At the very least, so I'll know what I'm getting into if something unexpected comes up."

"But we'll put it under a security filter." Jae tweaked his fingers at the screen, and a "security 4" signal appeared in the upper right corner.

Lina frowned at it. "What if I get wind of some juicy Level 5 stuff? Or Unlimited?"

Jae considered as Londo looked at him expectantly. "Give us a heads-up." He tapped his forehead to mean "telepathically." "You don't write down anything Unlimited without us standing behind you as you do so."

"Broccoli?" Londo asked as Jae scrolled down into new sections.

"You like it roasted with garlic, olive oil, lemon zest, and Parmesan cheese. Not plain and not raw in a salad. Mama Ruth told me that when we met. She wants to make sure you eat right."

Londo mumbled something along the lines of, "I might be able to stand it. Now and then."

"Good. Jae, do you like pie or cake? Or neither? Something else?"

"Ah… I take it you mean Terran?"

"Any."

"I'll get you a list of Sarastoran. You'll have to introduce me to the Terran varieties."

"Will do." Lina stretched. "All I want now is some serious sleep. I haven't been to bed yet."

"Not any?" Lon squinted at her. "Stims?" He gave her a deep frown.

Lina shook her head. "A little caffeine, sorry. Maybe six ounces. This had to be done. It does look kind of pretty, doesn't it?" The chart's intense hues against the white of the walls and floors created a primitive rhythm of color and shape.

Londo checked the half-drunk bottle of cola, gave Lina a fisheye, and drank the remainder to eliminate the temptation. "Flat," he pronounced, and then, gesturing to the banner display around the room, "It's lovely." He reached to take Lina's padd from her. He scanned the room and the symbols with their legend, and then checked his own to make sure it had copied to his systems as well as Jae's.

"Just recording for posterity," he said. "The Louvre might have an opening someday. And the cats might start tearing it down. Where's the hotel menu? You eat. We all eat. Then you can hit the sack, while Jae and I take in a little exercise. We need to go to Earth today, no matter what our Aldierran schedule says." He adjusted their schedules with some finger wiggle instructions.

His spouses looked at him questioningly.

"My lawyer," Lon said. "As long as we're organizing, we need to get other things done. Today."

"We need to start that communications center yesterday." Jae pointed at that purple box on the wall, from which string after string was strung.

"*Oui.* Communications is number-one priority, not lawyer," Lon agreed. "I'll set up channels in the military here. Jae?"

"I want to talk with Wiley, see who he recommends for the tech side as well as anything else he can think of. I've got a list of my own." Jae waved his padd at Lon, who nodded and again adjusted schedules for all.

"*D'accord*, we get communications set up on Earth," Londo declared. "*Maintenant...*"

"Training," Lina interjected. "That's going to take time."

"It will have to be short. We'll refine as we go. Lina, you've already done enough but I know you'll try for even more. Today, today, today, we'll do as much as we can. After Lina gets some breakfast and sleep.

"Jae and I will forego our exercise. We begin making hiring inquiries immediately, civilian and military. Send out requests for volunteers as well." He tied his goal schedule in to their padds as he set up newly prioritized bulleted points.

"We will find a temp spot for a Terran-based communications center. We'll hire for training. We'll arrange for the equipment and networks we need. We will get this organization in place." He looked up at them just standing there and waved his arms at them. "Hup hup!"

— — —

It was late morning in Montreal, but Lina had awakened on Aldierra an hour or so ago. Londo was making up for lost time there, knocking down city blocks as fast as the military could assure they were empty. He only paused to talk with Bracken about personnel.

Jae was slogging through some filthy river even as constant calls went back and forth between him and Wiley about interstellar communications, and between Jae and his office staff as to hiring. Otherwise Lina would have invited him to Earth for lunch. Besides, Jae liked to use most of his lunches to talk with his volunteered soldiers. He might interview a few for permanent positions. She wished she could have a leisurely talk with Jae, too.

Romantic Montreal and no husband to share it with. Double-darn it anyway. She'd grab some good food later and bring it home for them all to enjoy – whenever they individually had time, that was.

Montreal's InfoTouriste's front doors beckoned Lina, but for some reason she felt she shouldn't go in. It was as if a wall of air blocked any movement toward it.

This was not normal. It was Abby-normal.

"I need local advice," she explained out loud. "We have to figure out where our temporary center should go, so I need to know the lay of the city." Still that invisible wall persisted.

****_You have different priorities?_**** she drily asked the spirit guides who were always by her side. Turning in a circle, she felt another push, this one from behind, and she began to walk. Sometimes she stumbled, the pushes were so hard, but she kept–

"Oh! Sorry!"

She'd crashed into a woman barreling at right angles toward the crosswalk.

"*Pardon!*" the woman said, and bent down to pick up the briefcase and two bags she'd dropped.

…And knocked her head against Lina's as she also bent for them.

The two women laughed and sorted out the baggage. Then the other woman paused.

She looked early forties, comfortable in business clothes that were well-worn. Trousers instead of skirt; a pretty butterfly pin on her shoulder.

"You look familiar," the woman said in French as they both crouched over the bags.

"You do too," Lina replied. Where had she seen her? It was… It was…

"*Sacre–* You're Valiant's wife!" The woman's mouth fell open.

"And I saw you during my Investiture," Lina realized as both stood. "It didn't hit me until now." She laughed. "Literally."

"*Euh…?*"

Lina hoisted the last bag in her own arms so as not to weigh the woman down. "I'm Lina Starhart," she said. "Can we go somewhere to talk for a while? I need to find out something. Something important."

– – –

The soft ice cream was heaven. Because it was technically lunchtime here and not quite elevenses as it was on her Aldierran schedule, Lina got hers with a chunk of brownie at the bottom. And fudge sauce and pecans and whipped cream and a cherry that was the best one ever, just because. Let her guys have their booze. This was what life was all about.

"You wouldn't believe how bland most of the food is Out There," she told Wendy as they chatted in French. Wendy Cloutier, that was, an ex-Chief Warrant Officer of the Canadian Army, but she acted like a regular person and not some prickly Army type.

She had left the Army because she'd finished a creditable career but tired of all the red tape and bits of misogyny that any army still held. She was divorced, and her two kids had grown out of being at home. With her house empty she now spent her time overseeing a small startup for office temps, one that specialized in supplying government-adjacent agencies.

Lina nodded through the conversation, amazed at all the ghostly shoulder pats Wendy was getting. "I'm surprised you don't come with a halo," she told her.

"Let me get this straight: you've seen me before?" Wendy asked.

"It was a few weeks ago, way Out There," Lina explained. "Londo, Jae and I–" She'd already explained about Jae being part of the Three Worlds– "were getting Invested as the Three Worlds' Chosen. When I was, well, I guess you could call it 'anointed,' they gave me a vision. I saw It. Everything. The entire cosmos and a wonderful, eternal plan. It wasn't religious at all. Every person, every molecule, all are life moving together in perfect harmony until the universe and the evolutionary experiment ends in a few quint-zillion years."

Wendy's mouth opened.

Lina shrugged. "I forgot the particulars afterward, like I forgot the person-to-person communications with every living Aldierran – I'll tell you about that later – but I remember the wonder, the glory and especially the… bubbling *joy* of it all. So exciting. And when I saw you just now I remembered that you were there. I think you're supposed to be a part of this. The Three Worlds part, that is.

"But free will, you know. You are always free to refuse and do what you like. I think the Worlds have a number of people lined up as replacements available as needed, even for us three.

"But right now I need an assistant. An executive assistant as in practically a partner. Does that mean I'm an 'executive?' Ack!" Lina's eyes widened in shock before she went on. "There's so much to do. I need someone to keep me on track and do things when I'm not there to do them.

"They won't let me take stims for a few months. Technically I can't even have caffeine now. We're not going to tell them about the chocolate sauce on this, right? I mean, how much caffeine can it hold?"

The confusion in Wendy's eyes cleared slightly so she could garner a small smile at that over what remained of her own sundae. "I have a feeling I've just come in in the middle of a conversation," she said.

"Looney tunes, isn't it? I should sell tickets. We've been tossed into this, ker-splash! And we're treading water as hard as we can without a map." She frowned at Wendy. "Is it really Wendy? *They* say… That is, my guides say, spirit guides, there's another name."

Wendy thoughtfully stirred the last of the melted ice cream in her dish. "Kanti. But in the Army I went by 'Wendy.' I got used to it. Some people prefer to use our Anglo names."

"Well, I'll use whichever you prefer. Oh man, are my pronouns correct? So many things to remember. Do you live in Montreal? Our HQ is going to be here. Though I don't think Londo wants many people to know that. The price of real estate, you know."

Wonder washed across Kanti's face. "This is really going to be, well, a thing, is it? An important project. Not just for Montreal."

"Anyone I hire is going to have to live on Aldierra until Deadline passes. After that you're free to return to Earth or even Sarastor, where we'll also have an HQ. We hope to make some changes. Huge ones on Aldierra. Remains to be seen how big on Sarastor and Earth, but big."

Kanti was almost literally chewing over something. "I've sold my house. The new people are giving me until the end of next month to move out. I haven't signed a lease anywhere yet."

"Ah. The universe works in mysterious ways?"

"I need to know a lot more about all this."

"Right. Sensible. Of us all, Jae is the only truly sensible one. Lon makes decisions like–" She snapped her fingers. "I see the inevitable coming and complain but jump where there's usually no jumping back. But Jae puts on his inscrutable Thinking Face and ponders the problem until he figures it out.

"You don't have to decide right now. I can give you a Linguatape and a padd so you can begin learning Farrani right away, if you want to try it. The spoken language is easy-peasy sleep learning, but printed material and syntax and stuff requires sitting down and studying. It should take about three days to learn if you make it a priority, but the translator program will be updating like mad for the next couple weeks.

"We three have finished programming the language into AffSys systems for the most part, but Jae's plugged the system into Aldierran media records. It's scanning those to get to most of the remaining linguistic nooks and crannies. Jae says it'll be finished any day now. We can only hope."

Lina leaned in closer to confide. "I started by teaching it cuss words. For some reason the men of Aldierra start shrieking the most awful things when they bash each other and I have to wade in and straighten 'em out. Jae says that it's important to know how to curse fluently. Lon agrees with him.

"Now… Would you like to help me spend some money?"

CHAPTER

10

Kanti and Lina walked companionably along the St. Lawrence, more or less. There was a four-lane highway between them and it, plus a nearer utility road that ran as far as Lina could see, certainly up to a long, industrial-style bridge ahead.

They had to walk on the edge of that road, as there were no sidewalks. Modern, mid-rise office buildings lined the side they were on, and this one in particular had a "For Sale/*à Vendre*" sign in front of it. It stretched for some way back from the road. There was a small, multi-level parking garage as well as an even smaller ground level parking lot adjacent. A security fence surrounded it all. Spring was breaking out, and a line of young, almost-bare trees along the property line were thinking about blooming. Kanti regarded it critically as Lina stayed on her phone.

Lina thought the phone wouldn't be as spooky for Kanti to experience as watching a telepathic conversation, so she used it for an interstellar call to her husbands. "She says this is a great neighborhood for businesses like us. Good transportation routes, although the nearest Metro is quite a few blocks away. Not really walkable, as far as I'm concerned, especially when the weather turns bad. I hear it gets cold here in winter."

She hung up on the conversation. "Give us a few minutes," she told Kanti. "I'm going to look weird for a while." Then she handed the phone to the woman and pointed to the sign with the phone number on it. "Could you give them a call? Have him or her meet us as soon as they can?"

Five minutes later both Londo and Jae stood beside them, taking in the building, the highway, and the river. Jae was in his brown and violet Sarastoran work clothing, looking odd enough for Earth. He used his powers to clean the muck off himself, and gluts of dried dust plopped around his boots. Lon stood in his filthy uniform. He flew an angled path into the air to remove himself from the general area, then spun around like a top. He returned much cleaner. A car heading toward them swerved violently, even though they stood on the building's lawn.

The building next door also had a sign up: "à louer," *for rent.*

"If this works, we may need it as well," Jae remarked in the French they were all using. He scratched his cheek. "I don't think this one alone," he pointed at the one for sale, "is going to be large enough, even if it will be temporary until we put in the permanent HQ. We should get that one for reserve."

Without waiting for a request, Kanti called the number on that sign as well.

Londo grunted. Obviously he was busy poring through the building with his paravision.

"Let's look for ourselves," Lina insisted.

"We'll need keys," Kanti began as she ended the call, but Lina shook her head.

"We've got porting until the owner arrives and we can do things legally."

The owner of the rental arrived before the other did, so they completed their stroll around that building first.

"Call center in the for sale one," Lina whispered to Kanti. "It will require the most renovations and space. We need a lot of actual humans sitting in chairs, in addition to the basic computerized sorting system. Everything else would be in here, maybe."

"Call center personnel will need to live here, not Aldierra," Kanti said for confirmation, and Lina nodded.

"We'll bring in some Aldierrans for training," Lina told her. "But that's later, when we're setting up the local communications hub there. We can get calls routed from Earth to Aldierra easy. Just don't ask me how that works."

Both buildings had splendid views of the St. Lawrence on one side and rather disappointing ones of the city and its long background mountain on the other. "Security," Jae complained of the windows.

"We'd replace them with screens," Londo responded. "Maybe from a better viewpoint. People like nice views."

Lina leaned to Kanti. "Executive assistants get the best views," she whispered. "Not to influence your decision or anything."

Kanti chuckled.

"We'll institute a secure bus service to the Metro," Londo declared once the owner had backed out of hearing distance. "I'm tempted to put in an underground extension line, but not for a temporary base. This is a good location."

He pointed to something outside the building. "Cafes and restaurants. Probably a little too far for a normal lunchbreak, but all right for dining bigwigs."

"We can have a 24/7 food court in the rental, maybe," Lina offered. "Food trucks? Do they do those here?"

"*Oui.* We'll get a Timmy Hortons." Lon nodded enthusiastically. "And poutine. I love poutine. And bagels. And–"

"Healthy fare," Jae said before Lina could add the same. "Knowing you, I don't think those are too healthy."

Londo shrugged at that.

"We'll need a nurse on duty," Lina said. "And an HR department. Accounting. IT. Meeting rooms for employees as well as outsiders."

"A media studio as well," Kanti put in. "You'll be making announcements, right? You'll need that in a lower security area so the press can attend." As the others took that in, she asked Lina, "My staff will have nice offices?"

Lina looked at her. "How many are we talking?"

"I have seven employees. All extremely skilled at hiring as well as many other HR jobs. They're used to dealing with government and military honchos. One has had a lot of experience managing a Los Angeles police call center."

"Hey guys, we now have eight official non-military employees," Lina told her husbands. "We need an accounting department so they can get paid. Legal so we do the paperwork right. Lon, I'll give you Lt. Twofence. He'll like that."

Londo rubbed his nose but nodded. "Two buildings," he decided. He glanced at Jae and then Lina. "Maybe we should put in a buy offer on the rental?"

"I bet the price on that has gone up by about four hundred percent since we've been standing here," Lina said.

Lon grimaced. "Any longer and it'll get worse. Where'd Landry go? Let's get him in here. And Hebert too. After that we have one more thing to do today. All of us except Kanti."

— — —

The messages had been on Lon's voicemail for weeks now. The string of them was the reason why they remained on Earth, specifically Vancouver, this late afternoon:

"This is John Henry Rombard, attorney of record for Monsieur Londo Falcon Rand. According to recent news reports my client has not only changed his effing name without doing it legally, but also married and not told his poor, suffering lawyer whom he loves to keep in the dark one effing thing about it!

"Londo, get your ass over here. What the hell are you doing in the States, anyway? We have papers to draw up! Where's your pre-nup, or didn't you have one made, you unspeakable sap?! You'll need to change your will, too, before I kill you. I don't care if you're on some world-saving tour or not; I want your shadow darkening my door by the end of business Friday, or there'll be hell to pay!"

— — —

Londo closed his eyes. He could do this. Lina's hand squeezed his arm reassuringly before letting go. He took a deep, steadying breath and then strode into the high-ceilinged office without knocking. "You are many things, John Henry, but you are not poor!"

The Hawaiian Canadian looked up and actually jumped in his seat in surprise. After a moment he exclaimed, "I said Friday! Weeks ago!"

"We were busy saving the universe."

"F–, Londo, what are you trying to do to me?! What if someone tried to sue you this week? Oh hell, someone has. But what if you'd been killed on some mission? I wouldn't have known anything about this bim–"

Lina entered the room.

"Bim... Bim..."

"Bo," she finished for him. "Bimbo." She was wearing what she referred to as her Crappy Job Interview Suit, but Londo had had her add a spring green scarf to it, made her lose the untailored white shirt she'd worn underneath, and the end result looked rather sharp if he said so, especially with new black tights and shoes. *Eh bien*, the latter were not particularly stylish but Lina declared them comfortable, so Lon permitted them. He was determined to be a good husband.

And this might make up for things if he finally burned those pink overalls she coveted.

He himself of course was stylishly arrayed in a charcoal brown jacket over a dark tank top and slacks. He'd spent some time getting his hair perfect, but that was a habit he'd maintained for years. One of the first lessons Hal had taught him was that impressions were everything.

"Meet the bimbo, John Henry." Londo crossed his arms in front of his chest. "And please try to show a little more respect. John Henry Rombard, this is Carolina Starhart."

As usual in the confines of his smoky office, John Henry appeared as if he'd slept in his clothes. He was like this room. There were books scattered on every surface, some open, very few upright. An old-model PC slumbered with glamor-girl screen savers on his large office desk. His cigar smoldered in a glass ashtray. A half-eaten powdered sugar doughnut sat on a napkin next to a mug of coffee at his right hand, a flock of Post-It notes perching on the desk land line, a cell set next to them.

John Henry would only know about the original wedding, the one Lon had announced to the world. He wouldn't have any idea of what had happened less than two weeks later at Starhaven. The number of witnesses for the second, complete Triune ceremony had been minimal, and all had been sworn to secrecy.

Unfortunately Lon hadn't had time to warn Lina entirely about John Henry. "So pleased to meet you." She smiled dangerously. "I thought your type couldn't come out during the day."

"Okay *d'acc*, round one's a draw," Londo announced. "Lina, sit. John Henry, stay. We have arrived, somewhat late but per orders. Where's some coffee? Lina takes tea."

"Earl Gray, hot." John Henry gave her a dramatic leer. He and most of the civilized world surely had seen her on TV standing over the unconscious and near-dead body of Paul Granger, Earth's now-former Ruby Guard of the Galactic

Brigade, who had tried and failed to rape and murder her... but had damned near succeeded in killing Earth's preeminent woman parahero, Olympia. Lina had conducted the press conference at the hospital Olympia had been taken to, dressed in a bloody tee shirt that proclaimed her a Klingon Ambassador.

Londo knew that "Klingon" was some type of *Star Trek* deal and not a variety of dingleberry.

"Good guess," Lina said to John Henry, "but at this point I'm not allowed caffeination. Make it herbal, hot or iced." She turned to Londo. "He knows his *Trek*."

"Wonderful; that makes you best friends. Okay, John Henry. Tell us how big a hole we've dug ourselves."

John Henry pressed a button on his phone. "Steph, get us some refreshments. And see if you can find an old herbal teabag sitting around somewhere, will you?" He switched off and turned to Londo. "Just when I say that you haven't been sued for a while, along comes a Monsieur Grandee from Montreal with–"

Londo let out an angry sound. "I told him I'd have the building repaired within a month. Kurt bought some more time. The damage wasn't my fault, I've attended to all the residents' needs, I've called them all and they're fairly fine with things if we do run long, and I was paying for his damned insurance premiums. He should be kissing my toenails in adoration." He heaved out a breath. "I'm exhausted. I don't need this."

He pulled a chair for Lina and she sat, giving John Henry the evil eye even as he glared at her, like this was all her fault. She muttered like Marge Simpson.

Joke's gone too far, he told her. **Ease up.**

"He's citing you as a dangerous tenant, which is pretty odd that he's only now figured that out. If Grandee's had you paying for premiums, though, that would certainly indicate that he fully realized the danger when he signed you up in the first place." John Henry nodded to himself. "No sweat, then. We'll have this thrown out in no time, especially if you've repaired the building. Have you?"

"I was just over there, checking progress. If the final inspectors finish up tomorrow, tenants should be moving back by end of week. I hate to leave things hanging."

"Are you sure about him, Lon?" Lina asked. Her mouth pinched like she'd just sucked on a lemon.

"He's good, Lina. I've worked with him for years."

Her face showed more than doubt.

"He's not a misogynist. His attitude toward all of humanity sucks. He's an equal-opportunity defamer."

She frowned at Londo.

Steph, the legal receptionist, came bustling in with a tray, her smart, professional style in marked contrast to John Henry. His suspenders were wrapped around his mid-life belly and the top button of his pants was undone. Sweat stains shadowed his underarms and his curly dark hair was in Boris Johnson mode, as if he'd been rubbing his head all morning.

Cups were passed out; drinks were poured. Londo noted when Lina ported the smoky air out of the room and replaced it with fresh tropical air. John Henry automatically reached for the cigar on the side of his desk. Lina ported it and its ashtray to the other side without him noticing.

Lon enjoyed the game.

"What do you think of him?" Lina asked Steph.

"He's a real saint, if you're a Satanist," Steph replied. "God's gift to the paralegals of the world. They say that if you start off clerking for him, the rest of your life has got to be better."

"High praise." Lina looked at Londo.

"She's kidding, kitten," Londo said. "Give him a chance."

"Listen, Mrs. Rand..."

Lon could almost hear Lina gritting her teeth at that name. She had problems with being someone's property, even if it was his. Well, Lon had his own problems about living in Hal's shadow, so he'd jumped at the chance to change his last name.

"Ms. Starhart," Lon corrected before Lina could.

John Henry nodded absently. "...I get the job done, and I get it done efficiently. No muss, no fuss, no excess publicity. If you want one of those prissy liberal lawyers, I suggest you go down to the States to do your shopping. Me, I'm a down-to-earth realist kind of guy.

"Like I can look at the two of you and say, shit, they've not only changed their names without bothering to register them legally, but they also had the nerve to get married off-planet – wasn't Earth good enough for you, Londo? – and the bride's a freakin' American and not a God-fearing Canadian. What else, Londo? What else are you going to spring on me? Don't tell me the virgin bride's pregnant? I've got a bet riding that she is."

Lon grinned at Lina. "Imagine how he treats you when he doesn't like you, *chérie*. No, John Henry, there's no little bundle of joy due any time soon. See you Steph." Londo raised an eyebrow at her.

"You know who has to file all this," Steph sulked. "I'll find out."

"Not this time," Londo told her. "We're going to stand over his shoulder and watch him as he types."

Lina ported the cigar back across the desk away from John Henry's searching hand. The door shut very securely behind Steph.

"Good god," John Henry said. "Should I duck and take cover now? What's up?"

"What's up is that we'll use my spoken word program and link it to your computer. No one has to type anything. Lina? Commit, one way or the other."

Her lips slid from one side of her face to the other as she pondered. "Okay, Lon. I'll go along on this one."

"Good girl."

"Arf."

"Oh, be quiet. John Henry, we'd like to change my will and draw one up for Lina and do all those other things that married people do when they take a new name. But there's just one thing we have to mention."

"You're not legally married," John Henry guessed.

"Oh no, we're legally married, at least if I understand *Hol v United States*," Londo said. That was the definitive international ruling on the legality of extraterrestrial marriage.

"And man oh man, I hope you do," Lina said, almost under her breath.

John Henry reached for his cigar, but it wasn't there again. His subconscious still hadn't caught up with his conscious to tell him what was going on. "Spill it. You can't shock me, Rand."

"Starhart. We'll need all this paperwork done for the two of us, but there's another person in this marriage."

"Another... I thought you said she wasn't pregnant? You got a kid already, babe?"

Lon snorted. "The other person's about a year younger than I am. Do you mind if I bring him in?"

John Henry's eyes narrowed on Londo. "Is this April Fools?"

Jae appeared. He was wearing his Terran-style replicated jeans under a faux-leather jacket. Jae had seen some Earth fashions when he first came to the planet, and had replicated them at Legion HQ. His borrowed tee held the logo for the ParaNet. He looked good, real good.

He brushed long blond hair away from his startlingly blue eyes. "That didn't take too long," he said ironically. He glanced around the room, taking it in, and spotted the coffees and tea. "What, nothing for me?"

"What would you like, honey?" Lina asked.

"Some of that stuff I saw in the store out there, if you would. Cafe loddie? Something like that. Latte, that was it. Some woman was ordering it with a powder on top. It looked interesting."

"Would you excuse me?" Lina asked. "Jae, you sit here; I've warmed up the chair for you. Londo, please find an excuse to hit this man."

"Yes, *chérie*," Londo said. Jae sat down, taking the measure of this Terran lawyer. "John Henry Rombard, this is my husband, Jaeson Rallene Starhart. Out in the galaxy he's known as Neutrino; he's a megapara like me. He's not going to go public as Starhart."

"Yet," Jae said.

"Mm-hm. We want him kept secret."

John Henry faded back into his chair. "Ah..." he began and couldn't think of anything else to say.

Jae picked up the cigar from the desk. "Is this what I think it is? Tobacco? Monsieur Rombard—"

Londo smiled. "'Mister,' Jae. We're in western Canada; that's why we're speaking English." Still his attention remained locked on John Henry. The man looked ill. Or at least deeply shocked. Lon couldn't recall the last time he'd seen John Henry surprised, much less speechless with it.

"Ah..." John Henry burbled.

Would this be how everyone would react? Would they get over it?

Eventually they'd move to another emotional state. Acceptance or hatred toward Lon?

"English? Were we? All right. Mister Rombard, these things are deadly." Jae dissolved the cigar into smokeless ash that fell softly into the ashtray. "You shouldn't be smoking them."

"Hey! That was a Cuban!" John Henry raised up suddenly, but was too late to snatch it out of Jae's hands. "That was a fifty-dollar cigar, Rand!" He shook his finger at Londo.

"Starhart. So we'll talk for an extra two minutes. That's about fifty dollars of your time."

"My god, Lon. You're... you're..."

"That's not correct," Jae said. "He is not a 'faggot.' He's bisexual. Poly. Or queer. And so am I."

Lon pictured his closest friends reviling him. Turning away when they found out.

"And so is the... well, I suppose she wouldn't have to be. Well, in there in some way. And you're a telepath." John Henry regarded Jae and wiped the sweat off his brow. "Jesus, Londo."

"I'm a telepath too," Londo said. John Henry seemed to be emerging from the shock. He hadn't ordered them from his office.

He watched the lawyer closely. Felt the presence, but not the details, of his emotional state. Yes, it was dulling down to startlement without any spikes of hate or fear.

Ah. *Dieu merci.* Lon released a calming sigh as Jae glanced at him. With the worst over, he could enjoy John Henry's discomfort. He was pleased to have upset John Henry so, the man who could be a royal pain sometimes. "That is also something we're not going to advertise. Lina can be the public telepath in the family. Sometimes things go smoother when people don't know."

"Jesus, jesus christ, Londo. Holy moses. Mother mary."

"Why, John Henry, I had no idea you were such a religious man." Lina reappeared and handed Jae his latte, then turned to John Henry. "I got you something to replace your precious cigar," she said and flipped him a nugget of gum. "I got the bubble kind, not the regular. It seemed your kind of gum. I figure bubbles can be ever so much more obnoxious if they're used correctly."

"Thanks, doll," John Henry sneered. "Looks like you're having a lot of fun these days, eh?"

"I am indeed," Lina said softly. She sat on the arm of Lon's chair and he draped his arm around her hips as she rested a hand on his shoulder. "He's taking it well, love. Although he seems a few shades paler than when I left."

"He's just in shock because he's realizing how much money he's going to make off of us. Aren't you, John Henry?"

The lawyer pressed the button on his phone. "Steph, collar the nearest clerk and tell him I want to see *Hol v United States* pronto! Five minutes ago!" he yelled.

"I've already got them working on it," came the reply.

John Henry popped the gum into his mouth, thinking furiously. "First question:" he began.

"No, he doesn't," Londo replied. People's first questions to him, no matter what the subject, were always about his father. "He's not going to know."

"Soon," Lina corrected. She glanced at him as if she were alarmed at Lon's answer.

"Maybe," Jae said.

That was vague enough. Londo nodded.

"Good to see you're all in agreement," John Henry said snidely. "All right. Second question: Out There?"

"It's all perfectly legal," Londo said. "Out of the ordinary, but legal."

"Not out of the ordinary on Feith," Jae retorted. "That was my home world. It was quite common."

"But the problem is that Jae's the last one of his race," Londo said. "Everyone else was killed off over fifteen years ago."

"Ouch," John Henry said. "I see a loophole. Right away I see a possible loophole that everyone and his brother are going to point at."

Lina got up to go to the door. As the knock came, she opened the door a crack and poked her head out. "Thank you so much," they could hear her say, and she closed the door securely, having retrieved a thick book. She handed it to John Henry.

He leafed through it, settling on a page, flipping it to the next page and grunting to himself. He wiped his face down with his hand and glared at Jae.

"There's nobody else?"

"They're all dead."

"Shit. This whole thing hangs on doing things according to cultural norm Out There in the galaxy. If it's not the norm any more, it's invalid."

"It's normal for me. For my culture."

"Then, my boy, you're going to have to play up your Feithian–"

"Feithi."

"Feithi culture a whole hell of a lot between now and if you go public with this. Show everybody that you're not only Feithi, but you're the A-1, top-billed, pure-blooded, as Feithi as they get kinda Feithi. If your people used to paint themselves red and run naked through the streets every Tuesday night at midnight, start doing that, and get it on record."

He turned to Lon and Lina. "The same goes for you two. You married in a Feithi ceremony, so now you've got to take on Feithi culture. Who married you three? I'll need to interview him for my records."

"You're looking at him," Londo said.

"Eh...?"

"We split the ceremony up into thirds. I married Jae and Lina, Lina married Jae and me, and Jae married Lina and me both times. We have witnesses as well."

"I never heard that you went to seminary, Londo." John Henry was looking ill again as he chomped on his gum.

"Call me Reverend Starhart. We're all members of the Order of Uriel, all ordained priests. The Order used to be only on Feith. That's how Jae got in, but it moved to Earth once Feith had died."

"So you appointed yourselves priests of this order and declared it an Earth religion?"

"No," Lina explained, "it was here. It just somehow appeared after Feith died. It's been around for a little over fifteen years."

"Can we establish dates of ordination?"

"It's been about, oh, seventeen years for me, Terran," Jae said.

"I've been ordained for six years," Lina said.

"And I was ordained the day before the marriage," Londo added.

"*Halala.*" John Henry shook his head. "You couldn't have done it at least a year before? Just to establish that you weren't doing it only to perform an otherwise-illegal marriage?"

"Sorry."

John Henry sighed. "Well, what's done is done." He thought and blew a bubble.

Jae's fascination was centered on the expanding bubble, not John Henry's actual face. Lon watched the wonder bloom in his expression.

Jae grinned at Lina. **I want to learn,** he said.

Okay, we'll pick some up and teach you.

Me, too, Londo said. **I never learned.**

Then we'll pick up a handful and I'll teach you both. We'll have a contest for biggest bubble. I'll be sure to buy the nonstick kind for you.

Nonstick? Jae peered at the bubble so precariously close to John Henry's nose. "Do you mean that it–"

The bubble burst suddenly and they all learned at least one new word as John Henry peeled its remains off his skin. "Thank you very much, Missus Londo Effing Rand! Starhart!" he fumed.

He turned his chair to roll it along the wall behind him, settling down at the computer screen. "Get me set up here with your system, Londo. Let's get these wills out of the way first. Then we'll do the name changes. Mister Starhart with the ears, I suggest that you don't want to officially change your name until you make a public announcement whenever. Papers have to be filed, notices will have to be posted, and these days the name 'Starhart' will jump out and attract attention.

"In the meantime, I want you people to make a list of important points of Feithi culture and go out and do them publicly. If there's any naked running around, doll, I want you to contact me first so I can be there to supervise. Make a point that what you're doing is Feithi in nature. Emphasize that you're keeping Feithi culture alive."

"Got it," Londo said. "Jae, you're in charge of making the list. Anything hit you off the top of your head?"

"All I can think about is the annual slaughter of all practicing attorneys," Jae told him. "To make room for the younger ones just getting out of school, of course."

"Okay," Lon nodded. "We'll get a TV crew to record that one. People will cheer."

CHAPTER

11

Lon had ditched his jacket for a more casual attitude as they arrived in Atlanta. As Valiant he had to maintain a certain level of savoir faire even when off-duty, but this would do. And Lina had insisted. Jae also took off his jacket, leaving just the borrowed ParaNet tee, jeans and boots. Lina had gone to tee and jeans.

Individually Jae held their arms. Londo could sense the world clearing around him. He was able to breathe easier. When Jae did the same to Lina, he could see her face relax even as her eyes grew brighter.

Then Jae placed his hands on his own chest and began to breathe in four-second intervals. Finally he announced, "I don't like to do that without monitoring equipment to guide me. But we have a couple hours to go, and we're all exhausted."

"Not any more," Lina told him. "Thank you."

They visited a liquor store, purchased a rather large amount of alcohol since Jae wanted to test everything back home, plus Lon was curious as always about local brews, then wound up knocking at the door of a modest townhouse just shy of downtown. The front window held a small rainbow sticker as well as a larger one with a weekly "gay agenda" list that included being gay most days, extra gay on the weekends, and observing Taco Tuesdays.

Jae tapped on that as Lina ported the excess bottles and cans to Aldierra. "I haven't had tacos yet. I hear good things." He turned his head as a car with a particularly loud radio passed by.

"We will get you tacos. Many tacos." Lon would have said more, but the door opened.

A slender white man with receding strawberry blond hair and a small moustache greeted them. He was an inch or three shorter than Lina, which put him into normal male range here on Earth.

"Mace!" Lina exclaimed before catching him in a huge hug.

"Lina! Ah… Lina?" Mace stepped back to look at her quizzically.

"I can hug now. Isn't it great?" She pushed past him to give the living room a thorough scan even as she gestured her husbands inside. Mace stood back, his eyes wide as Lon and Jae nodded at him as they came in. "Nice place," Lina said. "Bigger than I'd imagined. We brought beer."

"Ale, actually," Londo corrected, and held out his right hand expectantly.

"Uh," Mace said but shook it. He glanced at the six pack in Londo's left hand and then up at Jae. He stumbled backward as his face glazed into awe.

Ha! Lon would never tire of people doing that when they first saw Jae.

"Mason Odell Lafayette, in times long ago called 'Mazola' but no more since we have all grown up into respectable adults," Lina said with grand gestures, "may I introduce the most honorable Londo Falcon Rand Starhart and Jaeson Rheoboth Rallene Starhart. My husbands."

Lon's gasp that Lina would spill the secret was drowned out by Mace's. Jae only let out a slight choking sound. Quickly Lon tried not to seem shocked at Lina's proclamation.

"And we just call him Mace these days," Lina added to the two. "Do y'all drink out of the cans or do you use glasses like civilized folk? You got some water for me, Mace? Ooh, cookies. Thanks. Does the water around here taste good? They're not allowing me real tea. They're mean." She headed to the couch and plopped as if she'd been there a thousand times. The vinyl cushion let out a loud fart and Lina howled with laughter.

"This couch is *you*, Mace. C'mon, c'mon, don't let the flies in!"

Lon had never seen Lina act like this with anyone. She'd just let their secret out, just like… that. This Mace and she must be very close, not that he was jealous or anything. The situation needed more scrutiny.

Mace closed the front door with a frown at Lina. "I was expecting you but I wasn't expecting *that*. I take it you didn't warn them. You could have warned me. Jailbait."

Lina laughed. "I'd forgotten about that. Red." She watched her husbands take seats on the couch and a chair as Mace trotted into the kitchen. "Those were our secret code names back when we were in college."

"You were in college together." Lon set the six pack on the coffee table next to the plate of cookies and arranged napkins beside it. Company napkins were supposed to be fanned out; Mama Ruth had instructed him in that long ago. There was also an open can of mixed nuts. Lon gave Mace a long look through a pass-through window into the kitchen. He couldn't be the same age as Lina.

She'd given out their secret.

But Mace hadn't gone into absolute conniptions at hearing it. Hardly a ripple.

"I was a little younger than the average college student," Lina reminded him. "Mace got me my first job so I could flesh out the scholarship with some real money. Waitress at a gay bar. Very safe."

Mace returned with glasses, including one with water. "It took them a full semester to figure out she was under age and fire her," he said.

"At which point I began to work in a Mexican restaurant."

Jae poured ale into his glass. "You lived there as well," he recalled. He looked thoughtful at the taste, and within moments his glass and the cans sparkled with condensation as the temperature of their liquids dropped. Jae sipped again and nodded in satisfaction.

"Well, the semester after that, until I graduated. Yes."

"So," Mace said. "Married. All three."

Lina grinned triumphantly at him and he shook his head at her.

"I would say that I should have guessed, but I never would have, not in a million years."

Jae took another sip before giving Mace a chin nod. "While you became a leader in the Terran gay movement."

Mace's eyes widened at that.

"Don't be modest, Mace." Lina seemed to be enjoying her circus.

"Well."

"He knows everyone," Lina informed her husbands, as if she hadn't done the same previously. "If he doesn't, he knows someone who knows someone who can fill in the gaps."

Mace gave a modest shrug. "Well, I do hand out the toaster ovens."

Londo blinked. Jae blinked.

"For when they come out of the closet. You get a certificate and a toaster oven."

"It's a joke from some old TV show," Lina said. "Mace kept me sane... well, mostly sane, during my first couple years at college."

"That must have been some feat," Jae said.

"He did. He graduated three years before me. Every time he came up to visit, he and I would talk and he'd reconnect me back with the real world."

Mason smiled at that. "Lina saved me from hell. Anything I could do for her, I was happy to do."

"How's Beth?" Lina asked.

"She's great. Third kid – can you believe that? – on the way."

"Mace was engaged to Beth when we first met. Beth was, let's see..." Lina crinkled her nose to remember. "Beth was the sister of Mindy, that was her name, who was my official roommate. The one I sub-leased to after our first year so her boyfriend could live there instead."

"You were married?" Lon was confused. That Lina would let loose the secret had still disconnected his brain.

Once again that brain noted: this Mace didn't seem put off by the news. Just surprised.

"I'm gay and I'm not married." Mace grinned. "Thanks to Lina."

"I turned him."

"Yeah, right. No, Beth had come to town to visit Mindy and me and take her to dinner, and Mindy dragged Lina here along – I thought she was babysitting or something, and then they tell me that no, Lina's a student. What were you, fifteen or so?"

"About that."

"Jailbait. I didn't like you right away, you young brainy snot."

"I spoiled you for other women." Lina bared her teeth in a grin like the Cheshire Cat.

"Well, anyway, Mindy and Beth get up to go to the ladies room, and Lina stays with me. And I'm thinking what do I say to a kid? And then she says, 'Why the hell are you going to marry a woman? You're just going to be unhappy and you'll start to hate her and feel guilty and then you'll have a messy divorce and maybe kids who won't have both parents around so they'll grow up to become criminals or rednecks.' And I asked her what the hell she thought I was, and she said, 'You're gay.'" Mace looked down at the beer he had and twirled it slowly between his hands, smiling.

"Lina's always subtle," Jae observed to Londo.

"Always. A Sagittarian."

"Sags stick together," Lina said and stuck her crooked pinky out. Mace linked his own with hers for a moment.

"*Mon dieu*, there's two of them," Lon groaned.

"Yeah," Mace continued. "So by the time my visit was over, Beth went home and I did some hard thinking. They have very good gay pride support at Carolina. I learned a lot, senior year."

"Things were so dull after you'd gone," Lina said.

"I was introducing Lina to all kinds of unsavory types," Mace said. "And her still underage. They would have thrown me in jail and tossed away the key." He paused. "Of course now all I hear are some rather interesting jokes about the three of you. The few clips we get here about what's going on on Aldierra have set off things."

"Jokes." Jae paused in lifting the glass to his lips. "What kind of jokes?"

"Tasteless ones, for the most part. Especially since no one knows you're married." Mace indicated Jae and Londo, and tried to wave it off. "Ignore them."

"How much do you trust this man, Lina? Can he keep his mouth shut?" Jae asked.

"He's going to have to, if he wants to head up this project," Londo said. "We handle a lot of secret material."

"Of course Mace can keep a secret," Lina protested. "He's not a blabbermouth... Well, he's not when someone tells him to keep his mouth shut about things. I told Kanti, and she can keep secrets too."

Time stopped for Lon. "You. You told Kanti? About us?"

"While you two were checking out your condo's progress. She's now my official personal assistant. She'd have to be told soon. I gave her a copy of our organizational structure, a list of our projects for the next month, and the info about us."

Lina reached out to pat Jae's thigh. "I softened her up with your baby pictures, the ones with all your parents in them. So cute. And you as a little boy with them. While she was oohing and aahing, I told her about the Feithi Triunes and let that sink in before I let the headline drop."

Londo couldn't catch his breath.

Lina gave him a long look. "She's fine with it. It took a minute, well, maybe four, but like I said: Jae's baby pictures. Gets them every time. They got me."

Jae wiped his face with this hands. "I hope I was wearing something in them."

"You were. Don't worry."

"Lina." Lon didn't know what to say to her, much less say in front of this stranger. She treated Mace like a brother, though. "When we want to spill the secret, we should discuss doing it first."

Lina shrugged. "Okay. Next time. Research completed: the sky didn't fall in. It didn't with that lawyer of yours either."

"That's different. He knows he's going to make a profit off us."

"He's your friend, Londo. It won't take him long to come all the way around."

"I agree," Jae said. "But yes, Lie, next time we discuss beforehand."

"Right. Agreed. I so affirm. Now to the problem at hand?"

The cat was out of the bag. Move along. "*Eh bien.* Nothing we can do about Kanti now."

"Valiant," Mace began.

"Call me Londo."

"You're... You're..." Mace shook himself a bit and sat straighter as he turned to Lina. "Well," he managed to say, "you certainly have gotten over that touching phobia of yours."

"I believe that's true," she replied gravely.

Mace giggled just a bit. "Sorry. It's just that I saw a picture of you, Lina, on the Web the other day with a caption, 'Why is this woman smiling?' and then there was a rather rough... and extremely flattering caricature of you, Val–Londo. Or part of you." He laughed again. "They don't know the half of it. Are you going to announce?"

"Where's this picture?" Londo demanded.

"Our plan right now is after Doomsday Deadline," Jae said.

"Or sooner," Lina quickly put in. "Depending on how things go."

"Sooner?" Lon asked, but Lina ignored him. He would talk to her later.

"So all this Gay Pride is to set things up so you'll have it easier?" Mace didn't look at any of them as he sipped his drink.

"Why, you–!" Lina sputtered. "I don't have a name rotten enough to call you for that. I'll tell them the Sonny's fried chicken story; that's what I'll do. No, this isn't for us. It's for you and those people on Sarastor who have to hide and those men on Aldierra who are executed because of this!"

"Executed? For real?"

Jae nodded. "Caught three times there, and that's it."

Lon said as he tapped on his phone, "We've issued an edict that any kind of consenting adult sex is now legal, but it's going to be difficult to ride herd on that. Too many people will slip through the net."

"And the women on Aldierra," Lina added. "Most probably don't even know there's an alternative. They're slaves. They're stuck on a, well, they call it 'marriage' but it's slavery – track to men they despise who mistreat them. That's multiples, Mace. I've met a woman with five husbands. The poorer you are, the more husbands you have. Poor women!"

"There are a lot of ways you could take that." Jae smiled.

"They don't marry for love, honey. I'm ecstatic with what I've got."

Londo let out a grunt of disappointment at the findings or lack of them on his phone. "Where's this picture?" he insisted.

Jae glanced at his husband and back to Mace. "He's just afraid they don't have it drawn big enough," he said. He dug into his jeans pocket and produced a padd. Its screen unfolded in the air to show the list of Three Worlds priorities.

Mace nodded and began to draw out small notepads from his own pockets, neatly labelled as to PROGRAMS, POLITICS/LEGAL, SUPPORT, PUBLICITY, AIDS ETC. He patted a larger binder on the coffee table with "CONTACTS" written in Sharpie across it.

"I didn't know how you wanted this organized," he apologized.

"Actually today we just wanted to know if you're interested in the job, and some beginning ideas," Lon said as he flipped through the Contacts book.

"If you think I can do the job, then I will."

"But do *you* think you can do the job?" Londo noted that there were people listed in these notebooks with organizations and parades and helplines attached to their names, from as far away as Asia. The thick binder was almost completely filled.

"I..."

Londo looked up at the hesitation, and Mace swallowed. "I have MS," he finally said.

"We know."

"Well, there's no telling with MS, you know? It's the relapsing recurring kind. I'm taking the latest drugs, and I'm in a study that has helped a lot. The research has come a long way but I've known others who were hopping around with energy one week, and the next they were in the hospital on their death bed. I can't guarantee you that..."

"Three Worlds has a medical plan," Lon told him. "Or it will, as soon as we can get it organized. Don't worry about it."

"We're not sure how medicine will work once we bring Earth in to the program," Lina said thoughtfully.

Mace had perked up; now he sighed. "Prime Directive stuff, huh?"

"*Ah oui*, I've heard of that in the last few weeks. Prime Directive." Lon shot a side-glance at Lina. "I see that there's a point. If Earth goes to Sarastor to get all its major problems instantly solved, you get an unequal co-dependency. We don't want to stifle the growth of Terran knowledge or culture. Besides, Earth might come up with something totally new if it continues on its own."

"So everyone else is stuck."

"What I was thinking," Jae said, "was that we could get some immune system boosters, packaged so that Terran doctors could use them, but in tamper-proof materials so that people couldn't peek and see what's inside. The disease would still exist, the need would still be there to find a cure, but people who could get to a doctor wouldn't die. In fact, they'd be able to lead quite normal lives." Before Lina could pipe up, he added, "And Three Worlds would cover costs, or most of them. We could include it in treatment that would cover a number of Terran diseases."

Londo rubbed his chin. "This packaging... It would have to be cheap. We need to stretch our finances."

"I was thinking of duesymonitha casings," Jae said. "With their own individual applicators. You pierce a case or stick the applicator next to something that's not skin, and the material melts into its contents, mixing and fusing with it."

"*Ouais.* It could work."

"One of Wiley's medical labs was working on something like this a few years ago. I'll remind him."

"We're going to have to start paying him a wage from the Three Worlds," Londo said drily. "And I bet it won't be long before Stoan starts to complain about taking away from Legion time."

"Who's Wiley?"

"A crazed scientist with five genius minds," Lina told Mace. "You'll like him. Lon, did you know that Wiley has over eight years of vacation time saved up? Vacation time that he has no plans whatsoever to use on taking a vacation?"

"Eight years?" A slow smile came to Londo.

"He's got a contingency in place to take it if someone starts kicking up a fuss. He'll take it in Legion Headquarters in his main lab, if he wants to."

Londo chuckled at that. Good ol' Wiley, best of the best.

"This is going to work," Jae told them all.

Lina poked a finger at Mace. "Get us samples of all your medicines. We don't want side effects from this."

"Yes ma'am, Miss Jailbait."

"Eat it, Red. You taking the job?"

"Uh. Yeah. Yes, I'll take it. Do I get a staff?"

Lina laughed and began pointing around the group. "You get a staff. And I get a staff. And he gets a staff, and he gets a staff. I guess I'll start hiring full steam, starting tomorrow. We need to get our shit organized. Fast. At least we have a structure now."

"We should celebrate," Jae announced. "Let's get dinner. I'm starving."

They ordered delivery Chinese and settled down to devour it. As they occasionally did, the vegetarian Starharts razzed Londo about the inevitability of him joining their ranks.

"Never," Lon growled as he hugged his carton close to his chest. "Mine."

"He refuses to believe it," Jae confided to Mace. "Lina and I – we can feel the animals' life vibes. Extremely unpleasant to eat."

"Plus there's the ethics of it all," Lina said. "Sure you're not ready to switch, Lon?"

"Never," Lon vowed. "Let me enjoy my delicious grilled animal flesh. You go chew on some carrots."

Jae chuckled and rose from the couch. "We should be getting home," he said.

"The cats' dinners are late," Lina agreed.

Jae bowed his head to Mace. He raised his hands to chest height, his spread fingertips touching but his palms somewhat apart.

"*Pelzire*," he said. "That is similar to your 'namaste,' but it is Feithi. That's my native language. It means 'I, a part of Source, recognize and greet you as a part of Source also. We are all one.'"

Londo made a mental note to substitute that for the "namaste" he had tried and failed to remember. Feithi custom, check.

CHAPTER

12

Their voices echoed in the tall, empty residential buildings. Now that he'd either helped refurbish or destroyed hundreds of polluting industrial sites, Lon's city bashing was increasing in scope. But Lina had gotten vague, iffy vibes for today.

When she'd checked with her pendulum as to where those vibes were coming from, it had indicated Lon's schedule with tight, fast circles. She'd drawn a tarot card for guidance and it had come up ten of Swords. That was never a good thing. It showed some guy lying face-down on the ground, ten swords skewering his back down the length of his spine.

She should double-check that these places Lon was destroying were truly cleared out. She made sure to bring five Aldierran bodyguards with her: Napyer, Ellis, Enn, Paglash, and… oh, Whatshisface. She glanced a certain way so that a hidden computer screen triggered and she could run through a list of names. Grego, that was him. He'd replaced Antong, who'd been injured on the job two days ago.

There were also three squads of soldiers on this floor, circulating through the building to ensure it had been vacated prior to demolition.

It hadn't.

Mounds of belongings remained throughout the various quarters, though Lina didn't see a speck of food among it. "Get someone to pack it out," she instructed the army crew after they'd called for moving vans. Had they run into this previously? Surely someone could use most of this. Lina checked local venues and found a good-sized storage facility. It wasn't in great shape, but it had a roof. It would have to do until things could be transferred to the local version of Good-will.

But something drove her on down hallway after hallway.

A child.

When she saw it she could not determine its gender, but they were filthy and had wrapped rags around themself. They let out a squeak of surprise, perhaps terror, at her, so she slowed her approach.

"Here now," she said softly. "Who are you, honey? Why haven't you left with your House?"

They shook their head. Maybe they couldn't talk.

Lina ported in a soft blanket from home and wrapped it around the child. "There, there," she told them. "We'll make a note of where we found you, but I'm going to take you to see a doctor, all right?"

When she put her arms around the child, they flinched hard and made a sound of pain. Lina bit her lip. "Sorry about that," she said and tried to hold them more gently. Poor little being, so few years on this world and having been subjected to this. "Here we go. You're safe now. Try not to be frightened." She nodded to her bodyguards and ported out.

There were only a few rooms operating in this new medical center staffed by AffSys volunteers, but Lina found an empty one and laid the child on its examination table. She called for a doctor.

"I think we have a little boy," she told him. "He's been through an awful lot. He's very brave."

The male doctor took the hint and impressed Lina with his bedside manner. The bone-thin child was indeed a boy, but malformed and badly bruised all over, even more than the average amount of bruising Lina had noticed among Aldier-rans. One arm was much shorter than it should have been. One leg had been broken at the knee as well as below. That must have been deliberate. His jaw was lopsided. And the boy's swollen midsection was covered with oozing ab-scesses.

Lina had to hold her hand over her mouth so she wouldn't get sick. Who would do this? Who would do this to a child?

She swallowed. "We'll get him better?" she asked the doctor, and he addressed his words more to the boy than to her.

"We'll make the pain go away and get some food and water into him, and after that we'll see what else we can do. Now, my boy, can you tell me your name?"

The poor boy could barely speak. "M…Mess."

The doctor frowned. "That's not a good name, don't you think?"

"If you could have any name in the entire world," Lina urged, "what would you name yourself?"

The boy looked at her.

"That's all right. You think about it, come up with a wonderful name you like very much, and tell us when you decide. That will be your name from here on. I'm going to leave you here. These people will take care of you. We will find your House and demand to know how they could have done this to you and what they're going to do to make up for it. You won't have to go back unless you want to. We could have someone, maybe your mother? Father? A friend? come visit you if you want. We will get you a loving home."

She smiled gently at him, trying to beam him white light and pure love. Angels gathered around him to cocoon him in their amazing energy, and she asked for more, please, and thanked them, knowing they'd come. "I'm afraid I have to go now. There may be others like you who have been left behind. I'm leaving you in very good hands. They'll contact me if you need to talk. You'll like it here." She smiled again, exchanged glances with the doctor, and ported out.

— — —

As the groups continued through the condemned community they found so many other abandoned human beings. Male, female; young, old. Debilitated and/or sick as the devil. Left because they were too much trouble to bring along with the evacuees. Unwanted.

Both Londo and Jae flew in to take stock. "I've always checked," Lon assured her. "Don't know why this suddenly began. Maybe it's micro-cultural. I'll keep a sharper eye out now. I will find *les bâtards* who did this."

That adults had been left infuriated them, though they talked with each victim soothingly. But an abandoned child – sheer fury rose in all of them, Jae with a sense of sickness and Londo with an elemental uproar almost taking him over.

"Here we are," they would tell the child as they lifted it in their arms. "You're all right now. You will be cared for." They would ask: what did the child need? What did they want? They'd assure them that it was perfectly fine for them to have been afraid, but that they could now relax.

Londo took notes of what each child asked for. He was determined to be Santa Claus. Jae notified child therapists in the AffSys to attend to the children immediately.

Londo called an Earth company he and other ParaNetters dealt with, and put in a huge order for teddy bears and other stuffed animals. They would signal Lina when the first shipment was ready to distribute to these poor kids. Some of the adults might need them as well.

For years a teddy bear had been Londo's only friend when he'd been kidnapped as a young child.

For each victim Lina made sure they received subdermal tags as to where they were found, and any information the person could provide as to which House, if any, they belonged. Few were Houseless, because Houseless people didn't live inside House buildings. The Houses involved in this dereliction would be punished, if the Starharts had anything to do with it. Which they did.

Then there were the dead babies.

Their bodies were discarded on open floors or as part of trash piles. Newborns or ones under three months old. All of those female. Toddlers with visible deformities and bruises covering their bodies; most of these were male. Some had been rotting.

The soldiers took DNA samples to be matched with Houses.

Londo stood there, his fists clenched, knuckles white. But Lina turned to him and huddled to his chest, gripping his arms. She began to sob.

"Sorry," she told him as she could. "Sorry."

He embraced her and rocked her back and forth. "Get it all out," he told her.

Jae rubbed her back even as he wiped his own tears away. Lon reached to put an arm around him as well. "These people will pay," Jae hissed as each dead child was carefully wrapped for burial. "There are rare times when retribution is called for, but this is one of them. We'll have to have public judgment, something others will learn from."

Jae triggered the subcutaneous tranquillizers stored in his left arm, and closed his eyes as the drugs must have begun to take effect. Then he touched Lina's arm. She gave a sniveling breath as she looked up at him and then nodded. He triggered her own dose.

"I'll get used to this," she said forlornly.

"No you won't," Jae told her.

"None of us will," Lon agreed. "This is not something you get over. This is evil."

Lina now looked to Londo. "You okay? You can't take drugs."

"What can we do?" Jae asked Londo as Lina stepped away so he could hug his husband. "Just tell us."

Lon took a breath. His bottom lip trembled. "Just be with me. Both of you, in your own way, have made such an impact in my life. You're my foundation. I need you."

He was engulfed in loving arms. "This is what will help me. Knowing you two love me. And my family and all my friends. Just… Just don't leave me, you two. Above all others, I don't know what I'd do–"

"Shh, shh," Jae crooned. "We are always with you."

"Beyond forever," Lina vowed.

They stood embraced for some time, gaining strength from each other as their minds meshed. Giving love. Who was it who decided to take a deep breath? They all did, and eased away to stand solidly in their world again.

Londo gathered himself, still looking sick. "You two don't have to worry about finding the people who did this," he assured his spouses. He wiped away the last of his tears. "I will track them down. I will have special troops assigned to find them."

"Lon?" Jae asked. He reached to rub Londo's back. "Make sure you check in with Adam tonight. You too, Lina, with your therapist."

"And you with Saichan," Londo ordered.

Lina took another look at the room where the last of the bodies had been cleared out. "Animals," she whispered.

— — —

Londo faced the camera, his features those of pure wrath. "I thought everyone had heard us the other day," he said. "The right of daughter refusal has been revoked. No exceptions. If you have a daughter who is unhealthy, you will take her to a medical center for help. If you don't want a daughter or even a son, medical centers now have places where you can leave the baby with no repercussions. They will be cared for. Was there something unclear in that, that someone out there didn't understand? Killing babies is murder. Leaving helpless children or adults to suffer is inhumane. We will track you down."

Londo took a full ten minutes after that to calm himself, but that allowed the staff in their studio to rearrange the set. Instead of a podium it now held a long couch with a low table on which to set drinks.

Jae had brought three cats in travel cases to join them, and released them. "Makes it look more homey," he said.

Lina kept her arms around Londo. "It's going to get better," she promised him. He could hear her telepathically reassuring Jae as well.

Over the cats Jae pointed two fingers at her and then at his eyes. She nodded. They would all keep track of each other.

Lon looked around, taking everyone in with his gaze. "We've set aside three and a half hours from a very busy schedule to do this," he explained. "It is essential to stick precisely to the timeline. We will cut when the time comes to do so. No exceptions."

While they were doing this, squadrons of soldiers were sweeping the next round of buildings marked for demolition. From now on, Londo wouldn't be bashing anything without it having been double-verified first. He wasn't going to take the Houses' or even his own senses' assurances that everything was ready.

The Starharts allowed three minutes to talk with each broadcast location and settle in before going live.

"Hello, Sarastor!" Lon gave a hearty smile to the camera. Only one was needed in the studio, since its picture gave a 360 degree view. Production teams on that planet could cut back and forth between angles using the one input.

They chatted to the AffSys audience about what they were up to on Aldierra, and referred to the footage they were sending along showing the state of the world and their various current missions on it. It was all upbeat, with no hint of dead babies or wars or scheming billionaires.

The footage of Londo battering through expanses of city were spectacular. Jae's clips were more nature-based, as he directed his armies to clean waterways and plant new forests. Lina's involved the ordinary people of Aldierra, especially its women, as they were shown how to begin to step beyond the confines their culture set upon them.

The news anchors were hungry for news of Valiant's marriage, and he and Lina smiled and gave quick anecdotes of the funnier moments from their attempt so far at being a couple. One of them was something Lon made up. He didn't realize he'd done it until Lina silently asked if that had been a story about Aiko. She laughed and went along with it for the cameras. He would talk to her about it later.

Jae gave a message that Aldierra would not be like Feith. He'd see to it that the world made it safely through Deadline. Lon and Lina's intense visages next to him drove the message home.

From Sarastor they switched to Earth and utilized three cameras so the studios there could cut from one to another, but because of the language problem they had to do four separate interviews: one in English, one in Mandarin, one in Hindi, and one in Spanish. Thank goodness and the orb for the Sentinels' technology! So far every language came through loud and clear. Lon had talked his spouses into doing a French one as well, so everyone back in his home province could tune in and understand.

At least once during every interview they had to pause to introduce whichever cat had just walked across their shoulders, curled into a lap to sleep, or, in one case, cuddled up on Lina's front shoulder and began kneading it.

"This is Fafhrd," Lina explained to the Sarastoran audience. "She's very old. She's doing what's called 'making biscuits,' which refers to a cooking process in which one kneads dough with their hands."

Fafhrd was so engrossed in what she was doing that she drooled, with bubbles coming out of her mouth.

"That's one of her best tricks," Londo said proudly. "The others can't do that." He confided that Fafhrd was the cat he was most scared to touch. "She's just so fragile."

Earth viewers got a chance to see Molly jump up on Lina only to turn and spit toward Londo. "We have had our differences," Lon admitted. Ember affixed herself adoringly to Jae.

For the Sarastoran and Terran telecasts, Jae moved ever so slightly away from the other two on the couch. Lina frowned at this but Jae insisted, never glancing toward Londo as he did so.

Lon made a mental note to keep track of Jae's stress level on all this secrecy. Good husbands wanted their spouses happy. Then again, Jae knew that at some point the secret would come out. Maybe that would be enough for him.

For Aldierra they made sure they didn't include any news of what they were doing or planning to do across the world. They already made many short daily broadcasts outlining that. Instead they gave the telecast a look inside their domestic life. For this Jae sat as close to the others as they did to each other.

They explained that Lina lived and worked alongside them and not apart, and that she had her own offices in which to operate as did the men. They showed the cat shit room with the charts for Three Worlds organization.

Lina laughed. "This is what we mean when we ask that if you have any ideas how we can improve our process, you should feel free to speak up. Look at what we're working with. Surely someone or someones out there can tweak this to be more efficient?"

The final timer went off and so did the cameras. All three Starharts let out a long sigh.

"Five minutes," Jae said as he set down Ember. "Then we get back to work."

— — —

"Lina's hired more employees," Jae remarked as he settled back to check his screen's daily reports. Outside their sleek new flitter's windows, the ground rushed by thousands of feet below.

After setting the music program, Londo eased closer to him. "I suppose it's a good idea to have a squad of female guards for her on occasion. Maybe we should get another flitter just to handle her guards."

"Two or three, since she's all over the place. Not as nice as this one; this is the family craft. With the others we can house guards on the continents where they'll be primarily working. We can put them to use between missions too, ferry important visitors about. That way we can save our normal transporters for other personnel, and Lina won't have to port as much.

"They're all hitting the ground running," Jae said as he read through the schedule. "More meetings with women's focus groups. Mace is doing some videos, so he must be finished with the first phase of his language tapes. I hear he brought five people with him from Earth. They've set up on the fourth floor. Looks like he's coordinating with our volunteers and not the army. That sounds wise. Hm. Today we have thirty army units assigned to finish work planet-wide on revamped elementary classrooms for the Houses and shelters as well."

"I've made sure they have skilled supervisors keeping track of them," Londo said, "plus everyone gets drug checked. But it reminds me that I need to contact some people on Earth and Sarastor about early childhood educational programming, and getting it adjusted for Aldierra. I haven't yet seen what's already available here, but I can imagine. Lessons on how to bully. Instructions for killing quickly."

The men of Aldierran Houses didn't take control of male children until they were six or seven years old, past the point of most of the random and uncontrolled squalling that men couldn't be expected to tolerate well. The women and too many of the men of those Houses also needed basic educations. They should be able to get it at home as well as public schools.

The two of them had decided to break in their new meso-cruiser, just arrived out of hyperspace shipping, with a real mission. The interior was the size of their tertiary conference room back in the hotel. Jae had equipped it with extra-lux seating including a store-away bed, and stocked the kitchenette with an extensive collection of AffSys adult beverages. A library included digitized books, games and vids, and a table could be summoned for impromptu meetings.

The sound system was also primo. They snuggled on a wide seat to listen to the latest compilation that Lon had prepared just for Jae. "Really, *chéri*," Lon said, "how are you doing? I know it's already a lot of stress and I've piled the secret on top of you as well."

Jae gave a little snort. "Doing fine."

"Really?"

He twitched his shoulders. "I can handle it. I'll let you know when it gets to be too much."

That seemed to satisfy him. "A fine motorhome," Londo mused as they flashed over the landscape, his arm around Jae.

He snapped the nearer contact point of Jae's cape off, then reached to take care of the farther one before leaning in to nuzzle at his neck.

"Let's call it an adventure flitter." Jae splayed his hand across the back of Lon's head to position him better. He leaned his head back to savor as Lon began to release his tight vest.

— — —

"I've always liked your adventures," Londo admitted as he reached for his discarded boots.

Jae chuckled. He set a rachet next to the seat Lon had brought back up. Then he placed one next to himself and sat.

"We need to work these sessions into our schedules."

Lon pulled on his left boot with an extra tug, to get his heel in all the way. "People will be looking at our schedules. I don't want them knowing what we're doing in private."

"So we come up with a code."

"Besides, I don't want to schedule sex. Do you?"

Jae sipped his rachet. "I prefer to have lots of sex. The only way we'll get that is to schedule it. Many if not most people do. I've had to do it in the past. It's the approach that matters, not the time frame."

"Did I approach well?"

The smirk Jae gave him was satisfied. "Very well, as was the follow-through. Keep it in your repertoire."

"*Bon.*" He tasted his drink. "There's something different about this."

"I didn't stock a proper rallo juice in the craft." Jae shrugged. "I'll get some when there's time."

"It's good enough. Just different."

They settled back, their feet up on the control console, to talk about drinks and then water and then the water quality on Aldierra. Jae told him some amusing stories about the more minor accidents his crews had seen these past weeks.

"That new man of mine is doing a good job so far," Londo mentioned.

"That Threefence fellow?"

"Twofence. He's all right. I can see where he caused Lina problems. I can handle him. I made him backup PA. I'm talking my new primary personal assistant."

"Uh… Ty? Trey?"

"Trey. Bracken recommended him and a few others. They're all Bracken's men in some form. Ex-Bracken's men, I should say. Not sure how their loyalties to us will measure up to those for him. Trey's coordinating with Rito this afternoon." Rito was Londo's new Legion Executive Assistant. His old one had transferred to another Alpha Team Leader when Lon had announced his leave to work on Aldierra. "I hate to say it, but Bracken's becoming a valuable asset to the Worlds." He took a breath. "And I do really, *really* hate to say that. I'm actually beginning to like the turd."

Jae lay his free hand on Londo's. "He wasn't directly responsible for Aiko's death."

"Not directly. Just responsible for the forces that tried to invade Sarastor. He indirectly caused her death."

"A man doing the job his government told him to do to the best of his estimable ability. And now he's working as much behind that government's gaze as he can, in order to help us."

"Yes, but…"

"Aiko. I'm glad we both got a chance to see her again. We saw her off well. She's watching over you."

"Euh, *oui*. Every now and then I get the feeling she's standing behind me."

"Maybe she is. Have you asked Lina?"

Londo rubbed his nose. "I don't want to talk about Aiko to Lina. I think Lina would get the wrong idea about her and me."

"That you were lovers?"

"That we were love-lovers. I really liked Aiko. Really. More than any woman I'd ever met up until Lina. I wanted…"

Jae patted Lon's hand. "I wasn't looking forward to her being the third with us, but I would have accepted it. For you."

Londo gave him a sad smile. "I probably would have forced you to do it too. I was a little…"

"Crazy. Let's leave it at that. All is forgiven."

Lon had even broken off things with Jae at one point after he decided to marry Lina. That had lasted all of five minutes. "No, I was *un osti de trou d'cul*. I'm sorry."

"You've apologized a million times and I've forgiven you. Only had to do that once, because it was an all-the-way forgiveness. You should talk with Lina one night. Pillow talk. She already understands, but you need to get it off your chest."

"*Oui*. You know, Jae-Bug, sometimes you are wise beyond your tender years."

That made Jae chuckle.

They'd instructed the flitter to make wide, continent-spanning circles as they attended to their unscheduled recreation, but now they set it back on course again. It was damned fast; the course was sub-orbital, but it still took another two songs before it neared their destination on the other side of the planet.

They dropped altitude and the landscape became one of forbidding mountains, so difficult to traverse that Aldierrans had avoided them when adding on to their cities. Here the mountains ringed a sprawling valley.

A pit of blackness.

As the flitter lowered the blackness seemed to stretch from horizon to horizon, the mountains made into a modest, circling barrier by distance.

"Hunh," Londo said as he looked at it.

"Hunh," Jae agreed. He moved toward the door, but as soon as he touched that, an alarm sounded.

A sign flashed next to the door. "Protective suit required," it said, with an additional "Complete coverage. Face mask essential."

Jae tapped his ever-recording earring. "Hey Wiley-mind," he said to alert whichever one Wiley might have on Three Worlds alert duty. If nothing else, this call would wake one up for communication. "This is interesting."

"Where are you?"

"That big black spot on the map," Londo replied to his own earring.

"Big black–? Why–?"

"We're on an adventure," Jae told him. "Who wants the complete story in advance when one is investigating something mysterious?"

"Whatever it is," Lon added as he checked his maps, "it's the size of Earth's Great Salt– No, a lot bigger. Ten thousand square miles." He translated that to Sarastoran units. "Not sure how deep it is. The map says, 'Great Shit Flats.' The locals must not think much of it."

"It's black," Jae added helpfully. He looked out the hatch as he activated his protective Legion armor. "Doesn't reflect much. The surface appears perfectly flat, though. Let's take a look."

The hatch opened onto a shoreline of black-spattered scree. Rarely a hint of green, or sickly brown-covered green, poked through the rocks. Once the blackness touched the scree, no vegetation grew.

Jae was about to step onto the rocks when behind him Londo gave a mighty, wordless shout. Jae whirled in time to see Londo bend over, retching all over the new carpeting.

"Close! Close! The door!"

Jae reached for the controls even as he realized that his ultra-sealed suit was letting some kind of... *smell* through. Putrid. Rotting.

Overwhelming stench.

Ultra-concentrated, aged *shit*.

Their earrings conveyed the sound of Wiley having the same reaction at his end. "Shutting off. Olfactory mode," Wiley managed to say between heaves.

It was all Jae could do to command the devas of the flitter's cabin to clear the air. Turn it into clean oxygen, nitrogen, all the rest. Holding his breath, he cleared the vomit from his armor's face mask. But he left the suit in place, looking pointedly at his husband and the puddles around him.

Londo wiped his mouth with the back of his hand. "Are you going to make me…?"

Jae dealt with that as well, and in moments the flooring was restored.

"Thanks," Lon said. "We may conclude that the name of the place is literal. And that our transport has officially been broken in."

"Armor doesn't protect against it, or at least some of it."

"I got a full nose-full," Lon complained. "I think you may have gotten a thousandth of that."

"I'll adjust next time. And maybe add an extra layer of gas mask. We forgot to order a kol-vanasche for this flitter. I'm not always going to be around for cleaning duty."

"Kol-vanaschen are illegal in extra-AffSys territory."

"Wiley? You still with us?"

Wiley's voice sounded weak indeed. "I'm cleaning up here. Great… orb. No, Gorgeon," he added to an intercom query where he was, "I'm fine now. The Starharts have just shared with me a… new aromatic discovery of theirs. I do not recommend it."

"Just think: it's ten thousand square miles of aromatic discovery," Londo reminded him. He set the flitter's operations on vacuum mode, to seal it completely from the outside.

Jae stood at the panoramic cabin windows. "Orb," he breathed.

"We'll have to do robotic testing, see exactly what we're up against," Lon mused.

"Yes. But whatever it is, this cannot be allowed to remain here," Jae told him. "We'll need to remove it somehow. Bit by bit? Dish it up and then spread it as fertilizer evenly around the planet with a giant butter knife?"

"I've noticed other shit features on the map. A few Shit Rivers, a Shit Bay, Shit Bayou… Are they like this?"

"This is the largest feature with the 'shit' name."

"Mm. How long did it take to get this way?" Londo scrolled through histories of Aldierra, searching for that of this place. "How did they allow it to–"

"Aldierrans," Jae said in a flat tone. "They allow whatever is easiest, no matter the cost to future generations." He glanced down at what had just lit up his padd. "What is this, Lina?"

"It's from my notes about city septic systems on Earth," she said from her meeting halfway across the world. "I heard you guys say… Well, here's a successful cleanup they're doing. I found this about a year ago and stuck it in my Dropbox because it was interesting. Didn't think it would ever come in handy. What do you think?"

It involved a toxic septic field near a city, where terracing and plants had been carefully introduced to create what now looked like thriving rice paddies. Slowly the vegetation was de-toxifying the area. Large parts of the project held water so clean it supported healthy aqualife.

"How long did this take?" Lon asked. "This mentions years, but not how many."

"Baby steps, dear," she told him. "We can schedule a visit there and ask."

Jae considered the view. "Lots and lots of baby steps for this, unless we want to start talking millennia. With lots and lots of people helping out."

Lina said, "We have those at hand."

"Ten thousand square miles."

"We should get protective gear designed that will stand up to this," Jae said even as he began to search for sources.

Wiley piped up, "I recommend hiring people you don't like to work on this job."

"Oh, they're definitely going to hate us," Londo groaned. He held his phone in front of his face. "Allo, Hal," he said brightly. "You should check out what we've just found. You have me on full sensory reception?"

– – –

Er'k Gallad's family were on the screen and Jae, as Erik's Team Leader, was allowed in when the Legion Medical team woke him from his healing cocoon.

"Uhh..." Er'k's heavy lids barely allowed his eyes to switch back and forth to take in his surroundings. "Legion Medical? Oh. Oh yeah."

"Welcome back," Jae said, and squeezed Er'k's left hand, the one Gorgeon had indicated would be okay to do so with.

"Er'k! Er'k!" The family on the phone shrieked. Well, his little sister did, and his mother's voice was a bit on the high side. Er'k's attention came to them. He assured them that he was in no pain, and that Legion Medical was the best place anywhere for healing.

"We'll give him four weeks of our full attention," Dr. Gorgeon assured the family members.

Eventually the family signed off and Lina and Londo came in, along with the other members of Jae's team. The Legionnaires made rude jokes about slacking off just because you'd had holes blasted through various parts of your body.

But Jae was more serious, as was Londo. "We deeply appreciate your standing guard during the Mind Control Tour," Jae told the red-headed Legionnaire. "Needless to say, we are in your debt."

Er'k tried to grin at Jae, but his mouth didn't quite make the right shape. "Legionnaires don't owe debts for duty."

"But this was Three Worlds and not just Legion, Er'k," Lina interrupted. "It was double the duty."

He gaped at her. "You said my name right," he finally said.

She gave an embarrassed shrug. "We have these built-in translators now. They let us make sounds we couldn't before."

Er'k checked Jae's expression. "True? Built-in?"

"The Galactic Sentinels," Jae said as if that explained everything.

"Wow." Er'k's eyes became even rounder. "I'd gotten used to being called 'Erik.' I think it sounds exotic. It's okay with me if you still use it. I might even change my name. 'Erik.' Yeah."

They went from teasing to Legion business to teasing some more before Lina had to step out because they wanted to discuss security matters she wasn't rated for.

She made her way down the in-patient hall to find Dr. Mart. Riz Gorgeon and her staff were just bringing him out of his cocoon as well, but no family call awaited him. Maybe they thought they wouldn't be ready for this. Another check let Lina know that Mart did indeed have family. They were even visiting Sarastor, so it seemed they'd be ready to come in for a visit when he was perhaps a little more awake.

Lina let the doctors talk with him, and he responded in medical-speak. He raised the stump of his right arm wonderingly. "Four months?" he asked.

"Maybe four," Gorgeon told him. "You're on full pay. Once you're feeling yourself, we'll see what kind of duty we can put you on. I know you get bored easily."

Lina thanked him profusely for his part in the Tour. It hadn't been his fault that he'd gotten in the way of Rikli-En's people who had mistaken one of her friends for her in their kidnap plot.

"You're off stims now though?" he asked her.

"Yes, yes. For three months, they've told me."

"Good. I don't have anything else to do in that time, so I'll be keeping watch on you so you don't cheat."

"Me, cheat?"

"I have heard things. I've also seen the Legion Betting Boards. Bet they're blasting away these days."

Lina chatted with him for a few more minutes until Gorgeon began making chin movements at her. Mart did seem a little tired. Lina wished him well and left.

She had Sarastoran people to meet with, travel to be arranged. Equipment to be ported to Aldierra. An, ugh, Legion Spouse meeting to attend.

These visits were tough to fit into her busy schedule, but they had to be done. If only she had more time. If only the days were longer.

Hm. Could she find a way to sneak stims back into her life?

CHAPTER

13

Lon sat on the edge of the living room rug, playing with a blue and white plastic truck. He knocked it against the bare floor, delighted by the hollow *clack* it made with each hit. *Clack-clack! Clack-clack!*

But other sounds made him look toward the door to the kitchen. Maman and Papa's conversation had increased in volume. They were yelling at each other. They always did.

Maman rushed out of the kitchen toward him. He couldn't see her well but he knew it was her. Automatically he raised his arms to her, and she pulled him up to settle against her shoulder.

He wished she'd stop shouting. Her mouth was right next to his ear. He could understand only a few of her words but he knew they all were mean.

Papa lowered his voice as he joined them, saying something about Lon. He smiled at Londo. That was the only part of his face Lon could clearly see: a kindly smile. Like a drawing.

But Maman kept yelling. Papa's smile turned into a frown. Then he bared his teeth like the scary wolf in the book Lon had. Londo didn't like that look, and he began to squall.

Papa said something to Maman, then to Londo. His words sounded like he was trying to coax Lon to relax. But Maman shouted at him unintelligibly.

Londo screamed and screamed. Papa left, and still Lon screamed.

Maman jounced him up and down, making soothing noises, but Lon couldn't stop screaming.

Then through his tears he saw Lina enter the room. "What's going on, Lon honey?" Lina asked, and he could understand her. He could see parts of her so clearly, unlike Maman and Papa.

"You're dreaming," she told him softly. "It's okay now. All okay. Take control of the dream. You can do it. What would you like to happen here?"

Lon bellowed his first wish. "I want Papa to come back!"

"Look, there he is," Lina urged. "He's sorry, can you see that?"

Lon saw the blurred figure, the impression of a giant man. He had a bouquet of flowers in his hand. Lon began to ease away from panic.

"He's sorry," Lon repeated slowly. "Papa. Papa's come back."

"That's right, darling. Isn't it nice. Papa's there. And so is Maman."

He breathed easier. He wiped the tears from his eyes.

"Take a while and enjoy them. Have them be nice to each other."

He was in charge here, and that was a good idea. He had them kiss. And laugh. And chuckle at him with pride.

"Don't leave again, Papa," Lon whispered. "Don't leave, Maman. I love you."

He opened his eyes. Next to him, Lina was also opening hers as she lay on the pillow next to his in bed.

Jae burst into the room, which would have been startling if Lon hadn't sensed his approach. "What the—"

"We were in the same dream," Lina told him.

"I was having a nightmare," Lon said haltingly. "About Maman… and Papa. They were arguing."

Jae sat on the side of the bed to stroke Lon's arm. "You've been stressing lately. Getting upset and holding it all inside."

Lon shrugged. "Adam said we might want to increase the number of appointments we have," he admitted of his therapist.

Jae signaled to the house system. "Talk with him now while the dream is still fresh," he gently ordered.

"Yessir."

Londo let go a breath and then another. Papa had left Maman and him to the danger that had destroyed his childhood. Left him to be kidnapped and then subjected to gruesome experiments that had eventually transformed him into Valiant. But Lon was now surrounded by the people who loved him best. And beyond Jae and Lina, there were Hal, the best father he could have chosen, better than Papa. He had the gRands, most wonderful of grandparents. His friends on various parahero teams, as well as in civilian life.

He breathed deeply, and his heart slowed from its racing.

— — —

Hal had ported in via Lina because he claimed his curiosity was killing him. With Jae "properly" sleeping in a bedroom they'd set up to be separate from the primary one, and with Lina and her staff busy coordinating supplies and equipment with various army personnel, Londo escorted Hal to see what he'd been up to.

They flew over the massive land areas Londo had cleared already. Armies moved across it, laboriously planting seedlings that were being grown as fast as greenhouses across the world could produce them. For the most part the things were tiny sprouts, but the Northern Hemisphere was in summer mode and the seedlings would have temperate conditions in which to flourish.

"In five years," Lon told Hal, "most of these will be as high as me."

"Hm," Hal said, and Lon could tell that Hal knew that the world needed better than that.

"Plants only grow so fast," Lon muttered.

"Better than nothing. So what's happening with the atmosphere they'll be growing in? And the dirt?"

For that Lon had some surprising charts to show him. "I've got most of the Majority Army working on this. Or I will before we're done." He made an annoyed face. "The best way to get them to do something is to tell the bigwigs what a great, terrific, fabulous job everyone's doing. They aren't. It's good there are so many of them. It takes ten soldiers to do the work a competent professional could do, but this world can afford the ten."

Hal flipped the webpage to the next one. "Lies are an efficient way to get things done. I've always told you that. It's not ethical but sometimes lies are your only recourse. Or the best recourse. The only difficulty is–"

"Keeping track of what you've said."

Hal laughed. "You and all these figures and focus groups. Who'd have thought you'd be satisfied working on information instead of action?"

Londo gestured to the bare land spreading below them. "This took substantial action on my part," he said, and then grimaced. "Plus there are a lot of near-Aldierra asteroids that will no longer be menacing the planet any time in the future. Space dust."

Hal nodded. "Adam's staying informed?"

"Adam and his AI self are putting in a lot of overtime."

Hal's approving smile at him reminded Lon again that he was a lucky man in finding the Rand family. It had been a while since he'd talked to his grandparents. He should call them tonight to reinforce that comfort.

– – –

They dropped by the hotel to tour Lon's team's design office, filled with long tables and electronics and building samples. The two paraheroes listened to a presentation about Western Libernian architecture, the region where new work was beginning. Lon wanted to make sure positive traditional design would be accentuated and that Aldierra wouldn't end up with cookie-cutter designs.

He basked in the glow of Hal's pride toward him. "The Worlds couldn't have chosen a better man for their purpose," Hal told him.

One of the large conference rooms downstairs held both live and remote focus groups from the area, who offered their own suggestions as to what they'd like to see to add color and interest to their cities. Bright colors or muted ones? Did the actual color of a House have to match its name, if it was color-centric? How much repetition should there be of House facades?

How many people did a physical Libernian House hold before they branched out into a new one? What was the optimal number of people in a living space?

Women's focus groups regarded both Hal and Londo with suspicion until Lina popped in along with Kanti and female AffSys sociology experts to ask for their ideas on comfortable interior design. Oddly enough, the women didn't want anything to do with change!

As he talked with the men, Lon kept track of the women's conversations. Lina finally put up video of the women's quarters she had encountered so far. She set the video side-by-side with the ones of the new plans.

"I wouldn't let a dog [she had to explain what one was] live in what too many of you live in now," she told them. "Please explain to me how the plans we see here, that you are welcome to adjust to your taste and needs, are worse."

She had to take the women into a separate room before they'd admit that they were desperate to live like human beings. They just didn't believe that men weren't playing a cruel trick on them: ha ha, get your hopes up just to destroy them.

Once the idea set in that they could design their spaces, they insisted on change. Then the hair-pulling and shouting began.

Lon couldn't help Lina there. His own groups were screaming. Which led to slugging and hard punching. These men refused to be moved to new housing, period.

"We won't go!" "You can't put us off our own property!"

Londo stalked around the room, eying the objectors. "For the duration of this emergency, we have the power to do this. This is what your planet wants, for there to be a better balance between human civilization and the natural world. It's the only way you stand a chance of survival."

They hated him for this. He felt their fury toward himself. The broken furniture some left in their wake showed it as well. They couldn't harm Lon, so they took their frustrations out on anything they could reach. He kept them from harming each other.

Hal had already commented that the furniture in the focus rooms was old and somewhat dilapidated even before the meetings began.

"This isn't our first rodeo," Lon said to him. "Different day, different furniture; same destruction." They had warehouses filled with discarded furniture from the demolition sites that they could use.

Lon nodded at any proactive comments offered. He even took notes and consulted with aides, most of them in army uniforms, who also took notes. Then he stood with his fists on his hips and waited. And waited. Finally the room and screens quieted.

"We have a Deadline," he announced in even tones. "We have a world that needs far-reaching changes that are going to affect almost every aspect of life. My spouses and I [he noted Hal's flinch at that] are trying to give you the best world that can be cobbled together in nine months, with a view for further improvement afterward. We will do our best. Your input is important – but not required."

The outbursts began again, the shouts. More than a few personal insults were thrown against him. Just one against Lina, and someone knocked that insulter to the ground for their heresy. No insults for Jae, though. Jae hadn't done much to irritate them.... yet.

Again Lon let the furor die down.

"If you have a historically important House that can withstand being moved, we will consider it. Choose carefully, as these will be the ultimate exceptions and not the rule.

"We will have these plans ironed out by locals by the end of the week, all the way up to supervising councils," he told them. "After that we will allow another week for each House, each business and service, to notify us as to final interior designs and finishes. If we don't get those, we'll use our own discretion."

He looked around the room, to all the screens and government groups viewing, and the group who was there in person. "Thank you so much for your time. You know how to contact us." He pressed his fingertips together in front of his chest. "*Pelzire*."

As they flew off afterward, Hal turned to him and said, "I don't envy you."

"Things will get better," Londo lied.

— — —

"Not everyone can get what they want," Hal told Lon as they settled in the Landmark hotel suite's living room. "There'll be many more as this goes on who are going to hate this. Going to hate *you*. Don't take it personally."

Grimly Londo shook his head. "It can't be helped. I didn't sign up to be liked." Was that entirely true though? Adam and he had discussed this.

"Better you than me, I suppose. You know you can always call on me for help. This is some construction project, refurbishing an entire planet."

"Thanks." Londo nodded as Bran-Bran jumped up on the couch next to him with the felt Mr. Mousie in his mouth. Lon tipped it gently side to side, resulting in an energetic game of tug of war for the cat. "We're trying to enlist the entire population in some way, get them working together. Twenty billion people, Hal. More than that by now."

Lon's father gave a noncommittal sound. "Maybe you could enlist someone to clean your place too."

Londo looked around at the Starharts' suite in dawning dismay as he imagined it through Hal's eyes. Cat toys everywhere. Jae's cape on the back of a chair. Books and padds, cups and empty flavoring packets left over from the meeting last night added to the clutter. "The cleaning squad is not doing well. Both Lina and Jae have complained." He shrugged. "At least they're not mistreating the cats. Jae put up cameras and we've had to get rid of two teams so far. I think the new one is afraid of the cats."

"Maybe Lina could take a few minutes a day and–"

Londo raised one eyebrow at his father, who'd paused at the look. "Finish that sentence."

Before Hal could add anything, Londo added, "I've already had this unfortunate conversation with her. I stand corrected. I will amend my sexist thinking. I will never mention this conversation to her."

Hal chuckled. "Yeah. Guess I could stand some of that too. Not to sound sexist still, but maybe I could send Else over?"

"Else? Have my stepmother assigned to cleaning duty?"

"She is not your stepmother, and she has nothing else to do."

"*Euh*... No. Thanks but no. I don't know how it would look. To Lina or to me."

"Your call."

They talked over drinks, father and son. Londo felt the tension ease in his shoulders and down his sides as he caught up on what Hal was doing, the ideas he had for Mama Ruth and Papa Mike's big anniversary coming up next year.

"So how are you and Lina?" Hal asked. He'd picked up the feather on a stick that Londo had offered, and used it to tickle the nose of one of the cats.

"Katie," Londo named her. "We're doing all right. We're busy."

"Busy? Or busy-busy?" Hal's eyebrows raised significantly.

Lon tried not to roll his eyes. "We don't have much time for busy-busy. We're trying to adjust our schedules."

"Hm. Schedules. How about you? How are you doing?"

"Super-busy. Things are coming up," he told Hal. "I'm having strange dreams. The other day Lina was caught up in one of my nightmares. She helped me restructure it, get out of it."

"Nightmares? Does Adam know?"

Lon nodded. "I called him right away. Told him that I was dreaming of my birth parents."

"Ah."

Lon shrugged. "As usual, I couldn't really see them, but I knew it was them. They were arguing. Shouting. It scared me."

Hal shook his head in empathy.

Londo went on. "And as usual, Papa walked out on us and left us defenseless. Though I doubt he could have guarded us when the Lectori kidnapped me."

"Your papa was an idiot, Lon. Forgive me for saying that, but he was. You are a fine man. You were a fine boy when I first met you. I bet you were even a fine toddler. No real man would leave his child. Never."

Jae and Lina were the rocks that supported Lon, but there was a significant corner of his life that only Hal could understand. He shared a comprehension of the scope and responsibilities their megapowers encompassed.

Lon's mouth tweaked at the sides. "I'm lucky to have landed with you, Hal. I don't tell you enough: you're the best father ever. I love you."

Again as it had all along, Lon's vision of how his father would react to learning about his true marriage rose in his mind. No. He mustn't drive Hal away by revealing it!

"And I love you, son." Hal's eyes looked misty for a moment before he took another sip from his glass. "Now tell me when I'm going to get some grandkids."

CHAPTER

14

Londo zoomed across the continent to arrive in the hills of Jezarun, in a city linked to the world capital of Drape-Tessay. It was known for its wide plazas and narrow streets. Blank-walled buildings crowded closely together in a remarkable absence of soul.

The pavement and rooftops were massed with men shouting and fighting. News cameras swarmed above the scene, taking it all in.

Lon strained to hear what the problems were. What he got was just: anger. People were furious with each other for so many reasons that it boiled down to no reason.

"Stand down!" he hollered from his sky position. They'd all be able to hear him. "Stop this! Put down your weapons! Step away from each other!"

Suddenly everyone was yelling at him.

Calling him all kinds of vile names. Telling him that he was running them out of their own Houses. Taking their jobs away.

Lon coordinated with the army and police troops that were already in the area, as well as the ones heading this way. Two by two, he swooped down to the rooftops to scoop up fighters, then deliver them to police vans.

Those on the ground could see what he was doing above them. They paused – some of them. Watched him as he made trip after trip.

Dozens of trips.

Finally he came to those on the ground. He ignored the ones who had stopped fighting, but few seemed to realize that as the others kept pummeling each other and shouting at him when he got close.

Army vans couldn't get through the crowded streets, so Lon had to cart the rioters beyond the melee, to where the vans waited. That took time.

When he returned for more, the people were shouting that he was a murderer. They claimed he'd killed those men. Would pretending he was doing so stop the fighting sooner? The next batch he took in four at a time. The hell with this; let these men have a rough ride.

Eventually he had to stop to catch his breath, more in wonder than fatigue. Why would they accuse him? Why would they continue fighting when it was futile?

Fear, Jae told him from wherever he was. **Doomsday looms, and they feel they are powerless to stop it.**

This isn't doing them any good.

Fear isn't logical, Jae said.

The news isn't helping, Lina's mental voice joined the conversation even as Londo picked up three struggling men. **Most of it is about how you're destroying Aldierra, Londo. There are crazy rumors about you killing people too. They're using the bodies left in the buildings as proof, among other things. There are a lot of just plain lies.**

You need a better PR department. As of yesterday. Jae's suggestion was not couched in humor. **Get rid of those clowns you have. They make you look menacing. They glorify your violent aspects.**

These people hate me.

They hate what they think you're doing, Lina said. **Let me ask around about good PR people.**

– – –

Lon, Lina and Jae appeared together in the gritty aftermath of the riot. Debris and blood patterned the streets behind them.

Jae scowled at the cameras. "Valiant didn't kill anyone through all this. He took them away. They're in jail, where they should be. The rioters are idiots," he said to them. "Londo's trying to save your world. But who gets the blame?"

"Valiant. Protector–" one of the reporters called out to get his attention.

"That's right, 'Protector,'" Lina mocked the man. "Keep that in mind. He's doing his absolute, amazing best to protect you all from any kind of Doomsday Deadline."

"But you're the one destroying things," the reporter told Londo.

Lon gave him a level look, trying not to reveal his emotions: anger, hopelessness. Fear. "We've explained at great length why we're doing what we need to do. My job at this point is to get rid of structures, pollution sources, and war materials. I'll be building up new structures, clean structures, within days. We'll be creating green spaces as well. But we need to make room for all that first."

"What could be wrong with that?" Jae asked. "The news shows me just as hard at work as Londo, but I'm with the Aldierra Corps clearing out waterways and soils. No one is against that, are they? People have been demanding that for years and years – though little has been done in that area.

"Lina has been providing supplies and support, and focused on women and other oppressed groups. There's powerful misogyny on this world, but almost no one complains, because a complaint about Lina goes straight to Aldierra's ears, right?"

"That's not how it works," Lina offered. "Aldierra is listening to everyone, watching everyone. You complain about Londo and she hears it. You fight a fellow citizen, and she sees it.

"You help someone, and she sees that too. You work to clean her environment, or make plans for a healthy future, and she notes it. I think I know how I want Aldierra to think of me and what I do. Why don't so many Aldierrans?"

One reporter called out, "Is it all a hoax?"

Lon scowled at him. He had orange skin; likely an Aldierran native. "Did you hear the Ultimatum?" he sneered. "Did that seem a hoax to you?

"Like it or not," Londo declared, "we have a job to do." He grimaced at the cameras. "You don't want to make me angry. I don't want to operate angry or defensively. That doesn't help anyone. I want to act like I want every person on this world to act, with a clear mind, positively focused on accomplishing the goals we've set."

Jae and Lina glanced at each other. **We'll get him a PR person who can suggest a softer approach,** Jae told her, and she nodded.

He should be doing more one-on-one communication, too.

That garnered a nod as well.

— — —

"Let's give them a little of this," Lon told Hal through his phone. He popped the air transport he held higher and let it bounce on his fingertips as he flew it and himself through the murky atmosphere. "Give the bastards inside a good ride. Hah! Two are puking." He repeated the action with more oomph. They deserved it.

And it made him feel better. He really needed to feel better.

"I hope they're miserable," Hal replied with a chuckle. "I shouldn't say that, should I? But I do."

"Let's try a little zero-G," Lon said. He took firmer hold of the vehicle with its hundred occupants and flew in that arc he'd mastered years ago, the one that made people float in planes if they weren't strapped in.

"I should have told them to unstrap first," Lon complained. "Well, maybe not. They might get injured."

"Still–"

"Ah, there's a puker. And another." The satisfaction was thick in Lon's voice, and Hal laughed. "Oh, three decided to go a little further. We'll have to have the suits thoroughly cleaned once we arrive."

"Should you be having so much fun with this? I don't want to interrupt it but–"

"Rands hold responsibility heavy on their shoulders. With great power comes–" Lon shrugged as his phone camera caught him. "It's going to help Aldierra."

"Really?"

"That's what I keep telling myself. These people really made me angry yesterday. They accused me of all kinds of evil while they tried to kill each other. At least for some things Aldierran justice moves quickly."

He frowned at himself. "This isn't forced slavery. It's punishment for crimes. The district high judge agrees with me. What the men in this particular group were doing was at the far end of the spectrum. Rioting. Attempted murder. A few actual murders in there as well. There are probably a lot of other crimes they've all been guilty of over the years. Their actions directly influence the fate of twenty billion people."

The idea of giving evil men their due lightened his mood. "Today," he decided, "I am karma in action."

Hal quickly berated him. "Don't let all this go to your head. You're in the center of the biggest spotlight there is. You need to set an example."

"I know, I know."

"Listen to me. We have so much power, it's up to us to keep ourselves in tighter check than others do. There can never be a speck of suspicion leveled upon us. Never, ever any scandal."

Lon heaved a heart-felt sigh that almost cracked the clear helmet he wore. "I *know*. You've delivered this lecture a million times before. It's just that sometimes a few people deserve a little nasty. I hear you, Hal. I do my best. Here we are; my first large creation here. Gotta go. *Salut*."

He signed off with more than a bit of relief and set the transport down in what might have been a meadow long ago. How was Hal going to take Lon's marriage? Talk about a scandal. Well, that wasn't happening today. Today was for happier thoughts. He walked around to hit the "door open" button.

"Hope you all have suited up," he cheerily called inside as a squad of sterile suited guards trotted out of the nearby facility toward the newcomers.

Londo certainly had himself completely covered. Head to toe he was encased in an odor-blocking sterile suit, fashioned to look like his usual uniform.

Inside the transport the suits were all white. Some men hadn't raised the hoods on theirs. They were easy to spot for they were doubled over, vomiting onto whatever was in reach.

"Hoods up!" Londo reminded them with raised thumbs and a grin they could see behind his mask. "Hup hup! Let's get you all moved in to your new home."

The guards reached the transport. They were quite secured into their orchid sterile suits as they waved weapons at the prisoners, urging them on their way.

There was a short boardwalk paralleling the edge of the black "lake" before they came to the expanse of the Great Shit Flats Penitentiary and Reclamation Project. Nothing here looked like a hotel, but it didn't quite seem a prison either.

It came across as a science complex, with varied heights for different buildings, and unbarred windows that looked out into the excremental waste. Oh, and the mountains beyond. Someday who knew when, this might be remade into a resort. There might be a picturesque lake out there, waving grasses, perhaps a forest or two.

But right now there was one hell of a lot of shit.

"You will be cleaning this up," Lon told the prisoners as they stumbled past. "No idea how long the job will take, but at least you'll begin it. Gonna be a beautiful site someday. We just have to get it to that point. You're just the group to do this! You're gonna like it here, *mets-en!*"

When the group had entered the complex, he waved to dismiss the accompanying guards. They broke into a trot to reach the transport. "Take it and get it washed!" Lon called as the vehicle lifted off, back to civilization.

Here the guards were volunteers, or mostly so. They were getting triple pay and their tours of duty would be shorter than normal ones. Their living section was behind odor barriers so they could get out of their sterile suits at the end of each day.

The prisoners were not so fortunate. Their side of the complex held a pervasive undercurrent of odor. It wasn't enough to make them sick; it was just enough to be a reminder. Perhaps in the near future Londo or someone would add an area of aroma relief for them. Lon admitted to himself that that day would likely come sooner than later, though he didn't like the idea. This punishment was too much fun; no, it was entirely fitting, to not only get them going on cleaning up the Flats, but in thinking about what they'd done and what they should be doing instead.

The back part of his mind, though, wondered how much reformation these men would truly be able to undergo during their stay here. It would be inhumane to constrain them in these circumstances for their lifetimes. And if no one ever heard their story, they wouldn't set a frightening example for others to avoid.

The goal was (A) to begin reviving the Great Shit Flats, and only (B) to make the men see the error of their ways and culture. In that order.

It was idealistic. Lon had made the penitentiary large enough to hold five thousand men. He'd been here on Aldierra long enough to know that there were far too many evil men here.

It made a large army to attend to the Shit Flats.

And a large experimental pool to see what kind of propaganda or psychological manipulation it would take to most efficiently heal the culture from a thousand or more years of rewarding hatred. And fear, Lon added in his mind. People didn't hate if they didn't fear. Yoda was right enough about that.

Jae was in charge of finding the best propaganda to feed them. He had sent out a call for criminal psychologists, human or AI, to see to reformation efforts. How were they going to be paid? Lon tried to rub his nose, but his face mask beeped in alarm before he could accidentally break through it to do so.

Still, Lon was going to have fun watching the footage that his film crews were going to send to the masses. There were likely drinking games one could come up with about how many times a man encased in a completely odor-guarded sterile suit, could vomit. Maybe one would set a record.

Should they hand out trophies?

— — —

They'd slotted three hard-earned hours for this, though Lon and she might have to leave early if something came up on Aldierra.

They were all three in Legion HQ on Sarastor, in a rec space lined with the Legion's usual dreary black walls. They'd now been decorated with colorful rocketing streamers and holograms, plus the occasional immaterial firework that zipped across the room.

It was Jae's birthday. He had never had a birthday party before.

Jae had decided to go by Earth dates, so this made him 29. Next year all this Aldierra mess would be behind them, one way or another, and they could throw a big zero-birthday blowout for him then. This one was just for close friends and colleagues.

Jae and Lon welcomed the guests as they arrived, primarily Jae's Alpha Team with their families, with the rest being various Legionnaires. Lina was glad that Jae's team medic, Scribbi, was included as medics had to tag along with their teams into the most dangerous of situations, despite the fact that they had no powers. They were the unsung heroes of the Legion.

The team had even retrieved Erik from Legion Medical, who came down in a floating recliner chair covered with blanket-like layers of regenerating equipment and with a nurse in tow. They could only stay a few minutes. Lina made sure they both got drinks, ice cream and cake, with a takeaway plate for later when Erik felt hungrier.

"Can you get me some rallo juice?" Erik asked her in secretive tones. At Lina's quizzical look, he explained, "It's essential for making the best ratchets. Jae makes those. He has a stash."

"No alcoholic drinks for a couple more weeks," the nurse admonished.

"I'll ask – in two weeks," Lina assured him and even noted it on her padd, which made Erik laugh.

A different, rat-a-tat laugh had Lina looking up. You always knew Jae was happy when he let out some of those. Nearby Lon was chucking as well, but his laughs stopped abruptly with the arrival of a new guest:

Stoan.

Actually, it was Stoan and Andri, commander and subcommander of the Legion. Stoan was wearing an obviously fake pleasant expression because he dropped it when he faced Londo, away from the crowd. Andri's expression was more a mix of agreement with Stoan and, when he looked away, a pained one for Londo. She was in on their secret.

Lina didn't have to hear the conversation to know that Stoan was chewing out Londo for their poly announcement. If Londo wasn't going to address the problem, Stoan wanted to put out his own statement to the sector.

Lina joined them, smiling as agreeably as she could at the scuzz. "Take your Legion business away from here," she quietly said. "This is a private party. You can talk some other time. Apart from selections you're familiar with, Subcommander, we have nachos, spring rolls, and Londo and my favorite kinds of cake on the buffet. I think you'll enjoy them." Lina turned and left, trying hard not to make it seem as if she were fleeing.

Her new Legion Spousal Assistant, Fennon Saltire, had worked hard on this party. Since Lon's Legion PA was new and up to his ears in work and Jae's seemed to be overwhelmed with tasks Jae had set for him, Fennon and she had agreed that he could handle this. The experienced PA listened to her suggestions of Terran foods to add to the Sarastoran selection, and to Lon's of drinks, and ordered a great variety for Lina to port in.

He'd been woefully underutilized until now, and likely feeling dejected for being assigned to the ostracized "Terran witchdoctor." Lately as her standing in the local news had elevated, he'd been calling to inform her of invitations to interviews and celebrity events. He certainly looked perkier than he had when she'd first met him.

Firmly he instructed her to move around the crowd. She hardly knew anyone here.

"Smile and be pleasant. If that's difficult, ah, do you know someone you could imitate?"

Well, there was Londo. Jae put on a good show among strangers, but Lon always truly had a good time in any crowd. He'd left Stoan's side and now was encouraging the kids who were enjoying all the flashy and mysterious techno-games that had been set up for them behind a sound barrier. Though the cakes and ice cream were scheduled for later, some of the children already exhibited streaks of brown, red and white around their mouths and on their fingers.

She couldn't do a pseudo-Londo on this crowd. Lina tried to recall female hostesses with the mostesses. Ah: Mame. Dolly Levi. Lwaxana Troi.

As if.

Swallowing, she pasted a smile on her face and approached these strangers, feeling like she was marching toward her execution. It was easy enough to chat with Wiley and Andri, as well as Chimrin – all in on the truth of the marriage. Actually, it was very nice to see Wiley attached to Andri's side. They made a nice couple. Were they one?

She'd handle the venue counterclockwise; always good to have strategy. As she strolled, she heard people talking about the poly marriage sham. "A blot on us." "Honor of the Legion." That old favorite, "Terran," was thrown in as if it were a terrible thing. Conversations stopped when she drew nearer, though once one of them let the word "scandal" remain in the air so she could hear it clearly. Then they regarded her behind a stony wall of silence.

Still she smiled and wished people a good time, then motioned them to the service table and servers, with food suggestions. She didn't let lack of response stop her.

Much.

Thank goodness the band finally arrived. Legion Lifestyle had allocated a certain amount of time for partygoer conversation, but now they set up and began to play. The AffSys didn't like much if any music besides percussion, so that was the performance.

Conversational groups motioned for sound dampening around themselves, but the band played at regular volume for those who wanted to dance. Guests arranged themselves into lines for the livelier beats, then split into couples for the slower ones.

After a while Jae sat down to the band's rialla, which was an intricate drum set. He began to pound on it with enthusiasm, laughing rat-a-tat-tat.

The rialla was so much more than just drums. It was every kind of percussion Lina could think of, and Jae expertly juggled through it all. Enthusiastic dances formed around it. Lina bounced her head to the beat.

She heard a familiar name as she approached one conversational group: Deegel, the traitor she'd helped uncover. Her trial was approaching. Legion PIC was trying to minimize the publicity impact. More mentions of "scandal." Were they talking Deegel, or her?

Jae joined her as she adjusted some platters after the servers had jostled them a few millimeters out of place. His face was shining with excitement and alcoholic consumption. "You don't look like you're having fun," he chided her.

"It's my first time as hostess," she said. "Are you enjoying it? I loved your set. Do we have enough food? Is there enough variety for everyone?"

No one had tried the Terran cakes until Andri had taken a slice of the german chocolate one, and then gone back for the red velvet. The woman truly was brave. Now she was the one pointing the Terran foods out to others. Good thing Lina had had the slices cut thinly so people could experiment.

Now everyone was sampling all the fare, including the drinks. The ice cream in particular was getting a good reception.

Jae replied with a delighted grin. "I've never had a dedicated birthday party before. It's always been a mention or a toast at some other event. Thank you. But do try not to make notes after people eat. Enjoy it."

Guiltily Lina put her padd away. It had given her something positive to do. "What can we do about her?" Lina asked, nodding in Mimik's direction.

The insect creature, Lon's second in command, stood alone next to a starkly ungarnished bowl of seeds and fruit watching everyone. Lina felt sorry for her. She was hesitant to go up to ask Mimik what food she actually preferred, and where it might be found.

"She's fine," Jae reassured her. "She's like that. I'll talk with her."

Mimik was a little scary. She was from more than a few galactic sectors away, which was why she wasn't more human-like. That sector had been influenced by different evolutionary waves than the ones Sarastor, Aldierra and Earth had experienced.

Jae and Mimik were joined by Baisley, who was medic on Lon's team, and were chatting well together, so Lina returned to her rounds. There were a few Legionnaires who were actually polite to her. She tried not to take up all their time just because that would be easier. She kept ambling.

"Scandal." "Stain on our history." "Honor," she heard instead of guests talking about how great Jae was doing. The alcohol was making everyone louder. Ruder.

Ordinarily a birthday boy would be opening his presents about now, but the AffSys didn't do birthday presents. Having people congratulate you on your day was supposed to be enough.

The three of them had decided that modest gift-gifting would be their norm, so there was a small pile of framed photos waiting back on Aldierra that she and Lon had gathered from Feithi records. They showed young Jae and his three parents, his sister, his slew of grandparents. They'd have Jae open those just before bedtime, which they were all scheduled to share tonight. She counted the minutes to when they could leave from here.

"*Skurny* witchdoctor."

People actually glared at her, their hostess.

Even Lon's grin as he circulated seemed forced. He must have heard the conversations. Finally Lina gave up on her route. She didn't want to be a wet blanket at Jae's event. Instead she settled in a far corner, where she wrapped energy around herself to hide from attention.

Chimrin, who had mentored both Lon and Jae, came up from the side as Lina was making just a few tiny more notes about who was eating what.

"Nice trick," the green-haired woman told her. "Can you teach it?" She sat down beside her.

Chim was a telepath, so Lina let her feel what she did as she explained the process. Chimrin nodded.

"I'll work on the technique," she promised. "Could be useful in the field. I hear great things about the Aldierran mission."

They chatted about that, and Lina scrolled through her padd to show her encouraging stats as well as what they were teaching about psychic work.

Chim nodded. "I wonder if anyone on Tishan is monitoring this," she said of her home world or maybe it was a large space station, that housed and educated the sector's better telepaths.

She gave another chin motion to the padd in Lina's hands. "If your padd is holding secure information, your screen should be on polarized view," Chim told her.

That was an odd remark. Lina's screen hadn't shown anything classified.

Chim didn't have to have that spoken aloud in order to respond. She tapped her head. "I've heard things, kid. From now on, Level 2 or higher: polarized."

Lina was going to argue that Jae and Lon's padds weren't confined to that rule, but they were Legionnaires. Perhaps that played into things.

"Yes'm," she said meekly as she adjusted the settings.

"Have you scheduled defensive training yet?" Chim asked.

Lina winced. "I have lots of personal guards." And she usually remembered to utilize them. "We haven't had any real problems yet. We'll get to it after Deadline."

"See that you do, all three of you."

That sounded like a command.

But it wasn't rude, or meant to be so — unlike the other conversations she interrupted as she made more rounds. At least Fennon hadn't asked that awful Ms. Yency from Protocol. Lina kept her smile in place and tried her hardest not to pray that the party would end early.

— — —

Lon also circulated among the guests, the good host. Many of these were good friends of his, and he valued them for being that. He joined in the dancing because he loved dancing. He even stood next to Jae in line because it was just a line dance. No one would suspect. They laughed and laughed. It was so good to relax, even for only a little while.

Jae had the greatest, warmest smile around. And he could make even the most formal of dances seem like an invitation to seduction.

After the dance Dellen Gorten approached Lon. "We hear great things about Aldierra," she said to break the ice. She wasn't a member of his or Jae's teams, but she was on an Alpha one.

He gave a pleasant reply and they chatted. Then she said, "So after this is over, after Deadline is met and won, Jae will have more time on his hands?"

"We'd better not keep up this pace. It's exhausting, and we're only a little way in."

She nodded and took a sip of her drink. "Jae's not… He hasn't found anyone… interesting on Aldierra, has he?"

Lon lowered his own drink. Dellen and Jae had had a torrid two-week affair a couple years ago, back when Jae would go full steam with someone before abruptly dropping them. Since then he'd worked on his manners and had returned to Dellen for a final night of sex and then a gentle speech about liking and respecting her but this wasn't really the best thing for them, goodbye.

"Maybe Lina could port me over there for a week and I could help Jae?" Dellen said, gazing at Lon's husband. "I mean, for the Cause and everything."

"Multiplex. Dellen." Lon had no idea how to address this, so he gave her as understanding a look as he could. "Perhaps this is a conversation you should have with Jae. I thought you'd broken up. He only has good things to say about you, always good things, but he said… broken up."

She lifted her chin. "Jae's interests skip around," she said. "Someday he's going to want to settle down for a while. Maybe even a year or two. I intend to be there when he makes that decision."

Londo licked his lips and then took another sip of his drink. "Definitely a conversation to be had with him," he muttered.

Her expression soured at that idea with its shadow of pessimism, so she soon found an excuse to talk with someone else.

This was not good. No revelation of the true state of their marriage meant that Jae would continue to get propositioned. Jae got propositioned a lot, Londo knew. And a man had his breaking point. Was it fair to keep Jae in a secret marriage when so many would be badgering him?

Revealing the secret wouldn't solve the problem of propositions, but it would significantly decrease them. It would not only lessen the worry load off Lon's shoulders, but ease Jae's life as well.

Londo rubbed his nose and tried not to hear the rumors and accusations that were quietly being circulated.

— — —

Finally it was time for everyone, including Lina, to lift their glasses for a toast to Jae.

"We will skip the traditional singing of 'Happy Birthday to You' because… well, you know," Londo announced. Sarastor did not approve of singing. "But we will observe this once we return to Aldierra."

Several in the crowd congratulated Jae in their toasts, especially on his work on Aldierra and with the attempted Aldierran Invasion. Many took the advantage to turn it into a roast.

By now Jae was quite sozzled but enjoyed it all, joking and insulting his tormentors with ease.

Lon and Lina stood each with an arm around each other, so happy for Jae. Excited because there would be a lovely night ahead, centered in the bedroom.

Standing by one of the serving tables, Mimik studied them all.

— — —

Lina waited until she'd received the "all clear" sign from her guard squad to port into the mountain village. Though this was only a sixth of the available entourage there was an equal number of men and women for this mission.

The guardswomen were from Sarastor, and held excellent defensive skills. Three medics from across the AffSys had already arrived with their own guards to double-check supplies at the location.

Kanti came with Lina as a part of her expanding training. Lina always found this funny, because Kanti was learning at the same time Lina was. Kanti was the best hiring decision Lina ever made; she was that good.

They all wore bulky fluorescent orange Three Worlds coats that protected them from the freezing temps. This Sha-Green village was actually that: a village not surrounded by city. The reason must be the forbidding mountain landscape, part of the Master Range, which had kept the area isolated. And rather breezy, which added to the freezing temperature.

The locals had the usual Aldierran tech, and Lina knew from checking records that the village had received food supplies as well as basic pure water units. Too bad their tech hadn't been utilized to update their buildings. House complexes and other structures were in sore need of repair. Cracks penetrated walls. Odd building materials leaned against foundations and littered the streets.

Even though the delegation had called ahead as well as posted their schedule, the four main Houses of the village were unprepared to hand over their women yet though their men seemed ready to be processed. That gave Lina and Kanti time to inspect the prefab field hospital that would be serving as a medical urgent care as well as small schoolhouse. Jae had told her that it was sturdy enough to last in good condition for several decades. Plus it was fairly cheap, always a good thing to her mind.

"They need screens to separate grade levels, adults from kids," Kanti observed even as Lina had also noted that. She scribbled on her padd as Kanti did the same on hers.

Lina raised her head at looked to her right. "Just a moment," she told Kanti, and ported.

Kanti spoke into the tiny bubble that always hovered by her side. "Speaker has ported," she informed it. "There might be trouble. Lina, report your location."

— — —

Lina ported into the middle of the village, paused only a moment to touch her earring to relay her location, and then followed the direction her spirit guides pointed toward. She ran.

Two Aldierran men roughly held a scrawny woman in each arm at the entrance to one House's compound. "Out of my way!" Lina demanded and rushed by them.

She chose the second building in the complex. Its interior was dark and the floor, uneven. The guides pointed. Lina ran as she could past the extended family, mostly males, inside. They followed her.

In one of those dank, claustrophobic cells locals kept for their female population's living quarters, Lina found an emaciated woman – hard to determine her age – cowering on the floor, covering her head with her arms. Above and behind her a man was raping her.

She made no noise, but her bruised and trembling body flinched terribly with each thrust. Crusted wounds opened, bleeding. Pants around his ankles, the man held a short, narrow pole in his left hand, adding a beating to his abuse. Lord knew if he was planning to use it in other ways.

The sound Lina made was inarticulate but loud. The man looked up.

Lina yanked his shoulders. "Get off her! Stand back! Stop hurting her!" She had to use her PK to aid her efforts.

She was so angry! It was difficult to concentrate. Her hands shook. She wanted to pummel this man. This animal. This evil.

A full spectrum of emotions, from shock to anger to astonishment and then fear, swept the man's face in waves. Finally he backed off, pushing the bloody woman fully to the floor.

"Oh, honey." Lina rushed to her and tried her best to cradle her in her arms. "We'll get you medical help. I'm so sorry. I'm so sorry. Poor thing." She managed to remember to touch her earring again.

Fury emanated from her as she faced the man. He was trying to escape.

"Stay right there!" she commanded.

He kept attempting to run, but she had control enough of her telekinesis now to stop him in his tracks.

"Rapist!" she accused. "Torturer! Did you not see our broadcasts? Rape is illegal. Punishment is–"

"She's just a *dizzen pod*!"

The words struck Lina hard in the gut. No time to translate it for the system now, though. "Keeping her from receiving help. Are you so frightened of her then? Londo?"

The man clawed at the wall in his attempt to flee.

"Where is that prison of yours?" Lina listened to something no one else could hear as the woman now whimpered in her arms. Lina held her tightly. "Ah."

The man looked behind himself at her. He was still trying to use his grasp of the wall to break Lina's hold. "She's mine to do whatever I want to with."

"She is a human being, deserving of dignity and safety. And love." Lina told him. "You have provided none of that. You have injured her. Greatly. Are you familiar with the Great Shit Flats? The terrain is much different from here."

"Great–"

"There is a large penitentiary there. Prisoners are castrated upon arrival." Lina *thought* their last discussion was that punishment was primarily chemical castration, but still… It would register hard with the men listening at the door. "They are sent to work in the Shit Flats."

"But–"

"Happy travels," Lina said and turned the woman so she could see as the man disappeared. "He's going to get what he deserved. Oh, where are those med– Here they are."

Three guards, two male and one female, plus a medic rushed through the gaping crowd into the room. The woman was crying uncontrollably on Lina's shoulder. "We have a patient. She's just been raped and who knows what else. She didn't deserve any of it, not a bit of it. Honey, you'll feel so much better in just a few hours. I promise. What's your name, sweetie?"

"Uh… Dung," the woman managed to reply before being overcome with coughing interspersed with her tears. The coughs obviously pained her, and she grabbed her sides before she broke into sobs anew. "Speaker. Speaker."

The guards gently lifted her onto a gurney, tucking a blanket around her even as the medic scanned her injuries.

"You'll choose your own name when you feel ready." Lina held her hand as she spoke to the woman. "These people will not harm you. They'll do everything in their power to help heal you. You'll have your choice whether to come back here or go to one of our new women's shelters when you're better. This was as bad as it gets. It'll be better after this."

The female guard took the woman's hand when Lina detached, and spoke soothingly to her.

Lina turned around as the gurney left, to discover that the House's inhabitants had followed her fully inside the room. "Who was that man? Which House is this?"

"Mid-Mount Green," one man said deferentially. He bowed to her. "He were Biz, Speaker."

Lina nodded. "Biz of the Mid-Mount Green House no longer exists," she told everyone. "He is now Houseless. Soon he will be castrated. He will have nothing more to do with any of you. Consider him dead with dishonor."

Silence.

"And you there, holding those women so hard. Let them go. They are human beings. Let them stand on their own two feet, if they can, and if they can't, kindly assist them to the urgent care.

"Who here allowed this torture to continue?"

The crowd shrank before her gaze, but the women gave her looks of defiant triumph.

"Who here should share in Biz' punishment?"

Silence.

Kanti arrived with guards in tow.

"I see. Well, we'll be getting testimony from the women of this House, as well as any men who have not been treated well. We will advise local law agencies and let them handle it.

"We are trying to change your world for the better. Trying to keep you all from being exterminated. Why aren't you working with us? Do you deliberately want to suicide?"

Again, silence. A few men shook their heads, but looked around first as if making sure that no one else saw them do that.

Lina tried to control her anger, her terror at seeing that woman. Her disgust at people who would allow such within their own House. Still her guides made gestures: toward the corners, beyond there. "There are members of your House who haven't been gathered. There are Houseless people nearby as well. Go and bring them to the urgent care. Use kindness. We need to get all this done quickly but not so quickly that we miss anyone or hurt them in our haste."

As Kanti supervised the exodus from the House Lina flagged down a likely-looking man. "Is everyone in your House getting the food supplies they need? Have you registered everyone? Seen all the Rules broadcasts? Has everyone been meditating, at least once a day?"

She listened closely to him, and then others dared to approach her with questions, which she tried to answer. The same questions came up from the other Houses in the village and she made notes to reiterate the answers on her next broadcast.

"If you have any testimony to give as to what has been going on within your House, or within this village, give it to…" She checked her padd and gave him the name of the local magistrate. "Don't go to anyone below that rank. Tell them the Speaker gave you instructions. Spread the word."

He nodded gravely and then gave her a low bow. Then she shooed him off to the urgent care to join the triage line with the rest of his House.

Tapping her wrist to dispense a dose of prescription tranquillizer, she also cleared an extra space in her schedule to check in with her own therapist. She had to watch out for exposure to this kind of shit. Mustn't have a breakdown like she did at the Mind Control Tour. She shut her eyes for a moment and took a deep breath.

"How are you doing?" she asked Kanti to bring herself back to business.

"All right, I suppose. You okay?" Kanti asked.

Lina nodded silently. Another breath. Another. The events of the past half hour fuzzed slightly in her memory, detaching itself from whatever brain center it was that triggered panic. "This too shall pass," she reminded herself. She just needed to make sure it had a happy ending.

— — —

Lina had only arrived at her desk ten minutes ago to start her day and its schedule. Yesterday in those mountain villages had been ghastly. There had been more incidents. More blood. More shattered people.

She'd made sure that the medics and guards all had therapist help at hand. Her own therapist, Carnie, had been called upon for as long a session as Lina dared to schedule. There was too much of this happening, and Lina wondered if her anti-anxiety meds could really handle the load.

Thank goodness she had them, though. Maybe she'd put off trying to sneak some stims. At these levels, the meds might interact badly.

Already her schedules were chiming at her, bleating in blinking code colors. At least Kanti was here to share her dismay at it all. Perhaps two frantic people weren't the best way to handle these straits, but it was comforting to have someone beside herself who was also freaking out.

They needed to deal with that.

"I've got to check with twelve more locations," Lina said as she pulled at her hair in frustration. "Plus a handful or two of focus groups, both men and women. I need AffSys medics – plus guards for same – because a lot of these guys will be high on drugs. Drug use is rampant out there, have you noticed? I don't blame some of them. People are stressed to the max. But I need everyone thinking clearly. The medics will ensure that.

"When it doubt, delegate," she told Kanti. "Ask Lon's PA, Whatshisface–"

"Trey."

"Yes, Trey. I *will* remember that name someday. –if he can get us army medics and guards for them to stretch what the AffSys has sent. That's Lon's bailiwick. He'll like it.

"And make sure that the equipment and supplies get delivered for everything we need to do in the next week. While prepping for the week after that and the week after that. I already gave you the preliminary contact list, but you might find some gaps in it. See that we have quarters and guards and supplies for the specialists Wiley is sending us. He'd better be including supplies with them, but he might forget. If he's not, remind him. You can talk with his PA if he scares you."

Kanti gave a faint whimper at that. Wiley could be intimidating to people who didn't realize he was just an ol' softie. They'd have to address this, but not now.

And as for her... "Am I being Bitch Lina?" she asked.

Kanti gave a short laugh. "No more than usual."

"Oh, terrible answer. Terrible answer. Kick me if, no *when*, I go too far. Already I need a long vacation. That won't happen for seven more months."

"And a honeymoon?"

Lina smiled warmly at Kanti. "Is it that obvious? Oh, a honeymoon." She allowed herself two full seconds to imagine happiness and peace. Tenderness. And lust. Plus a clean swimming pool, sparkling in the sunlight.

Then she said, "There are messages that I need to answer personally. Where's some time for me to do that?"

Kanti paged through her own digital notes on a screen they could both view. "I've got you scheduled solid, with a long wait list. There's no more room to fit anything in. At the very least, let me send out some of those replies. Or we could program an AI."

Lina frowned at the world, at her situation. At Kanti's. She drummed her fingers on the desk as Kanti waited expectantly and then offered, "I could–"

"No." Lina turned to her. "This thing isn't working."

"Which thing?"

"With you. You as my assistant isn't working."

Kanti drew back with a harsh breath, astonishment and hurt all over her face. "It's... not?"

"No. Not at all. Tell you what. You hire seven people to do what you're doing now, for me. That's enough to start, to cover shifts and workload. Hire two more than that, in case people get sick, want a vacation, we decide to carve the entire

Orchin continent to look like the Patriarch, whatever. And hire a staff for yourself. Hire from that point as needed in the organization and per job crush."

Kanti sat, confused, but she still took the notes as Lina continued.

Lina pulled up that organizational chart they'd put together. It sprang off the screen in 3D even as she motioned some portions of it to disappear. She made finger and eye signals to add new boxes to it.

"From now on you're my Chief of Staff. We might call it Chief of Speaker Staff. Yeah, each section gets their own; I like it." New organizational positions began to fill the chart in new directions. "Who came up with this thing? Remind me to inform The Boys." But she'd already motioned for CC's to be sent. "I want you to start hiring those assistants pronto. Bunches. You have my permission–" a finger wave alerted the computer– "to add them to this chart. Give me a yell when it comes to the final job interview of your top assistants and mine. I should be able to weed out the fakers. I can work from video if need be."

"Er. Chief of Staff. What's the job entail?"

"You're another me but in the office, not out and about unless you feel it's necessary or you need the steps. I don't want you in danger out there. I'll give you the authority. You'll be able to go further into our files than you can now. Security level… five, as far as I'm concerned, when it comes to Three Worlds, which probably puts you at a four for overall security to Lon and Jae's eyes. We'll work on that. If you find you've hit a brick wall security-wise, give a yell and I'll see what I can do. You see something that needs to be done, you organize ways to do it and drop me a line about it if you have time.

"This will free me up to get out there more, fine tune, meet with the people who have ideas about what we should be doing. Get a feel for the various cultures, so we don't erase them."

She finally focused to check Kanti's reaction. "Oh yeah, a big raise comes with the job. I'll tell The Boys. It's time they got their own Chiefs of Staff, take some weight off of us. They may be doing a helluva lot out there with their own hands, but coordination is a bigger bitch. We'll have weekly meetings as well, maybe twice a week, with the Chiefs, that will be different from the Boys' and my regular Tuesday meetings. You'll have your own meetings with your subordinates, and so on down the line. But not too many, because we need to get actual work done. Does that sound good?"

Kanti was blinking and Lina could feel her mind working as if it were an actual gigantic collection of mechanical clocks, ticking away the possibilities.

"The Boys?" Kanti decided to ask as her mind clicked away.

"I'm tired of trying to remember if the last time I said 'Jae and Lon' or 'Lon and Jae.' I don't want to make one feel left out or inferior to the other."

"'The Boys.'" Kanti nodded. "I'll never refer to them that way to their faces."

"And I'll try not to as well. You'll need a suite for your office, meeting rooms and staff. You want your office up here or on another floor?" Lina asked.

For the past week her office had been just outside the original suite, but now Londo had rearranged the outer hallway yet again so their territory stretched farther toward the lifts, effectively enlarging the suite as the three of them now had large offices at the entrance. "In here won't be very private. You've seen; people are always traipsing through and bellowing. And then there're the cats."

There were two sleeping on the desk in front of them, with another on a nearby chair.

"We'll take the floor underneath this one," Kanti promptly said. "No, we'll need multiple floors. Two for our command crew; Speaker, I mean. Maybe one each for Protector and Minister crews, since, as you say, their sections don't require that much coordination. Though we may be wrong about that. Maybe keep another floor open for overflow from them as well.

"Let's see, there's the floor for hotel and army staff, the one for the guards and more army staff, plus the broadcast studio, the floor for visitors and Mace's crew. Another two floors for what we don't know yet… I think we have enough floors to go around. Besides, the lower the floor, the nearer the hotel kitchens. People will like that. I'll warn the hotel staff about the impending personnel surge."

Lina laughed and stroked the cat nearest her. Molly. "That's what I like about you. You make quick decisions."

"We need an actual HQ on the PDQ," Kanti said. "We've got Three Worlds communications central on Earth, and the training is just about to end for the first round of Call Center employees, but we need an HQ here. It should also include communications, though that can be much smaller than Montreal and will coordinate closely with Earth."

"Communications is key," Lina agreed. "I'm sure this hotel is not happy having us all here, tearing up their walls and causing such a ruckus. They might as well rebuild from the ground up once we're gone. The other day Jae said something about finding an HQ here. I'll follow up with him, maybe give him a kick. A gentle kick." Lina smiled to herself as she made the note. Maybe a couple kisses on the boo-boos to accompany that.

"Make sure you wind up with a good balance of Sarastoran and Terran crew, but start with the Aldierrans." Lina paused and looked off into empty space, ignoring two people shouting at each other just outside her door. One of them was Bracken. "Communications needs to start with 100% Terrans. We'll have to bring some here as we start this center. Lots of women. The Aldierran men will see their skin color and not treat them the same way they do Aldierran women. The Aldierran women will see them and say, 'That'll be me someday.'"

Kanti gave a snort. "I once had to meet with one of those South African authorities from the old days, the white ones. He said that he could work with the Blacks in North America because they weren't like the ones in South Africa. He could respect them; they were somehow different in an evolutionary way."

Lina sighed. "Oh great. Just think: we'll be dealing with that kind of thing next year."

"Next year is far away," Kanti murmured.

"When we arrive there I bet we don't think that," Lina said. "Speaking of which, when we branch out after Deadline we'll need to pretty much triple staff. If everyone here and in the call center is up to speed by then, so much the better." She let out a groan. "I'll get Jae to talk with our finance people, see what we can do. But I know we've got enough to handle Aldierra. Guides always give me the thumbs-up on that."

"Can we get them to handle the numbers?" Kanti asked, and Lina snorted.

"Wouldn't that be nice? I'll give you a list of Aldierran possibles for staff," she said. "I've been working on one with people I'd trust enough to work closely with, and who seem trainable for all kinds of things. These are just suggestions from me, starter ones. I'm sure you'll come up with your own list. And oh," a new screen lit in front of her at her command, "I promised to take care of this woman. Tidda."

An incarcerated AffSys felon had died in Lina's arms and she'd promised to look after his wife.

"I'd like you or whoever you hire to assist you to research her, see what kind of work she could do. And whether we can trust her to do it. When you're through, give me a buzz and I'll contact her to offer her a job, if she's candidate material."

Kanti transferred the info to her padd. "Will do, boss."

"We also need an official Press Secretary. High time. With assistants. And someone like that, but different, you know? Someone who can go around and make powerful speeches when we need them to. Someone the people respect who can speak well and represent us to them. Maybe an actor would do, do you think? They could deliver the lines, and if they already had a good rep, well… You give us some choices.

"Ask Bracken. Ask Jae's PA, whatshis– Tanfield. Shield. Somebody Tanshield. We can't waste our time making too many speeches or media appearances, but someone's got to stand in the spotlight, keep the info and spirit flowing. They can bring us back info on what they run into out there, too. Someone to take the load off all three of us in those situations. We may want a woman as well as a man. You know how Aldierra is. Oh, make it four speech people, at least one of whom is a woman. We need to do a lot of yapping."

"We do indeed. I'll get on all that asap."

"Contact Lon. He's the big speech-maker in the group. He'll have some ideas about what kind of person – people – would best fill the job. And who to get to write all the speeches. Speech writer – add that to the list. Don't know how many of those we'll need, but he will. Gah, I didn't want to make a pyramid out of this organization. Where'd my flat structure go?"

Lina wiggled her fingers and waved her hands at the screen in a frantic dance. "We need to coordinate PR with Lon and Jae's folks at Legion HQ, no matter what Legion Regs think about the Aldierran situation. I've got a guy there now, too. He might like to be included. And… what was her name? Lon's PR lady in

Montreal." The screen changed in front of her. "Janet Chinn. She needs to be brought into the loop.

"Remind me to ask Wiley about the person his person said might be helpful in something. It was important." Lina frowned, unable to bring up the memory. "I'll have my AI find it, but remind me toward the end of the day, will you?"

"Will do. Thank god for AI."

Again with the finger-drumming on her desk. Lina stopped when she noticed Molly stirring, a tiny cloud of orange fur rising from the movement. Thoughtfully she told Kanti, "We've got someone coming up. We're still musing about it. Well, *they* are."

"Your guides?"

"The Boys. I'm convincing them. There might be another side on this pyramid soon, or at least a pyramid annex. I'll keep you posted so you're not caught unawares."

Lina chuckled. "And you do know that Wiley is the Fifth Beatle."

Kanti snorted at that.

"Don't know what we'd do without him, and he insists he's just an unpaid adjunct."

"Fifth Beatle."

"Right." Lina sat back in her chair to assess Kanti. "You get too stressed, give a yell and we'll do a little juggling. You have a therapist, right? If not, get one asap. Tell me when you feel you need some time back on Earth, besides just checking out the new operators there. You may not know this, but I sneak back every couple days just to regain my sanity.

"Don't tell Lon or Jae.

"Make sure you take time to eat and breathe. Maybe enjoy life around the edges if you can."

Kanti was still scribbling notes. "You too. We're in this together."

"Glad to hear that, Chief."

CHAPTER

15

As usual, neither spouse was around after Jae had finished dinner. Lina had joined him at its beginning, but for her it had been breakfast. Or maybe lunch.

There were vast new sections in their organizational chart that hadn't been there before, along with portable clothes racks in their bedroom, ditto.

"What are those?" he'd asked her. They were of a Sarastoran design. "Some of it is my stuff," he'd decided after looking it over. "I wore those boots day before yesterday. Those are my lucky boots."

"And now they're clean, even to Legion specs," Lina had replied around her granola. "I didn't like how the laundry here was being done. Especially Lon's clothes. He gets into everything imaginable. You know how bad his dirt works into the fabrics."

"Hadn't noticed."

"Well, it does. His laundry at Legion HQ handles it well enough. So starting yesterday – my yesterday, not yours – I am porting our dirty clothing to Sarastor and letting the laundry bots in Lon's apartment take care of it. It's like old California, you've been there. San Francisco."

"Hm?"

"During the Gold Rush some of the miners actually shipped their clothes halfway across the ocean to Hawaii in slow-sailing wooden ships, and waited for it to come back. How clean could it have been by then?" Lina made a goofy face at him. "But anyway. I programmed Lon's laundry so it would put our clean stuff on racks."

Thus the racks.

"I'll port clean racks back here when I port new dirty clothing to Sarastor. Each person is now assigned to put away their clean clothes when they come in. And use the hampers for dirty clothing. No more throwing things this way and that."

"You need to tell me these things when—"

"I put it on your schedule."

He'd checked. Sure enough, on yesterday's feed were the instructions for both him and Londo. He hadn't noticed it among all the new hires info.

"Sure this won't take too much energy for you?"

She gave him a small smile. "It's worth it. And it's not that much of a problem. I'll just add it to the daily ports for the equipment you guys order." She took a breath. "I need a yes or no on Chloroplast asap. Remind Lon."

Jae stifled a groan but nodded. When he went to attend to his clothing he found the racked things cleaner than they had been lately.

Ah, married life. No, it was more Aldierran life, dealing with the situations and people here. The laundry seemed a logical way to go about things, especially when they didn't have to wait for shipping. He'd have to look up this "Gold Rush" thing. Sounded interesting.

Where could they find a decent cleaning crew, though? At least the current military personnel who came in weren't bothering the cats, but the other day Lina had wondered if someone had been going through her dresser drawers who was not a husband. Jae had installed cameras that unfortunately confirmed that. A new crew was now assigned to the duty.

With no one else around, it was him and the cats. Each Starhart was required to play with the herd for twenty minutes each day, making sure that the pets worked off energy and got exercise as well as attention. Jae had to admit it was different. Maybe even fun, as the animals leaped into the air after feathers he managed on a stick. He ran a remote-controlled mouse in loops around the apartment to keep the others enthralled.

But other than that it was time for Jae to wind down from the day. Since dinner he'd spent almost two hours coordinating oceanic cleanup survey ships and then another hour overseeing the outfitting of a small fleet that would be performing surface trash collection. He wanted to see what worked and what didn't.

Plus he'd certainly done enough physical labor as he helped his small land army dig out obstructions in the Saba River. Well, he thought it was small. Lon told him the other day that from the air it looked like the legions of workers who built the Great Pyramids. That was another thing he needed to look up.

Jae had paced along the river's banks, sensing the chemicals in the ground and the water, before tracing them back to their sources. Sometimes he called for equipment to dig up long-buried containers of chemical foulness. Sometimes he had to sit on the ground and send his mind out to change those chemicals to benign ones. He tried to make them healthy ones if he could, but in a few instances the change couldn't be forced that far.

The aquifers of Aldierra were polluted beyond belief. Everywhere. It was too much for just him to do. They'd have to come up with another way to neutralize the problem.

"Wiley?" he asked his ring. "Got a minute?"

His good friend answered him via video screen, and the two Legionnaires talked a while.

"I know it's not Legion business," Jae said, "but you do have a lot of laboratories, some of which perform, you know, practical work."

"All my labs' work becomes practical… eventually," Wiley replied huffily.

"Yes, yes. But I'm talking practical *now*."

Through their discussion Wiley settled on asking a few of his more promising general assistants to see if they had spare time to work on the problem. He also recommended some ecologists who were working on similar projects.

"Thanks a lot." Jae's relief showed in his voice. "The sooner we can figure this out, the better."

Jae signed off, then signaled Legion Medical. It was Mart who answered, the doctor who'd lost most of an arm during the Mind Control Tour.

"I hate to bother you while you're convalescing," Jae began.

"Neutrino, your call only interrupted hours of boredom."

"I was hoping you could refer me to someone with AffSys medical training who'd like to learn *veterinary*… that means medicine for animals. It seems we have a herd of cats here, and all we can rely on for them is Terran medicine."

"Specialty medicine for animals?" Mart said doubtfully. "These are animals that live with you."

"Yes. They're called 'pets' when that happens."

"Tell me, Neutrino, are pets regarded as, well… No, that's silly."

"Pets are considered part of the family. Lina, I mean the Speaker, refers to herself as their 'mama.' They are her babies."

"Hm. Legion Medical is responsible for all Legion-related family members."

Jae chuckled. "Right. I think that's a stretch even for us. All I want is a recommendation for someone who might want to train in this. Maybe the Legion would give them the position of adjunct."

Mart's voice was thoughtful. "Who on Earth would I contact to get preliminary information? I mean, I assume Terran medicine already knows about cat physiology to some extent."

"Uh. I really don't know. Contact Mrs. Va– the Spea– Contact Lina directly and ask her. She'd know. And when you talk about cats in a scientific fashion, the noun becomes 'feline.'" Jae tasted the word in his mind. "It's something about Terrans relying on a dead language to categorize their sciences."

"Will do, Neutrino. 'Feline.' They're trying to keep me occupied, but it's by making me do boring things. This sounds intriguing, or at least different. I'll see what I can do. Mart out."

Jae stared at his Legion ring. Mart? A Legion doctor? Becoming their vet? No, he'd misunderstood. Mart was just volunteering to attend to coordination of the matter.

He went to the suite's bar, got himself a drink, and settled back on the couch as three cats made their way to him.

One let out a yowl of surprise as Lina popped onto the seat next to him and threw her arms around him. What was left in his glass splashed.

"Oh, you genius! You darling!" she exclaimed between kisses that landed all over his face.

He got her aimed at his lips and the result was very satisfying. He tried that again. And again.

"Are they really going to do it?"

"We are the Legion," he solemnly declared as he set down his drink. The cats had abandoned them, so there was now room for more thorough body contact.

"I'll see who I can contact on Earth. State has a vet school, very impressive stuff going on there, even if it's State and not Carolina. Oh, you're so hot. I can port Mart there for as long as he needs to look into this. You. Are. The best," she assured him.

They sank into a deep kiss, and their hands roamed over and under clothing.

"You have a schedule to attend to," Jae managed to whisper.

"And you need to get some rest," she returned. But her hands kept traveling. "You need to relax. Shake off some excess energy and stress. I need to attend to my sex beast husband."

He wasn't going to argue with her.

— — —

Despite the sound and debris barriers having been set up – and Lina knew they were far better than anything ever imagined on Earth – the BOOM BARUUMM BOOM of destruction still thundered through the valley city like a massive storm. Within this multilevel urban sprawl, the ground shook rhythmically. Taller buildings, completely emptied now, visibly vibrated with it above an impenetrable cloud of dust. It flowed through the hilly streets and alleyways like a fog.

Dozens of camera crews gathered around Lina and Jae, their focus alternating between them and the mayhem. Everyone wore masks that had been configured to filter construction dust in addition to the usual pollutants. Their goggles and bodysuits protected them. All wore bright Three Worlds identification vests.

Their elevated position allowed an overall view of the project. It was moving, expanding miles to the north even as they watched. Skyscrapers toppled in its path. Lina adjusted the large screen that showed the destruction from a drone's even higher point of view. "You can see a bit of the *pardeirs*. They take everything that has been destroyed and sort through it. It will become either new building materials or sent off for recycling in some other form. When that's done and buried infrastructure placed, the first sylviculture and landscaping crews will begin work."

Lina almost shouted so the audience could hear her above the din. "Jae will perform the final clearing of toxins from the soil and water table before planting begins. We hope to be getting some experimental neutralizing equipment by the end of the week so Jae can concentrate on other things. Civilian crews will be working as landscapers. Nurseries from all over the world are sending flora that is native to this district."

Jae triggered a video recording that took the attention of the video teams back to the screen. "This will be the edge of Reyda's primary north-south migration zone," he explained as the video showed the section of the globe involved. "Here we stand in a peninsula of city that borders it, but the zone follows the lay of the land and its watershed. We're taking into account normal wind direction – that is, as it will be after we dismantle Weather Control – and seasonal changes to shape the zone. You can see why we have to move the people who live in the Zone out of the way. We've already moved, what, Lina, four million all in all?"

She nodded and Jae continued.

"The way we'll accomplish all this is by revising existing cities. They'll either extend higher than they do now, or will go into the ground. It all depends on bedrock. We'll utilize some of the floating sea cities to house temporarily much of the displaced population. We hope they'll be comfortable.

"Here large new city structures will have ground-level openings that allow fauna to roam from one side to another, as needed, as what's being cleared will be just the Primary Zone. Minor ones will eventually feed into it."

The reporters began to barrage Jae with questions. They'd had an initial briefing on all this, and had come prepared to ask the things ordinary people would want to know.

Jae gave a discreet nod at Lina and she ported.

– – –

She divested herself of her Three Worlds vest, draping it over her left arm, but let her goggles and breathing mask hang loosely from her neck as she unfastened her protective hood to walk through Legion HQ, a human-made mountain of a building that sat square in the most important sector of Sarastor.

"Um, puter?" she asked the dark walls. "Can you send a kol-vanasche or something to get rid of all the dirt I'm shedding? Maybe clean me up a bit?"

She paused as a six-foot wide, blinking pancake slithered out of the base of the wall to crawl over her. Just being outside on Aldierra for an hour made you filthy, even if you didn't perform any hard labor. She'd been standing in a construction zone. Yuck.

She screwed her eyes shut and held her breath as it passed over her face, but then it was done and set about vacuuming the dirt she'd left in her path. Efficient.

Here on the second floor were various offices belonging to the Legionnaires. It was not a high-security level, but it was closed to the unscreened public.

Lina followed her husbands' directions. Past the Alpha Teams, past the Beta Teams… She finally arrived in the section reserved for the Gammas, the least important Legionnaires. These could be newbies or established members past their prime. They might be former Alphas or Betas who were training the Gamma teams full-time. Or they could be members with lesser powers or who hadn't yet shown the level of martial or mega skill that the Alphas and Betas required.

At least that's what Lina's Legion Spouse Manual said. She really needed to keep studying that, but first things first.

She stopped at one door. With a wave at its sensor, it opened to her. Inside was a small reception area, a fifth the size of the ones in Jae's and Londo's offices. She'd visited theirs. They were decorated with entertaining and impressive items that welcomed visitors.

This was utilitarian. Legion minimum. A blue-skinned man who sat at a monitor-lined desk looked up as she came in.

His face took a moment before he registered surprise, and he turned down the intensity of his monitors. "May I help you, Speaker?" he asked.

"I don't have an appointment," Lina said, "but we checked Chloroplast's schedule to see when she might be free. Is it possible to see her? I need to speak with her on behalf of the Three Worlds."

– – –

It took eight minutes before Chloroplast swept in. Lina's spirit guides had shown her impressions of the Legionnaire running and then slowing down in the hallway outside her offices, catching her breath and gathering her dignity before meeting with Lina Starhart.

She made a wonderful first impression, Lina thought. She was dignified and yet powerful-looking; in command of her presence. Lina had seen this in other Legionnaires, and thought it might be part of their training: the public persona. Very good. She should see if she could get in on some of those classes.

Chloroplast had orange skin that subtly changed in places above her bright blue costume to be lighter or slightly darker patches. There might have been a pattern to it, but the costume prevented Lina from seeing it. The Legion and AffSys didn't like revealing too much bare skin.

"Speaker," Chloroplast said as she bowed her head. "Ms. Starhart. Um, Mrs. Valiant?"

Lina bowed her head to the Legionnaire and brought her fingertips together in front of her chest. "Chloroplast. *Pelzire.* Please call me Lina." She glanced at Chloroplast's assistant. "May we adjourn to someplace… more private?"

"Please call me Nesh, Sp– er, Lina." Chloroplast gestured to her inner office.

— — —

The two emerged an hour later. Nesh was shaking her head.

"Take as long as you need to consider," Lina told her. "I'm sure you'll want to see the world first. I am available any time for transportation. *Any* time. If you agree, this could mean, well, night and day for our mission."

Nesh seemed dazed. Her assistant was poised at his desk, clearly brimming with curiosity. "I will contact you within ten hours, Lina. I have duties and a prescribed rest period until then. I also need to talk with some people. Several people. I do want to see this world first."

"She is anxious to meet you as well," Lina assured her.

— — —

Londo took Stoan's call, even though he was only dressed in a half-robe. His hair was still dripping from the shower, and when he wrapped the end of the towel draped over his head around his pinky to insert it into his right ear, it emerged ever so slightly dirty. He scowled at it and then tried to form an official, if pleasant, expression for Stoan.

Stoan was definitely in full scowl mode of his own. "What the blat are you trying to do to us, Starhart?" he demanded.

"Filthy work, Stoan," Londo replied, and displayed the grime. "You wouldn't believe how much dirt there is out–"

"Londo!" Stoan's face was as dark a blue as Lon had ever seen. "You are kidnapping. Legionnaires."

"It's not kidnapping when they volunteer."

"Coercion then."

Lon gave a gallic shrug, tipping his head to the side before he replied. "She was offered a job where she'll not only be able to work to her full abilities, but get a ton of respect. She'll be in the foreground instead of being shunted to the back. She'll be a planetary hero of historic proportions, far more important than she's been in any other role. Plus I think she'll enjoy her paycheck."

Stoan seemed as if he were trying to retort with a good argument.

"You've been wanting to see who else was out there for our Legion ranks," Londo said in a reasonable voice. "Now you have an empty slot to fill. Find someone who isn't good only for nudging an ailing onboard hydroponics system. Chloroplast's Legion days were numbered; you know that."

"Not enough places to use her," Stoan grumbled.

"Not for Legion work." Londo riffled his hair with the towel. "But Three Worlds – she's pure gold. You just wait. Phrase your press statement any way you want, and we'll agree that's how it happened."

He worked on his other ear and said offhandedly, "Lina says we should clone her."

Stoan snapped to alertness at that.

"Just a joke. But really, have you heard of any others like her? Any who have the same sort of powers? Who specialize in some phase of eco-systems?"

"I can check into it. I suppose. But for Legion to act against Legion–"

"It was the Speaker for the Three Worlds who hired Chloroplast," Londo corrected. "No Legionnaires were involved."

Stoan took a deep breath and then let it out in surrender. "We'll say that we worked with Three Worlds and offered the choice to her. With great regret–"

"And honor," Londo put in.

Stoan nodded. "And honor, and with an eye to her upstanding Legion record… for what it was… we celebrate her taking on a job that will… That will…"

"That could save an entire world, 20 billion people and more," Londo finished for him.

Stoan grunted. "I suppose."

Londo leveled an index finger at him. "Wait and see."

"But no more, Starhart. I won't have you picking off useful Legionnaires." His scowl renewed. "And I don't want to hear anything about how she's now your wife! Personally, I don't care anymore that you have to do this polygamy story to the Aldierran masses. I understand. But Legion PR has been stretched to breaking to explain it to ours. No more."

Londo held up his right hand in oath. "I so swear," he said, and broke out into a grin. "Three is enough."

Lon retained his grin long enough to sign off. How far would polygamy push Legion rules? Even if it were Feithi norm, would the iron-clad rules of the AffSys MegaLegion ease to allow this?

Would Jae and he be kicked out of the Legion? Would only he be, since this was a Feithi tradition and Jae was the only Feithi in the marriage?

Was it worth it to release their secret?

– – –

Lon's hair had dried and he'd dressed in civilian clothing by the time Jae arrived home from his duties. They gave each other a welcome kiss and tired squeeze, and compared their progress for the day.

Jae checked someone's schedule – turned out it was Lon's – and announced, "Training time."

"Hm?" Lon was still checking Jae's cleaning progress at Krakalee River on Limbernie even as he dragged cans of cat food out from their cabinet. He'd have to set up dust barriers to protect the river where it was close to his clearing route. The migratory paths in Limbernie linked by land to the continent of Orchin along an isthmus. It was the most important migratory route for land animals on the planet.

"Training," Jae repeated. He waved at the floor.

Londo looked down at what was a growing crowd of cats at his feet.

Yellow ones, black ones, striped ones, color-patched ones. Molly offered hisses to him as habit, but they weren't loud ones. After all, he controlled her dinner.

Lon sorted through cans of cat food to find matching flavors. "What are you teaching them?" he asked, not really caring.

"Not them. You."

Lon looked up. He had paused in opening a can, and the cats below voiced their disapproval. Or anxiety. Or hunger.

Jae made a whirling motion with one raised finger. "Proceed," he ordered.

So Londo continued to feed the cats, eventually accompanied by the sound of the herd munching away. He got out the milk and poured only an ounce or two, to find Fafhrd waiting expectantly next to his left foot.

He wrapped two towels that were now designated as not for regular use, around his hands and lifted her to the counter where she alone could partake of the liquid treat.

"The towels are to buffer you?" Jae asked with a mouth full of whatever snack he'd procured for himself.

"So I don't crush her to death. Does she get her pill now?" Lon shook his head. "The computer tracks that schedule; I don't." They had been keeping the cats on Earth time, which didn't synchronize with that of Aldierra. It had been discussed at length at their last family meeting. Which planet were they going to accustom the cats to?

Jae checked a floating screen to his upper left. "Lina will take care of that when she comes in. Let's deal with the towels."

Londo set them down at Jae's gesture.

"It's time you learned how to touch all the cats without concentrating so hard."

"We can do this la—"

"Now. After they finish."

Chrisse, but Jae could be pushy at times. Lon laughed to himself. He might have been the one to teach him that. But still…

Fragile, mortal rodent-beasts vs Valiant.

"Are you sure?"

"Training," Jae repeated, and tossed his white cape on a chair. He rubbed his Array wrist bands thoughtfully. "Who do you want to start with?"

"Molly. No one would miss her if I were to kill her. Accidentally."

Across the open room, the aforementioned ginger cat was giving Lon her best side-eye while she bathed herself, as if she could understand the conversation.

"Not Molly. Not Ember." Jae considered.

"Not Fafhrd," they said at the same time.

Katie scampered across the kitchen, kicking a tinkling ball in front of herself and playing both sides of a championship soccer game.

"We have a volunteer," Jae said.

— — —

Katie was not a lap cat. If she really liked someone she'd park in monorail position on the arm of their chair and let them pet her. Now she lay on the floor, suspiciously watching both Jae and Londo, who sprawled next to her. Jae petted her. Londo cooed to her and called her "Katie-Darling," like Lina did.

She didn't seem to be fooled, but she was compliant. For now. She seemed curious about what they were up to.

Lon frowned thoughtfully. "They aren't telepathic. They can't do a double-loop." That was how Lon and his spouses could touch each other without Londo accidentally mauling them with a tap.

"No, but you're a good teep now. You do the technique without a thought. With thought, with practice, I think you could learn to touch the cats."

So Lon tried it on a cat. Who was not telepathic. Who didn't know what he was doing.

Lon tried to feel his touch from Katie's point of view in order to regulate its force – and came up blank. She twitched.

He abruptly pulled back. "This isn't going to work. It's never worked before." He grimaced at Jae. "You remember."

Jae rolled his eyes at him as Katie settled again under his hand. "You rolled over on me. You were asleep. That broken arm was not your fault." He chuckled. That had been a few years ago. "But thank the orb you can't do that anymore."

"I am not going to break this cat. You don't know how long Hal worked with me so I wouldn't automatically touch people. 'We can't do this. We *don't* do this.'"

"Well now you do. Just try it. Ease into it. Erase your negative thoughts. Your past is behind you. The only reality is the present, and even that has iffy elements. You *can* do this."

Lon scowled at him, but took a breath. He considered Katie and then approached her warily, palm out. He sank his mind into her skin.

"Relax. Try it this way," Jae suggested, and did the same thing Londo had with the loop. "In stereo," he said. "Does it help?"

Ma foi, something was different. Mostly Lon could feel Jae's touch on Katie's back. He couldn't decipher his own.

They tried again and again. Different areas of the body. Katie fell asleep under their hands.

Lon blew out a breath.

"Take your time," Jae said quietly.

"I don't want to hurt one of Lina's cats."

"They're your cats too. And mine. And they're their own cats. Sentient."

"Not there." Lina's voice came softly from behind, so as not to startle anyone.

She set a paper on the floor next to Katie so they both could read it. It was a cartoon drawing of a cat with arrows and notations, likely downloaded from an Internet somewhere. The cartoon made note of where a cat wanted and didn't want to be touched. The arrow pointing to the tail where it attached to the butt said, "Oh hell yeah." The one at the belly: "Do you like having fingers?"

"Katie will roll onto her back when she's really feeling safe with you. This does not mean that you rub her there. It is merely a message to a cat's human that you take to your heart and treasure because it means she considers you safe to be around. At least at that moment. She doesn't do it often. If the stars are in correct position, it is possible to give her a belly rub and she'll enjoy it. But do make absolutely sure she's going to allow it. Katie. Katie-Darling."

Katie opened her eyes to see Lina crouching next to her. Lina spewed baby talk at her and then quieted. Lon could feel her trying to get the idea across to the cat: **Tell them what you feel. How does that feel, Katie-Watey?**

Lon felt Lina's go-ahead. He'd spent the last half hour trying to tune into this cat, so at least he now had experience at that. He touched her – on the back shoulder, where the chart said "fine" – and tried the telepathic connection.

He could feel Lina and Jae also in there. Katie definitely thought the pressure was too much. Just a bit. Londo eased back, and Katie relaxed.

"Scratch her."

Lon curled his fingers and gently did so. Katie eased into his touch so he increased the pressure ever so slightly. A little more.

Katie purred.

– – –

They danced alongside the cats that afternoon, except for Molly, who refused to get involved if Lon were part of it, and Fafhrd, whom Londo refused to even try to touch with his bare hands. Everyone else had received generous Londo rubs. He ordered knubby, thick hand towels to be liberally placed around the apartment so he could rub Fafhrd through those, though the technique helped that as well.

CHAPTER

16

"So in addition to you being 'married' to Neutrino," Mimik chortled onscreen, "you're now spiriting away Legionnaires? What, wasn't I good enough?"

"Hardy-har," Lon replied to his second in command. "As I told the commander, I didn't do that. Lina did, in her position as Speaker for the Three Worlds. Chloroplast – Nesh – seems very happy at the situation."

"Hm, hiding behind your wife." Mimik's startlingly focused eyes closed so she could let out more belly laughs. She'd practiced how those worked for quite some time, back when. Laughing like a human didn't come naturally to a giant insectoid.

But mimicking was Mimik's specialty. No one could copy others better than she, and Lon had seen some changelings in his time. She was sharp-witted, a great fighter, a crafty spy. Good to have her on his team, and he made sure she knew how he valued her both as Legionnaire and friend.

She reported as to the team's latest work and missions. Londo couldn't fault her leadership.

"So you're doing all right… without me?"

Leave it to her to spot the pause. "We look forward to your return, but we're making the best of things. People are stepping up. They're sharpening their skills to make up for the hole in our ranks."

"Ah. *Bon.* I guess."

"We still love you." She chuckled. "You have a huge job there that none of us want to take on. Or could. If you need help, of course, we'll be glad to tweak our schedules, go there and help out. Give us time to prepare."

"Of course. And thank everyone for me. Bad enough that I was parttime before. Now I'm… missing in action."

"Oh, we all know where you are. We watch the reports. Everyone's… No, there are two definite sides to opinions about this Aldierran ruse of yours. The polygamous marriage."

Lon stopped breathing and hoped against all hope that Mimik hadn't caught that. She'd been checking something out of the corner of her eyes as she'd spoken.

"Two sides?"

She set the table screen of whatever had caught her attention to the side and regarded him in that bobbing-shoulders way she had when she was amused. "We have all kinds of new jokes in our repertoire. The betting board is filled with rather obscene bets."

"Bets?"

"Calm down. They're just jokes. Everyone is having a good time with this situation. I believe it's to offset the seriousness of the Aldierran Deadline Doom. Besides, how often can Legionnaires make fun of Valiant?" Her head slanted to her left and her eyelids made slits as she regarded him. "Thank the great orb the boards are private."

Lon gave her a crooked smile. "I'll be sure to check them out. And clue Neutrino in about them."

The tilted head gave way to a shake. "Then there are the others."

Londo waited.

"They want Protocol to stifle any mention of your game. They say it besmirches the honor of the Legion. Some people are even calling for you to be officially reprimanded, though I don't hear much of that aimed toward Neutrino."

His stomach clenched even as he tried to maintain an amused but irritated facade.

"Perhaps you should speak to Protocol. Or the subcommander. Get this straightened out before it can affect morale."

"Or Legion honor." Londo licked his lips before he added, "I'll give it a long think. Thanks."

– – –

Nesh Inagar looked about, seeming uncertain in this deserted, hilly setting.

Was Lon whom she was uncertain about? He and Jae had sat down with her last night to explain the Triune. The news had visibly set her aback. Lon could almost see how she tried to shove the shock aside so she could discuss it with them in an objective way. But when they left her they could both feel the unease and doubt she radiated.

They'd told her she could back out of the deal if she wanted, but today she'd shown up as scheduled.

Londo explained to her, "These are fifty open square miles. Toxins have been cleared out. We've conditioned the soil to the best of our ability. Here and there I've transplanted established trees, but much of this has been newly grown, newly planted."

Chloroplast looked at him in that way so many through the years had. He was a hero to her. Still. He needed to act like that, or at least seem to be in control of himself. He had a world to save, and she was now on his team.

He'd always tried to be polite to her the few times their paths had crossed, but had never felt she was much use as a megapara.

That is, in the Legion.

On Aldierra she was another thing entirely.

Nesh knelt to examine the barely-leafed twigs set in the otherwise empty ground, approximately twenty feet apart from each other. Here and there were dots of smaller plants with a few leaves on them, some green, some purple or red. Even so, the land seemed stripped of life.

"It's been seeded," Lon lamely added. Would she care? "It rained last night. It's supposed to sprinkle a few hours for each of the next four nights."

She was still silent, but looked up and then around to take in the full landscape and its fledgling plants.

This particular swath made a wide arc along a river that – amazingly, for Aldierra – seemed clear and clean. Jae and his Aldierra Corps had been concentrating on watersheds through the area. A softly violet haze covered the ground, which Nesh would know was a temporary way of preventing erosion. The lines of orange fencing tracing the slopes provided a hardier level of erosion control.

A small squad of photojournalists grouped together out of her way, ready to take in whatever would happen.

"We can blow off the camera crew for a few days, if you want," Lon quietly offered.

She stood. "I'm glad you Starharts convinced me to change my costume." Nesh smiled shyly at Valiant. "This is something I can feel comfortable in. I think it will also photograph well." She sighed. "Publicity is important with this project in particular."

"It is. Good publicity, that is, like you being here," Lon replied. "I'm glad we could convince Stoan to let you keep your Legion Array. It will help with your mobility and range. Work at your own pace. Be sure to give us a call whenever you need us, and feel free to use our planetary transporters. They're now yours as well. We also have a flitter available, which might come in handy transporting…" He shrugged. What would she be transporting? "People, plants, guards. Whatever.

"I hope your quarters are comfortable. You can change them any way you like. Just give the staff orders. Or you can move somewhere else if you don't like the Landmark Fifty. Jae will see to security if you do that. Lina will have meals delivered wherever you are. Tell her what you like. Contact her if you need any other supplies. We have PR and media people available for you, and can link you with about any kind of expert you might need. Staff: Contact Lina or her chief. They hire good people. Contact Jae if you feel something is off in the landscape, and see if he can help. Call me if you need something, uh…"

"Moved." Nesh smiled at him.

"Or bashed. I'll leave you to it, then?"

He stepped back, unsure of just what it was she was going to do, how she'd present herself. Or even if she'd begin now.

She lifted slowly in the air. Her new costume was not the skin-tight Legion apparel he was used to, but layer upon layer of translucent, sparkling pastel fabric that unfolded like flower petals in the air. A pretty bodysuit under it all kept her modesty, and she wore an air filter necklace so she wouldn't have to strap a device to her face.

She rose in a lazy spiral as she raised her arms to the land.

Something began.

Lon felt it before he saw anything. It was like… Like tiny spots of joy peeking out from the ground here and there. Like… life awakening.

The twigs twitched around where she hovered. The tiny leafy things began to sway.

Then they began to grow.

Itsy sprouts emerged from the soil.

You could see it before your eyes.

It wasn't the entire landscape, just a circle around her, but things were growing, stretching toward the sky.

The camera crews gasped in awe. The happiness blooming in the air lifted Londo' heart. Some of the darkness that had gathered around him loosened its hold. Nature was celebrating.

When the trees got to about ten feet in height, branched out over the ground, leaves sprouting as quickly as they could, Nesh drifted on, there to bring more joy and growth to the plants Lon's landscaping army had planted.

It was jaw-dropping magic, a miracle that moved with her.

Nesh couldn't make the entire world grow but she could certainly start an incredible number of patches of woodland. They'd have to make sure she concentrated on the major nature paths, which were the ones they were working with first.

This. Might. Work.

— — —

Jae's Corps had progressed halfway down the Saba River and were making good progress as well on the Krakalee. He decided that everyone now had enough experience that he branched out to more continents in earnest and began an intense PR program to entice volunteers.

Lon went to Libernia to clear land to regain the vast grassy plains that had once been there, leading to the Bentmark wildlife corridor. Nurseries could only produce so many specialized plants, so he varied his venues so others could provide different output, and cleared land to house rainforests on Orchin and the Joice.

Lina recruited all-female companies to attend to marshes that looked out to the sea cities that lined the Geonie Sea coast. She found Terran and AffSys women who could direct them. They began in the north and worked their way south as spring approached.

Mace did the same with all-gay groups, but they took the central lowlands of Sha-Green to work. There they also helped grow the landscapes needed in other spots.

Nesh worked in everyone's wake here and there, spotting in greenery as healthy primary plots came available. Eventually those spots would expand to meet each other.

Lon checked everyone's progress and then their schedules. Maybe it was time to expand some more personal plans.

– – –

"Erik!" Lina exclaimed as she spotted him in the hallways of Legion HQ. They were in the living quarters section of the mountainous building. He was strapped into a stylish floating wheelchair. As he was now freed from all the lumpy healing systems he'd been connected to before, it looked quite comfortable as it zipped along about six inches above ground. Lina could see it had a food replicator built in and some symbols that indicated built-in massage and such. Erik was watching a video message as he came toward her, and she stepped aside in case he hadn't seen her. Or in case the chair didn't have collision-averting software.

"Lina!" Erik brought his vehicle to a halt. It swung around so he could proceed at her side, back the way he had come. "What brings you to Sarastor? You're not here to kidnap any more Legionnaires?"

She laughed. "If I were, you'd be first on my list."

He brightened. "Really?"

She paused to consider him. "It might be a good idea at that. Hm, a weather master. You know we're going to be doing away with the weather control there soon, right?"

"I hear Sarastor's also in line for it. I'll be interested to see how you manage to talk the planetary managers into that."

"Oh, we will. Somehow. But we do need you on Aldierra for more than just weather, Erik. We need more handsome young men with all their teeth, and a little muscly meat on their bones. You'd improve planetary morale."

He gave her a shit-eating grin.

"I'll ask Lon and Jae about it. Maybe after I get through chatting with Rainj. Do you know her? Kinesis' wife? I think his real name is Jikker."

Erik shook his head. Then he said, "Thought I'd talk with Jae, find out the good gossip about what's going on on Aldierra. He said he'd be in quarters about now."

"Oh yes. He's supposed to signal me when he's ready to return. I wonder where Londo is? Oh, I think he was going to talk with Jae too. Legion business or something I don't have security clearance for." She shrugged. "Well, you all have fun. Don't get Jae too drunk." She waved him off and strode down the hall on her own personal mission.

— — —

Erik stealthily entered Jae's quarters, knowing that Jae rarely locked them, as did most Legionnaires. There wasn't any reason to be afraid of thieves – except the occasional Legionnaire who wanted to borrow from Jae's famous stash of rallo juice concentrate, the only thing that would make a top-of-the-line ratchet. He could grab some and hide it somewhere before speaking with Jae.

He sat straighter in his float chair. Maybe Valiant was in here. If so, they were probably in the large office that was beyond the guest room. He'd idolized Valiant from the first time he'd seen him. Valiant and Maximus, the heroes supreme.

Of course if Valiant were here, there'd be no thievery. If not…

He floated in. Judging from the faint sounds coming from the back of the apartment, Jae had found someone to spend some downtime with. That meant Valiant wouldn't be here. He'd have given Jae his privacy.

Erik tried to figure out who was in there with Jae. Legion rules declared that no one not cleared at least through Level 2 security could be brought on these floors of HQ. Well, Jae knew everyone. He'd been through a good proportion of the Legion's membership, including – in Erik's early days – Erik.

For fairly straight Erik it had been pure youthful experimentation. Well, maybe not so pure. Since then he and Jae had become good platonic friends, and through the wiles of both and intense training on Erik's part, Erik had recently wound up a member of Jae's team.

So Erik decided to keep quiet and mind his own business. Ah, Jae kept the rallo juice in the usual place, hidden in the cabinet next to the trophy room. There were others in Legion HQ who would take it if they knew where it was. Superb stuff. Erik had been afraid it had been moved to Aldierra with many of Jae's other possessions. He tucked the container into a storage compartment within his chair.

Jae's trophy room was a thing of wonder. Erik wasn't sure if Jae had taken some of his trophies with him because it remained filled with every imaginable award, things Erik had only heard of and some he had not. Someday his would look almost as grand.

The noises from the back got louder. Two men going at it. He tried to turn around to leave, really he did, but his curiosity stilled his hand from making the proper motion for the chair's navigation.

Instead he inched down the short hallway from the trophy room to the bedroom, just to take a quick peek. Just to satisfy his curiosity.

Whoever it was grunted and gasped with frantic exertion. They were doing it under the covers, too, and the rhythmic, humping movements were those of... Valiant and Jae!

"By the orb!" Was it he who said that, out loud? He hadn't meant to. But bytheorb, it was Jae and Valiant! Great grigach, it was Jae and... Valiant. Invulnerable, mega-powerful Valiant. Too-strong-to-touch-anyone Valiant. Married Valiant, who had seemed so happy with Lina, the only person whom Valiant could touch safely.

"Chrisse!" "Kicking skurn!"

Jae's head twisted to look at Erik. Valiant's emerged from under Jae's, staring at him. His eyes were wide. So were Jae's, before they narrowed.

Now Erik's Legion training kicked in and he swiveled his chair around at a speed it wasn't programmed for. It tipped wildly.

And Lina stood in the hallway.

"Erik?" she asked.

Lina! Lina mustn't know about this. "Uh, go back," Erik told her. Then he summoned a commanding, no-nonsense Legion voice. "We should go to the living room," he told her.

He tried to herd her that way, blocking the hall as he could.

"Sunstorm!"

Erik winced at Valiant's bellow. Then he heard the two men in the bed arguing with each other.

"Are they both in there?" Lina peeked around him, first left and then right, as he tried to block her view. "What are they doing?"

She ported. He couldn't block that.

So he turned around. Could he prevent a murder? Could he lessen her shock? Valiant and Jae?

Her shriek came from the bedroom with a volume that made Erik jump in his seat at least eighteen inches.

"HOW could you do this!!! HOW could you DO this to me?!! Oh my god. Oh. My. GOD!!" If Erik had been the slightest bit familiar with *Star Trek* he might have recognized the delivery patterns of William Shatner.

His chair zoomed to the bedroom and into it.

Arms akimbo, Lina stood in shock at the scene. Valiant and Jae both had wrapped themselves as best they could in the bed linens, looking sheepish and shocked and agonized, all at the same time.

"Ohh!" Lina exclaimed again.

"*Chérie*, it's not what it looks like," Valiant offered, his gaze switching back and forth between Lina and Erik.

Lina crawled in to the center of the bed, separating them. "Don't '*chérie*' me! Oooh, Jae honey," she pulled Jae to her, enfolding his face between her breasts. "Did he hurt you? Did he try to hurt you? Are you okay?" She rocked him violently back and forth, not letting him leave his cage of breasts and arms. He started to giggle within his confinement. "Were you *trying* to kill him?" she accused Valiant.

"Can't… breathe…" Jae's voice came from the depths.

"Lina, kitten…" Lon said.

"Oh, you brute!! You BRUTE!!! Poor sweet Jae-Jae, tell Mama where it hurts..."

"I would if I could breathe..." Jae gasped.

"Lina, I'm trying to tell you that we can do it now," Londo said.

Lina stopped swinging Jae back and forth. "You can?"

"Just like normal people."

"Oh. Well." Lina released Jae, who fell back onto the bed gasping. She crawled to the pillows to sit with a man on either side, a pleased smirk on her face. "Well in that case, okay."

Erik just stared at the tableau, his mouth hanging open.

Then things began to click.

"Wait a minute," he said. "Jae told me to come here. No specific time, but this general one. And you, Lina." He stared her down accusingly. "You said you were going to visit a friend. Not more than five minutes ago."

"Did I?" Lina snuggled next to where Jae was rearranging his blankets to sit up. "I must have lied. This was going to be much more interesting." She turned to look back and forth at the two men in bed. "Sometimes I like to watch."

Erik's brain clicked double-time. "This was a setup. For me." His eyes squinted. "You're all despicable," he said slowly, gazing at the scene. "What the blat's going on?"

Valiant held up his hand, wiggling his ring finger. Lina held up hers, too. And Jae switched his matching ring to his ring finger and wiggled it.

Erik's legs decided he'd better sit down. Except he already was. "Oh, shit."

"Testing the water, as it were," Valiant said. He was closely studying Erik. Studying his reaction?

"Uh…" Erik let out a sigh. "What, now you kill me? I've seen too much?"

"Not with all these blankets," Jae laughed. "For really active sex I prefer being unencumbered."

"What they mean to say," Lina offered, "is this: Are you shocked? As in, ultimate horror shocked? On a scale of one to ten…"

"Uh. Ultimate surprise shock." Erik said. "I mean… Well, I mean a lot of things. Valiant and Jae? Valiant with anyone but Lina Starhart? How– Well, you know the rest of that question."

"But… Valiant and Jae?" Londo asked him. "The pairing."

"Oh. Homosexual." Erik looked blank a long moment, then gave a slow shrug. "Not as shocking as Valiant having sex. I mean with someone other than–" He grimaced.

"Valiant being gay? Or bi?" Jae asked.

"Shards, I can't even think about that. I think my eyeballs are never going to work in tandem again. Valiant, can you do it with… anyone now?"

"Take a breath, Erik," Lina said softly. "Do decide on an overall answer, one to ten. Rate your impression. It's important."

"Oh. Oh." Erik gave Valiant a good look. The legendary Legionnaire looked anxious. "I suppose… Well. Give me a few minutes. Let it sink in. You okay with this, Lina? Does the commander know?"

"What he suspects is an affair, not a marriage," Jae said. "Between Lina and me."

"So tell him. Tell everyone. Grigach's balls. Can you do it with everyone now, Valiant?"

"That's a damned personal question, Sunstorm. No, I can't."

Some startled movement of Erik's made his chair begin to do a slow turn in place. He let it.

"Married. A threesome. Orgy marriage."

"Not orgy," Jae corrected quickly. "Four is an orgy. Three is normal. Three is a family."

Erik laughed as he brought his chair under control. Then he laughed again. And again. Finally he sputtered, "You Starharts. You break every rule. You'll get away with this, too. When can I put money in the betting pool?"

"That's Lon's call." Jae raised an eyebrow at his husband. "He decides on this."

"You a Starhart too, Jae?" Then before Jae could respond, Erik said, "You're doing this. On Aldierra. It's supposed to be a sham, but it's real. Hunh."

"Hunh indeed," Lina said. "Now on a scale of, oh, one to eight, how…?"

— — —

Back on Aldierra Lon made the happy discovery that his workers helping to clear the land on the Bentmark isthmus were not only expert but sober. He credited that not only to his threats but to Aldierrans in general settling in to this great change. That would surely count in their favor to Aldierra.

Sunstorm hadn't been completely shocked at discovering that Lon was bi and they were all in a poly marriage. There were a few rough minutes in there, but Sunstorm had recovered and hadn't really seemed that concerned about it, all in all.

He began singing. "Shine on, shine on, harvest moon…" to himself as he worked demolishing structures. It was something Mama Ruth liked to sing when she was happy.

"January" WHAM. "February" POW. "June or July." WHUMP! WHUMP!

Was he happy? Yes. Things were going right. They were pointed in the right direction. They could do this.

Maybe he should tell some more people.

His earring beeped.

It was Trey, his PA. "We've got an impending execution," Trey blurted. "I sent Bracken to stop it, but I don't think he can get there in time."

Execution? Someone had four gay men lined up in front of a firing squad.

Lon swung around and hit the accelerator on his paraspeed, heading southwest. Past the shores of Limbernie, over to the foothills of the Master Range on Sha-Green, overlooking the ocean.

He landed with his shield out and extended fifty feet to either side – just in time to catch the first laser blasts. For a split moment he'd considered having the shield reflect the shots, but willed it to absorb them instead.

He stood in front of the four prisoners, facing a crowd that began to shout as soon as they realized what had happened. The terrified victims were tightly bound. Most were bruised and bleeding from having been beaten. One was on the ground.

He turned around to assure them, "No one will harm you."

The shouts turned into screams of sheer hatred.

"Valiant, you *kaket*!" "*Joot!*" "*Paggert!*"

"Quiet!" he shouted at them, and the sheer volume hurting their ears made them silence for a few minutes.

"Did no one hear us when we told you? Consenting adult sex is legal. You do not harm gays. What you're doing here is attempted murder."

Again the insults and profanities came, aimed squarely at him and what he could do with his proclamations.

"Have any of you *not* had sexual relations with other men?" he sneered at them. "Why aren't you in front of this firing squad? What makes you so holy?"

Screams. Shouts. Howls. Like animals.

"Have these men threatened you? Attacked you in any way besides just existing?"

There were murmurs at that, and Lon met the gaze of the men who made them. "Are you afraid of what they are? Afraid that somehow that reflects badly on you?" He stuck his lower lip out like a petulant child. "'Wah, they make me feel bad.' They scare you. They threaten you to question more deeply just who you are, and you're afraid you won't like everything you see when you do.

"Well. That is your problem, not theirs. We have mental therapists available to you, 24/7. You can begin to heal yourselves, not kill others. Or even bully them."

He triggered a giant screen to materialize above the crowd that gave contact info for those therapists. "Use. This. Service," he ordered.

He'd get nowhere here. Instead he changed the screen and replayed the Three Worlds' proclamation above the crowd about consenting sex. When it had finished, he asked, "Was that too complicated for anyone? Hm? Hm?" No answer. "Who organized this lynch mob? Point them out!"

By now his flitter was lowering from the sky, as he'd summoned it. Bracken's was still an ocean away. The crowd bellowed their hatred of Londo, their disgust at him and the terrible things he was requiring them to condone.

"Point. Them. Out!"

No one would.

"All right. Let the heads of Houses here step forward then. Who holds the honor of their House in their hands?"

That would get them. After a few minutes six men did indeed shuffle forward.

By then Lon had freed the prisoners of their tethers and urged them into the safety of the flitter. They helped each other get in.

Lon faced down the heads of Houses. "You will point out who instigated this farce."

One had the audacity to point at him. Two raised their hands. One of those said, "I take the responsibility for my House." But no one pointed at anyone in the crowd.

Londo growled to himself. "So this is how it will be. I will repeat for those in the crowd who need to hear: We have safe Houses for gays to go to if needed. Check our sites for how to get in contact with them. Where to go for safe transportation to such a House.

"As for the rest who are too cowardly to take responsibility for this illegal act of violence, I will leave it on your consciences, if you truly have any, that your heads of Houses will take the punishment for you. If anyone wants to confess later, I will take that into consideration. Until then, these heads of Houses will be taken to the Great Shit Flats and used for labor. If evidence shows that any of them are truly responsible for this, they will be physically castrated. For the next six months, though, it will be chemical castration until the case is fully decided. Your choice."

He shoved the House heads to the flitter. Three of them carried guns, but Lon used his parabreath to heat them, and all tossed their weapons away while they could still handle them. He stomped on them to make them unusable for anyone else.

How quickly his good mood had evaporated. Been destroyed, more like it.

He felt empty inside. They didn't like him, much less love him. The entire mob. He tried to bring back that vision of an entire world cheering for him; cheering for all the Starharts when they saved Aldierra. It took effort to visualize.

He wanted to hit something. Bash his head against something to get rid of the feeling. Ah, he'd vent on more buildings in the Bentmark. Handy.

CHAPTER

17

Maybe it was because Lina was on Earth that the signal came through so loudly: Chekov's spritely escape scherzo from *Star Trek IV*. Even though it was distinctive, it took her more than a few moments to realize:

It was a Terran cell phone call, not an interstellar one, and

It was Lina's sister.

She gave a "sorry, gotta step away" hand-stop motion to the AffSys workers in the building overseeing the machinery installing communications screens in the four hundred new cubicles that filled these floors. She tapped her earring for communications.

"Barb?" Lina answered the phone by touching her right earring.

Before she could say anything else, Barb screamed, "What the *hell*, Lina?"

"Hey, I'm doing great. How are–"

"What the effing hell doyoumeanmarriedtoValiantandbeingonTVandwhat-theeff–"

"Language!" Lina had to shout it into the air. The workers looked up and she waved them down. "Not you," she mouthed and they returned to their work.

Barb was incoherent. Shouted syllables with a few f-words thrown in were all that came through.

"Barb," Lina said. "Barb! Take a breath. Look around you. I mean it. Just. Look. Around you."

Ah, enough of a picture there. Barb appeared next to Lina, her phone still in her hand.

"Welcome to Montreal," Lina said.

"I–! It's–! Where–"

There were a number of miscarriages between the two siblings' births. Barb was eight years older than Lina. Others had told her that Barb resembled Lina greatly, though that was difficult for her to see. Barb had straight hair that Lina coveted; it never went crazy, much less frizzed. She had a real nose, unlike Lina's nubby one. And she was a few inches shorter than Lina.

"Let's go somewhere we can talk," Lina said blithely. "I was getting hungry anyway. It seems the only way I can have a serious conversation any more with people is by us both shoveling food into our mouths. Well, that's efficient. What do you feel like eating?"

Barb's lips flapped as any sound louder than a squeak refused to come out.

They appeared on a breezy street downtown with most traffic stopped at lights at either end of the block, and parking meters close to the street's buildings instead of the cars they governed. Lon had told her that was for easier snow removal in the winter. It was high spring here, though.

Lina opened a modest door under a sign that said, "Marcus Sous la Montagne," to reveal a flight of narrow steps leading downward. "It's a nice place," she told her older sister. "Act civilized, please. Screaming is not allowed. I hope we don't need a reservation."

Soon they were seated in the private, darkened corner of the cozy bistro decorated in deep reds and wood. Lina and the waiter, Michel, had a short French conversation with the word "anglais" in it ("Since when do you speak French?" Barb asked her), and Michel nodded to Barb.

"We are happy to serve you," he said in English.

"Feel free to try anything you want," Lina told her sister. "Lon brought me here the first time we visited the city. He likes this place because of the food, the privacy, and," she nodded to Michel, "the superb and friendly service."

Michel beamed and soon the sisters were involved in lunch.

"I don't know where to begin," Barb said. Though the food was excellent, she picked at it.

Lina wondered if Barb were truly tasting her lunch, the shock pouring off her was so raw. Lina didn't make that mistake and dug in. Earth food, yas. "Number one," she said around an uncouth mouthful, "I married Londo, who is also known as Valiant. Number two, we are in Montreal, where we're putting up a temporary communications hub for Three Worlds. Number three, you need to meet Jae too. He's part of all this. You'll like him. Number four… uh." What else did Barb need to know?

"You… have powers."

"Oh. Right. Yes, I port around now. Interstellar. I'm the taxi driver to the stars. Number four: I am now Speaker for the Three Worlds."

Barb shook her head at her plate as she speared more poutine. Lina had heard Londo rave about the dish, so she was greatly enjoying her own, this one a vegetarian version.

"And… you go Out There?"

Lina motioned Michel back to the table. "We're mostly Out There now. Just trying to get this communications center set up. We're starting everything from scratch and it's all an emergency and a royal pain in the you-know-where." She looked up as Michel arrived. "Could I get two, no, better make it three more of these? Take-out, please."

Three medium sized covered black trays appeared by her side. "If you could put a note in them, we will return the plates when we're done. I thought Londo would like a serving, but you know him, he eats enough for almost two."

Michel laughed. "He does have a hearty appetite."

"Lon's still not vegetarian, so keep that in mind. The other's for Jae, who is definitely vegetarian. I don't think you've met him. If he's really hungry, he'll eat his serving plus anything Lon has left over from his second portion. So maybe Lon's second serving should be vegetarian?"

She demonstrated the stasi-keeps to Michel by putting her glass of iced tea in one, securing the top, and then twirling the keep around. When she opened it again, the tea didn't have as much as a ripple on its surface.

"*Sacré–*" Michel gasped.

"Yes, absolutely," Lina said as she retrieved the tea. She'd been good and ordered it decaf. "They keep everything the exact temperature and structure as when you put them in there. Nothing goes bad. It's very handy. Londo's trying to collect as many of these as he can because there are too many times when we come home and haven't eaten and we don't want to wake the staff to get fed."

She paused to smile ruefully. "And when what the staff wants to feed us is just awful crap. I need to add to the stack more than I have. I get around more than Lon or Jae do."

Barb had watched the demonstration with a squeak. When Michel left, she said, "Out. There."

"For a couple months now. I was under house arrest on Sarastor for about a week and then a week here, and after that we had the Mind Control Tour and traveled to a number of different worlds along the border of the Affiliated Systems and the Yanist-Glory Empire. That was supposed to have been a week, but we used stimulants to keep us awake and stretched the daily schedule and it was different worlds with different day lengths, you know, and who knows how long it actually took?"

Barb slowly nodded.

"So now we've been on Aldierra for a while and will be mostly for the next seven-ish months. They're under a strict deadline." Lina touched her earring and paused for a few seconds as Barb stared at her.

"Sorry, I have to take this," Lina said.

There were problems with the supply lines and the portalets for the eco-armies on the move. "Refer this to Field Marshal Bracken," Lina finally decided. "I think the reserves on the Ivory and Gold units can handle this in their respective hemispheres. They're close enough to both the armies and the supplies. I won't be long here. I don't think. We want to move those ground scrapers into the Bentmark before tomorrow."

"What was all that?" Barb demanded. "You spouting gibberish. Are you trying to impress me? Think you're so important now that you've married Valiant?"

Lina's earring went off audibly. "One more," she told Barb. She tried to remember the proper hand signals.

A screen appeared in mid-air. Front and center:

"I was wondering when anyone in your family would notice," Hal said. He was in glorious full Maximus uniform and spotted Barb.

She sucked in a breath.

"Are you spying on me?" Lina asked. It wasn't particularly perturbing; not in this instance.

"Lon alerted me a few minutes ago."

"Ah. Maximus, my sister Barbara Yates. Barb, Maximus."

Hal nodded at Barb. "There are security procedures your family need to know. We've already installed a good amount of safety features in your homes and cars, Ms. Yates, but you need to learn the finer points and collect the portable units. Your children will have to learn how to act as well. We don't want harm to come to any of you."

"Uh. Uh. Yessir." Barb was obviously flummoxed.

Lon's screen came up, accompanied by Jae's. And wouldn't you know it, Wiley and Andri were together on a separate screen as well. All were in uniforms. Impressive. Well, maybe not Wiley's since his didn't look like a uniform, but rather lab wear. For once his hair was tame. Maybe that was because Andri was with him, Lina thought hopefully.

"Who won the pool?" Wiley asked. In English, the lout.

Barb stared at the blue-skinned man.

"You did," Andri said with the screen translating her into English. She crossed her arms in front of her as she glared at Wiley. "Most people gave up on it, it took so long for someone there to find out. I think you cheated."

"Wouldn't put it past him," Jae said. "So this is Barb. Hello, Barb. I'm Jae. You've met–"

"Hello again, Barb," Londo said.

"The Mega-Legion has its own security procedures," Andri said.

"Barb, this is Andri. Uh, cape name of Nurunori. She's the subcommander of the Affiliated Systems Megaforce Legion, kinda Jae and Lon's boss. And Wiley's, too. That's Wiley. Dr. Wilder Mem-Bazer, cape name and real name all in one." Lina pointed them all out.

"You'll coordinate with us?" Hal asked Andri.

"Lon has the info ready. I think Jae had some additional ideas."

"Good. Lina can port in the equipment I'll need to set up. When do you inform your parents, Lina?"

"Get some of that poutine to go, kitten."

"Already ordered, for you and Jae both," Lina reported.

"With meat for me."

It was time to tease him a little on this. "You sure, Lon?"

"You're not going to turn me, never!" Lon repeated his vow with a laugh. "Though I wouldn't mind a side of veggies with it. It's probably healthier that way. Gotta keep up my strength."

"Okay. I don't know about my folks, Hal. Maybe they'll never find out."

"Not good enough. If nothing else, it's for their own safety. You don't want them bumbling about, walking into danger when they could avoid it."

"Yessir." Lina looked at Lon and Jae. "Suggestions."

But it was Barb who spoke up. "A picnic. We can have a picnic this weekend. Do the announcement then. Invite Mom and Dad, have the kids there."

"And the smelling salts," Lina said.

— — —

"I can't believe they still don't know," Jae wrestled with the last few buttons on his Terran shirt.

"You're just angry because you lost the bets," Londo said. "*Eh bien*, I lost the bets, too. And I'm not angry about it. I'm angry about them." He kicked his new sandals nearer the bed, where they'd be easier to put on. "They mistreated her. At first I thought she might be... exaggerating a bit. You know how kids can misread things. Then I had dinner with them." Lon paused over his footwear in order to help Jae with the stubborn buttons, careful not to accidentally pop them off. "I looked up what I could. There's not much on record, but what there is, what you can infer from it, is messy." Job successfully completed, he patted Jae's chest and returned to his shoes.

"All Terran families aren't like this." It was more a question when Jae said it.

"No. Not to that extent. Many are great. Some are far worse, though."

Jae sighed. "She left them years ago. There aren't any more kids around for them to screw up."

"Except their grandkids. Except our kids, when we have 'em."

"So we won't let them near them."

"Hal thinks she should press charges. "

"Have they changed? Has *he* changed over the years? Lina said her father had a court order to see a therapist, but it was for some other thing, not child abuse. Did that help him any?"

"How should I know? According to Hal's research, everyone thinks Kelly is such a wonderful guy, a real family man. No one outside the family is going to be able to tell us the truth. And I doubt many within the family will do so either."

"Which is going to make it… messy." Jae turned Lon around so they were face to face. "We have a decision. We can go there and scare the flapping dermott out of him, maybe even rough him up a bit, threaten him with a lawsuit which will embarrass the family..."

"Which might not be a bad thing at all," Londo growled.

Jae put his arms around him. "Or we can pretend like nothing's ever happened. Like they were normal parents and that Lina grew up in a perfectly, ahh… *all-American* home. Normal folks, meeting their in-laws and their in-laws' friend for a normal, all-American picnic." Jae let his lips brush Londo's cheek. "Everyone's happy, everyone's polite, and maybe, just maybe, there's a chance for healthy relationships somewhere in the future."

A little smile came to Londo's face. He looked up at Jae. "You make it all sound sensible."

"It is."

"But they hurt Lina."

"They can't anymore."

"You should have heard them when I met them. He was sniping at her. Constant criticism. Her mother didn't defend her."

"I watched your video. So we can tell them politely that it's not okay for them to do that anymore."

Jae could almost hear Lon's teeth grind.

"Look," he told Lon, "think of them as... lord high ambassadors from the Unaffiliated World of Earth. You can be polite to ambassadors. And respectful, without letting them walk all over Lina."

"They won't walk all over me," she said as she came into the bedroom. "I think I may have learned a little self-respect over the last few years."

"And I've always heard that adults revert to being children again when they are around their parents." Jae smiled gently at her.

"So I'll watch it. Ambassadors. I like that."

"And then we've got to be the ambassadors tomorrow," Lon reminded them. They had a group of politicians and military honchos from all Aldierran continents meeting here. "What do we have for them?"

"The staff says it will be the usual high fallutin' officials reception fare," Lina said. "They're going to zhuzh it up for us though. Everything is on schedule. The appropriate specialists have been notified."

Jae secured the new cowboy hat Lon had given him, which was specially made not to abrade the tips of his ears. It hid them very well. In the kitchen Lina loaded Londo's arms with two long, glass-like dishes covered with aluminum foil.

"You cooked?"

"Absolutely, so don't drop these. I made two, count 'em, two casseroles because I bet you anything that Mom's fried a bunch of chicken or tossed some bacon grease into all her veggies for flavoring."

"You told her—?"

"—That some of us are vegetarians. Chances are that either she'll forget or that Dad'll bully her into ignoring that as some kind of comment, or that she'd just do it because you've got to have lots of fried chicken and bacon grease at a picnic. It's a rule. There'll be potato salad and slaw. Both will be safe to eat, Jae."

Solemnly Jae nodded at the information.

Lon adjusted the dishes so the top didn't squash the contents of the bottom one. "Let's get some drinks. If we stop at Starhaven first I can dig out some lawn games too. This place has a field, right?"

"I think so," Lina said before she prompted, "Now, everyone remember—"

"No announcement until dessert," the two men chorused.

— — —

Since Londo carried the casseroles on top of a cooler, Jae and Lina clutched ring toss and cornhole equipment, with Jae also managing a cloth bag filled with presents. Bribes, Jae guessed. Londo wanted to make sure everyone in the world loved him. Then again, perhaps this was Terran tradition.

They ported onto a small dirt and gravel parking lot surrounded by an open forest. A narrow, clean river meandered nearby.

Jae scanned the environs. The day was bright; the sky, blue. The weather and breeze were mild. Earth air tasted so fresh, and Jae gulped in as much as he could. Fairly aerodynamic ground cars of different styles sat near the grassier sections, often under some of the abundant trees. Congregating stations had been set up at equidistant points around the lot. Hip-high metal tables sent up spindly columns of smoke, while much wider wooden tables with attached benches allowed people to sit and eat. Food smells and children's playful shouts filled the air. And of course, this being Earth, music of different styles came from each group.

The three took a moment to collect their bearings and then set off, target in site. "Grill for cooking," Lon told Jae about the metal tables, and the word clicked into place. Lina pointed out the strangers to Jae as they approached. He'd already seen Lon's recordings as well as researched them, but he nodded all the same.

Mother: Emma. Father: Kelly, a shortened version of his surname. Sister: Barb; met her the other day. Brother-in-law: Bubba. Niece: Pegi.

From out of the parkland an animal galloped toward them. It let out a sharp, low barking sound and didn't look like it was going to slow down. It was manic. In less than a moment Jae dropped his equipment and bag and stepped into a defensive stance in front of Lina.

Even so, the black and white furred creature was entirely focused on his wife. Was it hungry? Crazed?

"MacDuff!" Lina called. "MacDuff!"

Jae's defensive posture faltered. Lina did not seem concerned about the attack, even as the animal almost knocked her down with its lunge. It went for her face, but its tongue seemed to be its primary mode of attack. Its entire body shook back and forth and it let out noises like "Ralf! Ralf!" Though it took a momentary break and regained its four-legged footing, it again jumped up, its forelegs planted on Lina's chest. Again with the tongue and the ralfs.

Its tail switched frantically as it hopped on its back legs.

But Londo was not worried at all. He glanced at Jae and his mouth formed an "o."

"Did I edit him out of the video I gave you?"

The creature's excitement extended now to Londo, who kept firm grip on the casseroles as he laughed, and then it was Jae's turn.

The animal jumped up at him. Jae reared back. "Do I hit it?"

"No! This is MacDuff," Lina exclaimed. "Down! Duff, get down."

"He's a dog," Londo said, and MacDuff turned his attention first back to Lina, and then to Londo. "A good dog. Good boy. MacDuff."

"MacDuff." Jae repeated. Dog. Domesticated animal, a pet. That made the tail movement a "wag."

"He gets excited," Lina said as the dog returned his attention to her. She knelt on the ground and… rubbed him. Petted him. The dog licked her all over her face.

Different from the cats, yet similar.

"I forgot the hand sanitizer." Her eyes clenched hard during licks. The ralfs became "wuffs." "Duffer. Duffer-dog."

"Starhaven," Lon said, and within moments a large bottle stood at his feet while Lina continued to pay attention to the dog. Londo used the contents and passed it to Lina when the dog backed off, tail still wagging.

Jae peered at the creature. When the dog looked at him, he matched gazes, trying to feel the difference between dogs and cats, and MacDuff began to growl. "Sorry," Jae told him. He reached out–

"Squat to his level. Give him the choice to smell your hand first," Lon ordered quietly, and Jae's hand froze in mid-air.

The dog sniffed it, then sniffed Jae's arm.

"Now," Lon said, and Jae patted its head.

"Good dog."

MacDuff shook himself and grinned a loose-tongued dog grin at Jae, wagging his tail.

"You have been accepted," Lina told him with a smile.

Jae looked up to see that Londo had given the entire situation one of his Grins of Approval. He hefted the cooler onto his left shoulder with the casseroles tucked into the crook of his right arm.

Barb was the first human to greet them. "Ah, I don't think that cooler's light enough to do that," she advised Londo. Her eyes were wide at him as the reality must have sunken in.

"It isn't?"

She shook her head. Londo lowered the cooler and slouched slightly to his side, as if he were carrying a fully-loaded troop cargo ship instead of lunch.

"Better," Barb said.

"Uncle Lon!" Young Pegi, Lina's niece, ran up to him. "I wanna Pepsi. They don't have Pepsi. You gotta Pepsi?"

"Please," Jae prompted.

"You're mean," she pouted. Then her lower lip stuck out for a different reason. "I don't know you."

"Pegi, this is Jae."

"Oh." She squinted at him, really got a look at his face. "Oh!"

He didn't know why he even took notice of such any more. Everyone did it. "Your Aunt Lina makes me say it, so I make you say it," Jae told her.

"Oh. I wanna Pepsi."

"'Please, may I have a Pepsi?' I don't know–"

"Yes, we have some Pepsis," Londo said. "Even though Coke is better."

They waited for Pegi to speak.

Finally she stamped her foot. "Please, may I have a Pepsi, Uncle Lon?"

He smiled at her, setting the cooler down on the ground next to the large picnic table. "If it's all right with your mom," he told her.

"It's okay," Barb relented, and Londo reached into the cooler to get her the drink. She drank two sips before setting it down to run after the excited dog.

Everyone turned as a small, paint-patched pickup screamed into the parking lot, brakes squealing and gravel spitting as it parked. A lanky teenaged boy Jae recognized from photographs as Lina's nephew, Drew, jumped out of it, leaping over the chain that marked the edge of the parking lot from the park.

"Aunt Lie!" His run slowed down as he spotted Londo and Jae. That was right; Drew hadn't met Londo yet.

"Drew!" Lina exclaimed. She rose to greet him.

No hugs in this family, Jae noted. Lon had mentioned the same thing. It wasn't just Lina who'd been afraid to hug people.

As Drew joined them, Lina introduced Londo. "Here's your new Uncle Lon." Jae could feel her almost introduce him the same way, but pause. "And here's Jae. He's a good friend."

Jae could definitely feel Londo clench at that. Good, that Lon could feel a little of the cost of secrets.

He held on to his faith in the dearest man in his world, and hoped it would prove true.

— — —

"Hands off the presents, Pegi!" Lina ordered for the twentieth time at least. Londo was engaged in a deep conversation with her brother-in-law Bubba, near to where Dad stood at the grill. Jae was over there playing with Drew and Mac-Duff now instead of guarding the gifts from Pegi. She considered porting everything back to Starhaven so that she wouldn't have to keep reminding the girl.

"I wanna see what you got me."

"You'll see when we open the presents. Right after we eat."

"I wanna see now!"

"You don't have to get a present. We can save it for your birthday or give it to someone else. You got that?"

Pegi stuck her lower lip out in a pout. "How 'bout these others?" she said, lifting a box and shaking it. She reached for the wrap.

"Pegi! Put it down!"

But Pegi kept going. Barb came up behind her and slapped her wrist. "Put it down!"

Pegi started to cry. Lina could tell that there was just startlement behind the tears, but Pegi milked them for effect.

"We'll stop and get you something extra on the way home," Barb soothed her daughter. "Stop crying."

"Don't get her something extra," Lina told her. "We got her a present. That's enough." Pegi turned to run to her grandma, to cry at her. "Don't reward her for acting like a baby. She's ten years old!"

"Eleven. And I'm not rewarding her."

"So you tell me what you were doing. Every time I see Peg, if one of you tries to discipline her she goes running to the other one and they say, 'it's all right. Here's a present.' How's she going to learn to grow up like that?"

"You don't have any kids," Barb muttered.

"That's right, I don't. But I will someday. And I see how covering up the family guilt with spoiling makes a kid turn out."

"She's not spoiled," Barb said as Emma came over, led by Pegi.

"She only wants to open up one present," Emma said as Pegi beamed at her. "Here, Pegi, you can open up mine."

"No!" Lina said, a little louder than she'd intended. She grabbed her mother's present and held it up, out of Pegi's reach. "We haven't given it to you yet. You can't open it yet, you can't have her open your gift. We're giving the gifts, Pegi, and we say you can't open any of them yet."

"And I'm your mother, Pegi, and I say you can't open any of them yet. You can't open Grandma's present for her. Just your own."

Pegi burst into tears.

"She's going to be a great actress when she grows up," Lina said sourly as she regarded her niece. Pegi gave her an evil glare and ran off to bedevil the dog. "Either that, or..."

"I know how she's going to end up," Barb said with a sigh. She looked at her mother. "I just feel so guilty all the time. The kids are treated so differently. It's Dad. He makes it so clear that Drew's his favorite. Dad's always been the problem."

"No, I should have stood up to him," Emma said tiredly. "And it's not his problem; his father was the problem."

"And his father, and his father, and his father before him." Lina stamped her foot. "Well somewhere along the line, someone's got to stand up and say enough! I'm through with this shit!"

"Lina!" Emma was shocked.

"Someone has to," Lina retorted hotly. "Otherwise when does it stop? How many people's lives does it consume? Have you considered some kind of therapy for her, Barb? Or even family counseling, so we all can stop this from going further. Lon and I have talked about it; we'll help finance it if you want it."

"But no therapy for miss perfect?" Barb spat at her.

"I got hold of two of the best therapists that have ever been born, Lon and Jae. They've helped me enormously. Lon got rid of my phobia all by himself.

As Emma returned to the picnic table, Lina said, "I'm also seeing a professional therapist. Just started a while ago, and she's been great. We all need it. I mean it, Barb. We'll help on the bills. Just find a good therapist and either just put Pegi through their office, or your whole family, or both. Lon's shrink has already given us some names of good doctors in this area."

"Lon has a therapist?" That stopped Barb. She looked around for Londo; there he was, talking quietly with Bubba.

"Since he was a kid, on Earth and Out There. He's been through dozens of them," Lina told her. "He says that there've been scores of books written about his problems alone, though they never named him. I've talked with the people who knew him way back when. His father. Jae. They've both told me about how he was – nothing at all like he is now. And Jae: same way, only more therapists."

"Jae? I know I've barely met him but he seems so, well, normal."

"Yes, he is. Now." Lina let that sink in and then laughed. "We're shoveling out therapists on Aldierra to everyone we can. I get a therapist. You get a therapist. Everyone look under their seat and get a therapist."

"Let me think about it," Barb said slowly as her daughter ran by them, grabbing a box out of the pile. She screamed in triumph and held it in the air.

"Pegi!"

Barb and Lina watched Pegi hoot as she ran deeper into the woods. Suddenly Pegi shrieked in anger. "What–?" Barb began, but a movement caught her eye.

Lina had ported the gift box into her own hand. Now she set the box back on top of the pile of gifts before others could see.

Barb considered her daughter. "Therapist," she said again.

— — —

"Damn it, Emma!" Kelly shouted across the clearing as he sorted through their own cooler. "I thought you said you had enough steaks!"

"I do, dear." She hurried to him.

Jae looked up from where he and Drew were playing tug-of-war with the dog. This was something you couldn't do with cats. Fun. And interesting that dog growls sounded so much like cat growls, only he knew that MacDuff knew he was playing. Cats growled only in deadly earnest.

"I just see seven steaks," Kelly pointed. "Count them! Count them!"

"Seven steaks," Emma repeated. "That's enough." She counted off on her fingers. "You, me, Barb, Bubba, Lon, Drew, Pegi. Seven."

"Jae and Lina. That's nine."

"They're vegetarians. Remember?"

"Vegetarians!" Kelly muttered. "Since when do we have to pander to vegetarians? They can eat what we eat, and like it."

"Actually," Jae said in his most soothing voice as he came up from behind them, "we find that we become physically ill if we get hold of meat. That might spoil the picnic. Londo doesn't go that far, but if you look closely you'll see he becomes a little pale when confronted by meat. I think he'll turn soon. Besides, I've discovered that vegetables cost considerably less than meat and meat products. You save money."

Kelly obviously didn't know what to say to this stranger in the cowboy hat. "I suppose guests can eat what they want," he grumbled.

Jae watched Kelly put the steaks on the grill, heard them sizzle and saw the steam rise from them. Cooking at its most primitive. "I've never cooked like this," Jae said. "How do you control the heat?"

Kelly showed him how to check the coals. "So you know Lon's family? For a while?"

"I've known Lon and his father for... oh, over fifteen years now. He's a good man."

"In security."

"Very good at his job. Rather well-known, too."

"But Lon was in security, and now you two are going into... what?"

"Oh, we're still in security. All three of us now. Lon's mentioned how he wants to fix your house up with a security system. He's doing that for Bubba and Barb. In today's world, it's so much better to do everything you can to make sure you're safe."

"Well," Kelly considered, trying to find a down side. "Okay, thanks. It won't cost anything?"

"Not a penny," Jae assured him. "Lon and Lina just want to know that everyone's safe." Jae had very good ideas about what this man had done to Lina when she was a child. How to get around that? How to leave that in the past? "Lina says you're a closet architect. Lon's got his license, and he's finally getting into doing something with it these days. You might want to look at some of his designs."

"Architecture?" Kelly eased back to search out where his new son-in-law was. "Residential?"

"He's working on some large public works kinds of things now, but yes, he does residential as well. He designed Starhaven; that's one of the nicest houses I've ever been in. Well, it will be when it's done. I've seen the final… concepts."

"Starhaven?"

"Where they're going to live. In Wyoming."

Kelly tried to think. "He used to live in Canada..."

"Montreal." Jae nodded. "The homestead will be in Wyoming. We're opening some major offices in Montreal. It's a very nice town. City. Lots of ambiance."

Lina walked up to give the steaks a look. Londo was beside her. "Why don't we open gifts now?" she said. "The steaks might be done by the time we're through."

"Presents!" Pegi shrieked. "At last! Where's mine?!"

She shredded the paper as she dug through, screaming in delight as she unearthed the selfie video kit.

"Neat!" Pegi settled down to unfurl its green screen.

"What does it say?" Drew wondered as he pulled a tee shirt out of the wrapping.

"It's French," Londo said.

Jae whispered into Drew's ear from behind him, and Drew laughed. "No, really," he said.

"Really," Jae told him so no one else can hear. "You're going to have to learn the language to find out the exact wording. Just never wear it near anyone who can read French. At least, not unless you're feeling very, very friendly towards them."

Everyone else oohed and ahhed over their jewelry, Kelly over his wallet, and Bubba popped one of the new "C'est tiguidou!" cozies on his can of beer, laughing at the thought of using it around his friends. Then again, it was guaranteed to cool and keep a beer ice-cold for a full day. Plus it could heat and maintain a mug of coffee for as long as needed.

"Genuine French," Lina assured him. "It means, 'It's all good.'"

"I'm going to have to get another display case for the new matchbooks," Bubba told them as he studied the ones he'd been given. "This is really from China?"

Barb drew Lina aside. "What the hell does Drew's shirt say? Is it really dirty?"

Lina told her, and Barb blanched. "He's not wearing that," Barb determined.

"Can you read it, now that you know?" Lina asked her.

"No, but..."

"Will he settle down and really study his French now?"

Barb made a face. "Probably. Until he can get a confirmation translation."

"And where around here will that happen? He'll have to ask a native about this one. It's extremely colloquial gutter slang and not European French at all. It's Montreal French."

Drew was already pulling his shirt off so he could wear the new one. "Oh, all right," Barb sighed.

– – –

They'd finally sat down to eat. Barb had pulled Pegi back down in her seat when she'd tried to take her plate and run off, and Pegi played with her food. The dog lay on the ground behind Kelly, watching them all for falling chunks of steak.

"Got enough gas in the truck?" Kelly asked Drew.

Drew perked up. "Maybe a quarter tank."

Lina got the impression that might be a fib.

"Here." Kelly reached into his pocket and handed Drew some tightly-folded bills. "Keep it topped off."

"Thanks, Grandpa. Thanks!" Drew pocketed it quickly.

Watching the cash exchange, Pegi picked up her steak with her fingers to eat it. "Use your fork, Pegi," Barb told her irritably. "Don't be a pig."

"You're not touching this money," Drew warned his sister under his breath.

Peg made a face at him and then considered the rest at the table. "You know," Pegi told her mother with her mouth half-full, pointing at Lon. "Uncle Lon looks just like that guy."

"What guy?" Barb asked automatically when she realized. She glanced up at Londo abruptly. "Don't point. Eat your vegetables." She shoved a serving dish at her daughter.

"They made us study the ParaNet in class," Pegi said as she pushed her green bean casserole around her plate. "And I said, 'My Uncle Lon looks just like that Valiant guy.'" She pointed at Lon. "You have to come to my school some time. They didn't believe me!"

"Now, Peg, Lon doesn't look anything like–"

"What did they teach you about the ParaNet, Pegi?" Lina asked. She could feel both husbands clench and then surrender.

CHAPTER

18

"Oh, they're a bunch of paras who guard the world. You know. We had to learn them all." She counted on her greasy fingers. "Maximus and Valiant. Dragonlord and all his guys. They work for him, but the Para-Net uses them too. Dragonwing; he's one of those. He's cute. White Puma and Olympia and Forte – howcum there are only three women in the Network, Mom?"

"I don't know, Peg. Eat."

"There are a few more than that," Lon said carefully.

"And, um, the Ruby Guard. But he doesn't count. He got kicked out."

"They don't kick out members," Emma corrected her granddaughter.

"Do so. They kicked him out. He's a bad guy."

"Who else, Peg?" Lina asked.

"Um. Jù… Jùfēng. He spells his name funny. He's Chinese. The Bolt and Blitz. Are they related? They have the same power. Ah. Who else? Who else?"

"Let's see," Lon said. "Jelena – that's another woman, Pegi. Black Magnum. Those are all the full-time members. Green Mage is one of the important part-time members. But Valiant's not full-time any more. He's auxiliary now."

"Auxiliary? Whazzat mean?"

"It means he only goes when they specially call him," Bubba explained. "Where'd you hear that, Lon?"

"Mrs. Deerfield didn't say…"

"It only happened a few days ago," Londo explained. "Maybe she didn't hear that part of the news. There's been a lot of other things going on lately."

Pegi nodded. "Au-xil-iary." She took a bite of potatoes. "Is he au-xil-iary because he got married?"

"Married?" Kelly reached for the steak sauce. "Pegi, Valiant isn't married. Don't be an idiot. Eat."

"Yes he is. Valiant is too married," Pegi said as she took another bite. "Mom?"

"No, he's not," Kelly said flatly. "You should study harder."

"Well, actually," Londo said hesitantly, "I believe he did get married. Fairly recently. When was that, *chérie*? We were out of the country then..."

"Well, let's see," Lina said, counting on her fingers. "Ah... I think it was March 21st. The same day we got married, honey."

Emma looked up sharply at that.

Lina had used the date of the Triune marriage instead of the first one just to Londo. Jae pointed at Drew, who had been staring at Lon. "Your food's getting cold."

"That reminds me, Lina, did you bring the photos?" Lon took a large spoonful of potato salad to plop onto his plate. "We managed to find some photos after all. A friend happened to take some shots of the wedding."

Lina reached down to her side below the tabletop and when her hands came back up, they contained two manila envelopes. She glanced at Jae, a look of apology. Lon grimaced at that, but this had to be done in stages. These photos would be of the first wedding, the one that was annulled later to perform the Triune, and that only contained Jae as the officiant. "Oh yeah. Here they are," she said and passed one to Barb, one to Emma.

"Oo, pretty place," Barb said as she let her husband see them too.

"Thanks," Jae told her. "I programmed it."

Drew peered around his mother's hands at the photos. "What, it's like a holodeck? From *Star Trek?*"

"Holosuite," Lon corrected. He was too busy watching Emma's reaction. The picture clearly showed Legionnaires in full costume attending. She wouldn't recognize the people, but they certainly looked paraheroish to anyone.

"Where—" she squeaked. "Where was this?"

"A planet called Sarastor," Lina said smoothly. "We really had just gotten out of quarantine; there wasn't time to bring any family in."

Kelly looked up at that and held his hand out for the picture, snapping his fingers. He looked at it for a moment. "This doesn't look like the South Pacific to me," he said.

"They just said, dear," Emma told him. "It's... another planet. Sara..."

"Sarastor," Lina said. "That place is inside the headquarters for a group called the Affiliated Systems Megaforce Legion. Lon's a member. So's Jae. Well, they're both parttime now."

Drew looked wide-eyed at Jae, then at his father, then back.

"I wanna see! I wanna see!" Pegi reached for the picture.

"Use your napkin, Pegi," Barb said as she passed more to Bubba. Drew leaned over to see them, his eyes wide in wonder.

Pegi hurriedly wiped her fingers and leaned as far as she could. "Oh!" she said as she saw all the uniforms. "You are! You're Valiant! Uncle Lon–!" She looked at the picture again and prodded it with an index finger. "Howcum you're not wearing your costume?"

"Because I was getting married," he tried to explain. "The outfit was a gift from the Three Worlds. They're who we work for full time now."

"You really are... Valiant," Emma said, her voice quaking. "Ohmigosh."

"Are you a Three World, Aunt Lie?"

"Ohmigosh."

MacDuff dove for dropped food.

"We work for them, but that's what everyone's calling us now because we sort of stand for them. I'm the Speaker for the Three Worlds."

Kelly held the photograph up in the air as if it were an indictment. "You're Valiant?! Lina, how could you?"

"Very happily, thank you."

"You... You aren't..."

"That man at church the other week," Emma turned to her husband. "I told you he looked exactly like... exactly like..."

Lon nodded. "Ah, is that what he did. Hal said he'd met you, undercover."

"Maximus," Emma said faintly.

"Ridiculous," Kelly said, putting the photograph down on top of a bowl of pickles. Emma snatched it up before it could be ruined. "Making like she's important."

"She *is* important," Jae said.

"If you don't believe her, maybe you should contact the ParaNet," Londo said very softly. He was not going to get angry at this man! He wasn't! "She was made an auxiliary ParaNetter."

"Auxiliary," Pegi said.

"What for?" Kelly asked incredulously. His eyes narrowed on Lon. "You're a ringer. You have to be a ringer. Has she been talking to herself again? Saying that she's talking to angels? Like she's God or something. Listen, Lon, or whoever you are, anyone who'd believe that would be a complete idiot!"

"I guess we really should have put this off until dessert," Lina said miserably. "Sorry. Everyone's dinner has been spoiled."

"Are you an... auxiliary ParaNetter, too, Jae?" Pegi asked.

"Uh huh," he said. "Same timeframe. Let them talk."

"Okay."

"Anyone who'd believe you were... Valiant, for god's sake... would have to be an idiot too!" Kelly jumped up, a tricky thing to do at a picnic table, almost ripping his napkin in half. He stepped out of the bench. "This joke has gone on far enough. Lina, you're a liar and you always will be. Always trying to boost your image! Always trying to be something that you're not."

Slowly Londo stood up. "You're not allowed–"

"Don't call me a liar," Lina said softly but defiantly. "I've put up with a lot of verbal abuse all my life, and I just will not have it any more. Enough is enough. If you want to yell at me, at least do it out of earshot of the children. But do not insult me and do not try to bring me down to your level."

"Why doesn't someone take Drew and Pegi away?" Jae suggested.

"Come on, Pegi," Barb insisted.

"But why?"

"Because there's going to be an argument. Bring your plate if you want to. Come on, Drew."

"Oh, Grandpa's always yelling at someone."

"Well now, someone's going to be yelling back," Londo growled.

"Lon..." Lina put her hand on his chest. "Ambassadors, remember? No violence."

Jae swung around on the table bench. "Ambassadors, Londo," he said quietly.

Lon growled deep in his chest.

"Pay him off, and his friend, too," Kelly pointed at Londo. "Or don't you pay them... in money?"

"Don't," Lina warned him. "Don't go there. Calm down, Dad. Sit."

"Oh, so that's what it's about? So you're powerful enough to give me orders, huh? Listen, little girl, I'm still your father–"

"Even though you tried very hard not to be." Lina gritted her teeth.

"Look, Dad," Londo began.

"Don't call me Dad, you actor."

"Look, Kelly, then..."

"Mr. O'Kelly to you."

"Then you can call me Mr. Starhart. Or Valiant."

Jae stood between the both of them. "Waitaminnit. Peo-ple. Let's get one thing straight. It's very simple. Londo here is really and truly Valiant. Lon, do something Valiantish. What would prove it to you, Kelly?"

"And you–" Kelly regarded Jae with a jaundiced eye. "What are you in this for? Do you just hang around Mr. Valiant there? Go on, Va-liant. Cut down some trees with your bare hands."

Lon leaned over to pick up the picnic bench with Bubba, Emma and Lina still on it. He lifted it over his head as Bubba and Emma grabbed onto it, exclaiming, and then set it gently down. "Is that good enough for you?"

"That's good enough for me," Jae said quickly as Kelly's mouth opened. "As for me, Kelly, I change things." He leaned down to pick up a beer can from where it had fallen off the table. He turned it into gold and then into a cloud of vapor. "This beer was a bit too gassy for my tastes," he said. "Lina, do something Starfleetish."

"I don't have to..."

"Just to establish a starting ground," Jae said. She nodded, and Kelly disappeared to reappear instantaneously on the opposite side of the table.

"There," Jae said as Kelly's mouth opened and closed like a fish gasping for air. "That establishes our credentials. We are the Three Worlds, and if anyone here besides Barb had even glanced at the news in the past weeks, you would have known it. As it was, Lon and I lost our Legion bets about it. Of course Lina said you wouldn't find out. Well, she's known you for longer than we have."

"It's a trick," Kelly finally said. "Somehow, it's a trick. You arranged for us to be here. You have it all set up. You're magicians..."

"Why in the world–?" Lina asked, shaking her head. "Okay, Dad's in total denial over there. Mom, how are you taking it?"

Emma just looked to Kelly.

"Mom does not have an opinion until Dad states his," Lina said. "Typical." She sighed. "I suppose this afternoon's activities are at an end for us. Y'all have our phone number whenever you want to talk. It will switch to our interstellar service and catch us wherever we are. In case you've lost it–" She ported in a business card and put it on the table, handing one to Bubba, too.

"Please say goodbye for us to the others," Lina told Bubba. She glanced at her mother. "And permission or not, you *will* be getting a security system in your house."

Londo pointed at Bubba. "Call me about that security we talked about."

Bubba still looked dazed from it all, but he came to himself. "Will do. Take it easy. Uh. Valiant."

The three of them popped out.

CHAPTER

19

The leaden sky glowered, just hinting that the sun might be up. The air was rank, per Aldierran norm. Rain was scheduled three days hence.

It was going to be a good day, Londo vowed to himself. He closed his eyes, took a breath, and recalibrated his attitude. Picnic had been yesterday. Done. In-laws told that they were paraheroes; step one accomplished.

But lord knew when the three of them would tell them about the Triune.

It didn't count on the "what will people think of me?" scale. Different subject; involved a couple of crazy people whom he really didn't think that much of. *Non.*

The three of them had had a thorough conversation about it last night. Lina had checked in with her therapist. She'd be all right.

So. Today: a different day. A day of beginning.

Below Londo, guidelines and digital markers gridded the area, perfectly matching the plans on the screen beside him. The land had been graded with many spots dug far below normal foundation depth. Bedrock in this area was particularly solid and could support deep underground facilities.

Springs had been marked and incorporated into areas that would become parkland. A dozen red flags indicated vents from which easy geothermal power could be collected. Pipes had been installed with temporary caps attached.

Lon checked the plans again and this time added the final view layer: that of a towering green city, though one that terraced down so a significant portion of it got a good view of what would be forested hills beyond. A monorail system would eventually enter that area to accommodate ecopersonnel, tourists, and even provide ground transportation to the next metro area, without unduly exciting any woodland creatures or flora. A narrow, primitive road ran underneath it for occasional maintenance equipment or hikers to utilize.

There was also an archeological site Lon had spotted but not informed anyone about, which was penciled in as a monorail stop for the future. Let the people of this world discover it in their own time.

He cued a street view to meander the city's future version. He'd saved historic front doors, entire facades. Unusual windows. New frontispieces had been programmed in the fashion of centuries ago. In some city quarters the building colors would be bright, eye-catching. In others they'd be sedate and layered.

The pending parks held fountains and flowers as well as playing fields and picturesque walks. Some roads were slated as pedestrian-only. Many buildings utilized unloading docks for aerial vehicles, to keep them off the roads.

He'd busted his butt doing all this. They all had. Now it was time for one final step:

Londo touched a button on his screen.

As documentarians and journalists filmed from above, an army of batchers, print boxes, gantry connectors, and tessercranes rumbled forward below him, followed by a larger one of humans to keep track of it all. The trucks holding raw materials formed the largest and most mobile group, already cycling from front to back to pick up new loads.

In his ear, Jae and Lina reported supply and personnel flows. Londo had made sure all workers knew what they were doing and were not only sober, but excited about working on this project. More people provided remote backup scrutiny from AffSys worlds.

Even as he watched, pipes and foundations began to emerge across the area as machinery crouched from above to mold plastic-like cements in the correct forms. The families and businesses that had been displaced from the river valley could begin moving into this new city next week.

"Allo, Hal." Lon couldn't keep the pride out of his voice as he reported the good news. "It's begun in earnest. We're building."

Life was good.

— — —

"You look great, both of you." Londo admired his spouses as they paused in the restaurant's lobby. Three days ago amid their hectic schedules he'd set up appointments at his favorite Montreal clothiers for them to get proper Terran attire for at least the few occasions they must attend on Earth before their duties branched out to include all Three Worlds on a regular basis. Lina needed a full range of pieces she could wear to business and social functions and Jae… well, Jae needed everything. He should schedule them to consult Londo's stylist, but for now they had the basics.

Sweet basics.

They were both tailored to perfection. Jae's glistening dark outfit made him look even sleeker than normal, dashing to the nth degree and oozing with sex appeal. And Lina's flared rose cocktail dress gave her the appearance of the princess she was in his heart.

"This is the fanciest restaurant I've ever been to," Lina murmured as the maître d' led them to their private dining room. Diners gaped as the group passed. Londo nodded graciously to some, as he'd been taught to do. Don't be a snob.

Yet this was Wadsworth, about as upper-scale a dining spot as one could get in London. It was a favorite of Hal's, particularly for this private room and a staff that could be counted upon for discretion. The quiet music was live, though the quartet was not set up near this area. Appetite-stoking aromas infused the air: spices. Meats – red ones. And alcohols. Londo could smell them all. Under comfortably high ceilings, Lon released a relieved breath he hadn't known he'd been holding on to.

Part of that breath was because his family wasn't maniac like Lina's. Here he'd be able to relax. He needed a break like this, and he was going to enjoy it.

Lon used a hand on her back to steer Lina through the open door, and then did the same for Jae, who'd paused to look around the main dining room. He was likely trying to catalogue what elements denoted "upper class" on this world.

Inside was the celebrated Octagon Room, with its dark, intriguing walls and their abstract wood moulding. Low-wattage lights dotted the ceiling, but abundant candles were also used for intimate effect. A round dining table sat midroom, large enough to seat eight people. Londo had seen a different table in here where twelve could comfortably sit. Tonight was just for family.

Now it was Lina's turn to pause. Maybe she hadn't had a chance to check out the deco– Wait; she'd spotted Else.

Oh damn.

Lon had forgotten to warn her. Too many things had been happening. He should have… Damn damn *tabarnac* damn. He– Too late now.

"Good evening," Jae said to everyone.

"Jae." Papa Mike stood up to welcome them. Hal did the same, but his grinned greeting to Jae was, "Shaggy," which made Jae roll his eyes as it always did. At least it wasn't accompanied by the usual noogie. Mama Ruth was there as well as Else.

Hal's wife.

Chrisse.

For some reason she looked particularly metallic tonight. Though she wore a chic black dress with tasteful jewelry, she still looked like a bald, steel manne-quin.

He could hear Lina's breath catch. Catch again. And then her face blossomed into that smile of hers.

– – –

Lina tried not to gape at her new mother-in-law.

An android!

Not one of those stiff and color LED-decorated movie ones, but one con-structed out of silver that shone and reflected every surface in the room under the candlelight.

Yet her… Else's… features were mobile like a human's, as she gave Lina a pleasant smile of greeting. Her face worked like anyone's would. She had straight teeth that were also metal. Her body movements were smooth, nothing mechanical about them as she fiddled with her napkin.

And she did fiddle with it. Was it an actual unconscious move, or was she trying to set everyone at ease?

She wore a pretty black dress with jewelry. Her lips and eyes were painted what should have been subtle evening shades but which stood out a trifle garishly against the metallic.

How long had Lina been staring? Please, Lord, make it have been a nanosecond.

"Hal. Mama Ruth. Papa Mike," she said as the maître d' pulled out a chair for her. "But we haven't been introduced." She nodded to Else. "I'm Lina. You must be…?"

— — —

Londo could have burst with pride.

"I'm Else," the android wife of Lon's father said. "So glad to meet you at last."

"I've been dying to talk with you," Lina admitted. "Not only to meet, but to get any advice you might have for me."

Else tilted her head to the left. "We are in similar circumstance, but only in some ways."

"In the important ones." Lina took her seat and gave Londo an accusing Look. "I didn't know you were an android. Is that the proper word, or is there a better one I should use?"

Jae's Look at Londo was hidden behind a polite mask of an expression. **I thought you told her,** he accused.

I forgot.

You forgot. Lon!

And then Lon caught Hal's glance. A raised eyebrow. *Chrisse.*

— — —

"I have a lot of questions for you," Lina told Else.

A raising of eyebrows, quirk at the corner of her mouth. "Questions?"

"Well," Lina said as she settled in her chair and the maître d' stepped away, "thank you, you married Hal. I figure you have a lot of useful advice on how to handle things. I don't mean it that way. I mean *things*. Life. Married life with a mega."

And how did Hal, with a build like Mr. Universe, get his suit to look so elegant? Lon's looked stylish and sexy, but Hal was considerably bulkier than Lon.

"Yet you're a mega as well, from what I've been told," Else replied. Her voice had a natural purr to it. Soothing and intimate. How nice.

"Well…"

"What she means," Mama Ruth interjected, "is telling her that she needs to have at least four copies ready of every piece of furniture in your home. Furniture gets broken very easily around certain megas."

Both Hal and Londo had the grace to look guilty.

Jae snorted. "I've seen Lon at work. Wiley can tell you as well. Lon's mangled a lot of Wiley's equipment over the years." He shrugged. "You come to expect it and be prepared. Me, I transformed most of the furniture in both our apartments to some form of impervion. Haven't had to replace anything in, oh, a half-year at least."

"Wish I'd had you around when Hal was growing up," Papa Mike said. "He's a good part of the reason why I had to be successful with my companies. We needed to pay for a lot of damage." Before Hal could say anything, Mike added, "But he learned quickly. So did Londo when he came to live with us."

Lina congratulated herself in feeling comfortable with Lon's genial grandparents. They were both so vigorous and youthful, looking not that much older than their adoptive, uber-famous son. Lon said that was because they traveled to Sarastor often for medical tune-ups. Good to know.

Then again, Hal also looked quite young for his age. Maybe that was part of being Maximus? Aging slowly? What would that mean for Londo? Would the treatments those aliens had given him produce the same results?

Lina nodded at them, trying to memorize their advice. "We have cats," she decided to say. "Maybe a fifth set of backup furniture would be appropriate."

— — —

Lon watched Lina and the gRands as well as Else chatting. It was good to see Mama Ruth and Papa Mike with Else. She so often missed family get-togethers for whatever reason. Hal's excuses – when he offered them – seldom seemed realistic. It was as if he wanted to hide his wife from his family.

The waiter was taking non-alcoholic drink orders. Lon ordered a special roast coffee for Jae with steamed milk and sugar, a good way to break into the taste since he wasn't used to it. Lina asked if she could get decaf tea, which of course she could since this restaurant offered everything beverage-wise, and then ordered it half-and-half. Else asked for coffee the same way Hal took it on special occasions: cold-brew Liberica, black. The gRands were finishing their coffees; they must have arrived before Hal and Else showed up.

While they were waiting, Hal ordered wine to be served after they'd had their coffees.

"We used the ParaNet transporters, dear," Mama Ruth was explaining to Lina as Jae listened in. "They do help us get around."

— — —

The single waiter made his way around the table with coffee and came back with Lina's tea. "Madame," he said as he placed the cup by her setting. A small pitcher of cream went with it.

She stared at it, for a moment uncomprehending.

Oh. Not the worst conundrum in the world. No need to make any kind of fuss.

"Is there something wrong?" Else asked her.

Oh dear, oh dear! Her android senses had probably computed Lina's micro-expressions. That's what they did in sf books. Right? "Um. It's just a cultural thing," Lina said weakly. She poured a bit of cream into the cup and looked around for some sugar.

"Cultural?"

"Ah, where I'm from… Did they tell you, I'm from North Carolina? Anyway, there 'tea' is iced tea. Hot tea is 'hot tea.' 'Half and half' means half sweet tea – you don't want to drink sweet tea because all too often it's just sugar with a little flavored water in it – and half unsweet tea. The combination usually brings the sweetness down to bearable levels."

The waiter had heard and rushed to her seat. He reached for her cup.

"No, no, this is fine," Lina assured him as she waved him off. "Hot tea is special. For winter evenings. For reading marathons and formal family get-togethers. I do enjoy it on occasion, especially tea, Earl Grey, hot."

"That's an odd way to put it," Papa Mike said.

"*Star Trek*," Lina replied. "That's how Capt. Picard orders his tea from the ship's replicator. These days he insists on decaf."

Mike looked blank for a moment, but then rolled his eyes. "Are you and Lonnie going to fight about that?"

"Fight about what?" Jae asked.

"*Star Trek* versus *Star Wars*," Mike explained. "Both science fiction, but the two fandoms can come to blows."

"I am aware of *Star Wars*." Lina tried to sound haughty. "But only take note of the good stuff."

"It's all good," Lon put in.

"It is not, and you know it. I might even admit there are parts of the *Star Trek* universe that might not be… exceptional."

"Is this the light saber stuff?" Jae asked. He turned to the others. "Lon and I are always having light saber duels. There was a program. A 'movie.' I fell asleep halfway through. But I liked the duels."

— — —

The conversation became centered around Jae and turned spirited as menus were opened and everyone volunteered what they thought Jae would like to eat. The only Earth food he'd really had was pizza, poutine, some Chinese take-out, a few tacos, and birthday cake. His reactions were all recorded on Lina's padd.

Eventually courses were ordered and delivered, conversation flowed, and the family settled back. Staff attended to the wines except for Lina, who held her hand over her glass every time the bottle came around. No one seemed to notice. Well, she might have been hiding her glass in that special way she had of hiding herself. She didn't want to make a fuss.

A new sommelier entered the room with a large rolling champagne bucket containing ice and a few bottles. Lina knew he was a sommelier because he looked just like the ones in the movies: a tux-like staff uniform without a jacket; black apron, white towel on his arm. No really, a white towel. And a black bow tie.

"Here we go," Hal announced. "We will have a toast before dessert. And likely several more toasts before we leave. Pace yourselves." He gave a Significant Look to Jae.

The sommelier came around the table, pouring fizzing champagne into the group's wine glasses.

Someone asked Lina a question she had to think about before answering. That was why she didn't see the champagne actually being poured into her glass.

Oh no. Lina hated alcohol with a vengeance. She hadn't dreamed she was this picky, but alcohol not only tasted awful; it put her to sleep. She couldn't go to sleep on everyone tonight. But she also couldn't insult her host and new family. She'd be expected to drink it. What to do? She and Londo exchanged glances.

Just don't drink it, Lon told her.

But this is your father!

Hal stood up. "A toast," he announced.

Lon gave a tiny nod to Jae, who pointed at Hal's glass. "No, that's a drink. Isn't toast some kind of bread?"

Everyone else focused upon them as a polite titter went around the table. Lon's glass hadn't yet been filled. As the waiter came to him, he gave a start to find that Lon held a filled wine glass. Lon flashed him a quick smile and put his finger to his lips. Shh.

In the meantime, Lon's empty glass appeared at Lina's place. She thought quickly and located a familiar convenience store back in the States. There.

Ginger ale stolen. Placed on the counter at Starhaven in the Rockies. Much more difficult to port when she couldn't see one of the ends in person. Cap ported off. Lina could sense the drink *shusshing* out of the top. Then… *That* much would fill the glass. It did, though it made a gassy sound as it arrived.

Jae coughed loudly as Mama Ruth joined the conversation. That distracted from it.

Lina relaxed in her chair. Whew. Another world-shaking crisis averted.

Then she caught the curious expression on Else's face. She'd seen! She would also have seen the panic in Lina's eyes. Else's gaze shifted to Londo, who put that finger to his lips again. She gave him a tiny nod.

Was Else required by marriage vows to report the incident to Hal tonight? Lina hoped to heaven not. She didn't want to rile up anyone, not now, when they were all bonding.

Well, all except Jae. Tonight was family plus Jae, when it should be just family, Jae fully included.

That was wrong.

But tonight Lina wasn't going to make waves. If she couldn't control a beverage crisis, she'd never be able to control that.

— — —

Hal led toasts to Lina and Lon's marriage. Papa Mike did one to celebrate the Mind Control Tour which had been so successful and involved Jae as well as Lon and Lina. Then it was Londo's turn to thank his family for their support through the harrowing past months, to which Jae and Lina both said, "Hear hear!"

The drinks were refilled, with Lina smoothly performing her switch-out and exchanging quick glances with Else.

"You know, I could de-alcoholize that for you," Jae whispered as the conversation on the other side of the table picked up.

"But it probably wouldn't taste as good," Lina replied.

— — —

Hal toasted the beginning of the official rebuilding of cities on Aldierra, and all the work that had led up to that, as well as the ongoing tasks.

Londo had tried to leave the non-vegetarian pate accompaniment for the others, but it was a favorite and Hal had ordered enough for a small army. Hal made a comment about Londo not eating enough of it.

For some reason the meat dishes tonight had not been as… Lon was *not* going vegetarian. Not him. Not after both Jae and Lina had razzed him over the past weeks about the inevitability of it. No, the main courses were delicious, and Jae voiced his approval at his vegetarian fare. Lina enjoyed hers as well.

It was important that Londo make sure his spouses got what they needed and wanted. He wanted them to bask in the love of his family as they joined it.

Of course there was Jae's predicament. Londo could feel a pang from his husband now and then as someone said something that hit Jae wrong, that left him out of things. Lina also resonated with many of them. But both kept up their happy expressions. Jae held out his glass for yet another refill and made short work of it. They were truly trying to enjoy the evening.

But the more he thought about it, the more Londo argued with himself. This could be the perfect testing ground: family. These people loved him unconditionally. They had done so since he'd arrived to them as a boy. If not with them, where?

He'd been testing the figurative waters lately, seeing how others would react. It had gone well. Better than he'd imagined.

If not now…

He could do this. No he couldn't. No by god, he was Valiant. He was supposed to be brave. Look at Lina; she'd done crazy things, jumped great gulches of danger in the past couple months, just to follow him. Jae was a danger-seeker, the brash Legionnaire who'd been on the front lines for well over a decade and never backed down.

Londo was invulnerable. He was liked by almost everyone. If not now…

Servers stood outside the room, tidying their stations and waiting for the signal to serve dessert.

Lon tapped his wineglass with a knife.

The gRands smiled at each other. "A toast, another toast!" Mama Ruth laughed. Was she the slightest bit tipsy?

Londo rose. He didn't look at Lina or Jae, whom he knew were watching him closely. He could feel their surprise. And their loving pride in him.

He stood straighter. "A toast, but first… Let's see. Give me a moment to figure how to put this."

He took a long moment to lick his lips as he checked his non-spouses in the room. Another moment. "I would like to toast two people whom I dearly love. One of them for many years. The other just for recently, but just as deeply. To my spouses, my husband and wife, Jae and Lina Starhart!"

CHAPTER

20

"It's a fun game on Aldierra," Hal remarked sourly. "But don't bring it up here."

"It's no game. We are married."

"Eh," was all that Papa Mike got out. Mama Ruth just sat there, her mouth twisted slightly open as if she were deciding if she had heard things right. Else's features were still locked on the expression she'd held when Londo first rose.

Hal shot out of his chair. "You're what?"

"Spouses," Londo said. "I think we just walked out of the closet."

"Your… But this was just to fool the Aldierrans. A game. Fake!"

"We got married the day after Jae first returned to Earth from Aldierra. When Lina had been released from Legion captivity. Well, when she released herself, that is."

Lina leaned over to the gRands. "It was on the Spring Solstice. It was a beautiful ceremony. We have video."

"Only a handful of people who would have found out anyway were invited," Jae assured them, assured Hal. "We wanted you all there, but… But…"

"But I was afraid," Lon began.

People began talking over each other.

"I knew he was gay when he was a kid." Papa Mike's voice seemed to drown out the others. "Or bi, whatever it is. He couldn't stop talking about Jae when he joined the Legion. It was those alien kidnappers. Their experiments. But then he kept talking about girls too."

Ruth shrugged. "I thought the girls cancelled out all the Jae talk. Was it just Jae, Lonnie dear? Were there others? Other boys?"

"Oh dear," Lina said.

"I really didn't know that we were doing this tonight," Jae remarked sotto voce.

Lina shook her head. "It was Londo's choice." She gave him that adoring smile of hers, and Lon's heart lifted.

"So it was."

Jae's eyes also held a spark of such pride in him. And relief.

"So it is." Straightening from how he'd slumped, Londo checked the reactions in the room.

Else was watching Hal, whose face had turned thunderous.

"This. Is. True?" he asked Londo.

"Yes. I'm not… We're not hiding anymore."

"Polygamy. Bisexual polygamy."

"Yes. A Feithi Triune."

"I was born and raised in a Triune," Jae said helpfully, but no one seemed to hear him.

"You aren't Feithi," Hal accused his adoptive son. "Don't pretend to be."

"We have been urged to…"

"Scandal!" The word came out as a hiss. "How often have I told you: no scandal? We mean too much to this world, to all the worlds we operate in."

"It's not–"

"No. Scandal! It's illegal!"

"The Affiliated Systems have recognized the marriage. It's not public there yet, but–"

Somehow Hal was right next to Londo. He poked him on his chest. "Never. Ever. We have an image to uphold. Even if it's false. We must appear to be… To be…"

"Back off!" Jae commanded.

"Frauds?" Lon asked. "What year is it? The world has changed. It keeps changing. Everyone keeps telling me that people will understand. People will accept."

"People relish scandal! They embroider upon it. They blacken the reputation of whoever it's attached to. What will happen to you? To your Three Worlds?"

"We are who we are," Lina said. "Take a breath, Hal."

The door to the room cracked open. Hal raised a pointed finger to it. "Out!" he commanded.

The door immediately shut.

"Yes, take a breath or three," Jae said.

Londo watched Hal as he began to pace, his teeth gritted.

The gRands sat back in their chairs, mouths agape, but mostly peering at their son. Fear at what he might or could do, etched their faces.

Else's gaze traveled from person to person around the room before settling on the countenance of her husband. Her expression betrayed no judgment.

Finally Hal stopped. His hands were fists as he crossed his arms over his chest. His eyes were closed; his head bowed; his shoulders, bunched. "Scandal," he whispered. Then he raised his head to open his eyes in a fiery glare. "How many times have I guarded this family from scandal?" he asked. "I've deflected, I've outright lied. Over and over again.

"Londo came to my home an emotional wreck." His features crumpled with grief. "He'd been abused, but the world couldn't see him that way. A mega with severe emotional problems. They had to be able to trust him. They had to believe he was sound. He had to be healed so he could… grow. Happy. So I took him to every therapist I could find, did everything they said to do so he could find his footing and grow to be a man. Not a monster."

He took a step and the building shook slightly. "A man who would betray his family like this. Bring shame upon them. The world will not forgive."

"But will you?" Jae asked. Ruth and Mike's heads snapped in his direction.

"We should think about this," Ruth said. "Give it some time to sink in."

Lina crossed her arms. "There's nothing to forgive."

"Lonnie is still Lonnie," Mike declared. "We can work this out. Come to some solution."

"We've already come to a solution," Londo said. "Instead of an open marriage, we made it legal. It fits the customs we're supposed to maintain."

"We found a marriage that allows us to express our feelings without shame," Lina said. "It will let us love and support each other through the years, protected both legally and socially."

Ruth and Else both gave her a long look at that.

"Our children will be honorably born into this marriage," Lon said. "They will be safeguarded by it."

Hal's expression had turned monstrous. "Ssscandal! You cannot just drop this bomb on the world. You dishonor our family. I will not have it dishonored!"

Jae interjected, "Am I dishonorable because I'm the product of a Triune? Triunes were the most sacred level of marriage on Feith." He targeted Hal in his gaze. "I always looked up to Maximus, even before the destruction of my world. And then you were the one who rescued me. Do you regret that now?"

Hal clasped his hands close to his chest. He seemed to withdraw within himself. "It's not so easy. Not easy to release scandal on the world. We are *history*. We are what history will record of us. We must inspire the world for generations to come."

"Can't we all be ourselves along the way?" Lina asked. "I think Londo and Jae are wonderful men. They have their little hiccups but they are so much more than those. And they're trying to be good people. They're always trying so hard. That's what made me love them in the first place."

"You too, *chérie*." Lon smiled at her.

But Hal pulled his palms down either side of his head. Lina realized she could see great black clouds in his aura. She didn't often see auras, but huge issues were coming up for Hal. There was also a gray smudge there. Were there more issues than just their marriage?

"Scandal!"

"We'll get through this, son," Mike assured him.

"You don't understand. You don't understand!" Hal pointed at Londo. "I kept it from *him*. I kept it from you all!"

Jae clutched Lina's arm. **Uh oh,** he said.

"I kept it all to myself. To avoid scandal. The judgment of the world. It wouldn't do, it wouldn't do! It would fuck up my entire career. Ruin what I've tried to do all my life.

"Scandal!"

And a blast of clarity seared across Lina, Jae, and Lina's minds as Hal's thoughts ripped out of the hold he'd held them in.

How many years?

"You're my… father?" Londo breathed. "My biological father?"

Mike and Ruth gasped in unison. Else's expression didn't change.

Hal faced Londo blankly.

"You're my fucking father?" Londo bellowed. "And you lied, LIED to me all these years?"

"Back OFF, Lon!" Jae yelled as Lon dove for Hal. "Stop!"

In less than a second Jae materialized his staff and struck it on the floor.

Everyone froze in place and turned to him. Lon's fist was inches from Hal's chin. Hal's hand was grasping for Lon's throat.

"Step away from each other," Jae commanded Hal and Lon. "Think. Don't do something you'll regret."

They didn't move, so Lina ported them to opposite sides of the room.

"He's already said the unforgiveable," Lon accused his father even as he lowered his fist. "Did I ever mean anything to you? Besides a threat to your precious honor?"

"Which you apparently have none of. Scandal!"

"You shut me up with lies so you could be safe!"

"Oh my god," someone said, but Lina could only say, "Oh. Oh." She shrugged one shoulder. "Stop it," she told her guides. "Not now. Not…"

Jae tore his gaze from Lon and Hal to look at her. "Someone wants your attention," he said. "Even I can feel that."

"There's… Is that… Lon's mother?"

She pointed at that smudge of vague energy only she could see, standing between Londo and Hal.

"Is… Is Lon's mother dead?"

"Did you kill her?" Jae asked Hal.

"Kill– Of course I didn't kill her!" Hal exploded. "She killed herself."

— — —

Londo's throat dried up. *Killed.* He managed to swallow. It was bitter, bitter. "You. Never. Told me."

"How could I tell you? She died after I found you. She killed herself. She was depressed. Clinically depressed, all her life. And your abduction was the last straw for her. There was a long spiral. She was in a hospital. There was noth-ing… nothing I could do. I didn't want you to see her like that. Didn't want you to do the same."

"Wait. She was still alive when I got back to Earth?" Lon's entire body shook. "You didn't take me to see her?"

"Oh Lon honey, I'm so sorry. He shouldn't have done that. At the very least," Lina said.

"Very least," Jae echoed darkly.

"You would have been scared. I wanted you safe. Cared for. Healing from your trauma. She wouldn't have helped. By then she was almost incoherent. She scared even me."

"When… When?"

"Almost five years after you returned. I let her see that you were back, that you were okay. But she didn't recognize you, didn't acknowledge you as her son." Hal shook his head. "It wouldn't have been good for you. It nearly drove *me* mad."

He kept shaking his head as he faced his son. "You didn't need to know. And if you didn't, neither did the world."

"Not even us?" Mike asked.

"No one. It was *my* scandal. My scandal she wouldn't marry me. My scandal that you got kidnapped. My scandal that I couldn't keep the mother of my son alive and healthy."

He bared his teeth at Londo. "But it is *your* scandal that you've gone and done this. I won't have you bringing the family down by doing this, not after all I've had to go through to keep mine secret. Get an annulment. Erase the records. Stop this nonsense! Remember your honor. Remember what you mean to the world!"

Lon's breath came heavily. "You could have been my real father," he said quietly. "You hid that from me. You lied to me. 'We'll look for your mother,' you always said. You kept promising me. Telling me that you'd done everything to find her. You. Lied." He took a breath. "To me. Your son."

He looked around to Lina and Jae. "Let's go."

They quickly stood up. Lina and Jae looked at the others apologetically.

"I'll send you that video," Lina told the gRands, and to Else she said, "I don't have your email."

They disappeared.

— — —

Londo struggled to focus as his day continued with zero sleep behind it. His concentration since That Night was getting better. Whenever he returned to their quarters, Lina or Jae was there to hold him and listen. They had him stopping on the job just to breathe every half hour or so. It was stupid, but it seemed to be helping. He'd made it through a half-morning's work smashing buildings with sheer fury. Jae had warned the associated crews to stay further back than they usually did.

Now that he was back in his office Mimik had reported in from Sarastor, as she did every other day. His team was doing fine without him. Better than fine. Yesterday they'd foiled an attempt to trigger a supervolcano on Arthree and this morning had accepted medals from that world's Guiding Council.

What did they need him for? They shouldn't need him. He was just some glorified muscle that they could make up for with their own powers. He'd trained them for years to be their best. His team was constantly commended on their work. He should be celebrating them, but instead he felt betrayed. Abandoned.

Everyone important had turned against him.

Adam had told him that these feelings were to be expected, and that he'd be able to see things from a different viewpoint as time passed. Lon found it difficult to listen to Adam right now.

"Valiant! Are you there? We've been trying to reach you," his PA, Trey Oanukstripe, said in his ear.

"Oh, I… I was occupied with something," Londo lied. He was shocked; he hadn't even noticed his earring buzzing to catch his attention.

He glossed over it and listened to Trey as he collected his things. Protestors had gathered in the Augurel Manufacturing Center in the Bentmark. They'd seen the schedule to tear down the weapons plants there to make way for the East-West Wildlife Corridor.

"They're not only in our way, but uber polluters. We've given them enough notice to move. If I recall correctly, I even offered to help them."

"It's only been three weeks," Trey protested.

Lon trotted down the hotel hallway to his top staff's offices, pulling on his repacked vest. "I could have had them set up and in full, *non-polluting* operation by now. Time for them to come clean."

That might make a good catch phrase here, if he were into catch phrases. "Time to come clean!"

That thought sourly cheered Londo for a few moments as he joined Trey in his new Chief of Protector Operations, Luten Farhome's office, though the wan smile on his face seemed to confuse both men.

"This is going to put a lot of people out of jobs. It's going to play havoc with the supply chain," Trey reminded him.

Lon waved instructions to a computer, and readouts displayed in front of them all. "Contingencies for the suppliers," he said. "People out of jobs? We'll offer them new ones as part of our conservation efforts."

Luten waved an additional info screen to life. "They could have been working at the new plant or in their new location by now. They aren't listening."

"This is not going to go over well."

Lon stood staring at the screens and considered. No, it would not, even after what they'd done with that Froregreen billionaire a few weeks ago. You'd think that would have put the fear of god into such people. He could literally hear the vile shouts tossed his way from the manufacturing site. There'd be more.

People would hate him.

Well, maybe he didn't feel so good about *them.*

"Have Batt and his staff put together a short documentary – say ten minutes, max – with the history of what these places have been doing, and for how long. Interview some people who have tried to stop them over the years. Interview some of the people who've been sickened by what they've put into the air and water. And their products."

"Yes sir."

"And have it show a map of the migratory route, as well as a timeline of when they were informed they'd have to move. And my offer to help. Show that this is all on them."

Londo gave his aides a watery smile. "Buck up, Trey. Things are only going to get worse. Luten, you might want to increase the size of your personal security staff. We are going to save this world, dammit."

"Yessir." "Yes, we are."

But Londo wasn't smiling as he kicked down the flue-gas stacks, then the walls of the factories. As he cut off water coming into and waste flowing out of the buildings. He may have ground the carnage into powder finer than it needed to be. By the time he was done, the vast complex was nothing but dust and debris, with his machinery sorting through it for recycling.

Outside his zone of destruction the people cursed him.

So what? They were all bastards. Every. Last. One…

He threw up.

His insides wanted to rebel. He felt hot and cold at the same time. Noises rang hollowly around him. His muscles felt like immovable rocks. His chest pounded.

Was he having a heart attack?

What was happening to him?

"Argh!" he shouted. "Ahh!" Then he cursed and cursed and let out inarticulate noises that shook the landscape around him.

He threw up again. Twice.

Then he leapt up and took off into space where no one could see him.

— — —

Jae and Lina hugged each other tightly in Jae's office, trying to observe and yet not be noticed as they telepathically felt their husband hovering at the edge of space above one of the poles. Jae could clearly see through Lina's clairvoyance: Lon wrapped in a fetal ball, gripping himself tighter and tighter.

So much anger. Tension. Hurt. Betrayal.

If he'd been granite he would have shattered.

His heart was torn in a place it had thought unbreakable.

Londo pulled at his hair before he burst into tears.

"At last," Jae breathed. "I've been telling him not to hold it in."

Lina clung to Jae. How she wanted to go there and soothe Londo! But Adam had advised them to keep an eye out for this. "Let him cry it out, if he can get it to come," he said. "At least the first time, let it happen without him needing to filter it or hide it from you in some manner."

After that they'd go to him and hug and hold him like he'd never been hugged before.

— — —

Their aides didn't know what was going on but knew that something was, as both Jae and Lina cancelled all their meetings for two hours. The three of them talked in their bedroom, and Lon was never without arms around him.

They cancelled more meetings. Lon settled enough that he got into bed. Jae worked on his blood and muscles. Lina worked on his energy.

Finally his eyes drooped. They lay on either side of him until he was well and fast asleep.

Then they called Adam to fill him in. Between the three of them, they would be by Lon's side whenever he needed them. Jae told Bracken the entire truth, and Bracken said he could handle Lon's staff and duties for the nonce. He'd inform Lon's staff as much as he thought they could handle.

He wished them well.

— — —

CHAPTER

21

Lina appeared in the Monitor Room of Legion HQ per the emergency summons. She got one or two of these calls each week. Usually they gave her enough warning so she could port into her uniform, but… super emergency. Otherwise she wouldn't have come, and would have stayed near Lon.

"Who's porting?" she asked as she looked around, for no team stood ready to go. She needed to get back to Lon.

The Officer of the Day – at least that's what she thought the title was – stood at a central monitor. She didn't recognize him, but there were hundreds of Legionnaires to learn. He motioned and a view of four Legionnaires standing ready somewhere appeared on a floating screen. "They're due for R&R here at HQ," he told her.

"I'm supposed to be reserved for crises." Lina tried not to sound pissed. She'd been interrupted, and every minute of her time on Aldierra was precious. Plus Londo might need her. "Is this a crisis?"

"Port them in." He didn't deign to give a reason.

Well, she was here. But Londo and Jae would certainly hear about this. Maybe they could–

No. She could put on her big-girl panties and do what had to be done herself. Lon especially had enough on his shoulders.

Lina ported in the four and then ported downstairs, out of High Security areas. She was only allowed in the Monitor Room for porting purposes.

Down here were the levels Legion family members could use. So she did. She marched her way toward the subcommander's office. Part of

Subcommander Nurunori's duties were to keep track of Legion family services, and that included spouses.

Here also a few Legionnaires made their way, though family members comprised the most foot traffic. Up ahead Mimik paused in a hall that crossed Lina's route. She reminded Lina of a praying mantis, though she didn't have the extra legs associated with that. What she possessed was an extra two arms, each with fewer fingers than a human. That totaled more digits than a human had.

Mimik held more substance in her form than a mantis that size would have. She was no stick and walked fully upright. She was all kinds of greens on what skin was exposed, and wore a shiny gold uniform. Bright salmon accented her skin as well as clothing. Her eyes were large and pearlescent, and she had the habit of gazing at someone as if she were logging their every detail. It was unnerving.

"Speaker," she said.

"Mimik. How nice to see you again. I haven't seen you since the party."

Mimik peered at her. Accusingly? Why did Lina get that idea?

"Yes. You have come to steal another Legionnaire?"

"Oh? Oh that. We made an offer. Or rather, I made an offer. No Legionnaire had anything to do with the business."

"Of course, of course."

"Do you often stare at others?"

Mimik tilted her head. "It's my job to be observant. Don't you read the minds of others?"

"Not without their permission unless they're yelling telepathically. It would be rude. As is staring."

Lina didn't mean to say that last part out loud; it was just *that stare*. "Sorry."

"Hm. Let me see. Who was it that was asking after you?" Mimik made a motion to trigger a screen that would be invisible to anyone else. "Ah. Ms. Yency."

Did Lina's hair stand on end?

"Ms. Yency. I will make a note–"

"Here she is, Ms. Yency." Mimik waved her upper left hand and a screen with Yency's disapproving features appeared on it, facing down Lina. Lina shuddered.

Yency was head of Legion Protocol, Spousal Division. It was she who ran herd over them in the manner in which they presented themselves to the public. Lina, the lowly Terran witchdoctor, had been on her shit list ever since she'd first arrived.

"Mrs. Va– *What* are you wearing?" Yency almost sputtered.

"I was called here for an emergency and didn't change. This is a new work outfit for Aldierra." Lina tried her best to sound professional and not like a child being reprimanded. Hey, she was a little stressed these days. "Focus groups and I decided upon this design and some variations, as might be accepted by their culture. They require modesty of their own, though a different modesty than Sarastor requires. I thought it would be good enough. My ports *are* emergency work."

"Unacceptable. Sleeves, Mrs. Valiant. Full sleeves at the very least! And… the pants should reach your ankles. No skin should show on your lower limbs!"

Mimik's outfit didn't cover her up, but no one was on Mimik's back about it. Insectoids got all the breaks, it seemed.

"My schedule had me in rather warm conditions today." As Yency's disapproving expression didn't change, Lina added, "We were in a marsh. And I didn't want to sweat to death. I have an even more abbreviated version available."

"Un. Ac. Ceptable," Yency repeated. "Demerits."

"You'll love the variations on this," Lina responded sweetly. "Long tunics, short tunics, short pants… I might even go *barefoot*." She gave Yency a little sneer. The woman deserved it. "I look forward to a new set of demerits for each. Bless your heart."

"You've missed Spousal Meetings and Events. You are not allowed to do that."

"I've been saving two galactic sectors, Ms. Yency. Priorities."

"We are the Legion!"

"We are also the Three Worlds, Ms. Yency."

Lina turned her back on Yency and gave Mimik a scathing glance. "Thank you *so* much."

Mimik's large eyes blinked twice at her. "You are welcome, Speaker," she said gravely.

— — —

Lina waited and waited in the subcommander's spacious reception area. She had to admire all the trophies and wall picture/videos of Legion action. Finally the receptionist said she could go in.

"Subcommander," Lina bowed her head, per Legion regs, as she stepped inside the office.

The pink-haired Andri rolled her eyes at her with a sigh. "What the orb are you wearing?"

"Something that's already gotten me demerits from Yency. At least," Lina said. "It's what I'm wearing on Aldierra today. It was damned hot there and today is being particularly difficult. It covers more than I'd usually cover in such conditions. I ported in because there was an emergency. There wasn't."

Andri was checking her screens already. "Hm," she said.

"You sound like Mimik. I just saw her."

"Yes. I see. No emergency; you're correct." She muttered something dark under her breath as her fingers moved to get more info.

"I have better things to do than port in people who want to start their vacation sooner than they usually would."

Andri looked up at her. "Have you been making enemies?"

"A few here and there. Granger the Ruby Guard, for one."

"I mean, within the Legion."

That took Lina aback. "Uh… Yency," she decided.

"Oh yes, Yency." Andri cocked an eyebrow at her. "Have you checked your demerits lately?"

"Demerits? Again?"

Demerits from Yency were something to mock. Demerits mentioned by Andri were scary. Get enough demerits and it would begin to reflect on Londo's record. Not on Jae's, thanks to the secret. That stupid clause that allowed the

Legion to annul Lina's marriage if she gathered too many demerits and thus cast dishonor on the organization...

Just let them *try* that.

But Londo and Jae had to be kept in excellent standing.

"I've hardly been here. Well, to talk to Nesh, but that's pretty much it. And to go to Legion Medical to check on everyone. Or did demerits come into play while I was on the Tour? That wasn't at HQ. What I did there wasn't Legion business. That didn't count, did it?"

Andri's mouth formed a serious line. "Apparently for some it did. I'll check into this. Into the emergency ports as well. I understand you have important duties elsewhere. You might want to check your record. But Lina..."

Lina waited.

"Come up with something else to wear. Maybe a special Monitor Room porting – emergency porting – outfit that precisely follows Protocol Directives."

"Yes'm."

– – –

Lina knew how to be subtle. That morning when the call for an emergency Legion port came in, she was ready.

She appeared in the Monitor Room seven feet away from the OD, more than the minimum distance the Legion Spousal Manual dictated for spouses vs Legion personnel whom they were not married to. The OD, again another Legionnaire Lina didn't recognize, had to turn around to see she'd arrived after she made a slight shuffling noise with her foot to notify him.

She'd seen today's demerits totals. New credits had kept her from being in the basement, demerit-wise, but she was darned if she was going to take any chances.

The small group of Legionnaires waiting to port out turned to her. Their heads cocked in various angles of assessment.

Lina bowed deeply and waited in subservient silence.

The OD also waited, perhaps to see if she had questions. Perhaps he was wondering who she was. Perhaps he was still taking in what she was wearing.

It was a 100% burqa in unrelenting, flat black. No designs relieved the heavy fabric. The length of the cloak was longer than normal, though, so her feet were more than completely covered with an extra fold against the ground. It would be difficult to walk in such a long garment if one didn't hold it up. Luckily for her, she didn't need to walk. The sleeves extended inches beyond her fingers.

The window over Lina's eyes was fully covered with a dark lens. Inside, her view was not shadowed, but someone looking at her could not see in.

She was just a short, black mass of clothing.

She bowed again in silence.

I am the Ghost of Christmas Yet to Come, she silently reminded herself.

"Uh, five to port out," the OD said and motioned for the monitors to show the target area.

Lina bowed again to signal she'd received the order. She ported the group to their destination. When they appeared two minutes later in the monitors, they only made a quick comment or two about the fearful dark wait of the port, and then checked her out again in silence for the few seconds it took for her to gather herself to port back to Aldierra.

Let's see them demerit her for *that*. Try to annul *her* marriage, would they? Chumps.

— – —

The first time it happened it took both Jae and Londo by surprise. They'd been having a whispered bedroom conversation about the coming day's activities. Well, in Jae's case it was the past day, as he was ready for bed while Londo was prepping to go out to begin his duties on the opposite side of the world.

Lon stretched and twisted his back, then did some deep squats as he tried to figure a way to attack everything on the rest of the week's to-do list… today. This was good. The more work he had to do, the less he obsessed about Hal's unholy treachery.

Lina was fast asleep in their bed, for it was her middle of the night.

This was not working well. They needed their time together, and scrabbling a few moments at a time wasn't working. He needed human contact more than ever. Londo felt bad because all he could offer Lina in the way of marital duties were quickies, and not many of those. Jae more often than not got more than that from him, but not by much.

He'd have to find out how often Jae and Lina managed to get together. Both Jae and Lina didn't have Londo's energy levels and when their days were over, sleep was the only thing on their minds.

Should Lon be keeping score? His gut said yes. He wanted to give both his spouses everything, even it if was something he selfishly enjoyed so much. He wanted to touch and embrace them; to have the wonderful adult fun and contact that had been denied him until he'd met Lina. He wanted to feel them hold and love him. That didn't make him selfish. He didn't want to treat them anything like Hal had treated him. Full disclosure; full love. They must always know that they were the most precious people in his life.

He'd make a note to check out those Feithi marriage FAQs Jae had downloaded for them. Feithi info was still available through the satellite storage system that world had employed. The population knew approximately the doom that was coming to them, and had uploaded everything as a resource library for other civilizations. It was an incredibly gracious act, but more info than any one man or even one group could ever sort through.

This morning Jae had put off his own bedtime a few minutes in order to inform Londo about some news from the Reyda migration route. Four animals thought to be extinct had shown up on cameras, and two more on endangered lists had been reported within shouting distance of the remaining nearby city, far enough away from each other that they had to be different animals.

A waft of cheer eased Lon's chest. "Maybe we are accomplishing something," he whispered to Jae.

"I pray that's so. Tomorrow I'll make sure that people don't straggle into that area to see for themselves. Should we set up security fencing?"

Londo rubbed his nose as he considered. "I'll arrange it. We can program some robotic slicers and installers. We don't want to impede the animals. Maybe the system will need manual help as well. I'll see what Bracken and Luten have to offer."

Jae nodded as he peeled back the covers, careful not to disturb Lina, who was turned from him. "Check with Kanti about materials."

"Right."

Then someone in the room spoke.

"I shall guide the animals to the routes. I will remind them of how their ancestors lived."

It was a deeper voice than Lina's, but it came from her mouth.

Both men went on alert, but Jae waved Londo down from asking questions. "Do you have any advice for us, Aldierra?" he asked.

"More forests. More open spaces for my animals to move to where they should be. Deserts should return to being deserts. Grasslands should be grass again. And so on. Tell Nesh she's doing excellently well, but she has distant cousins who can also help if they would. I would welcome them, though they are not nearly as adept as she. Keep opening up the world to my non-humans."

"Yes, Aldierra," Jae said, and Londo echoed him reverently.

But Aldierra said no more. The two men looked at each other.

Guess I'll do a little more clearing today than was originally on my schedule, Londo told his husband.

You do that. And remember to take meditation breathing breaks. I'll get some shuteye... Unless Aldierra wants to say something else.

They looked to Lina expectantly, but she only emitted the tiniest, most subtle of deep breaths, hardly enough to be called a snore.

— — —

As he began his day in earnest, Lon settled to his desk, screens spread all around himself. First up was a message from Legion Med and Dr. Gorgeon there. They had completely released Demi from her stasis cocoon, and after two false starts, she'd come fully conscious.

He breathed a sigh of relief that Earth's legendary heroine had not only survived Paul Granger's attack, but seemed as if she might recuperate. "It will be a long recovery," Gorgeon warned. Demi had been millimeters from death.

Demi's sister, niece and nephew were with her. The Legion was offering them quarters as Demi recuperated. Queen Otrere had made special arrangements back in Scythia in order to be with her sister. After all, she told Lon when he called, family was the most important thing.

"Some of your ParaNet fellows are here, as is Hal," Queen Otrere reported. "Would you like to talk with him?"

Hastily Lon formed an excuse and signed off.

He would have to come up with some lie to tell his ParaNet teammates as to why he didn't want to speak to Hal. Maybe the overwhelm of Three Worlds work would be a good excuse.

More mundane business now occupied him. He called Lina's assistant's desk to tell whoever was there about the animal sightings and thus the fencing project.

"I think I know several sources for that," one of the new women, Tidda, told him. "When you figure it out, tell me where to have it delivered."

As his screen blanked, a gray cat jumped onto the desk.

"Down, Ember," he commanded. Instead of picking her up – he didn't have time to stumble through the adapted telepathic double loop and he had no towels at hand to cushion his grip – he reinforced the command telepathically. How did you talk to a cat to have it understand?

Ember cocked her head at him. "Down," he repeated.

She considered and finally, probably seeing that she'd get no rubs here, jumped down.

Almost immediately Bran-Bran jumped up.

"Down!"

Bran was more cooperative. Good cat.

So Londo managed to get a few calls done before contacting Mimik for a quick team update. Things were still going well, unfortunately. Mimik was excellent as back-up Team Leader, but Londo wanted to be needed by his team. Did they not value him, or was he just being paranoid? He also wanted to get his job here on Aldierra done. Right now the two goals did not mesh.

One after each other, Obi and Molly jumped onto the desk.

"Down!" Londo bellowed as Mimik watched.

The shout startled Obi and he jumped down, only to begin licking his back leg to show that he hadn't really been all that startled. But Molly took a defiant stance, her butt facing the computer's camera, and hissed at him.

Londo hissed back. He added a growl to the conversation.

With a final, long hiss, Molly jumped down and headed for the primary bedroom at top speed.

"No! No!" Lon jumped out of his chair and ran after her, waving a silence curtain between them and sleeping Jae and Lina. Molly managed to direct a stream of urine at the last of his boots, standing in a long line in the open closet. "No!"

Lina said to spray water to deter them. Lon didn't know where the *ostie conne* bottle was, so he spat at Molly and found his target.

She ran away.

When Londo returned to his screens, Mimik had a very peculiar Mimik expression on her face. "Domestic bliss?" she asked.

"Cats!" The word held infinite darkness within it. "That Molly especially. She pees on my boots. I've learned to make sure my other clothes are secured, but the boots are out in the open." He added with a mutter, "Must get some kind of boxes for them."

His face ran through a variety of grimaces. "We have to strap everything down. They go through the house determined to knock anything that's not secured onto the floor. You can't set a sandwich down for a minute. They'll grab it."

Mimik smiled. "Cats," she said. "I'll make a note in case I ever get to Earth to encounter some."

Ah, he could talk to Mimik about his problems and she'd make the right noises that assured him that things weren't that bad. He hoped he was as good a friend to her.

The cats weren't truly his enemies. Except for Molly. Some of them were even nice to have around.

What about the other people in his life?

Was everyone truly against him? He knew he was treading water in a great black ocean of emotions these days. He might not be making the best decisions.

Time to take a new tack. Experiment to see what worked. Consider clearly the results and then – in a sober, orderly manner – toss away those people who refused to be on his side. Regain control of his life and to hell with anyone who didn't fit in.

Should he tell Mimik his secrets? Should he inform his team?

In the old days he would have asked Hal about important decisions, but what did Hal know of such things? Besides, Hal was beloved by all. Perfect Maximus.

Hal didn't know what not being loved was. What being loved and having it ripped from you felt like, especially when you couldn't talk to anyone about it. *Va te faire foutre*, Hal.

He knew he wasn't thinking straight, and was still a little nauseated from the other day. Adam had explained to him that it hadn't been a heart attack (they'd checked with Gorgeon at Legion Med to make sure. She now knew about Lon's paternity) and that it was all stress. So Lon had taken a few hours and watched Jae's videos about meditation, and Lina's friends' videos about centering and breathing. Lina had a video about an archangel named Raphael whom she said was in charge of healing. He glanced through it and bookmarked it to study later.

If he had to put a number on things, he rated himself an improving six on a scale of one to ten. He was able to get back in the Three Worlds swing of things, though he knew his spouses and staff and Adam were all keeping a close eye on him.

No, *because* he knew that. That was why he was leveling off.

They cared. They thought he was worthy of being cared for.

He had people he could talk to. Not only Adam, but Jae was there. Had always been there, forever. And now he had Lina as well.

He breathed easier. This wasn't the time to do anything stupid. He wouldn't be able to realize he was doing so. He should talk to Jae and Lina, take some baby steps first. Maybe this way he'd lose the bare minimum of those he regarded as friends and family.

CHAPTER

22

Lon was about to bash yet another complex to dust when the call came in over his earring. He reached to it to receive the transmission.

#Do not mess with your earring!# Jae's voice said.

"I was not messing with my earring," Londo growled at the AI as the message came in:

Five boys, lost somewhere near the southern hemisphere city of Hormu. Likely within it. That city was enormous with a dizzying network of highways, streets, neighborhoods, alleyways and worse, and active criminal gangs as well as rival military ones.

The boys were all around nine or ten years old. The message sent visuals of them: gangly kids, malnourished. Several of them regarded the camera sullenly as it took their photo. Bruises were apparent on two of them.

They were from three different but adjacent Houses. One of the Houses had reported their missing youngster the day before, and another had added to that today with their own children. The four had been friends, and a fifth that the first House had known of turned out to be missing as well. His House had not reported him missing. When police had approached that House, they'd been told that maybe the kid had run away, but he wasn't important enough to keep track of. No one had seen him, but no one would have noted him anyway even if he'd been there. Which he wasn't.

They'd been gone for four days now.

Kids. Lon's stomach clenched. Innocents.

There was a bit of money missing as well as scant food and beer. Clothing, but not all of it. Not any clothes with their House colors and patterns on them.

These boys were running away from home. But… toward what?

— — —

Lon sat in front of his office monitors to use his Legion programs to gather and compare street visuals. He fed it the kids' pictures as well.

There. But that was two days ago. Not five boys, but six. Similar sizes for them all. They darted from shadow to shadow around fights and packs of adult men. Perhaps "darted" wasn't the right word. Two of them had to be helped as the group moved.

At least they'd run with jackets, and the two injured boys also had blankets wrapped around themselves. The others wore hefty backpacks, and two extras were carried as hand baggage by the unimpaired ones.

He tried to figure their goal, but their movements had them circling here and there, doubling back – ah, food sources. Dumpsters behind restaurants – and then heading on.

Sleet was scheduled for Hormu tonight. Was there any way to change the weather programs? No. Those things were complicated, interconnected like hell.

Well.

Those boys wouldn't be lost by tonight.

— — —

Lina connected him to her psychic friend Yej Ham, a Korean-American who'd been on the Mind Control Tour. He had Yej find the communications devices they'd given all the Tour's members.

"Here's the map of the city," he told her as he uploaded it to her. "I need–"

"Six boys," she confirmed. "Give me a half-hour. I'll get back to you."

Londo spent that time communicating with his Operations chief. Good man, Luten. Recommended by Bracken, though Lon still wasn't sure who commanded more of his loyalties.

Luten assured him that land clearing and surveying would continue on schedule. With Londo away, Luten would coordinate with the Speaker's offices to move equipment to new sites and make sure the army had buildings scheduled for demolition cleared with public safety features set up around them.

Yej's call came at the twenty-minute mark. "Two possibles," she told him.

He examined the maps she'd sent. She worked by setting up grids over the maps and then running a pendulum laterally over them, then perpendicular to that. The maps now had circles, one large and one much smaller about two miles from the edges of the first one.

"Thanks, Yej," Lon said. Woo-woo stuff. But it gave him someplace to start. "Tell me if it works."

— — —

The smaller circle paid off almost immediately. The two injured boys were stashed in a storehouse, huddled in their blankets. Severely dehydrated and coughing. They hadn't brought masks to filter the putrid air.

Broken bones, internal bleeding, and the usual Aldierran bruise coverage.

The one could barely speak, but the other made up for it. "Don't take us home, Valiant! Please!"

Lon fished out his first aid transport equipment, compacted of course, from his pocket. "You're not going home," he told the boys. "First, you're getting medical help. Then we'll figure out what you need. And want. No one who'd treat you like this is going to get their hands on you again."

He settled the worst-off, Nikt, onto the now-inflated stretcher. "Comfy?" he asked, and the boy bravely nodded.

Londo signaled for a medical crew to report to his quarters in Plegerit. The suite's security team also had to be notified. Then Lon had the second boy stand next to the stretcher, and he joined them.

The planetary transporter units he and Jae had set up (with Wiley's help, of course) worked well if not as smoothly as Lina's natural power, and the three of them appeared in the Starhart quarters. By the time Lon guided the stretcher and had the second boy hold on to his shoulder for support so they could hobble to an empty guest bedroom, a small squad of medics arrived from their offices downstairs.

The ambulatory boy didn't know exactly where his companions were, but he told Londo that they were looking for medical supplies as well as food, water, and masks. Maybe blankets or a heat source.

Londo listened solemnly, made sure the medics were treating the kids right, and returned to the southern hemisphere. He signaled the family flitter to go there as well.

Yej called again; she'd gotten a strong new pendulum reading combined with her guides tapping her on her shoulders about it. Londo followed her directions.

The boys weren't there.

"Where are you? Where are you?" Londo muttered to himself as he searched with his paravision. He turned in a slow circle while checking near, then a bit farther, then a bit farther… It was a big city. Lots of walls and hidey-holes.

Usually he just, well, felt about where to look, if he had to define it. He'd never asked Hal the particulars of how he worked his own paravision, but come to think of it, Hal had taught him to concentrate on who or what he was searching for, and that would trigger some kind of brain-thing to recognize whatever it was. Hal said it was the recognition that did the trick; otherwise the world was a paravision blur of infinite possibilities.

Now that he considered, that was an odd way to search but it had worked for him for years. It was ever so slightly woo-woo. Even so, Lon wished he could tune into his guides like Lina and her friends could. They were strong in the Woo-woo.

Wait. Lon lifted his right hand and held out his index finger. He had a special woo-woo of his own. "Tink?" he asked. "Tinker Bell, can you get to Aldierra?"

A tiny fairy-like lady, a handy way to visualize the spirit, appeared like a wisp on the tip of that finger. She'd helped him with air temperature and such before, everyday environmental things that he was too powerful to sense. "Tink," he begged, "where are those kids? Can you show me where they are? Or bring in someone who can?"

She made shivering motions, wrapping her arms around herself. Then she was clothed in a heavy winter coat, pants and boots.

"Yes," Londo told her. "It's cold. It's going to get worse for them. Please, Tink. I need help."

Tink disappeared but… Beyond his invitational finger there came a slight glow. Was it really there, or his imagination? Lina had said the imagination was an important gateway to psychic work. The glow was golden, about the size of a softball.

"Thank you, thank you," Lon breathed. Maybe this wasn't Tink, but one of her allies. "The boys?"

Ever so ethereal, the glow began to move to Lon's left and Londo followed. If he moved too fast, the glow disappeared entirely so he tamped his desperation and forced himself to follow slowly. Calmly. With focus. Breathe. The boys. He covered another mile, maybe two, but it took so long…

The glow disappeared.

How he begged it to return! *Please… please…*

Then he heard a boy's whisper from somewhere. Another boy answered. Using his para-hearing, he had been trying to discern a boy's voice from among the thousands of voices around him in these streets. Lina said it was clairaudience but whatever you called it, it helped him to hear things normals couldn't. He could focus on sounds that otherwise would just be part of a worldwide chatter.

He concentrated on the whispers. Then the heartbeats accompanying them. The breathing.

Yes, multiple boys. Not too many. Two, maybe three. Talking about breaking into a building.

There!

"Thank you, thank you very much!" Lon exclaimed to the glow, even though it had deserted him. It had led him this far. He took off at full atmospheric speed toward those voices.

— — —

Lon only allowed one media crew within the hotel's suite that now housed the healing boys and their care crew, five floors under the Starharts' home. One boy sat in a wheelchair, both legs bandaged as well as his left shoulder. Another two sat behind the table with bandages peeking out from their clothing. The others stood behind their friends. All had various healing patches across their faces, necks, and the visible parts of their arms.

"This is how some Aldierrans treat their children," Londo told the cameras. "These boys thought running away would help. Maybe it did, but it wouldn't have for long."

Tomp, the leader of the group, said, "We were lucky."

The other boys chimed in their agreement and Lon couldn't hide his fond smile. He turned back to the cameras. "But don't you all out there do this. We have places you can call for help. We are adding children's rescue centers and orphanages as fast as we can to our lists of special residences. Gays, women, abused men... and now abused children can contact us, both boys and girls. We will see they're housed away from their abusers and given a safe place to stay. We will be offering educational resources as well as the best mental health help we can get."

"And doctors," the boy next to Nikt and his wheelchair put in.

"Doctors for physical conditions as well." Lon moved to stand behind the children. He held the shoulders of two of the boys to either side of him and addressed the cameras. "If your House does not prevent abuse toward yourself or others within it, mentally or physically, contact us. If your House wants to protect its own in a healthful manner, contact us and we'll give you the resources to start or strengthen what you do within your family in order to provide for it."

[Watching elsewhere, both Lina and Kanti made notes to hire, hire, hire more people. "Children's Services" was added to the organizational chart. Jae brought up residence plans and sent some to people he'd met to ask for their suggestions about converting them to make them into orphanages or group homes for children. "We will call them 'homes' and not 'Houses,'" he noted on his requests.]

"Houses that allow for persistent abuse will be punished. If you don't change of your own volition for the better, you must be punished to make you learn. That's the only way we can teach the stupid. Don't. Be. Stupid."

To Lon's surprise, the second-oldest of the group, Riad Sixdots, whose arm was in a sling, said in a loud voice, "I hope you punish them good, Valiant. I hope you kill them."

Immediately Londo went to his side and crouched to be at eye level.

"I don't kill people because I'm angry with them," he told the youngster. "Only if it's an emergency and they're trying to kill someone else, and there's nothing else left for me to stop them."

The boy digested this. "So how do they get punished?"

Lon shrugged. "We've been letting the courts decide, for the most part, and we usually urge maximum sentencing. We're in an emergency here, after all. Everyone should be helping and not hindering. But for the really bad guys, the ones who are doing things that this world particularly objects to…"

"What?" Riad asked breathlessly.

"I take them to the Great Shit Flats."

Riad and two other boys shouted their glee at that.

Lon wondered if they even knew what the Shit Flats were, but the place certainly had a descriptive name. "They have to live a good part of their sentences dressed in plastic hazmat suits," Lon explained. "Otherwise they'd puke themselves to death. Or in some pockets within the valley, die of asphyxiation. That's lack of oxygen. The prisoners there now work to clear the Shit Flats, make them into a healthy ecosystem."

"Eco…"

"Ecosystem. Where nature is peacefully living the way it's supposed to be. Where humans aren't trying to screw things up."

"Oh."

"Do you approve?" Londo asked him.

The boy looked up at him worshipfully. "Yes!"

Lon watched as the boys returned to their quarters, where they'd been promised a full dinner and soft, warm beds. He'd been terrified that he wouldn't be able to find them. Their well-being had wiped every other thought from his head. It had taken a half-day but now they were safe.

Londo had been kidnapped when he was three years old and still had no powers. The Lectori had taken him off-Earth and held him captive. They'd tortured him and used other innocent, non-para children as experimental controls. All those children, save one, had died because of Londo.

Kurt had survived because by then Lon had powers. It was sheer luck that Lon had saved both of them that terrifying day.

Hal had looked for him. History had written that absence as Hal exploring the sectors surrounding Earth to see who else needed help. Still, many people on Earth had screamed their complaints. Maximus was their protector, not that of people Out There.

But for years and years he'd been searching for Londo.

Hal had given up three years in, or at least been driven back to Earth by some pretty nasty stuff going on there at that time. He had a mission to protect Earth. By then he'd probably secured many eyes throughout the sectors who kept a watch out for Londo or the Lectori. He had disappeared a few more times after that; probably investigating a report.

How desperate must Hal have been during that time? How frantic?

His son.

And Maman, already so stricken with deep depression… How could Hal have helped her other than by making sure she was looked after by the best mental professionals? He hadn't discovered Sarastor's famed therapists until… Londo tried to calculate the dates… maybe a year after Maman had died. Maybe just months. How would that have affected Hal? To have been that close to curing her?

What would Hal have done to get his son back? How would he have protected him afterward, knowing his awful trauma?

– – –

Legion Medical had kept Lina's good friend Dinah Stewart under sedation much of the past few weeks. She'd first been completely in stasis after the Mind Control Tour, so they could work on Legionnaires and Demi who had higher priority than a civilian, and then in a combination stasis and coma while they concentrated on her.

It seemed to Lina that all too many of her friends had been sent to Legion Medical as a last resort. Well, thank God for Legion Med.

Dinah had a right eye again, but the area around it was black, blue and swollen. Micro-tubing covered her like a mat. Lina had been too shocked to note all her friend's injuries as she and Lon had escaped from that torture chamber with her, but everything under the mat seemed to be, well, no longer filled with holes or blood or unholy implements sticking out.

"You're safe now. You're safe now," Lina kept repeating as Dinah began to wake. "You're healing and so much better. You're safe."

Dinah let out a shriek that couldn't form well; it was stifled by her injuries.

"Safe!" Lina insisted. "You're in Legion HQ. Medical section. They've been working on you for some time. You're among friends."

Dinah's shriek now resolved itself into yips and yelps of pure fright. Dr. Junn moved forward to adjust some of the machinery around her, and her exclamations dwindled.

"They've given you a tranquilizer. There's no need to worry now." Lina explained that friends and family were anxious to be ported in when she was feeling better. Rikli-En, Dinah's primary torturer, was in jail. Because of his political position, he'd be extradited to the Empire but his father, the emperor, was pissed at him. Rikli might be executed.

"Good," Dinah tried to say.

"But the main thing here," Lina explained slowly, knowing that she'd have to repeat it, "is that we'll need you to give testimony on your ordeal."

A gasp of terror came from the woman.

"They'll take your statement and after that's recorded they can give you some medications that will let you forget as much as you want to forget. Even all of it."

Lina let that sink in.

"I had to make a statement about Granger, the rogue Ruby Guard. What I witnessed him do was… a nightmare. As gruesome for Olympia as what Rikli-En did to you. Afterward I opted for meds at about two-thirds strength because it was really messing me up. You missed me having a breakdown the day… The day after we found you. Here they can dilute those memories as if they happened long ago. Or they can have you forget them entirely.

"Plus Sarastor here has the galaxy's best psychiatrists ever. That's why Maximus sent Londo here when he was a boy. They've got me seeing one now too. I like her. We're already getting some good stuff done."

No reply.

Lina told Dinah about how their pay for the Tour was so much more than they'd imagined. Dinah could live in luxury. She updated her on what their friends were doing now that the Tour was over.

"Right now we want you to know that the danger is behind you. You're safe and you're healing wonderfully and thoroughly. You need to sleep and rest and take it easy. Olympia is in a room a couple doors down from you. She's awake and healing too. You two could bond if you want. I'll be by as much as I can. You know we're working on Aldierra now and it has a deadline, but I'll take time for you.

"You're safe. You're safe."

Dinah's eyelids slowly closed.

Lina sat there, so torn between emotions that she was numb. "She's one of my best friends," she told Junn. "They grabbed her. They thought she was me."

Junn checked his patient's readings on a screen. "She lived, and we'll have her back to full physical health in time, Mrs. Valiant. I'll have a mental therapist here for her the next time she wakens."

"Plus whoever needs to take her testimony," Lina murmured.

"That too."

— — —

Jae and Lina joined Londo as he revealed their plans to the next significant community to be relocated. Much of the presentation was interactively broadcast to the area by Internet, of course, but they'd set up a community conference in the home of the most prominent family of the district, who possessed a meeting area of impressive size. Their good opinions – and Lon hoped that was what they'd leave with, or mostly so – would influence the rest of the 150,000 their construction would be displacing.

Southwest of here, families and industries were already moving into the structures that had been CAM-built last week. The media was full of their praises for their new quarters, though their upset at having to move in the first place was not ignored. Fingers crossed.

"There will be no people left behind," Londo ordered. "Not the sick, not the aged, not the injured, not the babies, not the mentally disturbed. You can bring those to the medical facilities we will have in the area for the next week. Heads of House for any beings, alive or dead, that we find left behind will be punished severely."

He could sense the questions the men around him had. They were all fit men of medium age.

"Yes, you can abandon them at our facilities," Lon told them before they could ask. "This is just as we've done in many places so far. You can check with the people there to see if they can offer any advice we can't. We will provide medical services and aid as needed. Part of your new community will offer services and shelter for such."

"People without Houses?" came a question from the back as well as the Internet.

"We will have room for new Houses. Current House-less people can form their own Houses, name them. Join in a new community who understands what they've been through."

He didn't even have to see Lina's glance toward him. "And there will be safe houses for women, into which men will not be allowed. Those will have room for minor children as well. And, ah–" He felt Jae give him a mental nudge. "Men who want to come out as gay will have their own safe houses in which to live and work, if their own Houses will not respect them. Orphanages. Juvenile homes. Treatment centers for the mentally ill and addicted."

Jae answered more inquiries. He posted the variety of house plan templates they'd come up with. "Any architects or domestic designers from this region, please feel free to suggest your own alterations," Jae told the audience.

There. Everyone was now concerned with checking calendars of construction and studying the designs, and had stopped asking questions for a few minutes. Londo let out a breath and glanced about the room. Jae was pointing out something on some blueprints to a group of four men and video camera. Lina was in the back of the room. That's where the women and the more wretched members of this House had gathered. Lon eased back to talk with them as well.

But Lina was in her "zoned-out" state, and three women stood guard around her. They'd cleared a small space in the area. Someone must be porting in.

Sure enough, after a moment they appeared: a group of five varicolored people dressed in lab coats emblazoned with Wiley's private lab logo. They all stumbled slightly as they adjusted to light again after their dark two-minute journey. Then they looked around. Two immediately deployed their translators, but it took the others a few seconds to do so for themselves.

"Welcome to Aldierra." Londo stepped forward. He looked to Lina.

"Wiley thought it best to bring them in while we check out something."

"Hm?"

"Hapsburgs," Lina said, and gave a bob of her chin to draw his attention to the wretched.

Hapsburgs? A royal family from Europe's history. Lon checked out the people she'd indicated with that in mind. Then he looked around the room at the others of the same House.

"Habsburgs," Londo absently corrected his wife to fill in the conversational void as he considered the situation.

"'Incest is best,'" she murmured in return.

Wiley's people had fanned out, scanning the ones who were so deformed they couldn't stand, or who stood on unlikely limbs. Their faces were marked with long chins, ear lobes that reached their shoulders. Those shoulders were often off-kilter, with a hitch on the left. Fingers were long and knobby, compared with the average Aldierran.

Lon strolled to the head of the House, a person of fairly normal features, who bowed his head at him. "I was wondering," Lon said, not sure how to approach the issue. "Forgive me but as you know, I'm new to your culture. *Euh.* Do you keep track of your hereditary line?"

Serk Redfan gave a proud, satisfied lift of his eyebrows and shoulders. "Of course. We keep our House blood pure. Is that what you meant?"

"I suppose I did. This means that you make sure all babies born are…"

"Are Redfan House. Completely. There are no exceptions." What pride Serk showed as he looked over his relatives! Even the ones with bruises and other signs of violence.

"The Redfan House is a prestigious one."

"It is. Very. They know of us on the opposite side of the planet."

"Yes. I see. Now, does anyone here know about something called 'inbreeding'?"

Serk's face tightened into a stark mask.

"Inbreeding," Londo urged. "That happens when no outside genetic material gets into a bloodline. Recessive traits find a way to emerge."

"We have no inbreeding here," Serk declared stonily.

"On the worlds I'm most familiar with," Lon said as he rubbed his chin thoughtfully, "inbreeding results in, ah, let me think. Shortness of stature, lessened intelligence and lifespan, reduced fertility… Not sure what else."

Londo crooked a finger at one of Wiley's folk. He chose one of the men, so any report would be taken seriously.

"Hello. Your name is…?

"Henkor."

Lon didn't know if that was first, last or only. "Henkor. He is from Sarastor," he explained to Serk. "Tell me, Henkor, have you had a chance to peek at this family's DNA?"

Henkor held up his padd and then remembered to translate its screen into Aldierran for Serk. "This is very preliminary. As you saw, we only just got here. The Speaker wanted to confirm…"

Henkor checked the picture his padd projected and adjusted it, made it simpler. "See here? Very little fresh DNA has infiltrated this population over, well, generations it seems to me. Very preliminary. Ah."

He flipped pages as more data came in, and showed them. "Here. And here. Preliminary scans of a quarter of the room now." He gave a pained laugh. "Many of them are half siblings. More of them are also first cousins, and some are both." Then he peered at the screen's finer print. "Just a few sperm donors over the past few generations. Possibly the inbreeding has caused nonproductive azoospermia. There are only a few males left who can fertilize an egg. I haven't checked on the reproductive systems of the women yet. I'm sure those are just as, well, inbred."

Serk drew himself up. "I am not… whatever you just said."

"Oh, sir, I haven't checked you yet," Henkor said with apologetic tones, as if he'd just realized he was insulting this House, this man in front of him. "Until that happens I wouldn't know how or even if you'd been affected, except by superficial physical signals."

"But there is an inbreeding problem?" Londo asked.

Awe shone in Henkor's features. "Oh, very much so. I've never seen anything like this. It's amazing that this… they call it a 'House,' correct? We've been trying to keep up with most of your data… Amazing it has survived this long."

Henkor turned to Serk. "It shows that your House began with strong DNA. Very strong, to have weathered this and not died off completely."

"We are not. We are not," Serk sputtered. "Inbred."

"Do you keep genealogic records?" Londo asked. "Surely after all these deformities began to show up, and there must have been many who never survived to adulthood, someone in this House began keeping records?"

"We don't need any records. We are House Redfan. That is enough."

Sheer force of will kept Londo from rolling his eyes, though Henkor couldn't mask his utter astonishment at the statement.

"Twenty billion people on this world," Londo said, "and you couldn't find a few others now and then to give yourself some fresh genetic material to work with?"

Lina sidled up beside him. "Many of the people here are drug addicts, but we sobered them up for the moment. The women have all agreed to four-year birth control," she reported. "Shane over there is providing it right now. Dale is doing triage so we can get the worst of the bunch in to medical after the meeting."

"Our women!" Serk exclaimed. "What right do they have to make a decision?"

"They have their own rights," Lina said.

"The adults have the right to command their own bodies," Londo told Serk. "The children, well, we'll just check them out in our medical units and let them or their mothers–"

"Or aunts," Lina put in.

"Or aunts, closest surviving relatives of the maternal persuasion, give their opinions about what should be done. Four years isn't forever. By the time four years have passed, everyone will know more clearly where they stand."

"What's going on?" Jae's voice came from behind Londo, and he turned.

"Inbreeding."

"Oh, you noticed it too? Good to see you, Henkor. I want people working on DNA and other systems rectification courses. Let's get the worst of these cases healed and sort through the rest when everyone has time. Maybe some kind of general genetic treatment can be applied until we can sit everyone down for a specific one?"

Henkor raised his eyebrows at that and pursed his lips. "You have an inflated impression of what we can do, Neutrino."

Jae laughed. "You're on Wiley's team. That means you're beyond good."

"And I've got a fairly complex network of AffSys people who have said they're ready to help, including medical, and including medical research," Lina put in. "I'll link you to it. You've got Wiley's network available as well. I'm sure Aldierran resources have begun researching it, if it's so widespread. I've seen things. Or rather, people. It's everywhere, although in general not to the extent this is."

"Widespread," Londo whispered to himself. Inbreeding. Drug addiction. Mental illness.

Twenty billion.

"We will stop it in this generation," Jae declared.

Serk was pale to hear it all. His jaw worked as if he wanted to argue, but his shoulders and chest slumped. His breathing was not full and he didn't look anyone in the eye.

Drugs, Jae whispered silently. **I can feel the chemicals in his system. Tastes like anti-anxiety stuff.**

Londo took note of it as he moved to another side of the chamber. This Serk Head of House fellow was beginning to see that things would have to change.

Automatically he reached into his vest for his phone. This would be something interesting to tell H–

Lon put the phone back into its pocket and sealed it.

— — —

The transmission was earmarked as being an important announcement, and all three Starharts were scheduled. Early-comer Lina did a double-take upon seeing Jae arrive.

"Where's your cape?"

"Not wearing the cape," Jae said roughly. "Not anymore."

"You modeled that on Hal's cape, didn't you? Yours was longer, but otherwise the same."

Jae gave her a level look. "I've thought about this. I'm not honoring anyone who treated Londo that way."

"Oh." What could she say to that? "New look is a good one. No focus groups needed."

He gave her the faintest of smiles.

Lon came in right after that. He took one glance at Jae's appearance but didn't say anything. Instead he'd grimaced, and a glint of pain sparked in his eyes. Jae reached out and Londo squeezed his hand. He nodded at Jae and affected a small smile.

This was not the time for Lina to tell them that this morning her office – not her personal line – had received a mysterious message from Earth: an email address of "imntarbot@" a common email host, with the message "Now you have it." Signed just "E."

Lina added the address to her personal contacts and had sent the wedding video there without an accompanying note.

— — —

The studio's cameras centered on Jae in his new-version costume, also wearing one of his generic expressions: #3, patient but firm. "Aldierra currently has a population of twenty billion, rapidly approaching twenty-one. Perhaps another society could sustain this in a healthy way, but Aldierra cannot.

"Every expert we have approached tells us that the population must decrease immediately. There is no way around this. We don't want to kill anyone, so we're going to make this," he heaved a sigh, "declaration. This is no longer voluntary.

"All citizens must report to medical information centers for mandatory birth control. Medics will be coming around, much more of this will be done via robotic delivery, and local medical facilities will be provided the necessary supplies. If you have your personal doctor do the procedure, please make sure it's recorded in the planetary records. Proof will be required.

"If your House has not yet been checked for general health problems and recorded in our system, you need to do so immediately. We have a new bioscan system that will simplify all this. It should immediately be able to handle everyone who hasn't been seen."

Lina stepped in. "We've already told you about abortion possibilities. We thought we could put birth control on a voluntary basis, but this doesn't seem to be working. So it's now mandated. Sorry. At the end of four years we'll step back to see where we are.

"Women, by then you'll have a thorough understanding of what birth control entails. You may decide at that time to continue with it, either on a temporary basis or permanent. Men, same thing, but since the women are the ones who are carrying the children, we'll give them first choice in the matter.

"By then we'll also have good data of how far inbreeding has progressed on this world, and what kind of harm it has done. Perhaps you'll be able to choose a mate or just a sperm or egg donor who will provide more healthy reproductive material than you've been able to select from. I've now seen far too many people hopelessly harmed through inbreeding, and others who are a danger to producing such effects.

"Please understand that what we want is a healthier world for everyone. Healthier world equals happier families."

Into the silence that followed Londo stepped up. "Aldierra has a very lopsided sex ratio. In the months and years to come we'll be providing information on the wide spectrum that is gender. Gender and sex are different concepts. Those who believe they were born the wrong sex will get a chance to change that but frankly, that is not on the top of our priorities list. Give us some time on that, please.

"With this current sex ratio, women as a group have been victimized by men. Many men mistreat women; many men kill off baby girls. Men then wonder why it's difficult to find a female mate when there are so many other men competing with them.

"Effective immediately, anyone who kills a female baby or toddler because of 'tradition' or 'honor'—" he made a terrible face at the words – "will be caught, castrated, and I don't mean via chemicals, I mean surgically, and imprisoned to hard labor as befits any murderer.

"By now you all know how to get in contact with mental health professionals. I urge everyone who is affected by any of this to do so. We know the stress is great, with the Deadline and all the changes, and many people have been evicted temporarily from their homes. It's a difficult time, probably the most difficult in Aldierra's history. We now have the computer capacity available to give you the individualized mental treatment you need. Well, we think we do. Take advantage of it. Get healthier in all ways.

"Visitors to our world are seeing some shocking things. We welcome you as well to use these mental health facilities as needed."

Jae concluded their broadcast. He stood beside his spouses, and the director made sure all three would be on screen. "As you know," Jae said, "we Starharts are married. We married in the Feithi manner, not the Aldierran one."

He let that sink in. "On Feith, the normal way of conducting a Triune like ours was that all partners could have sex with each other, in any combination. Whatever they wanted and consented to.

"Our marriage is no different, though most of you may have thought otherwise. I enjoy expressing love, commitment, and physical attraction with either or both of my spouses. This is one of the reasons why we chose to enter a Feithi Triune." He gave a quiet smile. "The primary reason is that we love each other enormously.

"May all of you out there find the same kind of joy in your life. You may be asexual; in that case, I hope you find joy in expressing yourself in other ways and aren't forced to a sexual relationship just because it is expected."

Lon pointed a finger at the camera. "Consensual," he reminded viewers.

"Cheerfully consenting," Lina corrected. "Adults. Of sound mind."

"Yes." Jae nodded his head at them before he raised his hands before his chest and touched his fingertips together. "Now, as my wife often reminds us, be kind to each other. *Pelzire*."

— — —

Lina studied Londo across the conference table where various army types sat, their medals so bright on their chests.

He looked tired. Maybe defeated.

She knew for a fact that after that last broadcast he had messages from Stoan he hadn't answered.

Unobtrusively she touched Lon's arm. "How you doing?" she whispered so no one else in the room would hear.

He nodded and tried to smile.

Liar.

It had been another hard day for him. Today's news reports had not been kind, not any of them. It seemed that cameras had caught him at every unfortunate angle. Edited soundbites made it seem that he was callous, that he was doing the things he did on a whim.

Lon was the one destroying people's homes and workplaces. Lon was the one who wanted them to stop reproducing. He was the one who'd decided on castration, as he wanted to castrate all of Aldierra's straight men. Lon was the one most closely working with the various military groups, literal armies across the landscape. In most places there was an endless history of armies ravaging the populace. This was just another travesty taking place, but the Aldierran Protector was now leading the destruction.

It didn't help that Legion PIC was sending message after message to all of them demanding that they explain and counter the "fake" announcement about the Triune. Both Lina and Jae had blocked those messages at least from landing in Lon's offices. They didn't think they could block Stoan's without serious consequences.

She hadn't received bad press. Well, not much. People were afraid of her influence on Aldierra herself. Neither had Jae. Just Londo.

A large part of the Aldierran opposition had to be orchestrated by someone, or maybe someones. Large conspiracy theories were almost always headed by some kind of controlling presence. Lina checked with her guides, who in her focused imagination pointed out lots of amorphous figures, though they stood in organized patterns. Several groups, then, with each group having its own agenda.

And behind it all, she thought the image in her visualization was that of Patriarch Lupoff. She made a note and copied it to both Lon and Jae as a warning.

As the generals and majors seated at the table and appearing on the screens surrounding it were summing up what their troops had accomplished and where they'd be going in the next two weeks, Lina began to send texts to coordinate with the military about supplies and equipment. When the soldiers cleared out, she admitted the Three Worlds' PR chief for Aldierra, Wicker Greenweave, and two of his lead assistants into the room.

They seated themselves opposite Lon, and Lina stood.

— — —

Lon raised an eyebrow at her, but she began the conversation. "Not to be abrupt, but what the hell is going on with Lon's PR?" she asked them. "People are chucking all kinds of accusations at him. Making like he's a villain."

Wicker waved her down. "Some people need to sell scandal to get ahead. They don't want to hear nice things. They get a kick out of the seedy stuff. If a hero can be made to be scum, that's high entertainment."

"We aren't entertainment," Lina countered. "We need honesty. And the honest truth is that Londo's trying to save everyone's lives. It sounds to me like people want to bring Lon down so they can step into his shoes. Grab some of his glory."

"I can handle it, Lina," Londo said calmly. He radiated calm confidence. And fatigue.

"You shouldn't have to. I want our PR to correct these lies. If someone cuts a quote short to make it sound like what it wasn't, I want the full quote aired. I want people reminded that we've consulted with everyone we could over this. If they feel left out, that's because they haven't contacted us and shame on them, not Londo."

Wicker considered this as well as very many other things he had to handle, probably. He checked with his assistants and their padds, and then turned to Lon. "Could you be available tomorrow morning? I'm thinking we could film you talking with ordinary people who have had their ideas used in your projects. Get a few quotes from them. Inspirational. Thankful to have been heard. Interview the Houses moving into their new quarters."

"And it would remind everyone that they're supposed to have input on all this." Lina nodded. "Londo? Tomorrow morning."

"But I'm supposed to–"

"Tomorrow morning," Lina repeated. She turned back to Wicker. "He'll be there. See if you can film it quickly, because I don't have to tell you that we're busy. We shouldn't have to be fixing a rumor mill that shouldn't need to be fixed."

"We'll stop this before it can become a bigger problem," Wicker promised. With a motion to his aides, they left.

But Londo was rubbing his nose. That didn't bode well.

"I hate being Bitch Lina," she said before he could speak, "but this is important. You need to see that."

"Jae saw our interview this morning," he began.

An awful interview, done for the AffSys at Legion PIC's insistence. Lina had felt like crap as she gushed over Londo – a good thing – but had to ignore the fact that Jae was also her husband. The interviewer had guffawed at how gullible Aldierrans were to believe their Triune marriage lie.

Lina had twisted in her seat as she tried to look pleasant for the cameras. Lon had seemed confident, unperturbed.

"Jae said it was fine, but I think it bothered him," Lon said. He had been looking at the ground but now glanced up to see how she was taking it.

She took a breath and walked to Lon's chair. There was only so much lying telepaths could do to each other, especially when the bonds ran as deep as they did with them. "He's been drinking more than usual. Have you noticed?" she asked. "You know I've never liked the idea of a secret marriage…"

"Yes. You made that clear from the start."

"But. But Jae told me that I can't nag you about this. I didn't like that. I wanted to, maybe a couple times each day. Well, some days."

Londo cocked his head at her, waiting for more.

"But Jae is right. There is no one with a core of decency, of honor, as strong as you, darling Londo. Jae says he has faith in you. Sometimes… Every now and then. Very occasionally, I have to remind myself that I do indeed have faith in you too. Always. I just don't have Jae's patience. But I know as if it were already an established fact that you'll reveal the entire truth at some point."

She sighed. "I just hope it's soon. You need to have faith in yourself on this as well. I know you've got issue upon issue to work through, and I have a good idea of just how much pretending is benefiting you. This Hal thing is not helping, not at all, damn him anyway. I didn't mean that. But damn him for it just the same. But at some point this lie is going to stop being a benefit. It's going to be better for you to 'fess up. To clean your soul publicly and to hell with any repercussions.

"I am going to be even prouder of you then than I am of you now, and I'm so proud of you already I could burst. You've always been my hero, and you always will. Keep that in mind always. I'm so glad you chose me."

She took her husband in a tight embrace before he could say anything.

CHAPTER

23

"Lunch break!" Jae called down the line. The horn sounded. Five hundred men looked up in relief. They had been working in teams, hauling out the rankest of industrial and natural debris from the river. An old, medium-sized city overhung this side's banks. Half of it had caved in upon itself over the years as new construction grew up through and around it. Idle citizens watched curiously from nearby spots, while others proceeded through their normal city workday.

Jae waved to the pilots in two long boats, in case they hadn't received his call. They nodded, and the vessels swung into and onto shore.

An uninhabited clearing a quarter-mile downriver held rows and rows of tables. Trucks that were still unloading meals parked nearby, and a medical tent was always held ready. Jae had already had to use that himself this morning. It was just a cut. Maybe you could call it a laceration.

As the men came through they stopped at wash troughs, located next to a veritable shanty town of portalets, which augmented the dozens kept near the worksite. Terran and Aldierran music of a pop kind, using only male voices, began to play at low volume.

Jae circulated among the men. He inquired if they'd had any problems that needed addressing. A few came up to him with questions of their own. Two who were work partners even had a great suggestion they could put into play.

Finally Jae could sit down to eat his own lunch. It was fairly edible today. Lina's staff was in charge of catering the various missions, and they were doing the best they could. Crates of bottled water stood ready to be gathered up for the afternoon's work, and bins held used containers that would be washed and re-filled for another meal.

Jae chatted with his tablemates when he finally looked up across the river. He'd been too focused on his men to do so before. How could he have missed it? There sat a monumental but peculiar building. One end had sunken by what seemed the effects of some flood.

He pointed with a fork. "What's that? Anyone local here know?"

Everyone turned to look at the building. "That's the old emperor's health spa," someone far down the line called. He waved his wrist with its computer com on it at Jae, and Jae checked his own.

The information popped up. Six hundred years ago, Emperor Park-Mage had erected this spa to entertain his many guests. The emperor had spent happy child-hoods in the area, and thus had a fondness for the location.

Jae looked around at the city that sat on this side of the river, crumbled remains of previous buildings filling the gaps between the more modern ones. He tried to envision what it had looked like back then. Some edict must have prohibited building around the spa, for there was no new construction on that side of the river. The emperor must not have liked uninvited visitors.

The Web showed what the interior had been like when the spa was in its heyday. There were numerous bathing chambers; a hot spring rose under there whose waters were supposed to be healthful. Ballrooms. Feast rooms. Offices and guest bedrooms by the dozens. Much of the lower estate was devoted to security. The upper stories revealed vast, plush bedrooms for the emperor, his family, and his favorites.

The whole was topped by a forest of once-colorful onion domes. A veritable rainbow swirled upon each one, now much faded with time and disrepair.

"Hey, Lon, look at this," Jae messaged his husband.

Lon liked large architecture, especially if it was an interesting variant of more mundane types. He might get a kick out of it. He needed cheering up.

"Busy," came the reply. Jae took no offense. They often had to respond that way because it was true.

Yet two hours later Jae looked up to see Londo descending from the sky above the river. Jae put down a haul-rake, told the team he was working with that he'd be back, and flew off to join him.

They made a loop of the complex, then looped back to do it again.

"Isn't it ridiculous?" Jae said. "In an interesting way, that is. Onion domes had their day, a few centuries ago."

"*C'est fou*, but… it's kind of magnificent."

It certainly had a presence. But lying half-sunken on one end didn't do much for its prestige.

"We'll be tearing it down at some point," Jae surmised. "This is prime migration route here."

"A shame. It's of historical significance, you say?"

Jae thought his answer was lost on Londo, who was rubbing his nose, first rapidly, then slowly, then rapidly again.

"Uh oh."

"Let me do some research," Lon said.

"Uh oh."

"Let me see if all historical research on the place has been finished. I see some really old pottery and shards and stuff underneath, but there are lots of spots here that seem to have been controlled excavations. Nothing of importance left to dig up. Bet people used this spot for millennia."

"So we don't tear it down?"

Londo pooched out his lips and then drew them back in slowly. "Put it on hold. Yes, hold. I'll do some research." He looked to the river itself. "Need any help? I mean, as long as I'm here?"

— — —

After his supper a few days later, Lon reviewed the news services with a search for Three Worlds activities. Where did they all stand now? How much info was getting out to the public?

There was a channel for Jae's meditations. Lon had himself often used those videos, especially since That Damned Dinner. Very relaxing, and new ones from both Terran and AffSys sources were added all the time.

Jae had other channels where he explained the Feithi way of looking at the world, other people, flora, fauna. Spirituality. Lon bookmarked that one. He and Lina had had a few talks with Jae about just what was going on beyond what anyone could physically see, and had agreed that they had much to learn. Perhaps the Feithi could provide an angle on that. "There are many truths," Jae said cryptically.

Londo thought Jae always got a good private laugh out of being cryptic.

There were lots of subchannels that taught Aldierrans basic hygiene, basic cleanliness, basic manners, basic kindness. Lord, how these people needed those! There was one for sex ed and more for child care.

Mon dieu. Here were Kuttr from the Legion and two of his chief assistants, one male and one female, giving lessons on self-defense. Kuttr was a good if annoying friend of his. He'd have to ask him who had corralled him into doing these.

Blackmail, someone laughed in his mind. No, not someone. That sounded like Aiko. He stopped, breathless, and waited to hear the voice again.

No, nothing.

Here was Lina, dressed up to her eyebrows in snow-frosted green parka and fuzzy pants in some god-forsaken, wind-blown place as she paused to make her daily public update. This channel organized all such reports.

Hers were personal stories, pointing out Houses who had chosen projects to help out. Some cleaned their neighborhood streets; some made birdhouses; some worked with the Houseless.

She pointed Aldierrans to places they could go online to record their animal counts, for she had the entire planet walking outside to observe their world and the wildlife in it. There were birds and insects to be monitored in every season, and Lon saw that some types of fish were also being added to the mix.

Always scrolling at the bottom of her video were lists of sites with needed tasks and research that people could help with. They could join with other Houses in their area to work as small groups. "After you've finished for the day or for the task, take a few minutes to celebrate with the entire team. Post pictures. I want to see! We all do!"

And of course she reminded the audience that women were people too, and that everyone should try to do at least one kind thing every day.

Each video from every Starhart was interspersed with contact info for emergency medical and psychological help. They urged the citizenry to check their own Houses as well as streets outside and report anyone needing medical care to the contacts listed. All were worthy of being cared for.

"Please be kind," Lina reminded everyone.

Cameras followed wildlife as well as Jae's crews doing work all over the planet and its oceans. There were worker interviews. Lon was pleased that the interviewer always asked if the work were too hard, if the camps were comfortable, the meals were good (they seemed all right, and certainly not worse than average, Londo noted), and various services provided were satisfactory. Whether military or volunteer, the workers seemed proud to be serving their world.

Then there were his own videos. He thought his were more exciting than those of his spouses. There was less yakking: Lots of footage of him tearing down buildings, hauling monstrous mountains of debris away to be recycled, rescuing large oceanic life from fishing and transportation vessels. Here were some bits of him working alongside his troops when they needed more muscle, and even of him laughing with them, chatting side-by-side. *Bon.* He should drop Wicker and his staff a note of thanks.

He approved of his appearance. He looked commanding like he'd take no nonsense, but knew that the directors always reminded him to smile, and he had whenever possible. He wanted respect, not fear.

(He admitted to himself that he most wanted love. Adam had been driving that home a lot lately.)

Always Hal had taught him to choose a positive public persona and exemplify it. Image was everything. The two of them were too powerful to seem ordinary, for norms made mistakes. A megapara who messed up could destroy by accident. People would fear them.

He didn't really want to think about Hal these days, but Hal had taught him so much. Had he been worried about his own reputation when he'd been teaching Lon? Had he been telling him in other words, "Don't do as I do; do as I say"?

No. Hal could have no excuse for his actions.

Nesh had garnered large audiences as well. There was lots of footage of her walking – no, dancing – through newly-planted forests, her arms lifted up as if invoking heavenly energies. No wonder Lina had said the other day that Nesh needed music or singing or both to accompany her. He'd look into that. Earth could provide that kind of thing. Nesh would need to be consulted with the choices.

She also had her own focus videos, explaining to Aldierrans how to create a rapport with the flora of their world. Londo bookmarked a few of these to study later.

Hm. Any more Legionnaires they could steal? The Legion had a huge sub-structure of almost-made-it-ins, call-on-emergency folk, and affiliated organizations with members who had all kinds of powers. Some might be useful in this circumstance. If not them, perhaps some had relatives with the same powers who might be interested. Right, Aldierra had mentioned Nesh's cousins. He'd have to double-check on that, see what response she'd gotten.

He made notes and copied them to his spouses and section chiefs. On second thought, he copied them to Nesh as well. And Wiley. And Andri; she always expressed interest as to what they were doing. Stoan would likely not appreciate it.

– – –

It was a Tuesday, the day they coordinated their schedules to catch up with each other as to where they were on this project, which was why Lon had studied so much media coverage. He always wanted to come prepared.

Jae lugged a torso-sized vase with him as he returned to their hotel suite from his travels. He hefted it to sit on a long table between several pots of greenery. Yes, that would do.

Since his birthday the suite had been decorated with scads of plants, some flowering and some not. The afterparty at Jae's place had reminded everyone that Jae liked to fill his quarters with vegetation. It seemed he was now ready to settle in on Aldierra. All plants had been certified non-poisonous, for it seemed cats liked to chew on greenery.

They utilized Jae's finds for it: beautiful, hand-crafted pots, full of Aldierran culture. There were picture designs that seemed like stories being told. Jae scribbled a reminder in his schedule to track down the artisans to ask about them.

Lon had rigged anti-tip devices to each pot, though once it had been a near thing as Moosie had launched himself across the room, as Moosie did, and landed on one pot's rim. The pot had tilted dangerously but eventually righted itself. Moosie could be a little terror when he got in a mood, though it seemed done in innocence. Unlike Molly's crafty sabotage.

Ancient Fafhrd he couldn't do much about. Faf came out of her hours-long sleeps to eat a little, get a few cuddles, and then return to her rest. She didn't seem to be suffering which Lina said would be the signal to take her into a veterinarian's office to be "put to sleep."

"I toured Three Houses who specialize in this kind of thing," Jae proudly told Londo and Lina as they examined the new vase. "Look at the colors. The texture. The shape. There's a little old grandfather, his grandfather taught him, and his grandfather taught him… That kind of thing. They've been producing these for ages."

"Beautiful," Londo agreed.

"Where do we put it?" Lina asked. "It needs to be on display somewhere public. Where the cats can't reach it."

"Oh, I can store it," Jae said.

"Why?" Lina asked. "You keep bringing home all these, uh…"

"Interesting items," Londo suggested.

"Beautiful items with stories behind them. They all need to be honored in some way, so others can enjoy them too. And so we can see them often."

"You need to make a vocal record of why each item is important," Lon told Jae. "We'll put a checkpoint next to each item. I'll bust through a wall–"

He looked uncertainly at those walls.

"We're just renting," Jae reminded him. He liked that recording idea. "I'll get larger storage space somewhere."

"You are a pack rat," Lina accused. "Though one who knows how to spot good things. Or at least things with interesting histories."

Jae smiled. "I do love the stories the most." He squeezed Lon's hand. "That's one of the main reasons I married you. For your stories."

Lon returned his warm smile with a kiss before he got serious again. "How long have we been here?" he asked.

Jae tried to sort out the days but before he could reply, Lon said, "Too long. We have overstayed our welcome. Installed too much of our equipment. And our staffs. And visitors. It's a regular Three Worlds City here anymore. It's time to find our own place."

"And where would that be?" Lina asked. "Will we still have army personnel working there?"

"No," Jae said quickly.

"We need them. We will for some time."

Lina thought. "We'd need easy transporta–"

Londo waved her down. "Yes, yes. I've been looking at this one location. Not far from Plegerit, but not too near as well. I've grown fond of this region. Good views. Really good views – in the future."

"I do love a view," Lina said as she cast Jae a sideways glance. He glanced back and waited for Londo to continue.

"This is above one of the lesser migratory tributary routes. City behind us. River below and vista ahead."

"Is there a building there?"

"There could be." Lon made computer motions and a screen appeared before them. "Remember that spa, Jae?"

"Whoa!" Lina exclaimed as the image came up, the spa as it had originally been built. "Is that a palace? An imperial Russian palace?"

"*Ouais*, it does have similarities. It used to be a spa. Imperial, served all the bigwigs. Lots and lots of rooms, meeting spaces, and a tremendous family living area."

"And you'll move it?" Jae asked dubiously. "As I recall, part of it was disintegrating."

Londo shrugged. "It could do with a refresh, but I can manage it. Might need some help. I can get it."

Jae changed the video feed to show the current state of the interior. "Needs a lot of refurbishing. And extermination. How long will it take?"

Lina watched the views for a few seconds. "Ancient shambles," she determined, "though there are a few rooms that look only antiquated. We could live here until it's done." She gave a long sigh. "With all the staff and business, I admit that this place has become a bit, well, confining. Plus I always feel like I'm intruding here. The poor hotel staff."

Londo looked at her sharply. "*Vraiment?* You should have said something sooner."

"It's efficient. We need efficient while we're so busy. Here we have staff who can commute easily. It would be great if we could turn this into a full office building, but I'm sure the hotel staff and the owners wouldn't appreciate that."

"Unless they would," Londo said. "We haven't asked."

Jae settled the video on one particular section of the spa. "We can set up special transporters," Jae said. "As for the remodeling, if we used some smaller 3D printers that–"

"No. We remodel using care. Craftsmanship. Tradition. This is not only historical, but for *us*. We can rough in with the printers, but finishing will be done by human work."

They stood, staring at the videos.

"Really? Can we beef up the paint job, make it like it was originally? That must have been spectacular."

"Lie, it'll be spectacular again."

"Then again," she said, "I don't really need to live in a spectacular building. Maybe tone down the original a bit so no one hurts their eyes looking at it."

"We will do that. Now, where do we live until it's done?"

"Cats," Lina said.

Both Lon and Jae nodded thoughtfully. "Cats," they said in unison, mulling the problem.

"Does this spot you're thinking of–"

"It does have a good area of openness around it. We'd filter the air. They could play outside."

"Enough for a good-sized garden?"

Londo raised an eyebrow at Jae. "You want to garden?"

Jae couldn't help himself. He vibrated from side to side in such a burst of anticipation that he surprised himself. A garden! "I've been considering it. Winter is coming, a good time to plan and prepare. Let's have a garden with green meditation space in it."

"We will have a garden," Londo declared. "Maybe even a maze and formal grounds, like those fancy Italian and Chinese places have. A nice pool for Lina." His eyes brightened and he stood straighter. "We could get a dog."

Lina pressed her lips together before releasing them to speak. "Um, can we make small side-trip? To Earth? I once saw something there."

Two minutes later they all stood outside the conservatory at the US Botanic Garden building in Washington, DC. It was a late Spring morning, but a small tide of tourists rambled the Mall.

"In there," Lina said. "Somewhere in back. It's been a few years since I've seen it."

Walking just a short way in the building amid its various interior sample gardens and landscapes took much more time than Jae was sure Lina had estimated. They had him in tow, after all, and everything was so interesting. He had to stop and study the plants and how they'd been arranged.

A staff member didn't help their tight schedule when she trotted up to give them a personalized tour. She pointed out what the signage neglected. Even Lina and Lon were captivated.

Finally they came to the chamber with the thickly branched, low-spreading trees amid benches and walkways. Lina raised her arms to take in the entire section and said, "Cats."

"Cats?" Londo asked.

Jae nodded slowly. "Cats. I see." So much better than those two cat "trees" they had back at the hotel.

"These are indoor trees, out of the smog and filth, living their best life, or at least a good one. Maybe we could do an inside/outside thing. How much do forcefields cost to keep out the worst weather and pollution? The cats would love to have real trees to climb and scratch. These are low enough that they won't break their necks on them."

Jae examined said trees with their tangle of branches and asked the guide questions about light levels and diseases. Londo busied himself searching screens he'd called up. He crooked a finger at Lina. "How are these?"

Two scrawny trees sat on a rocky mount that held debris from abandoned buildings.

"Those poor things. But they've survived. Maybe we could help them along?"

Londo called Jae over. Jae searched on his own screens, knowing he'd seen the branch structure before. "Those are *oveng* trees. Native to the Plegerit area; they've survived current climate conditions. Long-lived, especially in normal climatory conditions. Modest in their growth extent."

"Put a dome over them…" Londo squinted first at the video picture and then at the trees in front of them. "A permeable one. Lets rain through, not pollutants. We can adjust for temperature when needed."

Jae said, "We'll set up optimal climactic conditions and give them cold if they need it. Not too hot, though."

Londo was slowly nodding. "So we have the location. With trees. For the cats. Garden space and a good-sized lawn. For a dog," he included quickly. "Easy transportation for the staff and visitors. And we have a house."

"A palace," Jae corrected.

Lon shrugged. "A bit of a palace. A small palace."

"A mansion of great size," Lina said. "Dog to be discussed, by both us and the cats. And where do we live while all this is fixed up?"

"Too bad you don't have a big white tent," the guide said.

They realized they'd been speaking English. "Tent?" Lina asked.

"Like on that baking show," the guide said. "My favorite series! It's from Britain. Every year they bring in a troop of amateur bakers and they cook and bake in this giant tent. It's got electricity. Refrigerators and sinks and everything." Then she tipped her head. "Not air conditioning, though. There was this baked Alaska fiasco…"

"A tent," Jae repeated. He'd spent his early childhood living in a tent. Good memories. Family.

"A tent," Lina and Londo both said thoughtfully.

The guide gave them the name of the show and where it streamed, then hinted about her favorite seasons. They thanked her, Jae finished recording footage of this particular section (adding it to all the other footage he'd taken of this building), took selfies for the guide, and left.

— — —

That evening they sat together on the main couch in the primary living room of their suite, watching Terran TV where people baked intricate cakes. Cats lounged across them and the back of the couch.

"I want some of that cake," Lon decided of the creations on screen.

"I need to cook something," Lina declared as she scratched the two cats on her lap. "Probably not cake to begin with, but something. I get urges. This place has nowhere to cook, not seriously. Not even as semi-seriously as I am on my best cooking day."

"We'll get you a kitchen," Londo said. "Big kitchen. For cakes."

"White tents should be easy enough to come by," Jae mused. "Sturdy enough to stand up to rough weather. Secured so no one can come in without permission… I'll check Legion records, see what suppliers are out there."

"A place cats can't get out," Lina added.

"Hm." Jae turned to Londo. "We've decided? We can live in a tent for a while? Everyone?"

"I think I can stand it, as long as it doesn't go on forever," Lina said.

"We'll need a pitiful story about our early married life to tell the kids when they get older," Jae said with a quiet smile. Family.

"Hunh," Lon grunted. "General area forcefields, but we'd have those over the house anyway, like we have here."

"Do we need more tents for meeting rooms? Offices for our staffs? We need to have some way to have private areas as well as public ones."

"Gonna be a lot of big, temporary tents," Jae said. He set Ember and Moose aside and stretched in his place. "Estimated move-in date for the building?" he asked as he reached for his padd.

"Ah. *Euh…*" Londo rubbed his nose and then his left ear.

#Don't mess with your earring!#

"Let me think about that."

CHAPTER

24

"I am tired of rotten food!" Lina declared to no one in particular. She had waited until she left the hotel's restaurant, which served the staff and visitors. She'd hoped they were serving the staff a lunch a little better than what the servers had brought up to her suite. They weren't. She hadn't eaten beyond a bite to determine that.

How could the food around here be worse?

That TV show had reminded her that Out There was food good enough to make your mouth water just thinking about it.

The food here was tasteless, bland if not repulsive, textureless, icky to look at... But this was a premier hotel, its base staff still on duty even as many other duties had been taken over by soldiers. Some of those were working in the kitchens, overseeing safety – making sure no one deliberately added a poison to the food – and even helping with the actual cooking.

Bracken had assured her that the cooks here were top caliber.

Lina spotted Kanti taking with Wicker Greenweave and their Communications Director, Batt Middleplaid, across the lobby, and went up to them.

"Food," she said.

"Gah," Kanti replied.

Wicker looked at the two of them, perplexed. "Are you having a problem with it? Did someone tamper with it?"

Lina heaved a theatrical sigh. "It may be because everything's so polluted here. It may be that at some point in the past, Aldierran cooks looked at what they had to work with and just gave up."

"Really gave up," Kanti said. "They probably committed suicide."

"Bad food?" Wicker asked them, giving Batt a shared glance. "I thought the food here was great."

"Great?" Lina asked.

"Maybe Aldierrans have different types of tastebuds than do Terrans," Kanti suggested.

That might be true enough. Lina called for four of the chefs from the hotel, one of them military, to join them and then ported them to Earth. Londo had suggested a restaurant that served good, everyday food. He called to warn the place that they were coming, and manfully volunteered to come himself. Jae scrambled to join them.

There they had an abbreviated meal. While the Starharts ate vegetarian except for Lon, who said he'd do mostly likewise though he wasn't on the vegetarian wagon [yet, Lina thought. Give him time], the others chose from the full variety offered. The restaurant was in the middle of dinner service.

And the chefs were amazed.

Now it was Jae who suggested a Sarastoran restaurant and made the arrangements. They ported. They went through another round of amazement, this time with a breakfast menu.

"So what can we do about the food on Aldierra?" Lina asked them as they sat back, digesting.

"We could have them all watch *Bake Off*," Kanti ventured. Everyone had ordered takeout for future meals and/or study, and Lina had ported in a stack of stasi-keeps. Kanti kept her own on her lap, guarding it.

Again with that show. Kanti was a fan of it, and she was serious. "They go for fancier food, though they do traditional dishes occasionally. Plus it's mostly desserts, and we need the full gamut of courses."

"We're not going to get the entire population to attend culinary school," Londo said.

"I want our people to eat well," Lina declared. "And by 'our people,' I mean the people who are working so hard for us. This includes your troops, Lon. Your Corps, Jae. And our staff. Plus the food in our hospitals and orphanages and schools and shelters should be up to snuff. Healthy snuff."

"It could spread out from there," Londo admitted.

Jae would have added to the statement, but his mouth was full.

The chefs discussed the fare they'd had. "For all those groups we could start small," one put in. "We could choose one item that everyone eats often. What about beginning with improving *scanners*?"

Scanners were pastry-wrapped savory fillings like pasties, empanadas, calzone, or even steamed buns. Lina had sampled a few from Aldierra's street vendors and she admitted that one or two had been edible.

"We could hold our own *scanner* contest," Jae was finally able to suggest. "I volunteer to judge, as long as the entries are vegetarian."

Lon was thoughtfully considering. "It might be an incentive," he decided. "'Come work to save your world, and eat good food.' I like it."

While they had their chefs with them, they took tours of the restaurants' kitchens. The chefs not only got to see how other worlds managed commercial cooking, but what kind of regulated cleanliness they kept. There was much nodding and discussion, plus a vehement shaking of a head or two over some issues.

That afternoon on Aldierra Batt made the announcement. He was youthfully middle-aged, had a pleasant demeanor, and never got mad no matter how many times reporters asked the same questions. He already lived in Plegerit and hadn't moved into the hotel. His offices were on the second floor, next to the studio. And he'd eaten an entire heaping plate of the food they'd brought back for him and Wicker.

Standing at a podium before a wall containing a large symbol of the Three Worlds, he announced the contest and that local judging would take place in a week and a half. Regional would be a half-week after that.

"The quickness is because we want our workers, our volunteers and staffs, to have appetizing food available as soon as possible," he explained before launching into more detailed instructions. "The final level will be overseen by Three Worlds. It's scheduled for three weeks after the first eliminations.

"Final judging will be on continental and not worldwide basis. We want you all to think about your culture and come up with satisfying food that is a part of that. Who knows, a winning recipe might be something you're already serving to your House. Thus we'll have multiple winners, and judging will be blind. We anticipate three or four winners per continent, perhaps more.

"At the continental level, the Minister for the Three Worlds has volunteered to help judge for vegetarian entries. Oh wait, I have received a separate note about this."

Batt fumbled in his chest pockets until he produced a small, folded piece of paper. He shook out the old-fashioned way of communicating with a flourish and then read it dryly: "Watch out for Jae. He cheats." Matt gave the camera a grin.

"My final item is to ask you to think about another type of everyday food you'd like to have in competition. We'll be announcing the next round in the near future."

– – –

The next day Lon had only three minutes' warning before Jae broke into a popular planetary broadcast. Damn, things had been going so well too. He hurried to comb his hair as he strode out of his meeting in the suite's conference room. He could hear Jae downstairs in the regular studio, along with technicians who had been tweaking connections to the new educational programming stages across the hall and now scrambled to get out of Jae's way.

"I've just been informed that there are parts of Aldierra that practice slavery," Jae brusquely told the camera and entire world. "No. A hard and inflexible 'no' on this. As of this moment, it is illegal – grossly illegal – to own another human being or to sell them. For any purpose."

Lina herself arrived next to Lon and ported them both to the studio. They stood behind Jae, coordinating the screens of their padds and pointing at various reports and areas on maps as they conferred.

"We had no idea this was going on." Jae declared, "Houses with slaves will free them immediately. They will provide for them. They will assure their safety. No one will be harmed in this transition. If an ex-slave wants to stay within the House and the House approves, that House will treat them as an honored employee with a good wage and a safe environment. If they want to leave–"

Though he hadn't had a chance to read the two major reports Jae had filed, Londo interrupted. "We'll adjust our plans for the new city sections to provide housing for the ex-slaves in those districts that have them." Though he wondered how in hell he'd accomplish that. So much was already under way… "Or that *used* to have slaves, that is, because as of this moment, slavery is no more. There will be education, if needed, training for new jobs, if needed."

"Medical services," Lina added. "And women of Aldierra, if you are being made to work in whatever way and are receiving no compensation; if you are being held within a House that you want to leave; if you feel you are in an unsafe situation you cannot leave: you are a slave, though your House may not call you such or have paid money for you. We already have a growing network of safe Houses for you. If you can't find transportation, call Three Worlds and we will get you out of there. Check around to see if there are others within your House who also want to leave. Don't forget the children and those with disabilities who are in imminent danger of harm or mistreatment."

Jae nodded at the camera. "You'd probably be surprised at how much we've managed to do so far in creating safe havens around the world. I'm pleased to report that Aldierra already had secret organizations in place that had been doing this general type of work for centuries. We are happy to aid them by adding them to our own networks. If you need help, contact us."

But Londo was rubbing his nose. Jae waited expectantly and Londo looked up, into the camera. "The ex-slaves need legal documents," he said. "Contracts about what the people who once enslaved you owe you. Contracts about how and if you will ever have contact with them again. Contracts concerning any children or other family you might have. We will come up with contract templates. Boilerplates."

Lina scribbled notes and sent off heads-up emails to their law staff.

Lon continued, "If you can't read or understand them, contact us and we'll have someone explain them to you. All contracts having to do with manumission – that's setting slaves free – will carry the seal of the Three Worlds on them. If any contracts are used that carry a falsified seal… Well, we will deal with the people who created those."

His scowl was almost feral.

Jae raised his eyebrows at the cameras, which added a mystic air of promissory justice to those who would try such. After he signed off he looked back at his spouses. Lina was still sending emails and Londo was already talking with lawyers.

"Great orb, this world," he sighed. "No one needed to sleep tonight, did they?"

CHAPTER

25

The announcement for the special session at Legion HQ had just come through an hour ago. Deegel's court martial was day after tomorrow. Imagine: Lon had actually forgotten about it, what with everything going on.

This was bad. This was very bad.

He and Jae had used the planetary teleporters to return home from an Aldierran emergency with half the Gold Army running amok in central Orchin and slaughtering civilians. It had taken most of the day to grab every last hiding soldier and either crush or vaporize their weapons. If they'd missed anyone, they were hiding so deeply they wouldn't emerge until Doomsday.

"Do I send medics?" Lina asked him over his earring. "We just got in another load from the AffSys. Forty."

Lon considered. "I'll have Bracken report triage results. Send the medics to the worst-off, but not to the ordinarily wounded that the army and locals can tend to. Not too many; not for too long. We have too much to do elsewhere."

In addition, small riots had broken out in spots around the globe where slavery had been a major element of society. Citizens were screaming to ask who was going to do essential work now? How were they expected to pay people who'd been working for generations for free?

It didn't help that complaints were pouring in from, well, everywhere, about the audacious idea of including *girls* in their new children's education programs and also broadcasting those so that grown *women* might overhear – and learn.

Then the Legion summons had arrived. Jae had splayed his fingers over his face and given him a fed-up-with-the-universe look. Lon had grimaced at him in solidarity. Jae got a drink before retreating to his office within their suite to organize his testimony. In an hour he was scheduled for his sleep cycle. Good luck with that. Londo still had a half-day's work awaiting him.

He took a few moments to stand in front of the bathroom mirror, automatically adjusting his vest before resuming work. As usual, he checked for any sign of thinness in his hair, his mind on the reason for the summons: Deegel and the blot she had made on the Legion's history. She had betrayed them – and tried to poison Lon's marriage as well. Why would she have done that? How could the need for fame have distorted her character so? Had she been placed under therapy for it?

It would have been so much better if Deegel had died instead of Aiko. Aiko had been a hero of historic proportions. She had taken out so many threats and guided so many out of danger. She had inspired and motivated people. She had loved him. She was–

In his mirror, standing behind him.

Aiko.

Though she was clad in her famed gold uniform, she shone from within with a golden light of her own. Her skin was as dark as Hal's; her short-cropped hair capped in golden bangles so it seemed her head glistened with golden light.

Her poignant smile for him was still as warm as it had ever been, and he wasn't sure if it made him gloriously happy or heart-rendingly sad or just guilty to greet her. She had died before his eyes, murmuring a love for him that he could never return at the level she deserved. And then she had reappeared in Legion HQ in, well, spirit form to tell them all about the Three Worlds and swear them to their service.

He didn't turn, afraid she would vanish. Her smile widened. She'd said she was safe and happy wherever she was now, past death's door.

"They've made memorials to you," he told her. "Foundations. Educational organizations."

She nodded.

"I really did love you, you know. I just couldn't... I couldn't... love you that way. I was trying. I was thinking about–"

Behind him, she nodded without losing that smile. Then she blew him a kiss in the way of her people: the blowing and then a pop on the lips with the middle finger.

His insides began to relax. She was okay. She was okay with him.

"You need to see to the way you present yourself," she told him. It wasn't telepathy; her voice came as clearly as if she stood where she seemed to be.

Londo resisted turning, having heard too many legends of fairies and ghosts disappearing when fully confronted. Instead he delighted in seeing her, looking so vibrant and joyful in his mirror.

"How so?"

"I am looking after you. You are doing well. Your life is progressing the way it should. But do think about whether you should show your angry face so often, or lose your temper. Appearances, you know. Setting an example not only to others but to yourself. Be kind. Be patient. Be forgiving. Everyone is trying their best in their own way. Billions of people see you. Who is the leader they will follow?"

"Are you talking about... forgiving Hal? Or that I should take on Jae's masks?" Jae had those expressions he would adopt so his inner feelings wouldn't show to the public.

"Be sure the path you're on is the one you wish to walk. Be true to yourself. Speak the truth about yourself and your goals. About who you truly are. I am so proud. Everyone here is so very proud of you."

"So I should—"

But she was gone.

— — —

Now Lon took an extra moment to check reflections every time he passed a mirrored surface. Nothing.

D'accord. Set an example. Even as he worked his hardest Londo contemplated the idea of impinging the honor of the Legion. The Mega-Legion had supported him in so many ways for so many years. Working with it had begun the process of separating his public identity from the image of Maximus.

Lon's hands formed fists when he thought of his traitorous father.

But… forgiveness, Aiko had said.

These days Londo was hero in his own right… though many still lumped him in Hal's shadow. This Three Worlds duty and Aldierran crisis would cement his independent standing. People would respect (or hate) him and not him-and-Maximus for it.

He had so many friends in the Legion. Comrades. Was his so-called ruse really harming their images? They had their own to maintain, just as he did his.

What would happen should the truth come out?

— — —

Lon's scandal could hold little comparison to that of Deegel. Fellow Legion member Neuron, aka Deegel Voke-Netton's case had finally come to trial. Deegel was a member of a well-known Beta Team. She'd just emerged from secret trial by a high-security Affiliated Systems court.

Guilty.

She had leaked Mega-Legion secrets to journalists in exchange for publicity. Before leaving for prison she faced a Legion court-martial.

This time away from Aldierra was necessary.

This was for Legion honor.

"This is family honor," Lina said quietly as she adjusted Lon's vest before porting them. "The Legion is your family as well as Jae's."

When Jae and he arrived at Legion HQ in full, spotless uniforms, Londo had to remind himself not to rub his nose so much. It was a nervous habit, a tell that he was overly concerned about something. He was about to berate himself when he noticed Jae adjusting his wrist Arrays for the sixth time.

He gave his husband a reassuring arm squeeze and Jae nodded at him. Then cursed.

"I know," Londo said quietly.

Damn Deegel anyway.

— — —

A helluva trial. Many of the membership's cubicles had to be blacked out when they got to the secrets too far up in classification category for some to be privy to. Odder yet that Lina's testimony had been taped yesterday for presentation today; she couldn't give it in person because, even though she had helped expose the scandal, she didn't have the security clearance to deal with what she had exposed.

Lon had to give his own testimony of how Deegel's perfidy had been discovered. Deegel had long been spying on him personally, breaking the rules of Legion privacy. Then had come that night when Deegel had tried to spy on Lon's marriage bed activities in order to entertain her private guests.

The others who had been with Deegel in circumstances defined as official Legion misconduct – a small orgy, only one person more than what was involved in Lon's marriage – had volunteered to collect evidence to atone for their actions. Legion Protocol and Security had worked together so their unpublicized sins had been forgiven. From there everything had gone to the highest echelons of Legion Legal Services.

Thank god Aiko hadn't lived to see this. Aiko had been the zenith of Legion honor. Seeing this would have killed her.

Why hadn't he been able to love her better?

Jae spoke from the podium in the Great Meeting Hall to present his own research findings. Actually Lon and Lina had both helped, but no one need know that. No one knew that Jae had telepathically overheard the scene in Deegel's bedroom where Lina had discovered the betrayal. He'd been in Lon's bedroom next door at the time.

The secrets Deegel had chosen to spill had shown her mastery of PR. She went for the flashy stuff. Who was going with and doing what with whom when Legion PR hadn't released the news. Details of Lon and Lina's rushed marriage, and that Lina was a Terran "witchdoctor."

But that hadn't been enough for her.

She'd leaked details of delicate missions that hadn't been reported because they were for behind-the-scenes matters that weren't meant to be publicized. Two of those had held great import, had been part of affairs in which the Legion was working to balance conflicting governmental policies that would affect hundreds of millions.

High-ranking names. High-ranking offices. Policies that had been secretly redesigned for the betterment of most involved. Deals and more deals made behind closed doors. There had even been a secret bargain struck with the upper strata of the Yanist-Glory Empire.

Juicy gossip.

Do we really know the extent of her powers? Jae asked Londo silently. **She can feel others' emotions through long-distance touch.**

Through touching her side of my bedroom wall within her apartment, and from there to the floor and to my bed. Or she tried, Lon told him. He'd had to install insulators under the legs of his bed and other furniture.

She could influence people's emotions. Has that ever sounded a little like Mind Control to you?

Londo was silent as he pondered.

It always has to me, Jae said without waiting for an answer. **That's why I avoided her. Plus she wanted to get in your pants. Badly.**

That's what turned me off her. She was creepy about that.

She had those breast enhancements just to please you. Of course...

It was just the one time. You know how desperate I was. Just an experiment. It didn't work. I made sure it never happened again.

Did you ever ask yourself, what if she can do more than just deal with emotions? What if she can leech information out of people's minds? There have been a few times when she knew things she couldn't possibly have had access to. I asked Chim about it once, but she said Deegel wasn't a telepath.

Maybe not a kind she was familiar with. Though Chim's the best-trained teep I've ever known.

It's something we should keep in mind.

Except that Deegel is going to a mega prison for a long, long time.

We should keep track, just in case. I'm sure Stoan will set up covert Legion monitoring.

Ouais. If I were him, that's what I'd do.

— — —

Through the legal proceeding Londo contrasted and compared Deegel's final sexual escapade to what the Legion would think about his situation. Jae wouldn't matter to the rumor mill because Jae was Jae. His being Feithi excused much. Lina was Terran, and thus of little import to most in the Legion.

But Londo was Valiant. Alpha Team Leader.

That was a high position from which to fall. A high position that could possibly drag others down with him as he went – and lift others up in its wake.

– – –

Accompanied by solemn ceremonial drumbeats, Deegel was escorted to center stage. The dark-haired ex-heroine did not wear her flashy Neuron uniform but instead wore simple gray tunic and tights. There was no heavy, trendy makeup for her. Her blue complexion was pale; her features, drawn. Stoan stood outside of the spotlight upon her and began listing her Legion benefits... Revoked. The many honors she had accumulated... Revoked. The list went on and on.

At last he held up the items that made up Deegel's Legion Array, the wrist and ankle bands and the ring that controlled them. They had been confiscated when she had first been dragged away, her position with the Legion suspended until evidence could be gathered and she could be brought to trial. Now it was official: her Array was officially denied her. AffSys courts were still to decide how much of a mind wipe she would receive to rid her of the higher level secrets she had accumulated through the Legion over her years of membership.

Do you think that will work on her? Lon asked Jae.

"You are Legionnaire no longer," Stoan announced to her and the Legion membership. "You are dishonorably discharged from the Affiliated Systems Megaforce Legion. May your shadow never darken our work again."

Accompanied to either side by AffSys guards wearing power-insulating gloves and boots, Deegel was marched off-stage to her fate. A Legionnaire no longer.

Would that one day be him, cast in deep disgrace, when the Legion found out?

– – –

Lina rubbed the sleep from her eyes as she ported into the Monitor Room for middle-of-the-night porting. It seemed like she had only ported Lon and Jae back to Aldierra minutes ago.

A squad of ten Legionnaires stood ready, and she thanked what gods there were that she'd remembered to switch to her burqa before the final port to the Monitor Room. She kept it in a closet in Lon's apartment where he probably wouldn't see it.

She had three personal credits left; there was no room for any demerits.

Erik sat on an ordinary stool, though the OD was supposed to stand at all times. They must be allowing for his injuries. He glanced at her outfit and shook his head.

"Lina," he told her, "give us one minute and we'll be ready."

Someone had given her demerits last time because she didn't respond to statements directed at her. So now it was: "Yes, Sunstorm, sir." Lina bowed her head meekly to him as his eyebrows raised in surprise. He had to help one of the team or else he probably would have asked her about it.

And oh bother, Stoan was in this team going out. He was giving last-minute instructions, as the primary monitor showed that the situation they were porting into was a darkened cityscape with bursts of laser fire silhouetting background buildings. A metal container that looked like a dumpster stood in the near distance. The Legionnaires all had weaponry, too, and two were checking the charges on their guns as Stoan turned around.

He walked toward her and she skittered to his right. "What I want," he told her, "is for us to come up right behind that– What the orb are you doing?" For she'd ducked again farther behind him. He had to keep turning around to see her.

"I'm trying to maintain the four paces," Lina said, and remembered to add, "Commander Magnos, sir," to it.

"And I'm trying to talk to you!" he commanded. "Stay there!"

"Yes sir."

"Now, as I was trying to say, I want the squad to come out right there–" He pointed to the screen and the dumpster object, which had a doorway-type of indentation along one side. "Everyone ready?"

"Um, excuse me, Commander sir," Lina squeaked. "Begging your pardon, and I'm sorry, but..." How the hell did she do this without getting more demerits? Contradicting a Legionnaire – not only a Legionnaire but Mister High-and-Mighty Stoan?

"What? What the orb is all this?" He gestured at her Ghost of Future Yet to Come garb.

"Excuse me, Legion Commander sir." Lina again gave a quick bow from the waist. "But *they* say that that's not a safe place."

"Not a safe– Oh, they say that, do they?" Stoan sneered around at his squad.

"Begging your pardon, sir," Lina groveled.

"Are you questioning me?"

"No sir. It's just that it's not safe. Give me somewhere else to port them."

"Arguing with the Legion commander…"

"I'm not arguing, Commander Magnos sir, I'm just telling you that–"

"You are arguing. You are questioning my command. This is insubordination!"

"I'm terribly sorry, sir. I hate to do this, sir."

Stoan began to rant about how she was getting too uppity for her position and she should realize she was merely an adjunct, a tool, and not a Legionnaire in any fashion. When he gave her an order, by the orb, she would follow it.

Lina cowered. "Yessir. Yessir. Begging your pardon, sir."

Stoan pointed into the doorway that was centered on the screen. "I am the Team Leader here, not you! And I want us placed right there. Not there, and not there." He pointed around the screen. "Not one millimeter farther away than in the shadow of that–"

His chin dropped as a missile fell onto the dumpster, utterly annihilating it and an area of about twenty meters around in a spray of fizzing lasers. Shrapnel exploded in sparkling arcs across the landscape.

The last fizzes finally died away some minutes later.

"It might be safe enough now," Lina offered, "sir." She shuffled away from him.

Stoan set his jaw. "I want to see you in my office when I get back!" he ordered. "Same position – now!" And Lina ported the squad.

In the silence of the room, Lina asked forlornly, "How long do you think this mission's going to take, Sunstorm sir? If I may ask?"

– – –

"Lina, what the orb's gotten into you tonight?" When she just stood there, gathering her robes tighter around herself, Erik glanced down at the mission reports. "Maybe a day," he said, "maybe not that long."

"Hell," she said softly. "The month ends day after tomorrow, sir," she explained to him. "I hope he doesn't assign any demerits until then. Good night, Sunstorm sir."

"Lina!" Erik called out, but there was no one there. He frowned and called up the personnel boards, scrolling down until he got to her name. A demerit warning flashed bright red next to it. "Great orb!"

"Puter," Erik told the air, "report to Protocol that tonight Lina Starhart saved the lives of ten Legionnaires by delaying a port. I want to commend her for it."

A minute went by, two minutes, before ten more credits showed up in Lina's column. "Only one credit per Legion life? We aren't worth more than that? What kind of enemies are you making, Lina?" he asked the empty room.

— — —

Lon dropped almost vertically through the Terran sky. He'd flown in at high altitude so no one would see him.

There was Drew in the park where the family had had their picnic that had ended so badly. He was sitting on a table, his hands clasped. No truck was in sight. Odd. Odder still that the boy would have called him.

Drew looked up just as Lon landed, fast as a bullet, soft as a feather. A swift, chill wind accompanied him and blew the boy's hair into a tangle. "Whoa!"

"All right. I'm here."

"Hope I didn't, well, interrupt you from something important. It's just that I'd heard you were on Earth today."

"For a while." Lon settled beside him on the bench. "Where's your truck?"

"It's, well. I, ah. Let me get this out. I was just thinking. You know about everyone there is, don't you? I mean, everyone knows you. Knows of you."

"On Earth and a few other places." Londo shrugged warily.

"That's great. That's really great. Listen, Uncle Lon," and he pronounced the "uncle" part very carefully to make it sink in, uh oh, "I've got a little... problem."

Londo arched his right eyebrow. "This wouldn't have anything to do with that community service you have to–"

"Oh, no! Not at all! This is just a misunderstanding."

"A misunderstanding."

"Um, yeah. And there's some old stuff, from last year. These guys – I mean, they're my friends and all – they just happened to grab some stuff at a quickie mart while I was filling up the tank."

"…And because you were driving, you got caught along with them."

"Um, yeah."

"Did you know they were going to do it?"

"Well…"

"That definitely makes you an accessory. Okay, Drew, so whatever's going on now has nothing to do with that…"

"Yeah."

"Something with that vandalism thing? The graffiti?"

"Jesus, no. That was ages ago, and I helped clean it all off. Did the community service."

"What did you get for the heist? New community service?"

"A fine. Probation until the middle of next year." The boy sat there looking miserable. "That was a mistake. Well, not quite a mistake, but…"

"What's going on now?"

Drew took a deep breath before he spat out his words. "I got this ticket last night."

"A speeding ticket?"

"Well…"

"What? Did one of your friends do something? Somebody in the car?"

"This guy I know... He was going to see his brother…"

Londo stood and began to walk in small circles as he rubbed his nose. "*Sacre…* Let me guess. He was taking his brother something? Something illegal?"

"Some pills. And when they pulled me over–"

"Why'd someone pull you over? You were speeding," Londo tried not to sound too accusing. After all, the boy was coming to him for help.

"Okay. Okay, I was doing 85 in a 55 zone. But–"

"I'm not too clear about driving law, but isn't that automatic suspension of license? Are you driving around today without a license?"

"No, no. They don't take it away until you've been to court, and I took an Uber here. I can get this dropped to maybe ten miles over the limit. I've done it before; it's easy. But drug possession. Hell, they weren't my pills!"

"Did you know he had it? Be honest. You should know that I read minds," Londo said, not looking at the boy.

"Well... Well, damn, we were just bringing them to him! It's not like we were going to take them too or anything!"

Londo nodded, a small smile on his face. "Okay. So you want me to call up whatever judge it is and say, 'Hi, this is the famous Valiant, and this kid's my nephew. Go easy on him, why don't you?'"

He gave Drew a scowl.

"Well. Yeah. I guess."

"And you want me to do this the next time, too, right?"

"Oh, man, there's not going to be a next time, Uncle Lon. Never, ever!"

"That's what you told your old man last night, right?"

"Right. I mean it."

"And what did you tell him the other time?"

Drew paused. "Well..."

"C'mon, Drew. What?"

"The same thing."

"And you went out and did something stupid again."

"Aw, man..."

"Don't try to slough it off. It was stupid. I know. I've done some really stupid things in my life and I knew at the time that they were stupid."

"So what happened to you?"

"I got punished. A lot worse than what's going to happen to you, apparently." Londo grimaced. "For example, if I'd been your father, you would have been slapped with revocation of driving privileges for one year if the state didn't do that themselves. For starters."

"Aw, jeez. I should have known better than..."

"Be quiet." Londo reached out his hand to grab Drew's arm as he tried to leave. "Sit down and listen."

There was no way Drew could get away from the grip of steel. He sat down, sullen.

"Two misdemeanors in less than one year, and then you come up practically turning your truck over as you sped through here the other day. What if there'd been kids in the parking lot? There's no way you could have reacted fast enough to stop. You aren't listening to your own common sense. I know you've got some, but it's buried inside your hard head."

"Just say you won't talk to the judge, and let me go. Valiant," Drew spat.

"Oh, I'll talk to the judge. And I'll talk to your parents, too," Lon said. "But it'll be just this once. Nevermore. I'm a man of my word, Drew. Ask anyone. I've put people I thought were friends behind bars in my time. This one time only, I'm going to intercede."

Drew looked up at that. "Why?"

Londo gave a crooked smile. "Because that beautiful young thing I married is your aunt."

"So... what does that mean?" Drew asked cautiously.

"It means that family is important." Lon closed his eyes in pain. "Infinitely more important than you can imagine at this point in your life. It also means that you're going to wish your Uncle Londo hadn't talked to the judge," Londo said. "It means that you're joining up with Three Worlds for a period not to exceed... oh, sixteen months, Terran. You may miss a little school, but we'll put you in Sarastoran school, which you can do during any free time you may have. If you ever have any." He gave an evil laugh.

"Hey, Lincoln freed the slaves."

"You have a choice. Face the judge as an ordinary citizen of the United States who's been caught in a felony or misdemeanor before he'd finished doing his punishment for a previous crime... or do it my way. Choose. Take twenty-four hours to decide. I have to talk to your parents about it anyway. You're still a minor, still under their guardianship."

"Aw, man..."

"There are times when you have to say 'I'm not a kid anymore,' Drew. You're still a kid in a lot of ways." Londo's lips tightened. "I had to grow up long before my time. But you've had the luxury of having a real childhood. You're not a kid. Not entirely. Not in this, not when you're taking on adult responsibilities."

Huff. Drew scratched his head, looking at the forest floor. "I should have asked Grandpa."

"Running to mommy." Lon shook his head. "Or somebody who'll mother you. Be a man, Drew."

"Grandpa's not my mother," Drew replied hotly. "Maybe I'll go live with Grandpa. He'll take care of me."

"Oh yeah, he'll take care of you," Londo growled. "I've heard about the good care he takes of his kids."

"You've just heard from Aunt Lie," Drew said. "Me, he likes. I'm his favorite."

"Grandpa's perfect grandson," Londo taunted. "They'll respect that when you're in prison, in the showers. You're a cute little thing, I'm sure they'll say. And where will Grandpa be to protect you? The same place he was when Lina was growing up. Maybe by then we'll have a son that he can dote on instead of you."

"He... He doesn't like girls too much, does he?" Drew asked quietly.

"No, I don't think so."

"He's kinda... rude to my mom."

"He's worse to Lina."

"Yeah. I heard about that." Drew nudged an acorn with his toe.

"What did you hear? What did he do to her?" Londo asked. "Tell me. Lina doesn't like to talk about it."

"Ah. You knew about her being locked in the basement all the time?" Drew asked.

"What about it? How long?"

"I dunno. Mom said that she spent an entire Christmas vacation locked in the basement once. That's when Grandma found her a keyboard, so she wouldn't make any noise. It had headphones with it, so Grandpa couldn't hear it from upstairs. They kept it secret from him."

"How'd you find out about that?" Londo asked quietly.

Drew kept kicking his acorn around in arcs. "I wanted a big room of my own and I asked if I could make the basement into a bedroom. Mom got really angry. She said that no one deserved to have to stay in a moldy old basement. She told me about it then, about how Aunt Lie got caught sneaking out one of the basement windows when she was going to the library, and so she got all her books and her keyboard and her art stuff taken away from her for a few months. No TV, no radio, no music. Just staring at the wall."

Lon had been tossing a rock in his hand. Now he threw it in disgust. It shot through a tree with the crack of closeup gunfire, leaving a small hole through the trunk. A little flume of smoke rose up from the opening.

"Jesus," Drew breathed. "Uncle Lon?"

"I'm sorry," Londo said. He looked at the tree. "I'm sorry, tree. I apologize. I was taking my anger out on you." He puffed in its direction, and the flume disappeared.

"If you think that was the worst he did to her, it wasn't," Lon said. "There's lots more. You don't need to know the specifics."

Drew gulped. He didn't want Uncle Londo ever to be mad at him! "Ah. I think I'll just be running along now," he ventured.

"I'll fly you home," Londo said.

Bubba was waiting for them as they arrived. His face flushed first with wonder at seeing Valiant flying, and then anger directed toward his son. "Let me guess," he said as they entered the house. "He wants you to make a deal with the judge."

"I gave him a counteroffer," Londo said. "Hinging on your consent and his choice."

Bubba shook his head. "I don't know what to do about him," he confided. "He's a good kid, he really is. And then every so often he runs off and does something stupid."

Londo nodded. "I understand. He hasn't figured out that he's not quite a kid any more. That with great power, yadda yadda. Unfortunately with the amount of power kids have nowadays, that's liable to kill him or someone else before he makes the transition on his own."

"So you're saying pound adulthood into him. He's just a boy, Lon."

Lon smiled through his memories. "By his age I was several years into my adult career," he mused. He gave Bubba a sharp glance. "How hard is it to raise a kid? In case someone was considering becoming a parent?"

"Damned hard," Bubba said. "I wish they had a school about it. Knowing what I know now, I would have gone and studied hard. Pegi..."

"Pegi." They both regarded the little girl as she shrieked for no reason and ran through the living room, not even noticing Londo in the entryway.

"I always thought that therapy was what saved my life," Londo said quietly. "I was a pretty lost case when he found me. Hal was a good father in that."

If you shoved the lie aside, that was true enough.

"Therapy. Lina mentioned that to Barb." Bubba's eyebrows knit together as he considered.

"Jae, too. He had just as much as I did, maybe even more. And Lina – she worked on herself an awful lot. We're all in therapy. We aren't the same people as we were before. Life is a lot better when you don't have to carry a pile of garbage on your back as you make your way through it."

"Therapy."

"Family counseling," Londo said. "Get everyone involved."

Bubba nodded. "I'll think about it. Now, what was this counteroffer you had in mind for Drew?"

CHAPTER

26

Judge Westcott adjusted his tie just before he entered his chambers. Had to look good for this! He opened the door to the familiar room and blinked at the sight of the world-famous parahero standing up to greet him. Even in a sedate suit, Valiant was readily recognizable. Behind him were a couple, still a few years from being solidly middle-aged, and a teenaged boy, all skinny and still growing, looking very uncomfortable in a suit and tie.

"Judge Westcott." Valiant shook his hand before the judge took a seat at his office chair. "I'm Londo Starhart."

"I think that's obvious," the judge said drily. "Pleased to meet you. I've been following what Three Worlds news we get. Everyone, please sit down."

Valiant looked at him questioningly and the judge nodded. "You may remain standing, if you wish."

Apparently he did. Valiant motioned to the others. "These are my sister-in-law, Barbara Yates, her husband Edward and their son Andrew." There were murmurs and head-bobs of greetings all around.

"And I've been told that Andrew is the reason why we're all here?" Westcott made a point of looking around. "I don't see a lawyer here."

"Yes, sir," Valiant said. "We'll bring them in once you've heard from me. I thought you might want to hear the story clearly without any legalese attached."

Westcott nodded. "Unusual but I'll accept it for now. I may stop you at some point, and we'll bring in the lawyers."

Valiant continued, "Yes, Your Honor. Andrew's in a lot of legal trouble right now. He hasn't finished paying for one misdemeanor he committed this year, and he's just been caught with another misdemeanor which may bleed over into a felony, as well as a traffic charge. Now, I realize that you must have a lot of people come up to you to try to get their friends and relatives out of fair justice, but that's not quite what I had in mind."

"You didn't."

"No, sir. The way I understand it, Andrew hasn't quite comprehended the reason why he's in trouble. He hasn't figured out yet that it's time for him to straighten out in certain ways. That certain behaviors can harm others, including himself. Any punishment the court gives him is going to go right over his head, even if it's harsh. It might even result in worse future behavior."

The judge had had time to look over the boy's record. He'd called the school and had the counselors there report any anomalies. An average kid who'd gotten caught. Too bad the average was dipping so low these days. Why, in Judge Westcott's childhood kids had had a little respect for the law...

"As you may know, Your Honor," Valiant went on, "my partners and I have a project called Three Worlds. My proposition to you is this: I'd like to take a group of boys with records similar to Andrew's, boys who haven't quite grown up in their heads yet, and assign them some tasks to do on Aldierra. Most of it's going to be boring manual labor, but some won't. These boys are going to be front and center in various tasks, assisting people to develop parks as well as helping to clear land and plant forests."

"Like the, ah, Civilian Conservation Corps back in the Great Depression? Only this would be made up of delinquents." The judge considered.

The boy's features twitched at being called a delinquent.

"Unfortunately, Your Honor," Londo said, "Aldierra is what I'd consider a combat zone for someone his age. It scared *me* when I first went there. Now and then it still does. The people have a poisonous attitude and tensions are such right now that small riots crop up before we can defuse them. We'll try to keep the boys in safe conditions, but I can't guarantee that any place is totally safe."

"How about schooling?" Westcott asked.

"I'd like to arrange that two days out of every six we give the boys video education that comes from both Earth and Sarastor. That's a very advanced and fairly peaceful world Out There where I often work. The curriculum will be wide-ranging and will be targeted to giving them something they can work with once they're adults.

"The boys will be locked in each night. One hour of television or videogames, and then they'll be given high school-level books that they can read for entertainment. Every month they'll be assigned to write a paper on one book they've read. They'll have time for recreation, and they'll interact with Aldierrans their own age. My wife Lina has talked about maybe bringing the boys back to Earth every month or six weeks to visit their families and to see some of the major points of interest on this planet, too. She thinks that kids today don't learn enough geography, and I hate to admit it, but I agree with her."

"Hm... Languages?"

"We'll give them linguatapes to learn Panlingua – that's the language of the Affiliated Systems sector, where Sarastor is located – and the general Aldierran language of Farrani as well," Valiant explained. "The linguatapes allow you to sleep-learn a spoken language, but to learn advanced grammar and written language, you have to study. My wife learned Panlingua in three days, but she studied extremely hard."

"And she's smart," Andrew muttered, then looked shocked that he'd said it out loud.

"She's extremely intelligent," Valiant said with a smile. "We're proposing that each boy choose one major Terran language during the course of their service and take a final test on it whenever they think they're ready. Those they'll also get from linguatapes."

Valiant could see he was considering.

"The Three Worlds project, with or without Aldierra, is going to open Earth up to a galactic perspective. The boys enrolled in this program will get a chance to familiarize themselves with these other worlds and in fact, become the first stepping stones to the stars. I'm sure they won't like to think of themselves as ambassadors, but believe me, Your Honor, after you've heard people mutter behind your back, 'So that's what Terrans are like,' you have a tendency to be on your best behavior."

"How long would you take these kids on for?" Westcott asked.

"We think about a year, year and a half, Your Honor. More if you think we should. We want to watch them for burnout, though. As I said, Aldierra's a pretty frightening place. I don't want to traumatize the kids when we're trying to calm them down." He added, "By now we have Aldierra blanketed with mental health therapists. We'll make some available to these kids, with assigned appointments every week. Some of the therapists are AI."

"AI?"

"I have a human therapist myself," Valiant said. "When he's not available, I use an AI version. It has worked well for me."

The boy's father spoke up. "My son's a good kid, Judge. I've talked with Lon, I mean, Valiant about this and it seems that this program, well, strengthens the good qualities Drew already has. I think that he's been stuck in a small town with friends who are in just as deep outside the law as he is, if not deeper, and that sort of feeds on each other. This could be a way to break him out of that, and he'd get a fine schooling on top of it, as well as helping out on a very worthy project. As for Aldierra..." Mr. Yates looked at Valiant.

Valiant took over again. "Aldierra is facing a deadline. If, at the end it looks like they're not going to make it, I'll send the boys off-planet. The Affiliated Systems has worlds that need manual help. The world of Aldierra itself has already assured us that they'll be safe even if she has to... do whatever she's going to do. But I'd rather not have them around for that. We won't have them gathering up body bags or... or..."

Valiant closed his eyes in pain. "No," he said. "That will not happen."

Westcott nodded. "And why no girls? People are going to look at this and say it's sexist."

"Because it's Aldierra. Misogynism runs rampant on the planet; we couldn't guarantee their safety no matter how many guards we assigned them. And we would assign them guards, as we do all women working for Three Worlds on the planet. It's all we can do to set up some protections for Aldierra's women, and we've got a long way to go on that score. When and if the programs we're setting in place begin to work – with the emphasis on 'begin' – we might talk about including girls."

"Maybe they could go to those Affiliated Systems worlds."

"Perhaps. We can think about it. I can ask around."

"We all pray that your Deadline works out well," Westcott said solemnly. "Do you have this written out? I'll need to present it to some other judges. They could give recommendations for who else would be good candidates for this program."

Valiant excused himself to open the chamber doors. In came two obvious lawyers, dressed as if they were about to plead a case before the Supreme Court. The beefier one introduced the two of them as John Henry Rombard and Edmund Donner. Rombard handed a sheaf of papers to the judge.

"You're licensed for US work?" The judge asked as he lowered his glasses so he could glance at the pages.

"Not in North Carolina, Your Honor, but I am in California and New York state. My associate Mr. Donner is licensed in this state."

"Very good."

Westcott looked up at the boy. "Andrew Yates," he said, and the boy's face showed his anxiety as he stood. "What do you think about all this?"

"Well, sir..." The boy's eyes moved left and right as he sorted out his thoughts. "I know it's putting Uncle, I mean, Valiant in a spot. He says that he's never allowed special privileges before, and that this is the only time he'll do it, no exceptions. And that this'll look pretty bad if word gets out."

"Not that bad," Valiant said softly.

"Don't interrupt," Westcott warned the parahero sternly. "Are you worried about yourself, or...?"

"I don't want to do anything to hurt Valiant's reputation," Andrew said, standing straighter.

The judge nodded. "A reputation is one's most valued possession," he told Andrew. "How is yours coming?"

The boy swallowed. "Well, maybe it hasn't been the greatest up to now. But I know I'll be representing Earth Out There, and I'll try to do my best not to mess up. And I know Uncle Lon and Aunt Lie and Jae are in a real jam with Aldierra, so if I can help them, that would be great."

"So you'd think it'd be very fine to be in with all these other boys and talk about your Uncle Lon and Aunt Lie?" The judge regarded him shrewdly.

"As far as I'm concerned, nobody else needs to know that," Drew said slowly. "It might get me more trouble than it was worth. I might accidentally call Aunt Lie Aunt Lie..."

"But it might be embarrassing to you if you did. Well, I don't think anyone on your team will connect Andrew Yates with Lina Starhart. Do you think you can handle the work as well as the schooling?"

"Oh yeah. I like to work with my hands, your honor. I already know how to garden. I came in red ribbon junior class for tomatoes in the county fair last year, so I can do something like that easy, if they need it. This landscaping they're talking about is pretty close to that. And I really want to learn French!"

The judge took a moment to make his decision. "You sound like the perfect candidate for this pilot program, then." He turned to Valiant. "I want monthly reports, including copies of all the book reports. I'll grade them personally on grammar and spelling, if you please. I minored in English."

Valiant grinned at him. "Yes, Your Honor."

"Maybe we should have a small media report on this. I think other judicial districts will be very interested in how this works out. When do you want the first group to leave?"

"As soon as possible," Valiant said. "Within a week."

Westcott scribbled a note on his pad. "Wednesday, then, I'll have a group ready for you and packed."

"We'll need to know the candidates three days in advance, so we can hand out Farrani linguatapes."

"Good enough. You know, Andrew, I envy you a bit. It'll be hard work every bit of the way, but by god, it's going to be the adventure of your life!"

"Yes sir!" Andrew made it obvious he was trying not to smile too broadly.

— — —

Lina hurried down the hall. Ms. Yency had told her it was against regulations to port into a Spousal Meeting – odd that they'd have a rule for that – so she had to use her feet to get there. She'd promised she'd be there on time today and stay for the entire meeting. But after she'd talked with Dinah in the medical section she'd wanted to check on Demi and Erik, and poor Dr. Mart looked so forlorn, as he couldn't do much with just his one arm as the other was being regenerated, and it would have been impolite if she'd asked him if he'd managed to find out about cat medicine yet, so they'd just chatted. They'd all been injured because of her. And now…

"Jae! What are you doing down here?" Lina skidded to a stop as her husband stepped around the corner in front of her. She'd left him a few minutes ago upstairs and on his way to check in with his Alpha Team. His eyes lit up at her as she smiled welcome, and he stepped forward, his arms outstretched as if to take her into an embrace.

In Legion HQ?

What–?

"You're not Jae." There was no familiar presence from him. Lina backed up quickly, her mind blanking in shock. Then the gears in her brain kicked in.

"Computer!" she called. "Security! Emergency! There's an impostor–"

"It's only me." "Jae" began to morph… into a human-sized insect wearing a gold and salmon costume. "It's just a joke."

It was Mimik. Lina caught her breath even as two Legionnaires flew toward them in the hallway. "Mrs. Valiant," the one said when she'd landed. "You called an emergency?"

"It was…" Lina stopped speaking. Mimik was on Lon's team. She couldn't get one of Lon's teammates in trouble. "It was… a mistake. I'm sorry. Cancel emergency."

"You didn't think." The one's voice dripped disgust as she gave her a disdainful look. "Security breech is a serious thing. I'll have to send someone to re-brief you on Legion protocol for reporting emergencies."

"Ah. Yes. Sorry. I really am–"

"I'm filing twenty demerits into your file for this, Mrs. Valiant. I'll notify Valiant also."

They flew off.

Twenty demerits! And Mimik.

Mimik was gone.

She touched the communications strip on the hallway walls. "I'd like to talk with Mimik, please."

A blue-skinned man in Legion civilian uniform, apparently Mimik's aide, appeared on the screen that popped up. "Do you wish to make an appointment?" He gave a little start when he saw who was on the line. "Speak— I mean, Mrs. Valiant. Ah, I could fit you in in two days, would that be good? What is the nature of your visit?"

"Mimik knows damned well what the nature is," she said, surprised her voice had been a snarl. Yeah. Yeah, she had reason to be mad! "Tell her I want to see her today."

"She doesn't have any—"

"She'll see me today," she said and cut the communication.

"Mrs. Valiant to Spousal Meeting," a speaker intoned above her head.

Damn! She was late. That would in all probability mean even more demerits. She sprinted to the auditorium.

— — —

But Mimik never responded to any calls. Her aide told Lina Mimik was out on Legion business and could not be interrupted.

She had to sit through an entire forty minutes of Protocol lecturing, looking meek while she seethed inside. False emergency reports, especially security breaches, were very serious affairs. *Yes ma'am, so sorry.*

— — —

Jae used the afternoon's trip to Sarastor to confer with his team members, leaving the recovering Erik for last. Erik was ensconced on what looked like a very comfortable physical therapy bed with small slabs of medical equipment resting against various spots on his body. One exposed colorful variants of green light from its sides for his body to absorb. Displays of narsaws circled him with rainbow notes sparkling in them, likely from his many admirers.

"Say, what's this about Lina?" Erik asked him after they'd gotten through the major team review and gossip as Gorgeon flexed his leg. Another therapist attended to the green light controls.

"What's what about her?" Jae peered around the doctor's hands, trying to see for himself how the damage was healing. He couldn't quite read the screen next to Erik. Physical therapy was getting close to the point of Erik regaining active status. He'd check after the visit. As Team Leader, he had the right to know his people's health.

"The emergency call she made. And then cancelled. Something about an impostor in HQ."

"Impostor? She hasn't said anything about that that I know."

"Happened just an hour or so ago. Word was she was getting serious demerits from it. Betting boards are buzzing as to how much."

How to respond without seeming too concerned? The therapist wasn't in on their secret. "I'll tell Londo and have him look into it," he told Erik.

Erik nodded after seeing Jae meaningfully dart his eyes from the therapist back to him. "I've been hearing rumors about Lina Starhart and demerits. I checked 'em out the other day when I was OD and did what I could to help. You might have *Valiant* see what's going on in that department as well."

"Demerits."

"I like Lina. I respect her and her work. Be a bad thing if the Legion drummed her out because some people are setting her up."

Drummed her out? Demerits could be used to annul marriage. That silenced Jae completely. He did notice that Gorgeon gave him a significant look and nod of her chin. She must be concerned as well.

"We both will look into this right now. Send me a rundown about what kind of special training you'll be needing with the team, Erik. Thanks for pointing this out."

On his way to join him, Jae spoke telepathically to Londo. By the time he'd arrived in Lon's Legion office, Londo had brought up digital records so Jae could examine them as well.

From almost the moment Lina had appeared on the scene, she'd garnered demerit after demerit. Often they came in bunches, from several directions. She'd checked them periodically while she'd been living in HQ. A couple weeks ago she'd gone to Andri about it.

Apparently Andri had deleted what negative points she could. Jae would bet that Andri had had a personal meeting or two with some of the Legionnaires who most often were listed as assigning Lina demerits.

Here was Yency, Lina's nemesis. The woman piled on the demerits with vengeance. Today alone there were some for being late to a meeting, for speaking up at the wrong time, for refusing to attend three different social events...

And here was another large area of contention. Demerits for dress code violation. Snippets of footage showed Lina arriving to conduct emergency ports, but dressed in either Terran or Aldierran or some combination of the two dress. Parts of her arms were exposed. Sometimes a little lower leg. A couple of times she had dared show some minor cleavage.

And on more recent footage...

"What is that?" Londo demanded from over Jae's shoulder.

On the screen, a person completely covered and then some in black cloth silently stood among Legionnaires in the Monitor Room, shorter than they. Whoever it was bowed occasionally as the OD gave them orders, but otherwise never made a sound.

"She's like Cousin Itt but with fabric instead of hair," Lon commented. Jae had no idea who "Cousin Itt" was, but that wasn't important.

Non-communication piled up more demerits, but fewer than vocalized communication had before the burqa was utilized.

Oddly enough, Lina's extreme fashion followed Legion Dress Code to the letter, but demerits still flowed from its use. "Mrs. Valiant is disparaging our rules." "She demonstrates that she thinks she is superior to Legionnaires." "We shouldn't have to deal with this attitude!"

"And yet she's providing instant transport for them to emergencies," Jae mused, "speeding up travel time by hours or even days." He looked up at Londo. "We should talk to Andri."

"Andri, hell. I'll talk to Mimik. And Stoan. Tell him what's going on. The Legion should be kissing Lina's ring for what she's done for us."

"Maybe you shouldn't put it exactly that way. Try a little subtlety. You'll get farther. He's not her biggest fan either."

— — —

"What the f– was that about?" Londo demanded as he faced his team's second-in-command in his office.

"Sir?"

"Don't 'sir' me, Mimik." Lon tried to stare her down, but her natural stare outdid his every time, so instead he glowered at her. "You pull this, then don't even report any demerits. You let others do that for you."

Mimik blinked as if that comment were unexpected. Maybe she blinked because she was playing for time in coming up with a suitable answer.

"You pulled in Eaton and Yorber on this."

No response.

"Representing yourself as another Legionnaire," Londo growled. "How many demerits is that? And yet I don't see you getting any."

"Records don't show me disguising myself as Neutrino," Mimik protested. "I have no idea what you're talking about. Your wife began to make claims about, well, me pretending to be Neutrino, when I never did any such thing. My question is: what does she have against me? Was she trying to stir up trouble for me? Is she anti-mantodist?"

"You know, Mim, that was something I didn't understand. She insists that you disguised yourself as Jae and made to come after her like, well, in a romantic way."

Mimik *hmph*ed as only Mimik could.

"Funny thing is—" Here Londo fashioned a screen-in-screen picture on a floating monitor showing the encounter. Mimik merely said hello to Lina in a hallway. As Mimik, not Jae. "I don't see a 'certified unedited' stamp on the sequence."

Mimik's stare increased in intensity. "I'm not used to having my testimony questioned," she finally said.

"Did you know that Dr. Mem-Bazer has us fitted so our actions are constantly being recorded?" he asked her. "It's for the historical record, he said. But it also comes in handy for other things."

The screen split into two views: one, Mimik's video. The other:

Lina was walking down the hallway in Legion HQ. Jae walked out from behind a corner, spied her, smiled and opened his arms to her.

"Note the stamp."

"CERTIFIED UNEDITED" displayed in a corner.

Mimik didn't say anything.

"I'm not used to having my lieutenant lying to me. Or to the Legion." Londo eased back in his chair to give said lieutenant a long, considering gaze. "Bringing in two of my team with otherwise spotless records to help you do your dirty work. You've always been completely trustworthy. I appointed you as temp Team Leader while I'm on this Aldierra mission. I never had any doubts about you. You'd never act against Legion regs. Well, not too much. We all like a little leeway now and then. So I have to think: someone of superior rank has given you an order you have to obey."

Mimik stood motionless. She didn't even stare at him, but rather straight ahead, over his shoulder.

"An order to lie. To create false material. In order to incriminate my wife."

Lon leaned forward over his desk. "My. Wife."

No response.

Londo was too tense to sigh, but he needed to. His guts were twisting with unreleased frustration. "I can form my own conclusions as to this episode. I can point my finger at someone who might be behind this."

"I... don't think it would be to your benefit."

"You do recall that I'm now a telepath?"

For the merest moment, Mimik's eyes widened.

"But I don't go around reading people. My wife tells me that would be the height of impropriety. Psyche says no ethical telepath would do that. Otherwise, people have to shout at me to make themselves heard." His jaw moved right; moved back left as he glared. "Sometimes I find being ethical doesn't get the job done. But... I won't do it right now."

They stared down each other.

"The commander has been suspicious of Lina from the start – though I thought he'd begun to reconsider lately," Londo added in a softer tone.

It didn't take a powerful telepath to hear Mimik's inwardly shout, **Stoan. Stoan!** but he wouldn't tell her that.

Lon pursed his lips outward, and gave a quick lift of both shoulders and eyebrows. "Bof. If the commander gave you an order, you couldn't disobey," he told her. "You were being a good Legionnaire, though I would have... Well, I'd have refused, but she *is* my wife. I like to think I wouldn't have married her if I couldn't trust her with anything." He shrugged again, this time with tension. "That might not be true. The marriage part, not the not trusting her part. I trust her with my life. The Three Worlds trust her with this mission."

Mimik made a sound like she was thinking of a response, but he waved her off. "I will carry on my own investigation of this, see what I can come up with. I'll begin with the subcommander, see what insight she can give as to this entire demerit situation my wife finds herself in. And then… Commander Magnos."

He gave Mimik a raised eyebrow. "I'll see if I can get him to rescind his order."

"As you wish, Team Leader," she said rigidly, and walked out.

— — —

Londo strode through Legion HQ to arrive at Stoan's offices. The commander's PA had had the temerity to delay him. Delay! When he could see through walls that Stoan was not doing anything of importance. He was just making him wait.

Finally the assistant let him in. "Dammit, I had to interrupt important work to come here," he complained when he finally got inside. Stoan had that infuriating "patience of a saint when confronted by idiots" expression he so often used on Beta team members.

"If this has to do with your wife, then–"

"Of course it does. And whatever you ordered Mimik to do."

"Demerits are a subject best taken up with–"

"Andri's doing all she can. It seems there's a concerted effort around here to bully my wife into leaving me so they don't have to deal with her."

"Rules are rules." But Stoan paused as Londo's certified video began to play over Lon's shoulder so he could see it.

"Doctored evidence," Londo growled. "In all likelihood, on your orders. No, Mimik didn't rat you out. It was easy enough to guess."

"I thought–"

"Turning three of my own team members against me. Isn't that against Legion regs? How many demerits should I assign you for that, Stoan?"

"It was–"

"Didn't Lina just save the entire galactic sector from Mind Control? What more does she have to do?"

The two stared daggers at each other, Stoan almost as frightening as Londo.

"I will not have one of my team leaders betrayed by another," Stoan finally decided.

Londo blinked. And blinked again. "Team… Jae? You think Jae's done something wrong?"

"He *looks* at Lina. She *looks* at him." Stoan grimaced. "I bet they're both getting a big kick out of your fake Aldierran three-way marriage. How far do they have to go in order to sell that to the populace, Lon?"

"You don't know anything," Londo managed around grinding his teeth. Damn this secret anyway. Should he tell Stoan? Stoan was a close friend, but he held so much power. Stoan could kick him out of the Legion. Him and Jae both. You didn't bring scandal to the Mega-Legion.

Did he love the Legion more than he loved Jae and Lina? It was different. The Legion was his base. So many of his friends and comrades were members or worked alongside the organization. As much as Earth, the Legion was Londo's world.

But he'd take Jae and Lina without the Legion, if it came down to that. No question.

It just didn't need to. Not yet.

"We have a mission to accomplish," Lon decided to say instead. "An entire world to change. You are interfering. We don't need this kind of trouble on the Legion's side. You don't need to be encouraging the Legion's riff-raff." He brushed his hand through the air, dismissing Stoan's rebuttal. "I'm not talking Mimik. I don't think she's enjoying her assignment. I mean the mean-spirited Legionnaires, the ones who are all too happy to create trouble for those whom they feel are above them in importance. Like certain people who have saved the galactic sector in recent weeks. Or the last Feithi."

Stoan took a few deep breaths before he replied. "I hate to see you… cuckolded."

"I'm not being cuckolded. Lina is my wife. Jae is my best friend. They are friends, and they are also telepaths, which might give the wrong impression sometimes."

"Well *skurnit*, talk with them. I've already talked with both, and it doesn't seem to have done anything. Maybe they'll listen to you."

Londo's mouth slid this way and that. He resisted the urge to fist his hands. "I will remind them of appearances. We can't have interference during this time, Stoan. Lina's already on edge; she's barely begun treatment for PTSD. We don't need her breaking down again because you and the Legion's goons are piling on her for not acting like the Legion would have her act. She's Terran, not AffSys. Give her some time to adjust."

"If she has to stay away from HQ for a while as she learns, that might be the best solution."

"You want her to stop porting for the Legion?" Londo asked.

Stoan made a sound as the consequences of that occurred to him.

"No. That outfit she has… What the orb made her dress that way?"

Londo shrugged. "Lina has… a thing about bullies. About authoritarians. She's just a little, ah, passive aggressive."

That brought a small smile to Stoan's face. "And she married you?"

"I am not a bully!" Londo instantly responded. Then he added, "She adores me."

"Despite it all, I suppose," Stoan muttered. "But that *thing* she wears…"

"Is completely within regs. Anything else and people assign demerits." He frowned at himself. "Although they still do with that getup."

"Can't we have one of our designers do something for her?"

"She looks good in black."

Stoan frowned at him.

"We're allowed to wear our uniforms when we work. Lina's Aldierran clothing is her Aldierran uniform. Aldierrans approved it, in various versions."

"Legion regs–"

"She also has her Starfleet uniform that goes by Legion regs. She doesn't like the sleeves."

"If she has time to change into that… that…"

"Blanket."

"That blanket, she has time to change to that. Tell her to use the Starfleet uniform. I'll put it out that it is not to be docked."

Londo rubbed his nose as he considered. "Done. I'm thinking about finding a few extra hours and holding a very large party. Invite everyone in Legion HQ… except for those who've assigned demerits to Lina. Let's see if that gets the message across as well."

Stoan drummed his fingers against his desktop. "That would add to the lesson. No Earth music at this party, though."

"What's a good party without a band?" Londo asked. His gut was still cramping, but he couldn't sever *all* ties. Not with the commander. This would have to do.

Stoan gave Londo that Commander Glare. "Nothing more than normal percussion. No Earth music."

Londo pointed his index finger at Stoan. "We'll see who's added to the 'do not invite' list."

Stoan snorted.

CHAPTER

27

When they heard Lon's update, Lina hugged Jae comfortingly, not him. They held it for minutes, their thoughts not going beyond themselves in tandem.

Finally they broke apart and faced Lon. "That's it," Jae decided. "I'm calling a team meeting for tonight. I'm telling my team."

"But–"

"No arguments, Londo. Just my team; this goes no farther. You can let your own team run pell-mell, but they aren't going to screw with my team's morale. I'm not going to have anyone tempted to pull a Mimik-style mutiny on me. I'll put them all on report if they even try."

— — —

Jae's team arrived in his Legion apartment. All but Erik – even Brügz – eyed Lina suspiciously from the position she had taken in the far, darkened corner among the thickest stand of houseplants. Over the screens she had displayed before her, where she was making some adjustments on tomorrow's equipment transportation and group meetings, she faced them down. She began to stand to leave after she'd cleared her work, but Jae turned and raised his arm to point at her.

"No," he said.

She sat back down. This was Jae's game.

He was under so much pressure, but she hadn't seen him trigger his usual meds today.

Jae was about to speak when there came a knock. Without Jae's permission Londo entered, followed by his people. Halfway through the column that reluctantly marched in was Mimik. Lina glared at her. She stared coolly back.

The other members of Lon's team regarded her in just as chilly a fashion. As a group, they placed themselves as far from Jae's team as they could.

She'd never met some of Lon's team. It turned out that the two Legionnaires who had reported her were members of it. How coincidental. Lina crossed her arms over her chest.

I don't like being Bitch Lina, she moaned inwardly, *but sometimes "bitch" is the only thing people understand.* Bitch it would be.

So she gave them all a Southern-style Evil Eye. Bless their horrible hearts.

Right fist extended, Legion Array ring facing out, Londo approached Jae. He raised his arm so that their rings met for an instant, the salute of Team Leaders.

"Neutrino," Londo said.

Jae gave a nod of acknowledgement. "Valiant," he replied.

"Request permission to sit in on your meeting."

"You may not like what I have to say. Neither may your team."

"This meeting concerns my team's conduct."

"In part."

Londo nodded and stepped back into an at-rest position next to his team members as they took seats.

"Very well," Jae said and let his gaze rake every Legionnaire in the room. "There was an incident this morning. Someone utilized my image to fake a security breach. Lina Starhart took the blame for it, but records show who was responsible." With a wave of his hand, the correct scene played again in midair between the two teams. Jae's teammate Brügz sucked in his breath at Lina's report of security breach.

Jae turned to stand squarely facing Mimik. Mimik's expression remained unreadable. "This was the culmination of a number of innuendoes aimed at me. And at Mrs. Valiant."

"Legionnaire versus Legionnaire besmirches the honor of the Legion," Londo began, but several members of both his team and Jae's exclaimed, "Honor!"

Londo stared them all down. "Honor," he repeated. "We are the Legion. We stand by our own no matter what. I thought I could count on you people, Alpha Team members all. Even more so," he turned to Jae's team, "you are Neutrino's people." Then back to his. "My team. My teammates do not betray me."

Mimik jumped up. Her finger stabbed the air toward Lina. "Your own wife betrays you! Your friend as well." She shook her head in short jerks. "Unacceptable. Legion rules slide off the two of them. It is past time to do something about it. Something... permanent." Her jaw clacked harshly on the word.

"So you acted without consulting your own Team Leader," Jae growled at Mimik.

"She was under orders. A higher authority," Londo quickly assured him.

"How many of you? Just you three?" Jae pointed at the others from the tape. "Or the entire team?"

Mimik spoke for the group. "We were all in place to release the tape," she said.

"Of the false security breach?"

"Of Mrs. Valiant willingly embracing Neutrino," Mimik reported.

"Which she never did," Londo said quietly.

"And you forgot that she is telepathic," Jae sneered. "Sloppy, Mimik. Pitiful. I can think of a number of ways such an ambush could have been far better planned."

"Mutiny is operating behind Team Leader's back," Londo reminded his squad.

"Even when Team Leader doesn't listen to his own people?" Yorber blurted.

Now Lina leaped to stand. "In this instance Team Leader is hard-headed. Team Leader didn't want to deal with something that needed to be dealt with." She turned to Jae. "And the other Team Leader couldn't."

Jae's chin-nod told her gently to butt out for a while. She crossed her arms again and leaned against the wall.

"Security for this meeting is now on Need to Know," Jae intoned. "Absolute secrecy."

People in the room straightened to a new alertness as Jae triggered another scene. It was their wedding.

Lina's anger melted instantly. She had to smile. Her wedding had been so lovely. Look at Londo, so dashing and brave; at Jae, so endearing. Present-Jae spoiled it by fast-forwarding through most of it, pausing only for some of the vows and his statement about children from the marriage being his heirs, no matter who their father might be.

He snapped off the scene too soon for Lina's taste, and silence held in the air. Bless him, Londo did not search anxiously from face to face as Lina had expected him to, but maintained command poise with a steely glower. How he was holding himself together!

"But... the Aldierran claim that you're married is false," Yorber said faintly. "It's just to enhance the Three Worlds work."

"The Sarastoran claim that we're not married is false," Jae snapped. "Any more comments about my private personal life? A personal life that should have no bearing on how my team – or any other Legion team – works together? Well?"

"Shards, Jae, give us a minute to digest this," Kembril muttered, to be echoed by grunts from her teammates.

"And how were we supposed to know?" Yullowei blurted. "Legion honor was at stake. You obviously don't realize what this looks–"

"I obviously do," Jae said stiffly. "I have several dozen people report the situation to me weekly. The commander is one of them."

"What's he going to do about it?"

Londo said, "Commander Magnos doesn't know the true situation. Subcommander Nurunori does."

"Finally," Erik muttered. People were beginning to relax. Nudging each other, exchanging secret facial conversations.

Lina had one of her own: she stared very hard at Mimik.

Mimik stared back.

"Any other secrets we should know about?" Mimik *dared* to ask.

Lon's face might have been made of stone.

"Just one," Jae said, and Lina could feel Londo's effort not to flinch even as she tried unsuccessfully to do the same. "But it is not something the people here who know have a right to reveal."

That was true enough. And it deflected Mimik's stare from Lina to Londo. She could live with that.

– – –

Jae was *not* stressed. He repeated that to himself several times as he sat in his Aldierran office. The worst part was over. His and Lon's teams now knew. He took off a glove to adjust the re-gen bandage under his left Legion Array wrist band. Just a minor break in his lunate. Nothing to worry about.

This was physical exhaustion, that was all. All right, perhaps a little stress. He took another sip of valbing. One of the AffSys documentary film crew re-porters had asked him (away from Aldierrans) (the hundredth time Jae had gotten this question in the past two weeks) how he felt portraying part of a marriage that was a lie to this world.

He had assumed Confident Expression Number Two, the one with a pleasant smile, and replied that they would do anything to see Aldierra through this crisis. This way they would seem to be more like the people they were leading. Jae then diverted the subject to give the history of Aldierra's polygamous marriages.

Hundreds of years ago a pandemic had wiped out millions. In some places, too many men were killed. In others, too many women. It seemed there was no balance to the carnage in regards to locale and gender immunity.

Where there were too few women, men banded together to assure themselves of at least one shared mate per household. This way they also protected females from marauding outside males, which ennobled the men even as those women lost their individual rights.

The areas that held a surplus of women developed family line marriages, where the few husbands were shared among the household. The continuation of family was valued over personal relationships. This idea of almost holy family honor was born, though that honor was centered around men.

When the ratio between the genders again overbalanced due to degradation of women, society merely set polygamy as essential, as normal. Too few women were shared by many men within an open House marriage. Then they were shared without marriage or any legal safety nets, though marriage-related words were still applied to the situation.

It was advantageous to men, who found their Houses now had built-in slaves for both work and sex.

"Of course the ratio made it essential that many men now had sex with other men," Jae told the reporter, "but at some point – we don't know how – this became forbidden. Odd, isn't it? With men ruling the world, you'd think they'd have made gay sex a priority."

"Maybe even celebrated it?" the reporter asked.

Jae gave a little laugh. "That too. We are trying to promote joyous, happy sex, as long as it occurs between consenting adults with full mental faculties."

At that point Jae explained that he was bisexual. It might be against Legion rules to come out like this, but Jae was tired of keeping secrets. This much he could do, and it wouldn't affect Londo.

Lon's lawyer's advice needed to be attended to as well, even if this wouldn't be broadcast on Earth. Besides, it was the truth.

"Polygamy was normal on Feith," Jae said. "I had a father and two mothers. There were many couple marriages, but threesomes like the full Triune were the most celebrated ones. The combination there could have been anything, even three of the same sex. Foursomes…" He gave a mischievous smile to the camera. "They likely occurred, but were not embedded in the legal code. Feithi could share minds, and balancing more than three in that kind of permanent connection was supposedly quite difficult."

Amazingly, the reporter didn't seize on the obvious opportunity here to ask if Jae was telepathic. Jae did not feel he had to point it out.

Of course the reporter asked Jae what Lon and Lina's preferences were. Jae raised his eyebrows noncommittally. "Lina would say 'TMI,' for 'Too Much Information,' and by that she means personal information. But you can see that they have married and are quite happy. Well, as happy as two overworked and overscheduled people can be when facing a crisis. Ask them and see what answer they give you."

How many months to go before they could kick this bloody *sharding skurn* of a secret out of their lives and get some peace?

C'mon, Londo.

— — —

They'd set up this children's home to be boys only. Varied areas provided spacious educational rooms in addition to more homey aspects. The central court made a good playground.

Psych experts had tested the men who applied to work there. They weeded out the pederasts, and it was simple enough to set up interior monitor systems so that an AI could report any questionable situations.

There were three rooms with enough space to house all the Earth teens, Drew included. They showed up just outside, breathless from their two-minute interstellar journey, then looked around with curiosity.

"It stinks," one decided.

"Yes it does," Lon said. He pointed at stacks of clothing and equipment. "You'll find filtering systems there. Wear them when you're not in quarters." He gave them the full "Aldierra is violent" speech as they entered their new home. There they were introduced to their proctor as well as the landscape supervisor they'd be working with in the city's fledgling parks.

Lon tested them on their Farrani, which seemed good, and answered their questions. He supplied contact information for when they had more questions, and showed them the library from which they could draw their required reading. They ran through a few exercises on Aldierra's computers and exclaimed not only at what they might be able to do with them, but that there would be a sharp learning curve involved in same.

He left them to get to know each other and settle in. At no point did he give Drew any extra attention, except the slightest of head-tilts, as if to say, "I'll be watching you."

– – –

That had been Londo's last job of the day, so the call that awaited when he got home was not a welcome one.

Mimik.

"We have a problem," were her opening words.

"Someone on the team has a problem with my marriage?"

"I think everyone does, but not in the way you think."

It was so difficult to read her. Lon bet she could read every tell on his face, every bit of body language he displayed. She could probably read each of Jae's numbered Expressions.

"Enlighten me, please."

She settled into her chair but her eyes seemed to tighten on him. "We agree that we can support your marriage, though it is not the normal AffSys way."

"*Bon.*" Lon's chest eased at that news.

"I have heard what the team had to say on this after you left, and I very much understand them. It's similar to what I've been through these past two months, more or less. Being torn between loyalty to you and loyalty to my Legion duty."

Londo perked up at that. "But this no longer bothers you personally?"

"I didn't say that. The subject's axis has shifted. Loyalty is still involved, and now the entire team feels it."

Obi jumped onto Lon's chair arm and he automatically drew him to his chest to pet him. Bran leaped up to be near his best friend, so Lon alternated absently.

"I'm not sure–"

"Now we are involved with your lie. It's good we can talk with each other about it, as long as we are careful. But now we must lie to our fellow Legionnaires, the ones who are not in on this.

"It seems to us… It seems to *me* a matter of being dishonorable. I do not like to lie, Londo. It upsets me on a number of levels. The lie has expanded in some fashion that makes it, well, rather suffocating. The others are very uncomfortable."

He was silent for some time, merely rubbing the cats, who purred softly. After a moment Mimik tried an astonishingly realistic purr of her own.

"I have been lying to myself," Lon finally admitted. "I was the one who insisted on secrecy to begin with. Then I said maybe we can tell the truth here, but keep the lie there. The truth has begun to spread.

"I then told myself I could keep it in balance until I felt comfortable revealing all to everyone."

Mimik tipped her head as she stared at him in her way.

"Now and then I thought I could keep it in balance forever. That way I wouldn't have to deal with repercussions. Ever. Jae seemed to be taking it well, and he was the most affected. Though I supposed Lina has been quite troubled by it. She's promised not to nag me – *euh,* not too much – and says she has faith I'll do the right thing."

"Surprising," Mimik said. "That is a large point in her favor."

"I think you two could become friends," Londo said. "But. All this has made me think… come to terms… confront… Yes, confront myself with my lie.

"Mim, I've been terrified."

She sat silently, expectantly.

"I thought people wouldn't love me or even like me if the truth came out. People are funny that way, judging others for ways they can't help being."

"Similar to my situation?"

A sad smile came to his face. "Come to think of it, yes. You chose to leave your world."

"'Chose' is a nice way to put it."

"*Oui.* I've lost so many people in my life, people I've loved. The last one was Aiko."

"Yes."

"Lost them in a living sense. Now I'm afraid to lose people from my life in an emotional one. A few weeks ago… A few weeks ago some people I love whom I thought loved me, were told about the marriage. And… And…"

Mimik let out a soft whistle. "They turned their backs on you."

"*Oui.*" Lon licked his lips. Rubbed his nose. That dream of a tickertape parade for them all had vanished. He no longer had a reason to believe that people would cheer for him. "We seem to have gone our separate ways now. I never imagined it would be that bad."

"I'm sorry to hear that."

"It may sound like a copout but another lie has been revealed recently – not one of mine, thank you very much – and it's thrown me ass over teakettle. It's been about a month and frankly, I'm not thinking straight still.

"But I'm working on it. I feel…"

Mimik leaned in. "Perhaps you need to go at this logically instead of emotionally."

He pursed his lips as he considered. *"Peut-être.* But I feel like if I can get this one lie sorted out, this other one will solve itself quickly. It's just that I… can't seem to…"

"What does Adam say about all this?"

He chuckled painfully. "Adam knows the other lie as well, and we're pretty much in the same position. But he does agree: deal with the one, and the other will, well, what I said. Maybe."

"You'll reveal your true marriage situation." Mimik's mandible worked left to right, down and back again. "Are you sure you aren't judging these people or this person in the same way they judged you?"

Lon waved that thought away. "I won't keep my secret all the way to Deadline," he huffed. "I came to that conclusion that the other day. We'll all go crazy if I do. I just have to be very careful that I don't reveal this other lie because it's not my lie to reveal. It would ruin the life of the person it belongs to if I divulged it. Even to you."

"Do your spouses know?"

"Ohh, yes indeed. Which is probably why they're going easy on me still."

"That bad, eh?" Mimik snapped her shoulders with a click. "I won't ask you about it then. I'll try to explain to the team–"

"Maybe I should explain."

"My excuse for you will be that you're too upset. Stressed. We all know you have this Aldierran situation weighing on you. This will buy you time. But Lon, don't let it go on too much longer. Not revealing at least to the Legion. You can leave the civilians out of it, if you want, but Legion loyalty should be solid. Deegel–"

Londo almost let out a hiss. "I was thinking about this all through the trial. Dishonor. I do not want to dishonor my Legion."

"Then try to right yourself soon, Lon. Your teammates deserve that much."

– – –

"You talk," Lon told Lina as he triple-checked the placement of this girder. "I can't and do this at the same time." Summoning heat, he blew on what would become a solid seam of metal.

"We need to announce. Now."

We're not going to announce. Not now. You agreed.

"I agreed to revisit the problem as it seemed prudent. We need to revisit."

"No we don't. Skip this subject, Lina."

"Darling, you're about to collapse from the stress. People are going to hate you when we do it. I don't disagree with you there. But some people will respect you even more. The vast majority won't give a damn after the first ten minutes. You'll be able to be you and not some image you concocted."

Hanging in mid-air, he used his paravision to check the weld's fusion. "Jae is fine with the situation as it stands."

"He's drinking more. And how about the number of injuries he's been getting lately?"

"Just a few; it happens."

"Not this much. How many times in the past week has he had an injury bad enough to be seen to? My guides say twice normal for him. Twice!"

He landed lightly beside her. "Twice?" He scowled at nothing. "I'll check. Port me over there this afternoon and I'll check in person; I'll ask Riz."

"Ask Dr. Scribbi, too."

"Jae's team medic? So you think he's... what?"

"Plus he's sneaking around. Using medics with the Corps as well so the records won't show up en masse and get red-flagged." Lina said slowly, "I think Jae's always had a death wish, since Feith died. Now all the pressure is making it worse. Maybe it's subconscious, but how much of it does he have to–"

"Before something serious happens?" His gaze at her was sharp. "And you think this has something to do with–"

"Yes. I do. I never get a chance to talk with him anymore, Lon. Much less have any sex; it's been forever. Our schedules don't mesh at all. Look at us; I'm screwing up mine just to get fifteen minutes with you. But your schedule meshes a lot with his. Talk to him about it. I'll cancel an appointment – hell, I'll cancel an entire day – if you think I can help."

He stood there for a moment before rubbing his nose. The movement left a black oil mark. "Jae always says that he's fine with this."

"Jae took a vow to do what's best for you," Lina said gently. She reached into one of his pockets to pull out a clean rag. "He doesn't want to hurt you, and he knows that coming out would do that."

"And you, love? Why are you always nagging me about this?"

As she worked on wiping off the oil she bit back a retort. "Because we have reached a point where I outrank Jae on this, sweetie. I took a vow to do what's best for you and him both. What's best for him right now is to announce. What's best for you – in the long run – is to announce. It'll hurt for a while, Londo, but you'll weather it. You'll come out shining."

"And why do you think that?"

"Because you're the best of the best, the most mega of the megas, the most wonderful of the wonderful." She tucked the rag back into his vest and then slid her arms around his waist, smiling encouragement. "You've withstood worse. And even you have to admit that we've got to announce sometime. Rip off the bandage."

"No." He disengaged and turned from her. He found the rag and wiped his hands with it. "It's settled. No announcement now. Not… right now. We agreed."

He listened to her silence, then her soft, patient voice. "Talk to Riz, talk to Dr. Scribbi. Please, Lon. Get their input, too. I just don't ever want to be a widow. Especially now when we're just starting out. Screw the Three Worlds – I'm just worried about us."

He rubbed at the dirt under his fingernails as he turned back. "So you'd let the secret out – because you want to do the best for Jae and for me."

"Yes. But I'd get at least one of you to agree with me first."

"I remember a time when you said you were going to leave me because it was best for Jae and me," Lon said quietly, looking steadily at her. "You were wrong then."

"I was wrong." She met his eyes so earnestly. "As wrong as I've ever been in my life. I didn't understand. I didn't have the whole picture. This time, I know. Now it's time for you to trust me. You'll have Jae and me both backing you up."

"Against the entire sector." Londo regarded his rag. "No, Lie. I can't do it now. Let's not bring this up again."

She was quiet and then nodded. "I won't bring it up for another week, how's that? Next Tuesday when we're all together."

"I suppose that's fair enough." He took her hand. "I'll talk to Riz today. About Jae. I really will."

"I'm glad, Londo." She sighed. "I'll try to be patient."

— — —

"I got held up," Jae quickly apologized to her the next day as he entered his Legion apartment.

"So did I." Lina ran to clasp him into a tight embrace, her pulse thrumming. "But we're here now. At last!"

"At last! No time to waste."

Jae returned her kisses enthusiastically, then more slowly. More deeply.

It was heaven to kiss him. To touch him like this. To release his tight vest and pull at it until it fell away from him, even as he was fumbling with her own clothing.

"You wear too much stuff," she complained even though the manual removal jacked up her excitement that porting it off would never compare to.

They giggled and laughed and paused to fondle and kiss and get serious as they stumbled their way to the back. Bits of clothing marked their path. Their final attempts at undressing may have involved some tearing.

But make it to the bedroom they did.

— — —

Stoan looked away from the communications monitor at his desk in front of him as his Array ring vibrated against his finger three sharp times. He'd set sensors to detect whenever Jae and Lina, minus Londo, were in Legion Headquarters in either Jae's or Londo's rooms.

Impatiently he continued the call, and tried not to drum his fingers against his desk as he discussed a problem of security with the president of Mime-jed, capitol of its star system twenty parsecs away. Stoan hurried through the conversation, more brusque than usual, just bordering on the impolite.

It took only a few minutes before he apologized to the president and explained that there was a quasi-emergency here at Legion Headquarters. He would call him up tomorrow, if he could.

Of course, of course. The president held the commander in the highest of respect; he understood that Legion business could supersede that of his world's.

He disconnected, leaving Stoan wondering if he were doing the right thing. Then Stoan left his office with Legion emergency override room codes ready on the top of his Array ring's priorities. He nodded to his receptionist as if it were just a little walk to clear his head.

But he walked quickly.

CHAPTER

28

The door didn't make a sound as it opened. Anyone inside wouldn't have heard anyway. Pulsating moans were coming from within, a woman's cries, echoed by a man's deep grunts. He had them. He had them!

Stoan secured the door behind himself and slipped down the hall, activating the record function of both his ring and his padd. He held the padd in front of him for best angle as he stood in the bedroom doorway. One minute. One full minute of recording. He linked it into his office's puter in case something went wrong here.

They were oblivious to him. Lina was on all fours and Jae knelt behind her, fingers sunk into her hips as he drove into her over and over. She screamed at him wordlessly, her hair flying and wet with sweat.

Jae's groans were coming from deep within his chest. "You want it harder?" he gasped in English which Stoan's padd translated. "You want it? C'mon, do it for me." Stoan could see the muscles in his butt contract fiercely for every pump.

Lina's shoulders sank down to the bed. She clawed the sheets as she cried out with the increased rhythm.

Stoan stepped into the room. "First just a friendly kiss," he said. "This is a friendly hug, I suppose?"

Jae froze before he turned his head with a look of pure hatred. "Get out!" he hissed. "Out of here!"

Lina – had she even heard him? – still clutched at the sheets. But no, she was catching her breath and finally moved her hair so she could see Stoan. Jae pulled out of her with a wet sound.

"Port out, Lina. Now. D'Artagnan!" Jae gave what was obviously some kind of emergency code word.

"No." Reaching for a corner of the sheet to cover her nakedness, she collapsed fully on the bed. She was still gasping. Other than that, she seemed totally composed – or was it shock?

"Port," Jae ordered as he wrapped the thin blanket balled up at the foot of the bed around his waist with a jerk. "This is between Stoan and me. Get out of here."

"No!"

The Legion Leader circled the bed like a lion his prey. He considered them, then his padd.

"Got some great action here," he said. "World-class sex. Wild stuff, very hot; mm-mm-mm. You should sell copies to help finance Three Worlds. I never figured you for a screamer," Stoan told Lina, enjoying his triumph. Was she actually blushing? He shifted his eyes to glare at Jae.

"Just three months ago I wouldn't have thought you capable of this, Jae," Stoan barked as the Legionnaire rose up on the bed over him. "Never in a million years. My god, she's your best friend's wife." Stoan leaned against the wall right next to the two lovers. What to do now? He'd never gotten this far in his plans before.

He began to laugh now. "So Jae's a homosexual, Speaker? Apparently you don't go by the same definition I do. A cheating liar and someone who'd betray his best friend; what a pair you two make. What a remarkable pair, the Speaker and Minister for the Three Worlds."

He could see Jae's teeth bared like a wild beast who'd been cornered, who faced the blasters of the hunters. "First Deegel and now Jae Rallene. And you're dragging Londo's reputation down with yours, Jae. Down with the reputation of the Legion. Have you no shame? How could you have done this? All because of... her?"

His eyes raked Lina's form, barely covered by the sheet that she pressed against herself. "Was she worth it? Worth the scandal, the blacklisting that's going to be on your name? How does the last Feithi become such an object of derision, such a disappointment to the legend of his people? What would you call it? A sour note at the end of a symphony."

Jae leaped out of bed. Stoan straightened to step into a battle stance, bred into his cells through years of training, and tried to deflect Jae's hands as they aimed for his neck.

"Jae! No!" Lina shouted. The two men growled as they pulled at each other, searching for the superior position. Jae finally knocked Stoan to the floor. He poised to leap on him, to grind his knee into Stoan's neck.

"No!" Jae's forward movement halted as if a wall had come up between them. "Stop and think, Jae! Stop!"

"You don't insult her," Jae growled. "Lina, let me go. He's got to be taught a lesson in respect. I'm tired of all this shit. I'm tired of him."

Lina had PK powers. She must be using them. Jae's body vibrated with anger. Her control was not perfected.

"You're exhausted, Jae. You can't think straight," she insisted. "Step back and I'll let you go. Come over here with me."

Stoan rubbed his neck as he rolled up to a sitting position. "Exhausted?" he said incredulously. "Exhausted?" After what he'd seen?

"Shut up, Stoan," Lina said, and her snarl was like Jae's. "You've been riding him for weeks."

"Get out of here, Lina. Just leave him and me here. I'll take him down a notch or six."

"I wonder what your Gay Pride movement people will say when they find out you're not the gay boy you pretended to be." Stoan's laugh choked from where his throat hurt. He tossed the blanket back at Jae for him to cover up. "Going on the media all over the AffSys and telling everyone you were gay!"

"I never said I was gay. I said I was mostly gay. I even said I was really bisexual. Or didn't you notice, you bastard? Hounding me, hounding Lina every way you could. I want you to leave her alone. Do you hear? Leave her alone. Leave us alone. You insult her one more time and it will be your last!"

"Jae–"

"I said, port out!" Jae turned to glare at her and Stoan took the opportunity to stand up. Lina leaned down to retrieve Jae's blanket and resecure it.

"I want Londo here, now," Stoan ordered. "Bring him in."

"No."

"Puter, as of now, Jae Rallene is officially–"

Jae shouted over Stoan's words. "Puter, note that Stoan Kinrol has violated quarters privacy."

"What?" Stoan's mouth opened in surprise.

"Furthermore, he has used the violation to embarrass a Legion member and to threaten them. Legion member being Jae Rallene. He has illegally recorded a private act without knowledge of the participants."

There were two beeps of acknowledgement.

"Are you telling me you're going to bring up charges against me, Rallene?"

"If you do anything except drop this matter, yes. How dare you come in here without permission? How dare you record us?"

"How dare I–?" By novae, they were going to brazen this out.

Stoan saw when Lina's eyes unfocused. She touched her earring and then took it off, gazing at the tiny ball that held the earring in place. "A proximity detector," she said softly. She replaced the earring. "So when you said you just wanted to help by giving us these, Stoan, you were lying. You were manipulating us. Jae, I thought you said that privacy was absolute within quarters."

"That's what I always thought. But here stands Stoan Kinrol himself."

"Legion commander has access to certain overrides, in case of security breaches," Stoan defended himself.

"Security breaches?" Jae's voice began to increase in volume. "Is that what you're going to claim? Instead of invasion of privacy?"

Lina stroked Jae's arm as she stood beside him. She'd knotted her sheet into a wrap. "So we won't do this in Legion Headquarters again," she said in a soft, compelling tone.

"They're my quarters," Jae replied hotly. "I'll do whatever I wish in them so long as they don't impinge on Legion rules. Carolina Starhart, Stoan," he said as if reporting in from duty. "Legion spouse. Level four security clearance. Private quarters, accompanied by a Legionnaire, front door secured. What in that is a security breach?"

"What makes you think that you're a functioning Legionnaire any longer? That you have any security level left? After this? We can't stand to have a breath of scandal now, not after Deegel, and here you two have been cheating on Londo under all our noses. Flaunting it in front of us. It's a breach of Legion ethics," Stoan replied, his face set in stone.

He turned to Lina. "I told you to stay away from him," Stoan snapped at her.

"As long as he was on Legion business. He is now in supposedly private quarters on Legion property, not on Legion business. That is not flaunting."

"This is not Legion business," Jae retorted. "We've done nothing to disgrace the Legion. We've gone to great lengths to keep this a secret. You're not going to stand in our way to keep it that way. Now is not the time."

"And when is the proper time?" Stoan mocked, moving around the bed again. "The proper time for hauling scandal down on the Legion? Down on Londo? When you cuckold Londo you cuckold the Legion, you cuckold the reputation of Hal. You bring down over five hundred people with you, you traitor! There'll be an AffSys investigation of this. There'll be reports on the news for years to come. We're drowning still in stories about Deegel, and now comes this on top of it all. There's no way we can get over this for at least a year, a year and a half. You've made the Legion a pitiful laughingstock."

Harshly he ran his hand down his face. "You said you loved him," Stoan accused Lina. "You said it was forever, and Londo believed you. Shards. You're just a lying whore!"

"I told you!" Jae started to spring forward, but Lina caught him by the shoulder and pulled him back down to her, using her entire body weight to stop his motion. The blanket began to fall away but came back by itself.

"Easy, Jae. I've been called worse things in my life. Well, maybe not, but this was his first time. Stoan, why don't you just toodle on out and do whatever it is that Legion commanders do? It's none of your business."

"Get Londo here now, Speaker." He assumed the most assertive position he knew, arms crossed across chest; legs firmly braced. He was used to commanding powerful megas. Like Lina Starhart.

"Everyone is running at their breaking point," Lina hissed at him. "I'm leaving Lon right where he is. That's the only way I can stop him in this. Unless you *want* to be torn limb from limb?" She paused as he took it in. "You're welcome."

Was she bluffing? "You're trying to tell me that… Lon knows?"

"He should. He was at our marriage."

"He presided over it," Jae said.

Stoan's legs lost their stability. He barely managed to make it to a large chest and sit on it, the air whooshing out of his lungs.

"Marriage?" Then, "What the blaze are you talking about? Marriage?"

"I annulled the original marriage," Jae told him. "I am a priest of Uriel. I could do it. Then we all married in a traditional Feithi Triune."

"He drew charts for me, for how it worked," Lina said in a weak voice before she straightened her spine. "We. Are. Married. Now go away. We haven't had time for each other in over two weeks!"

"No more games. No more bullshit."

Oh, was that what it was. "A threesome? A little sex partner for you and Londo, Jae, is that it?" Stoan asked speculatively.

Lina's eyes burned as he let himself look at her up and down, the sheet clinging to her, her hip and one leg exposed. He could swear that she growled at him under her breath. "At last it begins to make sense. And how much do they pay you for your services, Speaker? That added to your Legion stipends must make a handsome salary. Is that why you insisted on her being paid, Jae? Or is she the one who made you insist?"

He settled himself more comfortably on the edge of the dresser, crossing his arms easily in front of his chest. "The enslavement and/or hiring of prostitutes within the aegis of marriage is forbidden to Legionnaires. Even if it's done in private." Stoan's smile was cold. "It's in our corporate bylaws, requiring probationary status at the very least, depending on the degree of practice."

Stoan grit his teeth and tried not to look like he was. The Legion's two most powerful members, respected by all. Getting thrown out because of this… An in-house sex service. It would make for bad news for the Legion. A plummet of public support, of respect. A severe depletion of manpower. And two friends lost forever.

Fury radiated from Jae in spikes that even Stoan could feel. He advanced toward Stoan, the dangerous animal refusing to be trapped. Enraged. "This is not a marriage of prostitution. Not a marriage of slavery," he barked. "It is a Feithi Triune marriage. It's honorable for us to be seen together. It's honorable for us to love each other!"

Stoan had never heard of a Triune. Jae was trying to trick him somehow. He'd never pictured Jae as being an enemy before, but now images came up of how in the past Jae had managed to confuse enemies by depleting the oxygen levels in their brains, or by just talking his way around them. The man was powerful, skilled, clever. *Watch out.* And who knew what the Speaker could do if she were enraged?

Jae pointed at the communications night table next to the bed. "Triune. Check it out. Look it up. Hell, research how much we looked into it before we actually did it."

Lina came up behind Jae, hiking her sheet while she kneaded his back. "Easy, sweetheart," she said softly. Jae regarded her and his stance relaxed. He let her massage his neck and kiss his shoulder. He cupped his palm on her upper arm.

"I have a right to make love to my wife, damn it! I'm tired of this shit!"

Lina smoothed his hair and he quieted more.

"And are there any witnesses to this... so-called marriage?"

"We considered inviting you–"

"That was a joke," Lina put in bitterly.

Jae shrugged. "Maybe. Your name did come up, though, Stoan. Consider that. The recording is archived here on Sarastor. Even by the Terran judicial system the marriage is legal. We've had it checked out very thoroughly, there and here."

Lina took his hand. "So it's time to publicly announce. Finally."

"No. No, no, no. Not yet."

"I'm tired of denying you. You're tired of being denied."

"No. Lon still isn't ready. We announce from a position of strength or not at all."

She made a sound of frustration. "Men!" she whispered fiercely, and he gave her a small smile for it.

Stoan's mind still reeled. "You're... You're going to announce this? Make it public?"

"When we first discussed it we spoke of never announcing."

"No!" Lina shook her head determinedly. "It's got to be soon. We do this well before Deadline. You heard yourself."

Jae looked at her. "Heard myself what?"

"Something about being tired of this shit, unquote. Lon and I don't want it to be an overwhelming burden on you. He'll agree. He can take it."

"Can he?"

"You will annul this," Stoan declared. Simple. Easy. Solved everything.

"A Triune is indissolvable. And shared souls like us are to be celebrated, not hidden away as an embarrassment."

"Would you take someone else's opinion?" Lina asked. "Hal said he'd witnessed Triunes on Feith, and that they were honorable."

Stoan looked as if he didn't believe the statement.

With a huff Jae looked up at Stoan and snapped his fingers in command. "Triune. Look it up. In the living room; give us some privacy here. How much time do you have, angel?"

"I cancelled three appointments."

"Three. I'm honored."

"It's been a long, long time, love. I was going crazy without you." She wrapped her arms around his neck.

"In that case, Stoan, get out of here and look at the records in your own quarters!" Jae yelled. "If you're going to expel me, give me two hours grace. Sarastoran."

Instead Stoan sat on the side of the bed and reached out to the bedtable/puter top there. "Why don't you two get dressed?" he demanded irritably.

"Why don't you leave so we don't have to?"

Stoan set his lips together in a line and stared icily at the both of them. "Triune," he declared and turned to his padd.

"Here."

Stoan could hear the sheet being whipped around, people flinging themselves across the bed.

"Stop it, Jae! You're just making the situation worse."

"Yumyumymyum..."

"This is not going to make me leave sooner," Stoan declared irritably, his eyes never leaving the screen.

"You're going to make him madder. He's going to kick you out for sure if you sit here – lie here and shove this in his face like this. The Legion's your life, Jae. Think. Don't throw it away because for a moment your anger knocks you senseless."

A whisper: "The Legion is not my life. You and Londo are. Three Worlds is my life mission. The Legion is just icing on the cake now. Coconut icing with little shaves of chocolate and almonds. Yumyum..."

She giggled. "Jae! You're crazy!"

"You knew that when you married me, sweet."

The sounds of kissing. Of soft grunts as they shifted around.

Stoan didn't want to know what the new giggle was about as the bed shifted some more. He accessed how much information they'd gathered, and when. A lot. Right after the Three Worlds initiation, it looked like. Accessing from Sarastor and Earth both. Wiley had also accessed large chunks of information about it. And here were Andri's queries. Gorgeon's. More recently: Sunstorm's. There were other entries into this dusty section of files, entries originating this week from Legion Headquarters for the most part as far as he could see. Members of Lon and Jae's teams.

Stoan was not amused as he read access reports. "Am I the only one in Legion HQ who didn't know?" he asked, and dared to look around.

Jae snorted as he came up out of the sheet that had entirely covered them.

Stoan turned off the console and held his hand on it for a moment. Triune had been listed as a normal part of Feithi society. Feithi! The most spiritual people the galaxy had records of. Of course, Jae wasn't the most spiritual of people, despite officially listing himself as a priest. "I don't believe this," he said. "Not for a moment." His eyes flicked to Lina's in accusation.

"Mind Control, Mind Control," she sing-songed, rubbing Jae's chest. He laid his hand on top of hers.

"I just think it's strange that not only did you latch onto Valiant, Lina, but now you have Neutrino as well. The two most powerful Legionnaires..."

"Um hm," Jae said. "It takes powerful Mind Control to make anyone love a passionate, beautiful woman." He considered Lina for a moment, thoughtfully. "It occurs to me that both Lon and I had to put up a considerable fight to get Lina to pay any attention to either of us. I don't think Mind Control works like that."

She smiled as she rubbed his nose with her own. "If I had known then what I know now, I'd have thrown myself at you both."

"So now you three are going to say that you're preserving Feithi culture by having a Triune."

"We were given a directive, Stoan. We were told at the Investiture, in case you want to watch it again. We were supposed to keep Feithi culture alive. Yes, one of the ways we're doing that is by our marriage."

"I am leaving now. I need to think about this." Stoan left, his mind whirling.

— — —

Daydreaming in afterglow, Jae and Lina were engrossed beyond each other's eyes and stroking each other tenderly, when Jae muttered, "Uh oh." A mildly irritating buzzer went off, coming from all the walls.

"What is it?" Lina asked as Jae rolled out of bed. He turned and gave her a quick kiss, then came back for a longer one. So niiice.

"Emergency meeting. I've got to get dressed and run." He reached for his clothes and then turned to her. "You come, too. You can sit in my cubicle in your official capacity."

"Are you sure? I'm allowed?"

"I say you're allowed. That'll be good enough. Now come on. Hurry up."

"Is this something to do with us?"

"Not this kind of emergency call."

Lina sat in bed and was instantly dressed in her costume. "Now who's the slow poke?" she asked. A tug to her bra strap secured the change. Wait, a comb, she needed to comb her hair. And wash her face at least. Jae grumbled as he tried to get dressed the fastest he could.

They ported to his cubicle overlooking the grand meeting room. Member cubicles filled the walls, stacked like a beehive. Down on the central floor, Stoan and Wiley and some others stood conversing with uneasy movements.

Jae? Lina? It was Lon from Earth. He'd been making final changes on the call center buildings after he'd made sure his spouses were okay.

Still on Sarastor, darling, with Jae. There's some kind of emergency meeting starting here.

We're involved here, too. I'm at ParaNet HQ. We've got an incoming message. You're not going to like who it's from...

Lon, same thing here. Jae beamed before Lon could finish his thought. **Stay tuned.**

Jae gestured at his console that put the scene at the ParaNet up on a side screen on the main floor. Some of the people on the floor looked startled as the auxiliary screen lit up, just as those on the other side of the screen were startled by seeing the Mega-Legion there, but from that central area Wiley looked up to see Jae and Lina, and nodded. At his glance, Stoan looked up too and saw Lina. He only gave her a measuring look, then returned to Wiley.

The main onstage screen had both English and Panlingua captioning. Lina tried not to cross her eyes as she settled on one language. "Granger?" she breathed as the ticker told her from whom an incoming message was originating. "But he's imprisoned by the Galactic Sentinels." Her heart clenched, and she breathed out the panic only to have it replaced by a slow, cold fury.

Paul Granger, the renegade Ruby Guard. Lina hoped the recovering Olympia downstairs didn't know he was free.

The member galleries had filled quickly. Within seconds the main screen cleared into a picture of Granger, the stone at his throat emitting an evil green glow instead of a red one. His dyed-red hair was moussed to spikes as usual above his stubble beard. "All set, are we?" he leered into whatever camera he was using.

He was dressed in a mocking imitation of his old Ruby Guard uniform. Instead of solid colors, the red areas were now mottled green. "First of all, let me just tell you that if you have any teleporters in your groups, that I have partners who are not with me but who are holding hostages who will be killed if I suddenly disappear from here."

"Damn," Lina whispered.

"Hello, Londo." He could see the group in ParaNet HQ. Hal stood next to Lon. "How's your wife? I do hope to see her again. I hear she and you and that other one put on quite a show after I left. Vegas night on Aum."

"Lina," Jae whispered to her. "Port us down over there. In front of the primary feed."

She did. There was a quiet stir in the gallery to see her there. They stood right next to the screen to ParaNet HQ. "Granger, what do you want?" Londo demanded back on Earth.

"Oh, I see we're joined by the rest of your trio. Neutrino, was it? And beautiful Carolina, how nice to see you again. You're looking well. Do not try to talk to my jasper; I have a new stone, as you can see, and it will respond only to me." A palm-sized, green-swirled gemstone was affixed to his neck where a Ruby Guard's ruby was usually set.

"How did you get away from the Sentinels?" Londo demanded.

"That's my affair. The fact is: I'm out, they can't control me, and I have very powerful allies. Allies who all have grudges against you, Londo. And your friends. We're all looking to settle them finally."

Lina tried to contact the green jasper, test it, see what its limits were. Instead it hit her with feedback, and she jerked at the recoil. Jae steadied her.

"What's that? Oh, Carolina, did you just try to do something to my loyal gemstone? I do hope you weren't overly disappointed. I told you," he grinned at her, "Jasper here is totally under my control. Not even the Sentinels have anything to do with its power.

"I'd like to test this power... against you, Londo. I've never liked you, I'm afraid to say. Although I particularly like your little wife there. I like the way she feels under me when she's naked and her legs are spread and ready."

"And unwilling," Lon hissed. "I saw what you did.. and didn't do to her. Don't try to pretend it was any more than it was."

Fear. Disgust. Terror. *Stop and think. Breathe. **He's on a planet called... Arient. Do you know where it is?*** she asked both husbands.

They did. Far, far across the galactic sector. It was in the later processes of being terraformed for human habitation.

"What are you up to, Carolina, my love? You have that strange look in your eyes. Just remember those hostages..."

"Earth has banished you for life, Granger," Lina declared. "Remember that. Her sister planets of Sarastor and Aldierra join her in that pronouncement. Set foot on any of these and it will be with the last breath you draw. Even you don't have the power to fight a planet. Arient can be persuaded to side with them."

"Ah, you've located me. Well, Arient is a long way from any of those worlds, isn't it? Maybe it won't join yours."

"Hiding is the coward's way," Jae began.

"It is also practical and serves my purpose. And my purpose is to wipe you off the face of the galaxy, Londo. You've been in my way for too many years. Taking all the glory. Making all the headlines. Just like Maximus.

"Hal, I thought by now you'd have slowed down a bit. Too bad I was wrong, but I'm willing to put you in your place, too. And as for little Carolina, I'm afraid I have a score to settle there too, but I think I'll settle for just getting a fair price for her... eventually."

He used his stone to make a replica of the power-nullifying shackle that had once imprisoned her. "See this, Lina? It's all for you. I figure I can get at least three star systems, maybe an entire sector, out of selling you to the highest bidder."

"Name the field, Granger!" Londo demanded.

The mere sight of the shackle made Lina feel faint, but she summoned her anger to fight against the fear. It was a white-hot blaze.

"You know the battlefield, Starhart," Granger said. "Arient. And make it within the next three days or so; those hostages aren't going to get fed or watered until you show up."

The screen went blank, and all that was left was the Legion meeting room and the screen showing ParaNet headquarters.

The four of them stared at each other in the screens: Hal, Londo, Jae and Lina. Londo clenched his fists. "Conference!" he hissed from behind gritted teeth. The four of them vanished in two blinks, leaving uproars behind them.

Londo and Hal appeared in the unfinished living room at Starhaven. Two minutes later, Jae and Lina joined them.

Immediately, communications buzzers went off. Large screens appeared on either side of the living room, one showing Legion HQ, the other, the ParaNet.

"Clear these channels!" Londo commanded. "We will contact you when we're ready."

The heroes on the screens took his measure. The screens vanished.

Lina realized that this was the first time she'd seen Hal since the big fight. They were on business now; it didn't count.

There were people here in Starhaven – construction workers. Jae waved imperiously at them and they scattered to the home's far corners.

Lon ignored them. "Number one:" he began.

"Find up what we're up against," Hal told Lina.

"I need something to start–" Lina said, but Jae was already handing her a padd. On its screen lay the picture of a green-blue planet. She put the padd through its paces and its screen enlarged to lie flat on a table like a map.

Lina held a crystal pendulum over it. She closed her eyes and breathed deeply. The tension in her shoulders and back melted but not entirely as she tried to center herself. **Arient, I need your help with this,** she called. Then she moved the pendulum over the map. Laterally. Perpendicularly. Back again.

The pendulum reacted in several spots, so she tried them again. In five more minutes a general area lay under the crystal, which traced a small circle above it.

Jae took Lon's padd to gain a closer view. There was a small village there of blocky, two-level buildings. The village was surrounded by parkland consisting of medium-tall forests that covered high hills.

Londo checked weather conditions for the area. Wildlife and vegetation that could be dangerous. Communications.

Hal called up blueprints for various village structures.

"Not in a building," Lina said in a distant voice. "Underneath. Within the ground." She touched her throat and sucked in air. "I think there's limited oxygen. Lots of hostages."

Both Lon and Hal looked skyward, then repositioned their focus utilizing their padds. The system was low on Earth's horizon, parsecs away. "Got it," Lon said, and in moments Hal echoed him.

"I see three guards," Hal said. "Not sure who some of them are, though."

"Maybe a hundred hostages; maybe more," Londo reported. "Women and children as well as men."

Hal held out a hand and Jae placed Lina's padd in it. He scrolled through lists and then began to call out names.

Jae winced at two of them. Londo didn't look happy at any of them. "There," Lon said. "Granger's got an air vehicle. Maybe that jasper of his can't provide transportation. There are four people with him." He named them all: Ded-Convex, Aktel Gaed, Birefringe, and Gold Matrix, names that Lina was unfamiliar with.

Hal and Jae's faces got sourer and sourer at the roll call.

"Might be a few more elsewhere on the planet."

"Probably," Hal said. "It's a big planet."

"A dozen?" Lina asked the air. "*They* say twelve total. I don't have names for them."

Londo and Hal nodded. "We'll just have to expect to face World War III," Hal said.

Jae looked up from the padd in his hands. "Ruby Guards are contacting the Sentinels to see if they can supply more info. Maybe all of these are escaped from their prison. Maybe just a few are. Last time I checked, Black Blade and the Matrix were in Rimhold, not Daq-qu-a."

"Any info is good info," Londo said.

"They're on heavy stims," Lina reported. The buzzy feel of stims sang in her visions. "They won't be taking shifts. Could be they're going to go four days straight. Maybe more. We could lose one of them; I keep hearing 'overdose' when I ask about the stims."

"Right."

"Then again, it could be some kind of random event," Lina mused. "*They* keep saying "random."

"Random." Lon exchanged a troubled look with Hal and Jae. "It's a name."

With a gesture, Jae brought up the screens to the two parahero organizations and reported in. Hal headed the ParaNet's discussion; Stoan, the Mega-Legion's.

Wiley asked, "Jae..."

"The new stone's not Ruby Guard material, but it's close. It may be just as powerful, but it's a different vibration. If it works for him like the Guard's rubies, it's borderline-intelligent sentient. It won't change states willingly. It'll be tough, but if worse comes to worst, I… think I can do it."

Both Lina and Lon glanced sharply at him. Neither thought he'd had time or experience to make such a declaration.

Stoan nodded at Jae. "Good. Hal... your team's job is the hostages."

Hal bit his lip and nodded. "Call on me the moment you need me."

"As soon as the hostages are out of danger," Stoan told him.

Lon asked, "Has anyone been to Arient?"

Hal said, "I have. It's been a long time, though."

"Someone in the Legion has probably been there recently," Jae said.

Andri came on the Legion's screen to say, "I'll check on that."

"Okay," Lina said. "Can the Legion launch a hyperspace cruiser now to Arient? Maybe more than one?"

Hal looked at her quizzically. "Why? It will probably take three days to get there. Arient's a far piece away, even from Sarastor."

Lon looked at Lina. "She means in case she can't port us back. In case things get out of hand."

Lina nodded, and went back to what she'd been doing.

Wiley checked the electronics at his disposal. "Arient is newly terraformed. It can't offer good transportation for passengers. Penred's a day out."

"We have an outpost there," Andri said as her fingers gestured to instruct her communications. "They'll send three cruisers from the local defensive forces. Immediately."

"It'll make a good diversion," Londo said grimly. "If they can track it coming in, they might think we're aboard and go after it. But Lina stays here. She's an observer only."

Lina knew that was incorrect. Something shivered down her spine.

Jae nodded absently at Lon's proclamation as he scrolled through his padd, but Andri stepped forward. "She'll take an observer position, but on Arient. We need her there. Easier coordination."

"Absolutely," Stoan said.

"No," Londo and Jae said together.

— — —

It took less than ten minutes for both organizations to receive a communique from the Galactic Sentinels. Yes, there had been an unprecedented breakout from their prison, Daq-qu-a. In all the eons the Sentinels had operated, breakouts had only happened two handsful of times. High-security interstellar prisons like Rimhold reported individual breakouts soon afterward. The Sentinels had their Guards on full alert, but this had been their first report of the prisoners' locations. Guards would be dispatched to Arient, but they too would have to gather info and extra weaponry. Travel times would likely place them there after the Legionnaires and ParaNetters would begin operating if the mission began immediately.

"We have backup. Thank you," Stoan told the Guard who'd relayed the message.

— — —

Wiley went through the list of escapees. "All from local sectors," he noted. "No nonhumans or fully nonhumanoid types."

"All right, we know who we're up against now." Londo named the people, and Lina could see by the reactions that their adversaries were Most Wanteds, Armed and Extremely Dangerous.

Quietly Lina separated herself from the others and called her offices on Aldierra. "We'll assume Backup protocol immediately," she told Kanti and Lon's and Jae's top staff, as well as Nesh. "This is not a drill."

CHAPTER

29

"Not sure how long this will last. A day? A week?"

The ten people Lina talked to, including Field Marshal Bracken, looked grim. "We want those migration corridors cleared and then planted. Medical aid needs to move along. Let's see if we can get more help from AffSys medical schools. The wars in the western sectors of Limbernia– They're still flaring up. They must be stopped."

She gave them a small, encouraging smile. "It will be up to you, even you, Field Marshal, to make sure the people also get messages to lift their hearts. Encouragement. Maybe we need a home decorating contest for the new quarters going up. Prizes go to whoever represents their Houses and region best, as well as provides comfort for the displaced families. Let's not leave out the people who don't have to relocated. Redecorating for them, maybe. Multiple prizes to reflect multiple cultures. We are very open to ideas.

"Y'all don't forget to check the 'upcoming projects and ideas' folders. We have to keep moving forward. Oh, and someone… Tidda, please, call my guards to care for the cats. They have instructions, and Greggo and Ellis know how to give Faf her meds."

There were minor questions. Lina directed them to various people and organizations who could either supply answers or investigate the matters. Finally satisfied, she signed off as they wished the Starharts success.

The two organizational forces were finishing their discussion as well. Stoan asked for volunteers who had specialized knowledge of their enemies, any targeted techniques that could be utilized. From the ParaNet Forte, Bolt, Jùfēng, and Blitz immediately volunteered to go.

"Not you," Hal told the young Blitz kindly. "Your mother would kill me."

From the Legion they got fifteen more, including Stoan, Wiley and Andri. Stoan was the one Legionnaire who had been to Arient within the last five years, having been curious about the terraforming and helping with the colony's energy systems. He brought current map data with him as Lina ported them all in to Starhaven.

Hal and Wiley pored over the maps while Londo headed the assault teams and Stoan ordered supplies. More ParaNetters were ported in with directions to focus on getting the hostages out. Heroes were assigned their targets. Reluctantly, all agreed Lina had to go but she was told to stay away from all action; she was their only transportation in and out. There would likely be injuries that would need quick transport to medical facilities on Sarastor. They planned to harry the enemy, too, and Lina would keep tabs on them and port them about like wasps around their enemies... but from a safe distance.

So she listened to the plans, and then to Londo's heart as he outlined his own private plan against Granger. He and Jae would go up against Granger and whoever the ex-Guard would have protecting him – they were sure there would be someone, maybe even a third person doing that. And it seemed logical, and tactical... but Lina could read the murderous rage in Londo's heart and could see his deeper plan.

No, Londo, she beamed to him, not willing to undermine his authority in front of the people he was going to lead into battle. **There will be no murder in this. You aren't a murderer.**

Jae chimed in. **You'll regret it the rest of your life. The Three Worlds' plan is not going to commence with a premeditated murder besmirching our reputation.**

Across the room, behind a loud discussion between Hal and the Bolt, Londo looked at his spouses. **Lina, he almost raped you. Twice. He did rape Demi, and almost destroyed her. And now he's after you again, and Hal. He's like a rabid animal; he's got to be put down.**

Then let the universe put him down, Lon. Not you, Jae instructed. **There will be no murder here. That is not subject to compromise.**

Londo walked over to Lina as casually as he could, even as Jae approached her. "I will not have that man threaten my family ever again," he said adamantly to her in a low voice.

"Then come up with other options," she answered, "but make sure murder is not among them."

— — —

They had Lina take her time porting so she wouldn't exhaust herself. They set up three camps on Arient, all far from the hostage site. One was strictly for medical emergencies, though the other two had med equipment available. Six very brave Legion team medics took their posts in them. Each camp got a small stack of stasis cocoons for storing the injured and criminals once they'd been defeated.

The world of Penred set up evacuation centers, awaiting freed hostages. Lina ported there for a few minutes to familiarize herself with the surroundings and thus make for easier future ports.

Communications were interconnected between personal padds, Legion HQ, and the ParaNet. As the heroes began to position themselves Lina monitored them as best she could, skipping from one transmission to another, waiting to hear someone calling her name if they needed help or to be moved. She'd have to work fast, even faster than the Legion teams were scouring this world.

They'd gone over their plans in detail before leaving, then as the camps were being set up, then as they searched for and spotted their prey. Four villages hadn't been touched by the villains. Lina ported in guard units to protect them.

The escaped prisoners had to be first removed from the area where the hostages and villages were. As soon as that signal was given, Lina would start porting hostages. After that, the heroes were free to let loose with everything they had onto their foes.

Everyone was so tense. Lina hopped in place, trying to dissipate her own surplus energy.

One by one, Legionnaires and ParaNetters reported in that they'd lured their targets away from the hostages.

"Not yet," Wiley murmured to Lina as they stood next to the main monitors. "Estimating ten minutes. We need to wait on Hal. This will be tight."

Lina gave a jerk of a nod.

"Granger's chasing Forte across the southwest continent," a Legionnaire reported. The Legion had given Forte an individual flyer for this mission, but so was Granger. Could his jasper weapon catch her?

C'mon. C'mon.

"Maximus just knocked Force-Off into the eastern ocean," came a report. "He… He… Location confirmed."

"Go!"

But Lina had already ported, even as Wiley gave her the order.

She ported to the cavern to make this end clearer. "Here we go!" she called, and ported five people. Then another five. A bunch of kids and someone who might be a mother. Another five.

Over and over, porting. She had to pause to catch her breath after the twenty-fifth passenger.

Every second counted. Every second was a chance someone would return and begin killing.

There was a group of injured who couldn't walk. She ported them one by one, calling through her communications to the medical personnel on Penred as to whom to expect.

Another. Another. Another two. Another.

Then… She sent her mind out, searching. That was it.

She sank to the floor, exhausted.

"Back to Central Command!" Jae's voice barked at her even as Londo's mind sent the same message. Taking a breath, Lina ported to safety.

Now it was up to everyone else.

— — —

Wiley kept track of them all. He coordinated with first Stoan and then Andri, once Stoan went off on his own mission. Forte came limping back to rest after another hero took over for her.

Lina had food, drinks, some cots, and of course a portalet, waiting at every camp. She knew right where to get those. Keeping things stocked made her feel less useless when it came to the real action. Her services were almost as important as the rest.

Still she listened anxiously to the reports coming in. Jae was doing fine as he harried Entangler. Lon was tossing bedrock at his targets and trying to avoid the fledgling flora of this terraformed world. He really wanted a giant tree he could bash someone with, but he made do.

Two targets were captured and rendered unconscious. The medics rushed to ensure that those targets were encapsulated into the medical cocoons, which put them out of action until released.

Great sonic booms rattled the ground, though battle was nowhere near.

Bolt's Achilles tendon was cut, which put him out of action. Forte announced she'd take over from there for him and rushed out on her air scooter.

eMage got tangled in her own spell and was taken down. Odom had been backing up Jae, but had to retreat for medical treatment when he got doused with caustic chemicals.

Even from within their shelter, Lina blinked as the light suddenly brightened. When she peeked outside, a sulfuric glow crossed half the sky and didn't fade for long minutes. Falling daytime stars pulsed across it.

The booms continued at random intervals, some sounding very far away and some far too close for comfort.

Boroh had bravely met his match and then some. His Legion Array sent out an automatic distress call when he went down. Londo managed to break away to get him to a camp.

The ground shook with an ominous rumble, hard enough for both Lina and Wiley to grab onto the camp's equipment to stay upright.

Lon had to work twice as hard to regain the ground he'd managed to win against Aktel Gaed. He reported that Gratika had joined in against him. Andri finished up her target and flew off to help.

Jae worked with the stims some had taken, upping their power. Causing overdoses. One major villain went down. He targeted another.

For ten long minutes everything outside turned dark. High-aimed lasers traced a webwork through it.

"Should I start porting the rest of the population off world?" Lina asked Wiley.

He actually paused before answering. "It takes a long while to completely destroy a world," he surmised. He gestured to a sub-communications channel. "I'll call for arks from Penred. Just in case. If needed, I'll direct you to whichever village is in imminent danger. Hal and Londo might be able to make temporary, air-tight shelters if it comes to it. Give you and the transports time to work."

– – –

An hour later. "What's that?" Wiley suddenly asked. They'd captured four more of the escapees, but the ones remaining were the most powerful.

Wiley let Lina see the screen he usually kept in invisible mode. He touched his rings in a pattern.

Lina recognized the symbol at the head of the popup window as being for Magnos, aka Stoan. Notations reiterated the common knowledge that he was a master of electromagnetism. The odd lines and notations next to those didn't look good.

"Is he hurt? Dead?"

Frowning, Wiley shook his head as he expanded the window. Those over there were medical indications, Lina knew, though she didn't know what they were saying. She could read the words "respiration," but didn't know what the numbers meant.

"Anyone near him?" she whispered to Wiley.

"Not so they could disengage to reach him."

"Give me a location," she said.

His lips tightened, but he touched more rings, waved his fingers over his screen. "Picture from his Array," he said as the screen changed:

Marshland. Tall grasses in the twilight.

Stoan lay on the ground, half in the water and half out. His position was sprawled. His uniform was bloody. Two rivulets of blood in particular traced his face from the top of his head.

"Head wounds," Lina murmured, remembering the sayings about how they always looked worse than they were. She didn't think that might hold true here.

She'd never seen the man striding toward him before, but she'd felt his vibe.

"That's one of the guys from Rimhold Prison. He has a—"

There it was: a sword of black metal that had two ribbons of red glows running through it.

"Black Blade." Wiley named him. "That sword can cut through practically everything. He has a telepathic connection to it. It has computer reactions and—"

"Give me a few minutes," Lina said before Wiley could contradict her. Unless he wouldn't.

— — —

She would bet money that Stoan had been thrown across a terrific distance. This Blade guy looked like he had enough muscle to toss an elephant about. Stoan was ghostly pale blue under the blood. He didn't seem to be breathing, though he was trying hard to. The air must have been knocked out of him.

The Black Blade was tromping through thick grasses hundreds of feet away from him. Searching. Lina aimed her port at behind him so Stoan, if he was still conscious, could see her. Stoan's gasping attempts to catch his breath were going to lead the Blade right to him.

She heard him then, in her mind. He was concentrating mightily, knowing that focused thought could be picked up by a telepath.

Stall him! he shouted at her.

Just stall? Lina blinked, just a microsecond of a pause. Legion commander. Order.

She ported all of the Blade's clothing off him.

Odd: the blade itself remained attached to him as if it were part of his body.

But the abrupt nakedness startled the man. He stopped in his tracks and looked down at his lower torso, then at the arm that held the blade.

Out of... Out of the water! came the call.

What, the Blade? Oh. Oh!

Lina ported up the nearest hill, where not a trace of the marsh's water reached. The Black Blade was nearing Stoan.

"Hey!" Lina yelled. "I see London, I see France…"

As the Blade whirled to her, she ported three hundred feet to her right onto more high ground.

"I don't see no underpants!"

He pivoted to take her in, but she ported again. He raised his sword. Could he throw it like a missile? Did it shoot rays? Should have done her homework. So she ported yet again.

There was a shallow river behind her. She ported a good section of it right over him.

It drenched him. He caught his breath and began to turn back to Stoan.

Almost instantly, the air crackled. Lina clenched her eyes hard shut and threw up her arms for protection. A flash of lightning struck almost ground zero. Every hair on her body stood as far out as it could.

The thunder from the blast tossed her backward.

It was a few seconds before she could scramble to her feet, and she stood weaving back and forth. Finally her eyes focused on Stoan. Then on the Black Blade.

He was out cold.

Naked and out cold.

Lina ran to Stoan. "Got your breath back yet?" she asked, and he shook his head.

Not. All. The way, he said in that careful manner non-telepaths could speak with telepaths. **Tranquilizer. Tranquilizer!**

"Legion Array, please tell Wilder Mem-Bazer that I need tranquilizer," she said to the air, and hoped Stoan's communications picked it up if her earring hadn't. She ported back to Wiley, who was fishing for an adhesive dot.

He slapped it in her hand and she ported back. "Where?" she asked, eying the naked villain. "You have your choice of spots."

Stoan tried to say something, and it sounded like "chest," so that's where she slapped the dot. The Blade gave a shuddering sigh and relaxed.

But the sword visually vibrated. The lines of power within it shifted.

It became an axe.

Stoan was pointing at the axe, likely utilizing his power, weak as he was. "It isn't that magnetic," he told her. The axe seemed as if it were trying to move, but it just vibrated, mostly in place. "I can't hold it. Port him. Separately," Stoan managed to say as he struggled to sit up. He was drenched with blood and water.

Lina tried. The axe would not go separately. She shook her head in defeat.

Stoan lifted a trembling arm and pointed. "Back there," he commanded. It was where Lina had been before, the dry, non-conducting high ground. She ported.

A snap of electricity split the air. The sword's power lines disappeared. For how long?

Lina separated axe from man. The axe could stay here. The man went to Wiley's camp, where she knew he stood ready with a cocoon.

"You good for a minute or two?" Lina asked Stoan, and he nodded. So she ported to Wiley and helped him load the naked Black Blade into a cocoon that expanded but still barely contained him.

"We don't have many of these left," Wiley said, troubled. "I need to check our inventory. When you get a chance within the next ten minutes, port out and get us some more."

Lina ported back to Stoan. The sword had moved from its previous position. "It's... trying to reunite with its master," Stoan explained.

She thought hard. "Do you have a homing device?" she asked.

Stoan fumbled with the belt of his uniform and handed one over. Lina went as closely as she dared to the axe, which seemed to sense her presence and began to turn about on its own, and ported the tiny dot into the path it was taking. The dot adhered to it.

Even as the axe began to rise menacingly into the air, Lina ported it to Aum, the world where the Galactic Sentinels lived. She breathed a relieved sigh. "Hope it didn't come as a surprise to them," she told herself. "If they can't contain it, who can?

"Okay, now for you," she told the commander, and ported them both to the main medical camp.

– – –

At last – Lon got great clearance and screamed across the sky to land a cosmic blow against Gaed. His personal force field couldn't stand up to *that*. It left Gaed wobbling through the thermosphere on a path that could become a low orbit of the planet.

Andri came up from directly below Gaed and belted him as only she could. He veered off at right angles. Blood ran from his ears, nose and mouth.

Time to finish him off. Andri was already gathering his devices as they fell through the air. Lon flashed up to intercept Gaed and –

Jae.

Jae'd just been hit hard. Londo felt it in his head, in his shoulders.

And yet Lon knew Jae had only caught the very fringes of the blast, wherever he was.

"Andri, you've got this!" Londo called and took off, throwing Gaed Andri's way. She stared at him for a moment but rushed to gather in the villain, letting the weaponry fall. Londo's ring relayed her communications to have someone catch those while she dealt with the unconscious man.

"Where's Neutrino?" Londo demanded of his own ring. It was Wiley who answered with coordinates. Lon could feel Lina's explosion of concern.

"I'll get there in minutes. Maybe five," Lon reported even as he sped up to the highest planetary speed he dared. He had to duck out of the atmosphere for a few moments to make the best time.

He doesn't have minutes, came Lina's response.

Wiley signaled to everyone that Lina had ported to aid Jae.

He was battling Granger. Granger and the rogue jasper of power.

Londo poured on the speed and dove, trying not to mind the atmospheric damage he left in his wake.

He could only watch as he approached. Granger held his palm-sized gemstone by a harness wrapped around it. It left an opening through which the jasper's energy could pulse out.

Jae tried to take flight, but still caught the edge of it. The blast knocked Jae backwards, sent him rolling in aerial somersaults until he fell flat onto the ground, groaning.

"I'm the one you want, not him," Lina announced from behind Granger.

Tabarnak! **Get out of there!**

She ignored Lon and kept her attention on Granger as he whirled.

Get out, get out!

"What's the matter; scared?"

Granger actually hesitated. Then he shook his head to himself. And moved quickly.

The jasper slid Granger around this way and that, in an unpredictable pattern. Lina's head turned left and right, trying to keep up.

Port out! D'Artagnan!

"I bet that husband of yours is rushing to your rescue." Granger let out a laugh as the jasper blurred the image of him. Lina kept turning her head, as if she were looking at him moving around. She likely didn't know that the Sentinels had said that the jasper could form illusions. Granger was probably standing still by now. Plotting.

Illusions, Lina. Wake up, Jae. Wake up, Jae!

Even as Lon slowed for landing, the jasper set a sickly green dome around Lina, Jae and Granger. Lina glanced up just as Granger's linked fists came down toward her head. Though she managed somehow to avoid the main blow, she sprawled hard.

Lon landed so abruptly the world shook for miles around. A freezing hurricane backwash blasted in his wake, followed by clouds of falling ice crystals. "I'm here!" he bellowed, and indeed, he caught Granger's attention. Granger's face twisted in sheer hatred. He raised his fist holding the jasper.

But Jae jumped onto him, reaching for it.

From the other side, Lina rose up to plant her hands to either side of Granger's head.

"I've got it," Jae said.

"I've got him," Lina said.

Londo punched the green dome, trying to get through. Again and again, calling on a level of strength he so rarely used. Full asteroids couldn't stand up to that kind of power.

Granger shrieked soundlessly, but Londo could hear it in his mind. What was Lina doing? He ignored it and battered away. It hurt. His knuckles burned with pain, so he turned to the side and used his shoulder to bash his way inside.

Then a thin whine began to emanate from inside the dome. It was metallic, unearthly.

It was the jasper.

Jae held it fully in his hands, staring at it with a blank face. What–

When Londo looked back at Lina, he thought he saw figures beside her, above her. Shining figures he could see echoing out in all directions, into this world. He was seeing them with another form of vision. And within them all stood Granger. No, an energy being.

An energy being who was Granger.

The energy within him was mottled with darkness. It looked sick. It was twisted upon itself. And it was fighting whatever it was Lina… and those figures… were doing to him.

Lon felt like he was watching the diagrams Lina used in her classes come to life. He could see Granger's chakras, cloudy rainbow energy vortices widely strung like lopsided beads down his body. A thunderbolt of intense white light crashed down through the top of Lina's head as well as Granger's. She directed the light within her into him. It crackled about the space that made up his body and accumulated in the chakras as well as smaller energy centers that Lon thought must be the minor chakras that Lina sometimes mentioned.

Granger screamed soundlessly. He jerked as if hit by wave after wave of electricity. Lina held on. The light increased.

Jae was speaking to the stone. Commanding it. Jae commanded Nature, and Nature obeyed him. He was Feithi. That was what he did.

But the stone was not listening. No, *trying* not to listen.

Jae cajoled it. He commanded. Sweat poured from Jae as he crouched with his hands clenched around the stone, eyes closed.

He made some kind of joke, trying to divert its attention, but the stone's intelligence – and it did have some kind of intelligence – came back to focus.

The stone released a blast of green energy at Jae, and Jae flinched hard.

But he held on.

And he commanded it.

From above Lina and Granger, then stretching into the very core of the planet, came another long burst of blinding white light. Londo shut his eyes against it even as he started to pound again with his fists. He knew where the dome was. He didn't have to see it to feel it, solid under this powerful desperation.

Someone was singing. Many were singing. Voices. Coaxing voices targeting not only Granger but the jasper as well. Jae was inviting them to help him.

The light was so bright even Londo's eyelids couldn't mask it. Instead he tried to reach inside himself, to the light that both Jae and Lina had told him was his true being, to join with what was going on inside the dome.

Yet the entirely physical part of him still pounded the dome with all his might. His hands and forearms were going numb. When he switched to his right shoulder, it didn't take long for that to do the same. So he switched to the left. He kicked.

He could feel people behind him now. Hal. Stoan. Andri. Forte. Wiley.

Hal, Andri and Forte joined him in trying to pound the dome into submission. Stoan couldn't use his lightning with the people around, but instead tried to reach into Granger's body to pull it apart magnetically.

Lon's mind was completely open to his spouses and their situation. His energy self reached out.

"No," he ordered Stoan. "Don't interrupt what they're doing."

He didn't understand why he said that, but his energy self did. Something behind him patted his back as if he'd done a good job. It was not one of his companions.

"Breathe," Lina told Granger over and over. Were those toxins, the dark mottling that oozed from the man when he exhaled? The tar of evil, the stench of unbridled ego?

Londo beat on the dome. He pounded and he slammed.

Nothing.

The light inside the dome grew so brilliant that the others could see it now, exclaiming. He could hear Jae's constant wooing of the stone. He could feel the stone's fear. Granger's terror.

"Don't be afraid," Lina murmured. "The light is pure love. There's nothing to fear there. No judgment. Just love. And joy."

Then… Granger let out a huge huff, as if his lungs were collapsing, and he dropped to the ground. Lina stayed with him. The white light poured through him, wrapping him in its glory.

Jae's orders increased in power. They beat through the jasper, through the geologic ages that had formed it. But it didn't want to devolve to a powerless thing. It enjoyed having power.

So let it evolve instead, someone said, and Lon was surprised to think it might have been him.

Jae grabbed onto the idea. His insistence increased, this time with a feeling of hope, of excitement to it. Time to evolve. Time to shift, to discover the new. Time to slough off the past and its negativity. Step into the light. See what's next. Here was the light for it. Now was the time.

Jae poured his very self into the job.

Come back, Jae, Lon pleaded. **That's enough. We can't lose you.**

But Jae remained entwined with the jasper. Melded with it. Was he showing it… things? Places in the universe Londo had never dreamed of? Maybe… different vibrations of existence?

Then Lon felt he was falling, falling from somewhere so high it was beyond time and space. The singing faded. The figures in the light dimmed to nothingness when he hadn't noticed.

All was silence.

The dome dissipated and Hal caught Londo before he could hit the ground.

— — —

Lina was soaked in sweat, her hair plastered against her head. White as a sheet. "Jae…" she whispered. She tried to reach for him, but her hands merely twitched. Londo propped her up to a sitting position and wondered if she should remain lying down. He turned to Jae.

Hal knelt beside the Feithi. Jae was unconscious. The jasper was clasped his grip.

"He's still alive," Hal said quietly. "We need to get to serious medical help. Now."

"There are no more cocoons," Wiley told them.

Everyone looked to Lina, but her eyes were rolling about.

She was burning up inside. Too much white light.

"Can you port us to help?" Lon pleaded with her. "Just two minutes to port, then I'll take you to help."

"Dunno. Fuzzy. Focus…"

Jae lay limp and still in Hal's arms, his breathing so shallow. Pulse weak. Londo could hear it.

"Lina, you've got to get us home. Jae needs help. Come on, Lina, focus!"

"Home?"

"Yes, home." Londo looked around. "Small group so she can handle it," he told the people around him. "Everyone else step back."

She was really trying to focus. "Home…"

This was going to be rough. "You can do it," he urged. "Think of home." And then because it seemed right, it was the one thing she truly could focus on for the two minutes she needed to make a clean port, he began to sing softly, *"In my mind I'm going to Carolina…"*

He kept his link with her clear and strong as everything else around her spun out of control. **Home, Lina. You and me and Jae and these others. You can do it. You can do it.**

Darkness suddenly descended for a long, long two minutes as Lon wondered if they'd ever emerge. Lina had that five minute limit. After five minutes… there'd be nothing.

Then he felt the breezes of Earth surround them. It was dusk and they were on a brick walkway surrounded by neo-colonial brick buildings and lawns, people strolling by. The few who saw them arrive stopped in their tracks. The white petals of a magnolia floated by in a gathering moonlight. Rhododendrons bloomed next to roses, spreading a soft perfume on the night time.

"Where are we?" Hal asked. He looked around. "Earth? Why Earth?"

"We wouldn't have made it otherwise. Who came with us?" Hal. Stoan. Wiley.

"Carolina," Lina whispered, and Lon nodded. "Nearest hospital? A really good one, Lina. Hal, do you know?"

Lina seemed like she was going to faint, shaking her head to wake up. "Memorial's... on south campus, tall building... next to a big parking deck. Or Duke Hospital is... is about ten miles northeast. Both... good." Hal was already taking off with Jae, heading northeast. The others, Stoan and Wiley, followed him. Lon was about to take off, when Lina pulled at him.

"Salt. Salt water. Big, big."

She often used salt water to rid herself of excess energies after healing. "Where? Atlantic Ocean?"

"Ah. Yeah."

They reached the ocean in under three minutes, and Londo held her head above water as he immersed her. He saw black streaks of energy like lightning rip through the water, light of every color explode off her.

"Is that good?"

"Can't... get rid of it all. That's... it."

Lon watched helplessly. He could feel her bloated with far more energy than a human was meant to contain. What could he do?

Earth! Earth, help us! he called. He imagined the warm mother love he'd felt from previous conversations with the planet through Lina, and then sank his consciousness into her. He felt the energies boiling inside her, hovering around her, threatening to overwhelm. **Release!** he ordered. ***I'll aim them; all you have to do is release!***

Somehow she loosed the energies, groaning as they peeled away. Lon felt Earth reaching up for them, and it was as if he reached down to take the earth's gentle hands, letting the energies travel down to her, where she could deal with them.

That's enough for now, or at least that's the idea he got from the planet, and Londo thanked her as he whisked Lina up and back toward Jae and Hal, this time slower. Lina was unconscious. He held her closely to him, for she no longer glowed with heat; she was deathly cold, and the water and airspeed were doing little to help her. He used his parabreath and Legion Array to try to warm her, but she was blue by the time he reached the emergency room. He stepped back to let the doctors get to her. One even gasped at her condition.

CHAPTER

30

L on stood in the corner of the emergency section, watching. Barely breathing in his panic. Hal held him by the shoulders. "Steady," he told his son.

"Are you all right?" Lon heard a woman ask behind him. It hadn't been directed to him.

Wiley and a bandaged Stoan stood nearby, with Wiley frantically gesturing to his invisible monitors for information. Stoan leaned against a wall for support. As Lon turned back to his spouses, Hal said, "They're aliens. They have blue skin. It's normal."

Wiley must have said or done something because Hal announced to the room, "We have a doctor, an off-world doctor, who can see to Jae and Lina." Medical personnel caught Stoan before he collapsed.

So Wiley joined the staff around the two beds. He peered and scanned and checked his monitors, then investigated what was available from the equipment within the room. The oxygen units that were brought in he approved of, and then reached into his pockets for the bits and bobs of advanced scientific paraphernalia that he always carried with him.

"I can begin some treatment," Wiley said carefully. "But–"

"Gorgeon is on her way," Stoan said from the doorway. He sat in a wheelchair, looking dazed.

"ETA?"

"Eighteen hours."

Wiley set his mouth in a grim line. "I'll try to keep them alive until then."

"He still has a grip on this. What is it?" one of the doctors asked. It took two of them to pry the jasper out of Jae's hands.

It had been a sick green mottled with dark veins and lumpy in shape. Now its form was triangular. Smooth as if it had been polished by a river for centuries. The stone itself was a translucent, honey-gold color that sparkled under the harsh lights.

"It's… It's…" the one doctor tried to say. Carefully Hal took the stone from him and turned it several times. Stoan wheeled past everyone to take it from Hal while Wiley issued orders and asked questions of the staff.

Stoan's translator hovered near his face. "Amazing. It's so… tranquil. Holding it, looking at it makes me feel good. It's almost hypnotizing. When has Jae ever…?"

"Makes you feel good?" Londo took the gem from him and puzzled over it a few seconds. Then he carried it back to lodge it between Jae's arm and body. "This might help. It stays with him. If nothing else, he's earned it."

He regarded his husband as his heart truly began to lose hope. Not Jae. Not Lina. They couldn't die. They couldn't… "No. No."

Pain welled up in his chest like a storm, larger than what he could contain. It began to move upward. Toward his shoulders. Toward his head. His knees began to weaken. And his arms… His right arm felt numb and yet on fire from all the blows he had dealt.

Misery. Utter black despair. Londo wobbled forward and back, side to side. Unformed words in the shape of a croon came from his mouth. He was going to be sick.

"They're going to be fine. We'll have the best people working on them. Here." Hal took him by the shoulders again.

"Ow!"

Hal dropped his hand from Lon's right shoulder, replaced it along the back of his ribcage, and guided him out of the room. There was a small waiting room a few doors down, with a door that could close.

— — —

Three chairs didn't survive Londo's weeping collapse. He tried to hold back. He'd always been taught to control, control.

"Don't worry about it," Hal told him with his arm around his back. "Papa's here. Let it go. We'll worry about things after."

Londo had no idea how long he wept and cried out in his pain. He began to emerge from it, only to plunge back into hopelessness.

Finally he felt emptied. Of everything. He sniffed and accepted another wad of tissues. How many had he gone through? He pressed the heels of his hands against his eyes. Or tried to. The right hand wasn't... working well.

"What is it?"

"It... It..."

Hal gestured to Londo's Legion ring and its medical scan appeared before them. As usual for Londo, the visual results were vague, the telemetry slightly unclear. The system had a difficult time penetrating his invulnerability. But...

"That looks like a broken arm," Hal breathed. He checked his son using his own paravision. "Broken in several places, from your hand to your humerus. The humerus is the worst, crushed in one place, though the metacarpals and carpals... Pretty close in the amount of damage. You've got other places hurt as well."

Lon let his head fall back. He didn't care. There was only one worry... two worries... taking all his attention. "What's happening?" he asked. "I need to go back."

He returned to Jae and Lina.

— — —

Stoan and Maria, the White Puma, were waiting for him at the intensive care room. They made him sit down and stay out of the doctors' way.

"We called your grandparents," Maria told Londo. "They're going to be beaming over shortly. I know she'll be all right," she added. "They both will."

She sat next to him and patted his left hand. He tried to smile and nod his head to lessen the concern on her face, but he couldn't. The misery gripped him too hard, the fear of what might happen.

"I should have–" He didn't know how to finish that. He didn't know what else he could have done.

Stoan eased over. "Earth, Londo? Really?"

"Magnos!" Maria chided.

Londo shook his head. "We wouldn't have made it to Sarastor. This was the only focus for her I could give. I had to sing to her mind the whole way."

"Ah." Stoan's eyes worked back and forth as he considered. "Sing."

"If Sarastor had any familiar songs about itself, I would have used those."

Wiley set down an instrument and walked to them. "Damn it," he said when he reached them all. "If she'd just taken us to Sarastor, I wouldn't have to work with these..." He shrugged. "They're both in deep neurogenic shock. We can counter a little of that here, but... There's damage the likes of which I've never seen. I'll try my utmost to keep them going until Gorgeon can get here. If I know her, she'll be able to handle things."

"Neural damage?" Stoan asked for clarification.

Câlisse de tabarnac. Neural damage... Londo could only half-listen to Wiley's reply. It was too much. He couldn't take any more. Lists of conditions, of injured body systems, of...

"Wiley," Hal said sharply, and Wiley's head jerked in his direction.

Wiley licked his lips. "They're young. Healthy before this happened. Exhausted from all the work they've been doing, but..."

"Gorgeon will arrive." Stoan sat at resolute attention in his wheelchair, as if he could direct the universe. As if Gorgeon was the answer to everything.

"Lonnie? Lonnie!"

They all turned to see the gRands rushing down the hallway toward them. "How are they? How are you?"

Mama Ruth enveloped Londo as she could in her hugest hug, and Papa Mike hugged the both of them from the back.

"Watch his arm," Hal directed. When they turned to him, he added, "Broken bones."

"Lonnie? Broken bones?"

"I'll be all right," he assured them. He wanted to cry again just because they'd understand. Because it was so good just to have them here.

They stepped away from the room. Chatter overlapped but eventually everyone caught up to speed.

Wiley said, "These people here, they're pretty good, considering the level of technology. And Lon, one of the nurses says that she knows Lina, has attended some healing classes with her. She'll try some kind of psychic technique on her later on. I'll want to watch that, so I can compare and contrast techniques." He checked Lon's expression. "It couldn't hurt."

"Sure, Wiley. Anything." He looked up at the staff inside the room. "Can I stay with them? Not just now, but tonight?"

A staffer in the hallway who had stopped to stare at the crowd piped up, "Let me get you something." Within moments he and a friend had retrieved a bulky lounge chair from somewhere, and ensconced it in the room.

"*Merci*. Thank you."

Lon moved it to the foot of the two beds and took his place. When personnel came to move Jae and Lina to a larger unit, Lon one-handedly carried the chair with him, but this time placed it between the beds, so he could reach out and hold his spouses' hands, even if it was just their fingers between plastic tubing and even if he could barely feel anything with his right hand.

— — —

Stoan and Hal watched as the two gurneys were wheeled into the large room, Wiley giving calm orders to the doctors who hurried in behind them. An orderly came up with a box of equipment; more wheeled some electronics in on carts to add to the technological plethora. Wiley pointed the way into the room, tinkering with the equipment even as it was still rolling down the hallway.

"They're going to live," Hal declared, as if he could order the universe to his will.

"Just a few hours ago," Stoan told Hal in a low voice, "I was calling her a whore. Threatening Jae that I'd have him and Londo both drummed out the Legion."

"So they told you about the Triune." Hal sighed as he steered Stoan's chair.

"I found out on my own."

"Is he... Are they really going to be expelled?"

Stoan rubbed his chin. "Ask me that this morning when my proximity alarm for them went off, and I would have said absolutely. But now... I have to think about this, do some research before I make my decision."

"I'm asking now. Between the three of them, Arient wouldn't have happened. You wouldn't have all those felons locked away. Hopefully forever this time."

"Arient wouldn't have happened," Stoan agreed. "It's going to be a landmark day in the history books, so many threats to the peace eliminated. A maddened ex-Ruby Guard with a doomsday weapon utterly defeated by just two people."

"Lon's… wife and husband." Hal shook his head. "Just tell me if they're going to be expelled or not, so I can stop worrying about that at least."

"If they survive? As it stands now, with all the secrecy... There are Legionnaires who know, but most don't. Some people have been joking about it. Everyone has been; they've been terrible at keeping this secret."

He gave an unfunny chuckle. "Turns out Aldierra was the only place that knew the truth, twenty billion people. But how does this reflect on what the Legion stands for? Hal, Lina said you'd been to Feith, seen Triunes there…"

"I saw, I saw," Hal said tiredly. "Jae tricked me, you know. Tricked me into saying that Triunes were a spiritual form of marriage and family."

"But it's different when it's your family." Stoan grimaced.

"Yes, it's different. What do we do?"

"I'm open to suggestions," Stoan said quietly. He looked up to see a screen blossoming in the air.

It was Andri, back on Arient. She wouldn't leave until he was back at Legion HQ, and had been tuning into Wiley's medical updates. "So you found out," she said. "I take it you're considering expulsion?"

Stoan's eyes were haunted. "There are grounds for it. Give me reasons not to. I'll listen."

Andri thought for a moment. "I can think of many reasons, some historical, some emotional. Some having to do with Feithi traditions. But there's one more important than any of those."

"And that's...?"

"I've thought about this a long time," she said. "I've done research, asked experts… obliquely, of course. The Three Worlds, the mere concept of it, of the forces that went into its creation, boggles the mind. Explodes all previous theories of how the universe is structured, about theology and philosophy and physics. Have you seen some of their plans? Of what they've accomplished in the short time they've been on Aldierra?"

"Not much. Just some things."

Andri gave a wry smile. "Their goals are monumental, on the scale of Windishao's Manifesto of Society, of Christin's Laws and Behaviors. If they can get even a fraction of it accepted, the repercussions will spread out from the Three Worlds in waves. I don't have to be a sociology expert to know that in three, four centuries, the entire socio-political-ecological-theological-philosophical-etcetera axis of every world in this end of the galaxy will have shifted in some way. For the better, in my opinion."

She looked at Stoan. "You don't understand, do you? If you take Jae and Londo out of the Legion, someone will just have to form another Legion with them in it. Chloroplast was just the beginning. Paras and megaparas are going to follow them. They're both – they're all three – natural leaders, the kind that can lead people by their hearts as well as their minds. People will give up everything in order to follow wherever they go. Legionnaires included. You take them out of the Legion, you'll lose half your Legionnaires. Don't force them to make that decision, about which project is the more important."

Stoan considered her for a moment. "And if the Legion were to expel them, where would your loyalties lie?" he asked quietly.

Andri's eyes were sharp on his. "I'm glad I haven't had to make a decision about that. I am quite content and proud to be a Legionnaire."

Wiley strode up, having heard part of the conversation. He looked tired as he reached into a pocket on his lab coat and retrieved a cloth to wipe his brow. "And I'm content to be a primary consultant for the Three Worlds." He took the opportunity to sag into a chair against the wall of the hallway.

Andri sniffed. "Hmf. And their unofficial historian. I remember."

"They should be on special status, not restricted by the more constraining rules Legionnaires have. Consider each group a resource for the other. Closely linked, but not the same. Working for mutual advantage."

"So you're saying... expulsion, but put them on a retainer."

Andri spoke up. "My vote is to keep them and put them on special status."

Stoan considered and then glanced sideways at Wiley. "How many bets do you have riding on this?"

"I'm willing to cancel all my betting activity on this subject if it will make your decision any easier."

Stoan sighed and leaned back in his wheelchair. "Nothing's going to make this decision easier."

Hal watched Londo through the wall as his son stayed out of the doctors' way. He could tell by his posture how helpless he felt. He looked at Wiley. "Do we call her parents?" he asked. "They have a right to know."

"And what would you tell them, Hal? Hi, Mr. and Mrs. O'Kelly. Your daughter, whom you don't give a damn about, was injured on a planet a hundred parsecs away, after attacking one of the most powerful megavillains this galaxy has ever seen."

"I'll call 'em." Londo ran a hand through his hair as he joined the small group. He sank into a chair next to Wiley's. "I'll tell 'em something. That she's had an accident and is in the hospital. We'll see how they take that." He shook his head. "I don't think they'll care. But her sister; I'll call her too. I need to check in on Aldierra, just for a minute or two."

He walked to the waiting area, where his grandparents, Maria, and some other ParaNetters were waiting, and the others watched him.

"By the way," Hal told Andri, Stoan and Wiley. "I'm Londo's biological father."

$- - -$

Wiley directed the hospital personnel on the next phase he tried. Jae and Lina remained in the same room. Computer screens surrounded Wiley, with Legion medical personnel joining in via video to advise. A snap of his fingers translated the commotion into English, so the Terran health workers could be part of the conversation.

Lon stood by helplessly. Dr. Riz was a few hours into her journey. Could Jae and Lina wait that long? Could Riz help them?

"We don't have any stasis cocoons on Earth," Londo told the screens. "We've been using them elsewhere. Should have replaced them, but we just haven't been… operating on Earth." He dragged his left palm across his face to wipe away the tears.

"I believe Gorgeon took some. Unsure. We're sending more now." Dr. Benton motioned to someone off-screen to follow through. "What else do you need from here?"

"A miracle."

"I should have the ParaNet keep a stash of the cocoons," Hal told him. "Too late for wishing." He put his hands on his son's shoulders. "All we can do now is pray."

"Raphael," Londo said. "That's the archangel of healing. I watched the video Lina made. Raphael and all your angels, all angels who can, please help her and Jae. Please heal them. Please…"

He wept into his left hand.

The Legion medic looked away.

Hal pressed his head against the back of Londo's. "I'm with you, son," he murmured. "I'm here with you."

— — —

Lon woke in his chair between the two beds as Riz bustled into the room. When had he fallen asleep? Someone had spread a blanket over him. He checked the time; couldn't have been out for more than an hour.

Floating carts of equipment followed Riz, along with Hal carrying a load. Riz flipped a handful of translators into the air, which sped to the Terran staff. "Plenty of barbarian magic here," she declared as she examined the Terran machinery. With a cup of coffee in his hand as he strode behind her, Wiley gave brief explanations of what the equipment around the room was doing, how the patients had been treated so far. Riz snorted and motioned to the Terran medics to explain the finer details.

Three of Riz's assistants entered, more floating platforms of tech ahead of them. Riz conducted as to its placement. The room was a large one by Terran standards, but the equipment filled it up so people had to shuffle carefully through.

Riz examined her wan patients, both with her padds floating around her and via her own observation. She quizzed Londo on what they'd been doing before their injuries. "Hm. Hm. All right. And then? Has this ever happened to him before? Did Lina say anything after she got rid of the energies? Hm. Hm."

"They were refining vibrations," Lon told her. "That's how it seemed to me. They were working independently, but the energy was combined at some points. Both were pulling their targets – Granger and the stone – upward in vibration. You know, more spiritual. Giving them loads of white light to wash out their lower vibrations. The sickness in their energies. There were hundreds, maybe thousands of spiritual beings adding to it all. I can't really tell–"

"Excuse me?"

A female nurse in floral scrubs stood at the door, gawping at them. "Uh," she said.

"You're Lina's friend," Wiley announced.

"Um, I took a class with her. From her. Once. Plus I have certification in Reiki. Level two. I'm Wade Marks. Can I help?"

Riz spared the room's readouts for a second to look at her. Then she motioned her in. "You do your thing while I work out a plan of action. Right now I'm more concerned with physical injuries than spiritual ones. Whatever you can do can't hurt."

"Um, what happened?" Wade asked.

"They got hurt."

"They were raising the vibrations of some very evil… things. A person and a thing," Lon quickly explained. "They invoked some kind of… heavenly energy to clear out the evil. There were beings. Angels, maybe. You tell me what I can do to help you."

"Wow. We have a remote healing circle already underway, across town and a few people from across the country," Wade said. "I called around as soon as I found out. Others are calling too. There are three prayer circles that I know of."

"Do they know there are two patients?"

"They know." The woman nodded her head. "Can someone move this chair?"

Lon lifted it with one hand. It wobbled in his grip. Not important. He then stood beside her as she told him about energies and prayers and angels and white light and things he wished he'd worked more with in the past weeks. He helped as he could, but thought he was doing it all wrong.

"No, you're fine," she insisted.

As the two worked and Wiley recorded, Dr. Gorgeon and her staff set up veritable webs of wires and tubes and lights around both prone Starharts. Jae lay gray against his pillow, while Lina was paste white. "Keep up the oxygen levels, whatever you do," Riz instructed her assistants. "Where's that turzing beam? Let's begin with that, see what results it has on Neutrino."

"Are they going to be all right?" Londo demanded.

"Concentrate," Wade reminded him.

Riz turned to Lon just long enough to note his exhaustion. And his arm. "Unknown at this point. We'll do our best, you know that. If it were anyone else, I wouldn't bet on their odds."

"What about stasis cocoons? You brought some, didn't you?"

"Let's start without them. We'll bring them in if needed. I want to see what level we can get them to here. Besides, the trip back will be another eighteen hours, and it's all through hyperspace. With these kinds of… spiritual injuries I'm not sure how the cocoons might keep them from receiving the energies they need right now. We have no data on cocoons and psychic injuries, much less adding hyperspace to the mix. We'll save those as a last-ditch effort."

The assistants aimed laser-type equipment at both Starharts, and rigged more energy networks around them, weaving them around Lon and Wade as they worked. Riz consulted three large screens hovering in midair.

"Let's use the mentart on Lina," she instructed. "And Mem-Bazer, see to Londo now. He's healing when he shouldn't be. He's healed. Wrongly. We should interrupt his energy work; it's that important that we get to this stat. I need that main break re-broken so it can be set properly and healed right. Plus I want to look at his other arm. Maybe his feet as well."

"*Ouais…* What?"

"Londo, let Ms. Marks do her work alone. You can view the record later and reinforce what she's doing then. Not now."

Hal and his parents stood outside the room. Hal had rigged a screen so all could see what was going on inside. He perked up at Riz' command.

"I may be needed," he told his mother and father. He peeked around the corner of the door. "Wiley?"

"Yes," Wiley said as he motioned for Hal to join him. The room was overflowing with equipment and staff.

"Everyone who isn't doing something directly, get out now," Riz ordered. "Ms. Marks, stay."

When there was room for it, Wiley pointed to a position next to where Londo had taken a stance beside Jae's bed. "Here." Hal obediently took the spot, out of the way of the others but still near to Jae.

Wiley motioned for two monitors to appear before him. One showed the equivalent of a vague x-ray of Lon's arm.

"That looks worse than before," Hal said. Bones were still broken, not in proper position, but were expanding toward each other.

"Don't bother with me," Londo insisted. "I'm not important here."

"Shut up," Hal said. "Be still. This will probably hurt. Wiley?"

Wiley showed him an animation of what and how things should be done. "Lon, I want you to hold Jae right here."

They taped Londo's left wrist to Jae's ankle. "As if that's going to hold."

"Whatever you do, don't break the tape," Wiley warned. As Lon groaned, Wiley positioned his right arm and made sure Hal took hold of it correctly.

Lon gripped Jae's bed with his fingers to steady himself.

"We need to break the bones here and here." Wiley didn't show Londo the screen.

"Break them." Hal's face contracted in pain. "I don't think I—"

"You can. Break. Not tickle. His invulnerability is weak now, remember that. Break."

Hal nodded.

"Ear protection," Riz commanded everyone, and handed out dots that went on the front of everyone's clothing. Terrans and Sarastorans applied them. Jae and Lina also received some. She nodded to Wiley. "Go."

"Braced?" Wiley asked Londo.

Lon nodded with a gulp.

"All right. On three. One. Two."

Hal snapped Londo's bones.

Lon let out a bellow. The walls rattled. The metal lower support on Jae's bed squished under Londo's clench.

"Next spot," Riz instructed in a loud voice.

Hal took care of the second break without a countdown.

When the room stopped vibrating for Lon's yell, everyone snapped off their protectors, even a confused Wade. "Quickly," Riz warned from where she stood next to Lina.

Riz' assistants aided Wiley and Hal in manipulating Londo's arm into place as Lon grimaced but remained mostly silent. One assistant wrapped flat wires around it.

"Impervion splints," she explained. "We keep them on hand."

"Is that all?" Lon asked through some gasps. "Is it over? Can I get back to…"

"Quiet," Hal commanded. "Let's get this done."

He stood by his son's side as they pried him from Jae and then adjusted an armature around Londo's arm, secured by the splints.

One of the Terran nurses rigged a cloth sling, which the Legion assistants reinforced with more impervion.

"One full day in this," Wiley informed Londo. "I don't know if we'll need to go in later to undo all the false healing that has been done."

"I didn't hurt him, did I?" Londo anxiously eyed Jae and then took back the chair he'd been using.

"You have more breaks," Riz told him. "More minor than these were. Are." She wrinkled her nose and squinted as she pondered. "I have a theory but we'll have to wait until Lina wakes up to try that. It requires a more precise approach."

Ah, multiple breaks might explain why Lon felt just a trifle uncoordinated. Now that he thought about it, it did feel like something wasn't quite right.

"Muscle injuries seem to have healed well in, ah, most cases, but they've healed over breaks that are still out of kilter."

Londo didn't know how to respond to that, other than determine that he'd think about it later. After Lina and Jae were awake and on the road to recovery.

The staff had positioned their energy webs in a close mesh, and Wade regained her place.

"I think you can rest now," Wade told Lon. "You work after I leave. You were doing really well."

Londo had to duck to get back to his chair, but he stoically took his guardian position by Jae's side and his sling held steady.

— — —

"Lon needs to rest," Hal announced a few hours later.

"No."

Lon had angled his chair so he could lean against Jae while holding Lina's fingers.

Riz examined Londo. There were dark bags under his eyes. His facial muscles showed debilitating fatigue. "Your... situation," and she wiggled her eyebrows to mean that he was touching his spouses, and thus negating his invulnerability, "is tiring you more than usual. It's slowing your healing, but that might be a good thing. The fimrit–" she nodded at the two inflated strips fastened to his right arm – "and those nanobots have been able to correct much of that premature healing. It's not perfect, but I have ideas about that we can try later. So we can disconnect you from everything, including *them*. I think we can rig a bed here, maybe in that corner. You'd still be near. You could regain your vitality."

"No. They need me. I know it."

Riz and Hal both tried to argue, but then Lina's lips moved.

Jae's voice came from her mouth. "We are healing," he announced.

Lon gaped at Lina. Hal, Riz, and everyone else left in the room did the same.

"We are... somewhere else. Spirit is healing us. Light and joy is all around us. Give us time."

"Jae, Jae *chéri*, you're okay?"

"Not now, but I will be. Lina should wake up tomorrow, we think. I'll take more time. Get some rest, darling. Let your papa coddle you like he wants to. Now and then we all need to be pampered."

"Coddle," Hal murmured.

"Are you sure, Jae? Oh, I'm doubting even you. You'd better get better. I'm giving you four days. Is that good?"

"Get some rest, my dearest. We worry about you too. We're sending angels to help you as well."

And with that, Lina/Jae became quiet.

The conscious people in the room stared at them.

"Does this kind of thing happen all the time?" Hal asked.

"Something weird every day," Lon said. "It makes life interesting." Hospital staff were bringing in a cot, and he ducked around the machinery and light web to get to it. Once he lay down he took in the room. His spouses. The workers. His father. Back to his spouses.

Then he closed his eyes and fell into a deep slumber.

CHAPTER

31

Lina's eyes fluttered. Then they opened halfway, seeking…

"Lon." The corners of her mouth twitched as if trying to smile.

"Lina, my love." His hands encompassed hers as he sat next to her. "You are in hospital, getting better. Jae is here, also getting better."

Her eyes closed but with visible effort, opened again. "I… Have we done this before?"

"Maybe a time or three, yes."

"I think I'm awake now. Well, not all the way. I think I'll remember. Where–?"

"Duke."

"Oh. Not Carolina. Too bad." Her brow creased for a moment. "But they have a chai place in the basement."

"I will get you a chai if you stay awake."

Now that was indeed a smile. "Sweet caffeine. I'll stay awake for that." Her gaze took in a fuller view. "Riz? On Earth?"

"And yet they managed to keep you alive until we arrived," Riz said with a smile. "How are you feeling?"

"Wrung out. I need to breathe extra deep today, suck in energy. How–" Her gaze swung behind Riz. "Wiley. Thank you and Riz and her staff and the hospital staff and Hal and everyone, everyone. Thank you."

"You're welcome."

"Lon, you're hurt."

"Just a little." Before Lina could say anything else, Londo told her, "Two of your guards are watching the cats. Leefe and Kanti are overseeing today's schedule, with Bracken backing them up. Nesh is directing extra efforts."

"Oh. Good. Good. Someone should remind Leefe and Bracken that portapotties are not to be scoffed at. They're important." Lina twisted her head to take in Jae.

Londo guided her hand so she could lay it on top of Jae's while he held her other one. Lon felt as if his heart were coming alive again. "He's improving. He did that ventriloquist thing with you yesterday and said Spirit was healing you both, but he'd take longer."

"Ventr–? Oh. I remember lovely light. Presences. So much happiness and joy." She gave Londo a brilliant smile. "That is true Source. Thank you, Source. Thank you, angels." She squeezed Londo's hand. "Thank you, Lon. In case I haven't said it yet today, I love you so much."

"You are my heart, *cherie*."

– – –

Riz had set up a full 180-degree montage of holographic monitors. She explained them to Lina as well as the Terran hospital staff, who stood behind things to observe. They hadn't been told about Londo's vulnerability process, but that couldn't be helped.

Some things had to be kept secret.

Still, Lina reasoned that these people were intelligent. They'd likely guess. But they were also doctors. They had ethics. She would have to trust them.

"He just ingested a large number of nanobots," Riz said.

"They did not taste good," Lon said. His glum expression announced that he held serious doubts about what was about to happen.

Riz's monitors cut the air between Lina and Londo. Her legs were taped to his as they both sat. The screens faced Lina and Riz, though Lon's side might also have had screens. Probably not. He might flinch.

One of the monitors displayed the nanobots dispersing throughout Lon's body. They targeted his arms, hands, legs and feet. One small section went to his jaw. He must have been clenching that pretty hard when hell had broken loose.

Something like 3D x-rays showed the various bones in different frames. The pictures were a little fuzzy but Lina could see how malformed they were. The bones had tried to reconstruct themselves to health while Lon had been separated from her and Jae. They'd succeeded, but only partially.

Now with Riz (and some brilliant green angels) guiding her millimeter by millimeter, Lina began to port those growths that were out of position or in an incorrect shape. She shaved off the parts that were new-grown and wrong. They went into specimen jars for Riz and her staff to peruse once they returned to Sarastor. Everything else stayed. Now and then PK nudged fragments closer to their proper position.

At one point Riz stopped her, and her staff triple-checked the progress. The nanobots swarmed into that area to guide Lon's body to heal correctly. Lina could *see* the bone grow under their guidance.

Again and again Lina ported. Bit by bit. Check by check.

"I want to leave him with *some* kind of skeleton," Lina muttered, and she could feel Londo's alarm. Or was that Hal, who was peeking in from down the hall? Both of them.

"You're only removing the incorrect spots," Riz reassured them all. "Have faith that Lon's body will know what it's doing when you're through, even without the nanobots. I'm giving him those to work while you're touching him. Otherwise Valiant will heal too quickly. This way we control things better."

So Lina kept on, working as meticulously as she had ever done.

But just to make sure, once they released her from Londo she performed as thorough a ko-laimni energy healing on him as she could from a sitting position, to remind the cells of how they were supposed to function.

When it was all done, Riz examined miles of digital information. Then she turned to Lina with an approving nod.

"That will do nicely. You may have one dose of caffeine."

$- - -$

"Riz says she's sticking around until you wake up," Lina told Jae, who hadn't stirred for an hour. "I bet ten dollars that you'd do that this morning. I'm not going to tell you what time. You might cheat."

She sat in a wheelchair next to his bed, and looked up when Londo entered the room, hot drinks in a carryout tray. He was walking fine and looked a lot better than he had yesterday.

Lina continued, "Riz says it'll be this afternoon, maybe tonight. I don't know when exactly she put her money on. She told me that Stoan had an hour ago. He was here for a while. Did you know that? Wiley and he left last night, so now Andri's just started taking the slow way back to Sarastor. They don't trust me to port yet. Here's Londo. What do you say?"

Lon sat in an adjoining chair and passed Lina a chai. "I signed up for 12:04 PM." He leaned over to speak closer to Jae's ear. "What time do I put you down for, Jae?"

But Jae didn't respond.

Lon tried again. "I think I've gone vegetarian. It's been creeping up on me for a while now. When Papa Mike brought in some take-out last night, I just couldn't. It was like you said, I could feel the poor cow in its death throes there on the bun. You won the bet, Jae. You said it would take me a while. You need to wake up so you can name your reward. I give you permission to gloat for five minutes."

But again: no response. So the two conscious Starharts chatted about what was going on around the hospital. Londo updated them both on Aldierra's business.

"I get to check in myself this afternoon," Lina confided to Jae. "About time."

When they'd gone through chat subjects, and after Mama Ruth and Papa Mike had visited for a while, they were left alone.

Lon let out a sigh. Then he began to sing, "I've got sunshine on a cloudy day."

Lina joined in with harmony and when they got to the chorus, it was "My guy."

On the final chorus, the final echoing, "My guy," it was Jae's voice that joined in.

His eyes were closed. His expression hadn't changed.

They switched to another song and he sang along.

Riz came in at Lon's ring signal. She and her assistants watched and checked status as the Starharts continued their soft concert.

Eventually Jae petered out, and the others let the songs drop.

Wiley checked in from Sarastor, as his monitors had picked up the change in Jae's condition. Then Hal wandered in.

"I hear he might wake soon," he said, and Lina nodded.

But Lon was studying Jae's face. Had a muscle twitched there, an eyelid fluttered? If so, it was so subtle he wasn't sure.

"Jae," he said. "My dearest *chéri*. You wake up now. You start building your strength. As soon as you can sit up comfortably for forty-five minutes, we're going to hold an interstellar press conference. You hear me? Time to wake up. We're going to announce."

Jae's eyelid definitely fluttered.

"Jae? Jae?"

Lina grasped one hand and Londo, the other. "Jae?"

"L… Lon." It wasn't a song. Jae whispered, "I'm tired of secrets."

"No more secrets, my heart, my everything. I'll bring everything out in the open. I promise."

"Just get well so we can do it," Lina urged.

Jae's eyelids opened slowly. His eyes moved so he could take in the room, the people. His gaze remained longest on his spouses. Then he noticed Hal.

"Good to have you back, Shaggy," Hal said, and Jae gave a weak smile. "I knew you couldn't die. What with the entire sector thinking you're the greatest hero around, the savior of Arient."

"Oog. Arient? Arient." Jae raised his head slightly and peered down at the golden jasper wedged by his side. "Hello," he told it. "Well, isn't that interesting."

"We thought so," Lon said.

"It's humming to itself. Quite content." Jae eased back onto his pillow with a sigh.

"You're in hospital," Lina hastened to tell Jae. "You're getting much better. You'll be fine soon. Everything's in order."

"We'll aim for Sunday afternoon or Monday morning for the announcement; think you can be up by then? We'll miss the Sunday morning commentators that way."

"I have no idea what day it is."

"You take all the time you need," Lina insisted. "There'll be another Sunday if you're not up to it for this coming one."

"All is well," Londo assured him.

Jae saw Hal's hand resting on Londo's shoulder, and he let out a held breath. "So it is," he said.

— — —

Cameras. Lights. Almost assured condemnation looming.

Large monitors floated above the back and sides of the crowded New York division ParaNet briefing room, showing that many other worlds were tuned in.

The room had fairly hummed when Lina came in leaning heavily on Lon's arm before he seated her at the long table. How her eyes shone with pride at him! "I had faith," she whispered.

Then Londo collected Jae in his wheelchair and placed him on his other side. A few swoony inhales emerged from around the room.

"Easy," Jae told him. He placed a soothing hand on Lon's arm and gave it a squeeze.

But Lon's pulse was thundering within. He could feel the sweat collecting on his forehead, and shook it as only Valiant could, to dry himself.

"*Que sera, sera*," Londo muttered with a sinking feeling.

"There's a song about that," Jae whispered back as he adjusted his position.

Londo took a breath, his hand on the back handle of Jae's chair. Lina's reassuring thought was like a hug and a kiss.

Then he moved to the podium. The ParaNet symbol on it had been replaced by that of the Three Worlds.

"Good morning. We are the Chosen of the Three Worlds. Valiant." He placed his hand on his chest. "Starfleet. Or do we call you Speaker? Does anyone use that Starfleet name any more?"

"I do," Lina said. "I like it. I have the tee shirt. Most people call me Speaker, though, since I'm the Speaker for the Three Worlds. I prefer 'Lina.'"

Lon nodded. "And over here is Neutrino. Someone pass the smelling salts to the audience."

Jae rolled his eyes at him.

Lon continued. "Hello to everyone watching. *Eh bien*, we've been busy. These two are still recovering from our last mission, which had nothing to do with Three Worlds. I'm not sure how much footage of our current operation has been broadcast on Earth. We've been working to save a world for a couple months now. It goes by the name of Aldierra."

Lina waved to the cameras. "Hello to the people of Aldierra, and all the soldiers and volunteers, both native and off-world, who are working so hard there. Keep it up. We'll be home soon to boss you all around."

Lon had to laugh at that. "*Correct.* We'll be upping our news distribution to tell Terrans about that in more detail than what I think you've had so far. I believe that by now the Affiliated Systems have fairly complete coverage of the mission. That's–" Lon jigged his head to the left – "The next galactic sector over, and one next to Aldierra's sector."

"They're getting about thirty percent of the news," Jae volunteered.

"Ah. We'll see what we can do about that." Londo then thanked the hospital staffs from all locations, as well as various healing groups for their aid these past few days.

"And," Lon added with a smile, "I suppose I should formally introduce our third more formally. As I said: Neutrino, civilian name of Jae Rallene. Or I should say, Jaeson Rallene Starhart, the Minister for the Three Worlds. My very dear husband."

He paused as he'd been instructed, to let it sink in, let the gasps begin.

"We are married in a Feithi Triune, it's called. Some of you out there have been told that this is fake news, but I assure you it is not.

"The Triune is an honorable and usual form of marriage practiced on Jae's home world of Feith. Tragically, Jae is the last survivor of that world, as its population was destroyed through the plots of some madmen. Who might not have wanted to go that far. Part of it might have been an accident, but only part. But that's for another time to tell, with a thorough investigation that has been delayed far too long."

Lon licked his lips, regarding the room, the monitors. "Accompanying our instructions as the Three Worlds was an edict to carry on the culture of Feith. We made this marriage as cheerfully consenting adults who adore each other in all ways. The recording of Lina's and my wedding? That was annulled right before the Triune took place a couple weeks later. This is how Triunes worked, with the annulment of any previous partnerships, so that all three could enter the marriage on equal footing. We have a recording of the Triune ceremony available for you."

Shouts and raised hands from everywhere greeted Lon's pause.

He ignored them. "We love each other. We have shared minds, which brings the relationship to an entirely new, deeper level. And we've all been invested as primaries into the project called the Three Worlds. We are in to both the marriage and the project for life. There is no backing out. No divorce. Nor does anyone involved want us to back out."

"I'd like a honeymoon please," Lina said.

"After we get Aldierra past the Deadline," Jae told her. "A nice long honeymoon."

Londo continued. "We've posted information about Triunes for Earth's Internet to access. There should be a url on your screens." There was, he saw. "The rest of you can access Feithi information on this through your regular channels. Jae?"

"I've released all Feithi information for the Affiliated Systems and for Aldierra," he said. "Not just for specialized research."

"I can hear AffSys historians going crazy even as we speak," Londo said. "So much information to dig through. The Feithi were a very wise people. They were quite spiritual as well. So spiritual that they chose to die to make a point about… well, I'm sure Jae and others will be having press releases and papers about all of that in the months and years to come. How about release to Earth, Jae?" Lon knew the answer.

Jae shook his head. "That will have to be filtered, which will take time to sort through. The Prime Directive is involved."

"Absolutely Prime Directive. Cupcake! But that's not what we're here for today."

Now Londo let the shouted, even screamed questions fly. Jae had tutored him for three expressions that he cycled through, twenty seconds apiece. They truly helped serve as a barrier against his fear and the accusations.

"Is it legal on Earth?" "Who married who first?" "Are you suggesting that Earth people should have polygamous marriages?" "Where do you get off thinking you can do this?" "What does Maximus think?"

At one point Jae touched Lon's elbow and then leaned forward to his mic. "Let's just combine some of these questions," Jae said pleasantly. He was using Expression #2, or was that #1? Lon couldn't think straight with all the negativity being aimed at him. "Yes, we have sex in threesomes, twosomes or onesomes, as we please."

Many reporters sat holding their breaths, recorders quivering in their hands at the revelations.

"No, Lon cannot have sex with anyone else besides us; it's a special technique that we can credit to Lina's fervid and desperate genius. You need to be taught by one of us in order to do this, and even then you have to have the right training and powers. Okay?"

The silence in the room was deafening.

"Glad that's over," Lina muttered. "And it's *qapla'*, not 'cupcake,' Lon. That's Klingon for 'success'," she added for the reporters' sake.

But Jae went on. "Lon was Lina's first and Lina was his first, and it was not an easy first time."

"Jae," Lina admonished, but he waved her down.

"Both cherry-red virgins when they met, does everyone have that? And I was both of their second, and there've been no thirds. I'm not going to tell you which numbers they've been for me; that might frighten the more faint-hearted out there."

Lina set her chin on her palm and Lon felt like doing the same. It seemed that Jae had more to say. He deserved to get things out of his system. Londo leaned back from the podium to glace at Lina. She shrugged and made a face at him.

Off to the side, on the main floor next to the stage, Hal gave him a "This is going so well" ironic grimace.

Jae still had the mic. "Those women with the so-called children of Valiant – all liars. I believe there were genetic tests to prove that, since some didn't take Lon at his word. Yes, we are planning children, but we haven't decided parentage order yet because we're way too busy to bring kids into this yet. We have enough with all the cats. Please do not send us cat gifts. Anything else?"

Londo heaved a sigh. It was terribly embarrassing, but at least it was out. Wait – Lina was pulling the mike towards herself. The reporters waited with breathless anticipation of the next revelation.

"No, I have not had a boob job," she said.

Lon guffawed.

"Some of the nurses gave me some tabloids to read. Lies, lies, lies. I should sue. *BortaS!*" Lina shook her fist in the air theatrically. Probably another Klingon thing; the audience liked it.

With that, the energy in the room lightened. Lina was good at that.

"All right, my turn again." Londo sighed. The worst was over? No, reaction had barely begun. He set his shoulders and leaned toward the mike. "So sometimes I don't wear clean underwear. I get busy. I get far away from home. Sometimes I do yell at the cats. Sometimes.... Um, I don't really know what else there is to tell, besides the fact that I was the one who bullied the others into not telling about the Triune. Lina's been begging to get the truth out right from the first, and Jae... I could see it was bothering Jae and I didn't do anything about it. I was afraid, okay *d'ac?*"

He scowled at the audience. "There's a hell of a cultural skew against gays, and people don't even want to mention bisexuals, much less polygamy. I don't like being disliked. But I'm out now for better or worse, and I should have done this a long time ago since I'm part of the new gay pride movement on Aldierra. If anyone wants to blame anyone about keeping this a secret, they should see me; I'm responsible.

"Does anyone have anything else to say?" Londo looked at his two spouses.

"I can't dance," Lina said.

"We're working on that," Londo said with a smile. "It's not an incurable condition. Jae?"

Jae thought. "As long as we're baring all, there are some minor infractions of the law I could probably plead guilty to – and you too, Lon – but the statutes of limitations have probably run out by now. Just little embarrassments for other people who deserved every one of them."

"Just a few," Londo nodded. "Well, one kind of big one on my part, but that was an accident, and nothing really bad resulted from it except that Maximus had me on punishment duty for a hell of a long time. Forget I mentioned it."

"Anything else?" Jae looked at the two of them. "I think we've covered everything that's been mentioned in the tabloids and then some."

"I shudder to see the headlines tomorrow." Londo made sure his confident smile seemed genuine. "But all our secrets are out and nothing's going to get worse. So there, rumor-mongers of the worlds!" He swept his hands at the cameras in a banishing gesture.

"Ah, just a minute," Hal said loudly so the microphones would catch it. Slowly he emerged from his screen and mounted the steps to the stage.

Londo froze and then said, "You don't have to do this."

"Sure I do." The easy grin Hal gave him belied the terror underneath. "Give me the mic. Don't be stingy."

"Always trying to upstage me." Lon stepped away from the podium. The mic relayed his comment at low but understandable volume. "You realize who's going to get the main headlines now."

"They'll read that the whole family's gone to hell in a handbasket." Hal laughed at him, then addressed the audience, poised expectantly over their notebooks, recorders and phones. "Okay, listen up, people."

He took a breath. So did Londo. "I've been guilty about a few things, lied about a couple of things in my time. Most notably was a time, oh, just over thirty years ago. I was in college and let's face it, feeling my oats, when along came the most beautiful, most exciting and intelligent girl I'd ever met..." He gave a sad smile, his eyes unfocusing a little. "What can I say. I was smitten. I wanted her to marry me, but she refused; she didn't want to become a footnote, or more likely a target of the Maximus legend. Even later, after Lon was born, she'd never say yes to my offers."

Multiple intakes of breath around the room.

Hal stared out above the heads of his audience. "She died a few years ago. When Lon was taken from us, she couldn't stand it, couldn't take the stress. She was always such a warm, feeling girl. No, she couldn't bear it, and then much later she had an accident, so Londo doesn't have a mother any more. But he has me. He never met her after his return. She knew he was back, but she couldn't have taken meeting up with the boy whose disappearance had torn her mind apart."

Now he came back to himself, straightened up there on the podium. "Her name was Valorie. Let's leave it at that. She has extensive family who haven't been informed of all this. Londo was born in France, not Canada. Sorry, Canada. 'Londo' was a family name from her side. I have baby pictures if he'll let me release them to the press."

"No naked shots." The reporters in the front and middle rows could hear Lon's comment even without the mic.

"Okay, no naked shots, no little Londo tushie." Hal smiled at his son.

"It's not the tushie I'm worried about."

Hal's crooked smile matched that of his son as he turned back to the corps. "But she died a long time after she insisted that I not see her again. I'm married now to Else, as all of you know. What you don't know is that Else is an android, made on the space station called Lexota by the late engineering genius Mishan Bab, who should go down in the history books for her generosity and brilliance.

"Else is a beautiful woman who can give your average genius a run for his money. She was the first person to alert me to the potential trouble our darling new telepathic daughter-in-law posed to the family secret. Which I'm happy to say didn't happen. Lina's been far too busy to think about such things. She'd have found out soon though. It was my angry mouth that spilled my secret. There have been some... rough family times since then. But we've come to terms with it, I think, Londo and I. His marriage and my fatherhood. We're still working on it."

Lon rubbed his nose.

"I just want to remind you all that these three are in love, crazy in love is more like it. In my opinion you'd have to be crazy to marry two people at once. One person's difficult enough. But those Feithi did it. I remember visiting their world, back when I was searching the sector for Londo. More than half their marriages were three-ways, what they called dual-Triune, which was a lot more informal than the Triune. There were very, very few people in full Triunes.

"I remember meeting one Triune family and saw how those around them deferred to them. They were the most respected of people and yet..." Hal smiled with the memory, "they weren't stuffy at all. Jae tells me that that's because in a Triune you get double input; you're never balanced for long, you're always moving forward with each others' help. 'Three is a dynamic number,' Jae told me this past week. I suppose that's numerology or astrology or one of those Lina things."

"Sounds like *Schoolhouse Rock* to me. Three is a family," Londo put in, but Hal waved him off.

"Whatever it is... These kids are working as a team. They know they're in that team for the rest of their lives, and they know that there can't be any secrets between them. You shake up that mixture and add the fact that they're committed to each other in all things..." He shrugged. "Who am I to stand against love? Against expressing who they truly are? Who is anyone? I say it's a relief that they found a legal way to do it.

"It's definitely keeping an important aspect of the Feithi culture alive. They're trying to take Feithi ideals and adapt them so they can become the ideals of the Three Worlds. Every world is different, every world has its own individuality to demonstrate, but they're taking ideas from Feith to use as a rough framework to shape those goals."

He gave everyone in the room and on the monitors a good stare. "So that's it then. Secret's out. All of them."

Jae shrugged and looked toward the heavens.

"These three are married. And happily so. And I am the very, very proud father of a man who has exceeded my every expectation."

He turned to take a step toward Londo. After a pause for permission, he gave him a fierce hug. Cameras caught tears in Hal's eyes as Lon hugged him back.

Lon held his lips together hard, desperately trying not to break down on camera. "Papa," he managed to say.

CHAPTER

32

Londo glanced back when Stoan caught up to them as they checked into Legion Medical for a final time before returning to Aldierra. The staff was gathered around a metal table holding an open stasi-keeper loaded with Terran cakes, cookies, crackers, and cheeses. Three cases of wine sat next to it. Everyone came to attention as they noticed the commander's presence. The goodies in their hands and mouths made it somewhat difficult.

A separate stack of stasi-keepers stood next to Lon, this one coming up to shoulder height. It contained sealed Sarastoran meals, favorites of Jae's and his, to take with them. A box of security devices sat nearby, along with communications add-ons and two state-of-the-art *friads,* which Nesh had requested.

Stoan looked at them all and, instead of telling the Starharts to come to his office or for the staff to go away, he waved a privacy screen into position.

Lon waited. Jae kicked at his mobichair impatiently while Lina's face held a curious expression. "And?" Lon finally asked, since Stoan didn't say anything.

"I have decided," the commander said slowly, "not to kick you people out. Though you deserve it."

Jae was about to say something, but Lon put his hand on his husband's shoulder and Jae shut up.

"Causing so much controversial publicity. Not checking in with Legion PIC before you made these… announcements. No, decisions. This should have been caught much earlier."

Lon's hand tightened on Jae's shoulder.

"But what's done is done." Stoan heaved a melodramatic sigh. "I've sought advice for this decision. What almost everyone – everyone who didn't tell me to kick you all out on your sorry asses, that is – agreed is that I will announce that the Three Worlds, all three of you, are working with the Mega-Legion in a one-time-only paradigm. You two–" his gaze addressed the two Legionnaires – "will still be members. Full time or part time; we'll say as needed for the nonce, as schedules permit until this Deadline of yours goes away. We will see what the situation warrants after that. The rest of my Legionnaires will not be recruited by you –" here he gave Lina his evil side eye – "but will be permitted to work with you as situation, inclination and schedules permit, provided it doesn't happen too often to adversely affect Legion operations."

Oh. Lon checked to see how Jae was reacting, but of course he had one of his Expressions up. Jae was still taking it in.

Stoan turned to Lina. "You will continue to port Legionnaires on emergency bases only. No frivolous requests will come to you. I will make this crystal clear to them. If you happen to port in not dressed according to Legion regs, no demerits will be assigned. Unless you come in naked. Do not arrive naked."

Now it was Lina's turn to consider.

"And your security rating has been raised to a five."

She brightened at that, though both Lon and Jae had discussed that she should have proved herself Unlimited by now. Well, they'd work on that.

"Ms. Yency would like a long conversation with you, though."

Lina's expression turned into a grimace, and Stoan smiled in satisfaction. "She says your absences from Spousal Meetings are not acceptable."

"We'll have to attend now as well," Jae put in. "Lon for me, and me for Lon."

Stoan's eyes closed in emotional pain. "There is a section in the bylaws for Intra-Legion marriages. Follow those."

"All right, we'll look those up," Londo announced. Time to take control again before the full backlash from their announcements set in. "Anything else?"

Stoan was about to open his mouth when a circular red glow appeared in the air at eye level.

"Uh oh," Jae said.

It stretched out until it reached pretty much Stoan-height, -width and -depth, and stood next to him. Within it coalesced the image of a Ruby Guard. She was dressed in the corps uniform of red, white and black, with the palm-sized ruby secured to the neck. The scarlet light of her transmission masked any non-reddish skin color she might have.

"Excuse me," she said politely. "May I interrupt? I didn't want to set off your security system. I bear a message from the Sentinels."

Stoan hesitated only a second. "Of course. We honor the Galactic Sentinels and their Guards."

The Guard nodded. "I went on Arient to collect Granger and the stone."

Jae raised the golden jasper so she could see it. "I have the stone," he said.

"Yes, we tracked it to Earth. The Sentinels would like to see it in its current state. They are curious about it."

"It has evolved," Jae told her. "I don't know if it can do anything like your rubies, but it emits an aura or field that makes one feel… content. Safe."

She pursed her lips. "Would you mind if the Sentinels studied it? For a while?"

Thoughtfully Jae turned the stone in his hands. "They may have it for as long as they wish. If they discover it has powers, it would probably be too dangerous to leave with us anyway."

"Could the Sentinels store it or display it, whatever, near to our Ruby?" Lina asked. "The Ruby needs to rest and recuperate. I should think that this jasper could help it. Maybe they could become friends. I'm not that familiar with the sentience of stones."

Lon nodded his head at her while the Guard cocked hers as she took in the idea. "I… I should think that might be arranged."

"Then tell the Sentinels to prepare themselves," Lina said. "I'll port it to the place we went on Aum. Ah, is that okay?"

"I'm sure that's good." The Guard swallowed. "Thank you."

"Okay for you?" Lina asked Jae and then Londo.

The Guard allowed Lina two minutes to complete the port.

"I'll miss it," Jae said. "Things feel different without it nearby. Now, can we get a report on Granger?"

"I got reports that he was in a mindless state," Stoan said to Londo's startlement.

"Not quite," the Guard said. "A blank slate, perhaps you'd say. His life has been wiped away."

"No," Lina whispered.

"And yet he is constantly muttering words of apology, of regret," the Guard said.

"So he's not quite so mind-wiped," Lon surmised.

"Is he standing outside his self?" Jae asked. "Looking back on his life, as if he's an outsider to it?"

The Guard looked thoughtful. "I don't know. I will inquire for you."

"I'd appreciate that," Jae said before Lina and Londo could chime in.

"But he's no longer a threat to anyone," Londo said as a question. "He won't be able to continue his terrorism.

"Not in any way," the Guard assured him. "He is being taken to Daq-qu-a, but this time will be in a section special unto him. He will be assessed to the best of our ability. He will be treated as we can surmise. And he will *not* escape again. No one will from that complex. Someone at some point centuries ago discovered a weak point in our security and built upon it. It took a long time for them to exploit it fully, enough to gather accomplices from outside Daq-qu-a to help them and escape.

"The accomplices have also been tried and placed within the prison complex. It is the most secure–" Her mouth twisted. "It is *now* the most secure prison in the entire galaxy."

"Which is saying a lot," Stoan said. "Our thanks to the Sentinels and the Brigade for seeing to this." Upon reflection he added, "We may have to send a delegation to record their conditions and sentences for our records."

"That might be arranged."

Lon looked at Lina. **Which means they'd need you for porting.**

I'll go along, of course. They're saying I essentially erased Granger. I mean, is he a semi-vegetable? Did I do something wrong?

No! You did exactly right, Londo insisted. **Whatever you did, he deserved it.**

We need to go with you too. I want to see the situation.

"Well sure," she told Jae out loud. The non-Starharts eyed her curiously.

Londo shrugged at them. "Give us a couple days' warning. We do have a situation on Aldierra to take care of, you know."

The Guard nodded deeply. "The Sentinels are closely watching that situation. As is the entire Brigade. Do you really think you can save that world?"

Lon gave her a reassuring smile. "We'll get it done."

And he hoped to all hell that he wasn't lying.

ABOUT THE AUTHOR

When you think of strong women and strange worlds, think Carol A. Strickland.

Although born in a small town in Illinois noted for its Nineteenth Century demonic possession cases, Carol claims that all those voices inside her head are a result of having stories to tell and books to write. Even so, her strange devotion to and study of Wonder Woman would seem to indicate an abby-normal brain.

A one-time comics letterhack and outspoken member of various comics message boards, Carol has found herself the basis for two comic book villains (at times her opinions have not been taken well by the books' creators) (both villains were soundly thrashed) (and both, for some perverse reason, were male) and had one superhero wear her costume design. (Light Lass!)

Carol has also become an award-winning painter and certified tarot reader. Her primary talent, though, is procrastination. See what else she wastes time on at her website: www.CarolAStrickland.com or check out her other books at www.CarolAStricklandBooks.com .